MW00575931

SUPER

Arca Book 1

KAREN DIEM

Copyright

Copyright © 2016 by Karen Diem

All rights reserved. No part of this publication may be reproduced, distributed, or transmitted in any form or by any means, including photocopying, recording, or other electronic or mechanical methods, without prior written permission from the author, except in the case of brief quotations in critical reviews and certain other noncommercial uses permitted by copyright law.

This is a work of fiction. Names, characters, businesses, places, events, and incidents are either the products of the author's imagination or are used in a fictitious manner. Any resemblance to actual persons, living or dead, or actual events is purely coincidental.

Crock-Pot is a trademark of Sunbeam Products, Inc. Taser is a trademark of Axon Enterprise, Inc. These and any other trademarks appearing in the book are the property of their respective owners.

Cover by Deranged Doctor Design.

★★★

eBook version 2.2 May 2017

First paperback printing: May 9, 2017

ISBN: 978-0-9975740-1-2

To contact Karen Diem or subscribe to her newsletter, go to http://www.karendiem.com.

Dedication

Dedicated to my family.

Table of Contents

Chapter One

Sometimes, Zita Garcia wished for the kind of blind date where the guy threw up, and she could leave.

Instead, her date, the world's most boring cherub with a badge, continued his monologue while she schemed to escape. Her plans had been locksmith work for an infusion of cash, followed by dinner with her two brothers. Instead, they had thrown her to the dogs—or in this case, her oldest brother's puzzling choice of a blind date: Dr. Justin Smith, an FBI psychiatrist or whatever. A question penetrated, standing out from the other blathering. "What? Oh, Miguel told you I'm an underachiever. No, I'm a tax preparer. My brother exaggerates."

A flicker of movement and the angry growl of a car without a muffler caught her attention, overriding the nearby bustling buzz of a highway. Before she could look, however, Zita's other brother amended her statements from where he shamelessly eavesdropped.

Metal chair legs scraped pavement as Quentin rose from the table next to theirs on the sidewalk of the trendy café in the outdoor mall. He closed in on them. Innocence shone from her brother's face, but his words were pure devilry. "I couldn't help but overhear as I passed. Don't let Zita sell herself short. Baby girl here speaks four languages and trains for the Olympics in her free time. I'm going to get something sweet, so if you take off together, don't worry about me." His eyes strayed to the interior of the restaurant, and he winked at someone there.

Zita gave her brother a death glare. Trying to be nice but uninteresting was killing her. *Carajo, Justin's all hopeful I'm a brain trust now. Please brush me off soon. Some adorable little nerd is pining to scoop you up.* She cursed herself for accepting her brother's offer of a ride to and from dinner; since her sprained ankle prevented use of her motorcycle, she should have taken a cab or bus.

Her date widened his eyes and gave her a pleased smile, increasing his resemblance to a pug. "Miguel had said you're athletic and super intelligent, so we should have that in common. Tell me about yourself," Justin burbled at her hair. He had been unable to pull his bulging, over-large eyes from it since they met. His preoccupation with her hair lost him any respect he might have gained for ignoring Quentin's hovering presence and not ogling her generous chest.

Zita's traitorous brother patted her on the shoulder, undeterred by the glare she gave him. Quentin's grin widened, exhibiting the smile the siblings had in common. His whiskey eyes danced. "Have fun, kids." He abandoned her for his own admirer inside the café.

Based on the subtle detachment in Justin's eyes, his title, and the forced enthusiasm in his voice, Zita suspected he might be legal to drink. Despite that, she doubted his smooth face had ever known a razor.

He adjusted his crooked tie. It hung from the neck of a suit apparently purchased with unrealistic expectations for his eventual full growth. As he sat back, his jacket flapped open and flaunted a gun that coiled tense on one scrawny hip, inching toward the moment of escape.

How could he miss that the firearm is undersized for its holster? Why didn't he fasten the strap to keep it in place? Even though he said today was his first day with it, you'd think he would know that much. Zita snorted as the intelligent comment caught up with her. Her reply came out clipped. "I only speak four because I lived all over."

She flicked a blue-and-white-dyed dreadlock out of her eyes. With a mental curse at both her brothers, she tried a more frightening tack: reality. "The Olympics are a dream. I like extreme sports, exercising, and the outdoors. I work out for a few hours every day, switching it up between a few different things: acrobatics, martial arts, rock climbing, and so on. Last October, I climbed Mount Washington."

Social obligation done, she fussed with the hot pink athletic wrap on her sprained ankle and took a wolfish bite of her sandwich to avoid further conversation. The headache that had been teasing her with small bites of pain intensified with every word the man spoke. And he liked talking. Sweat trickled down her back inside the makeshift sauna of her wilted blue work coveralls. Unwilling to risk encouraging him by unzipping even a little, she prayed he would leave so she could remove it and cool off.

Another rev of the loud engine drew her attention. Shops and small restaurants faced each other across two roads running in either direction. Perhaps to discourage jaywalkers, the mall planners had crammed spindly bushes and oversized flowerpots down the center of the grassy area separating the streets. A muscle car with stripes idled outside the jewelry store on the corner opposite the café. The orange paint job was vivid and happy, like the world's sleekest pumpkin, but the ski mask the driver wore ruined the cheery effect. It reminded her of biting into a cookie to find out it was wax. She hated when that happened. *Fake cookies should not look so real.*

Oblivious, her companion did not notice as he took up the burden of conversation again. His gun slid farther out of the too-large holster. Experience had taught her that men never took suggestions well about how to wear their weapons. She reminded herself to stop obsessing about the man's firearm. He wiggled in his seat with enthusiasm. *Pues, he spent several minutes telling me how he's a prodigy at his calling, and he's not even practicing it.* "Hang on, I got to call the cops about that robbery over there. Can you get the

license number or take a picture if you've got a camera phone?"
Distracted, Zita thumbed toward the car and the jewelry store. Not
waiting for his response, she pulled out her phone and flipped it
open. She watched him in her peripheral vision, most of her
attention on the car.

Justin jerked around and finally noticed the two men enter the
store as Zita began to talk to the operator. "You call. I've got a job
to do," he said, leaping to his feet and snatching his ID from the
table. With a clatter, his chair fell to the ground behind him, and
the little green metal table rocked. Coffee sloshed out of his cup.

"Seriously?" Zita blinked in disbelief.

Each of his limbs tried to go a different direction as he sprinted
across the street.

A white sedan screeched to a halt to avoid hitting him.

She winced.

The sedan's driver flipped him off and kept going.

Justin almost fell crossing the grassy strip when a bush snagged
the straggling edge of one pant leg.

Zita spotted his gun falling out as he untangled himself, but he
continued across the next road. She smacked her head with her
hand. Her stomach tightened, a hard, cold knot in her center.
Suddenly dry, her throat could barely swallow. *Do I want to do this?
I can't let him be murdered, not like in Brazil. Justin has the
coordination and muscle tone of a born desk jockey; he needs help.*

"Pretty certain Behavioral Analyzers or whatever your title is
aren't supposed to do that. I would know if I'd been listening
better, I suppose. He's been watching too much TV," she grumbled,
setting aside the mangled remains of her sandwich and limping
over to the gun.

The operator on the phone said, "What was that?"

In reply, Zita did not bother to explain. "Send an ambulance.
An overconfident FBI civilian is playing hero. Armed robbery.
Gotta go." She rattled off the location and snapped the phone shut.
Reaching the bush, she crouched to extricate the weapon, a Glock

22. One new scratch marred the finish. With a mental tsk, she tucked it into a pocket of her bulky coveralls.

Justin's voice was loud as he identified himself and demanded the robbers stop when they exited the store. His eyes widened, and his talking sped up as his hand patted the empty holster.

Zita sighed, and pulled out a utility knife from a zipped pocket on her leg, concealing it against her body. Her stomach clenched again, and she exhaled, focusing. *I've been through worse. This is an exhibition against amateurs.*

The robbers stopped for a few seconds and stared at the young FBI specialist, who tried to glower back.

Zita lowered her estimate of their ages. *Older teens, and they must be new to robbery if they're using that car and wearing pants that will slow running. The ones on the sidewalk should be high school or college football players, not robbing a hole-in-the-wall jeweler four blocks from a cop shop. Maybe I won't die.* Her stomach eased as a scheme formed. *I'll have to be obnoxious and loud.* The corners of her mouth quirked up. *Finally, a plan that plays to my strengths.*

Exaggerating her limp, she struggled across the street, ending with her leaning against the hood of the orange car. "Sweet ride. That color is all kind of cool," she yakked at the driver. The hood radiated heat under the hand she stroked down the edges. With the hand he couldn't see, she drove the blade of her knife into the wall of the front tire and pulled it along to make a considerable gash.

From her peripheral vision, she saw the two boys on the sidewalk glance at her, and then away. One clutched a common brand of semiautomatic 9mm gun, probably selected because it was easy to find, cheap, and held ten rounds of punishing inaccuracy in a shiny nickel frame. He barked at Justin. "You better move out of the way and go give your daddy his ID badge back before I shoot your skinny ass." He raised his gun, holding it sideways. *You'd think they'd leave the guns home until they learned how to shoot; everyone knows a man who can't handle his gun, can't handle other things. Of course, if they knew anything about shooting, they would use a better firearm.* The mental heckling helped her focus.

Justin raised his hands and tried a soothing voice. "Now, we got off to a bad start. I know you don't want to do this. Grand larceny with a weapon gets you extra time. You know, if you put that down, we can find a better solution than this. Keep your life on track."

Disbelief held the driver speechless for a minute. "Get away from my car, bitch, or I'll run you down," he snarled.

After withdrawing her knife from the tire, Zita limped toward the back of the car. With her voice pitched higher and whinier, she complained as if she were the densest person on the planet. "Hey, I've got a bum leg. If you're gonna be like that, you shouldn't pimp out your ride." She heaved a deep breath, keeping as much of the car as possible between her and the idiot with the gun. With a flick, she shut the knife and dropped it into one of her pockets as she moved. Warm sweat trickled down her back, not all due to the muggy May air.

"Are you stupid?" the driver said. "Get lost!"

The group on the sidewalk glanced at her, but their attention was on Justin. The beefy leader gestured with the gun. "You know what? I do want to do this. And I think you want to shut your mouth!" He shook his weapon, with the last few words escalating in pitch before he continued. "Toss over your wallet and badge, and kiss the sidewalk before I shoot your head off!" His voice rose to a shout on the threat, and the other kid on the sidewalk shifted as if he had to pee or wanted to rabbit anywhere else.

"We can go. Don't need to mess with nobody else. We got the bag," the nervous one urged the others. The driver revved the engine.

Reluctant to obey, hands still in the air, Justin caught sight of Zita. His eyes widened, and he shook his head at her in mute appeal as he dropped to one knee.

"Don't say no to me! Wallet!" His face red, the leader of the robbers wore the glazed incomprehension of a bull ready to charge.

Let's hope Justin is smart enough to dash for safety. Zita let her gaze turn toward the corner of the shop where he could find cover from the weapon, but she continued her slow amble to the sidewalk. She ignored her common sense urging her to run and hide; sometimes her brain was no fun. When she had cover from the gun, she stopped behind the orange car and slapped the trunk. With a toss of her hair, she raised her own voice. "Since you're blind, which is a dumbass thing in a driver, I am behind your car. That means I'm not in your way, and you can go wherever without running my sweet ass over. So stop insulting me before I scratch up your cherry paint job to prove to you who's smarter." She affixed a sneer on her face. Her heart raced. *Come on...*

The armed kid snickered. His weapon dipped. "Let's get in the car before the gimp beats up Dylan."

Tension reduced, check.

Sirens sounded—she'd guess four blocks away at the precinct station. *Must've finished the donuts.*

The other teen nodded and dove for the safety of the car.

Since he had mentioned her, she figured even a moron would notice the sidewalk tableau. Zita opened her mouth as if to berate him further, even lifting a finger. With a dramatic gasp, she let her eyes fall to his (terrible grip on his) firearm, and shrieked, "Gun!" Ignoring the angry ache in her ankle, she hopped and hobbled into the closest store, trailing shrieks.

Masculine laughter sounded outside.

Justin had better appreciate me acting a fool to give him a chance to escape or pull a clutch piece. Even with my ankle, I could run the distance faster than the cops are getting here.

A gun went off outside and glass shattered. She dropped to her knees.

The others in the clothing store cowered in the back, except for one entrepreneur, who was creeping toward the front with his phone. Flesh smacked against flesh, and something clattered.

Zita peeked out.

Tangled in a vicious wrestling match, the leader and Justin rolled around on the sidewalk outside of the store. For a collection of bony arms and legs with no coordination, Justin used his excess of elbow to his advantage. Despite that, he was losing to the teenager, who had at least fifty pounds and a few inches on him. The car engine revved, but the two inside the orange vehicle seemed to be having a whispered conversation. The robber's gun had skidded to a halt not far from her.

"Come on, we going," the rabbity one in the car shouted. The sirens got louder, then cut off. The bull of a kid now sat on top of Justin, gripping the hair on the back of the FBI analyst's head. Red stained the sidewalk.

Justin's dead if someone doesn't stop him. Shit. Guess I'm someone. Careful to avoid inching out of cover any more than necessary, Zita set her foot on the robber's sleazy gun. With a gentle nudge, she prodded it into the store to reduce its visibility. *Please don't let there be any more guns.* With another deep breath, she stepped out of the shop. She angled her body to present less of a target from the direction of the car. "That's enough. Go on. Leave him be."

The leader sneered, one hand poised to pound Justin's head into the sidewalk again. "What is this? Junior Detective needs his spic partner to rescue him?" His pupils were dark and dilated against the whites of his eyes.

Who even says that? She put her hands on her hips and let her indignation sound off in her voice. "Oh, hell no. I'm not his partner. I'm his blind date. Why don't you take off and let me get a piece in? I got plenty to say to his pasty ass."

The robber snickered. He released Justin's hair too, so Zita counted it as a step in the right direction. The driver hooted, but the rabbity kid urged his friend to get in the car. A whimper sounded from beneath the big teenager.

She huffed and drew Justin's gun. "Fine, let him go, or I'll shoot. I'm not playing no more." While silence might have been wiser, she had to add one more thing. "Notice I know how to hold a gun, so it won't break my wrists too." Zita turned her head to the kids in the car and lifted her eyebrows. *I look threatening. This is a gun. Be frightened of the loca and do as I command.*

For all of a second, she thought it had worked.

"He's all yours," the bully on the sidewalk said, throwing himself into the car. Tires squealing, the orange car howled off.

I totally deserve a reward for this, maybe a piece of... oh.

Three of the four police cars that had been sneaking up to surround them followed, lights reigniting and sirens ablaze with sound again as the pursuit began. The fourth pulled up in front of her with a screech.

Zita looked from the gun to the cop car. She set the weapon down on the ground in front of her and took a couple steps back, holding her hands up in the air.

Inside the shop, the enterprising man continued to point his phone their direction.

"No, don't help, keep filming," she spat.

Another moan came from the pavement. His face a bloody mess, Justin pushed himself up to a sitting position and glared at her from eyes swelling shut.

Guess I don't have to worry about letting him down easy. "Dude, you should have run or pulled your clutch piece. Are you okay?" As the cops circled her, claiming her attention, she kept her hands in the air and obeyed every shouted command.

Despite the endless rebukes for her actions, the police were gentle in their questioning. The number of times they called her *girl* was galling, but Zita took the censure without complaint. She smirked when the police radio announced that the thieves' car blew a tire less than a mile away, but she refrained from admitting her part.

Forty-five grueling minutes later, she extricated herself and limped back across the street to the restaurant. The admonition to stay in town for a statement rang in her ears as she hobbled. The remnants of her sandwich and pickle had disappeared, though her scowling brother sat at her table. She grimaced. After that fiasco, she deserved a snack.

Quentin frowned at her, setting down his half-empty coffee. "What the hell were you thinking? You could've been killed!" No hint of a smile appeared on his usually sunny face.

Tilting her aching head back, Zita exhaled and ran her hand over her hair. "I'm five foot nothing, and I've been called cute more times than you've had sex." She settled into her chair.

Anger gave way to thoughtfulness. "Unlikely, but possible. You are so adorable that it is a constant struggle not to pinch your little cheeks and coo at you. What does that have to do with you trying to die? Climbing mountains and jumping out of planes is one thing, this is..." Quentin waved a hand in the air as if words failed him. At five-foot-ten, he had the height she lacked, and he had the good fortune to share the striking Quechua features of their mother and oldest brother. On him, the effect was soulful. Zita was the only one to sport a mestizo pixie face, courtesy of their father. Regular workouts kept Quentin toned enough to please his dates, without being much stronger than average or spending a minute more in a gym than necessary.

"My point is, nobody looks at me and sees a threat. People don't realize I'm twenty-six, rather than twenty or even eighteen. Sure, they like me, but they don't want me doing their taxes or anything that requires brains or maturity. I have to work to be taken seriously, neta? If the situation had turned into a farce, those kids would be less likely to hurt anyone or get hurt. Justin may not be my type or even resemble an effective agent, but he doesn't deserve to die. So, you know, comic relief to the rescue." She eased her sore foot back up and took off her shoe.

Quentin stared across the street with the expression that told her his mind had drifted somewhere other than the dying confusion there. He sipped his coffee and grimaced. It was probably cold.

While he was silent, she sent Miguel a brief text. "No on the baby agent. He can't keep his gun in his holster." As expected, she got no reply. Some people were too responsible to reply to personal texts at work; the concept was alien to her.

"If the Marines taught me nothing else, it's that any situation can go to crap at any moment. You're not invulnerable. Don't make us lose you yet." Quentin's phone chimed, and he dug it out of his pocket, all dreaminess gone. Wielding his second-best angelic grin, he hugged her. One hand stroked over her hair. "Don't you remember our rule? Don't be a dumbass. Miguel will harangue you later and then some... when he finds out. If his latest serial killer case weren't giving him fits, he'd already be here to do it. Tell you what, I'll get you something sugary for the adrenaline crash if you can stay out of any more trouble. So, relax, I'll be right back." He disappeared into the café.

Suspicion flaring at his unusual willingness to pay for food, Zita tried to unwind while she tightened the athletic wrap on her ankle again. A few minutes of people-watching, and her shoulders began to relax.

Gleeful evil interrupted her salacious appreciation of the derrieres of several fit men in tight biking enthusiast gear as Quentin returned with a bear claw pastry and a sweating lemonade. "So, admit it, Iggy may have been bad, but he was a better pick for you than that epic fail getting his nose set. You want me to call Iggy back and see if he wants a second date? I bet he seems more appealing now."

Was fratricide really a sin? Zita seized the food. She took a fortifying bite of the pastry, then another, before he could steal it back. With a snort, she shoved a blue dreadlock aside. "Inky's a no go, Q."

"Why, you got plans tonight that don't involve working out in a gym?" her brother replied. "His name is Iggy. He likes climbing. You like climbing, and it couldn't hurt for you to climb on each other. How long's it been now, my little Two-Date Disaster?"

She counted. *Four years, one month, one week, not that he needs to know. I could figure out the number of hours, but I'm not obsessive. Much.* Zita countered, "Hombre, some of us don't have to buy STD tests in bulk. Sweet hands and a sexy rear can't stop the whole thief thing from turning me off. So did you need me to do more tonight? You're on the hook for my pitiful paycheck on the lock changeover earlier today." Fatigue washed over her. She took another bite and washed it down with the drink. Her brother's voice interrupted her musing.

He had the audacity to say, "Your paycheck would be bigger if you could commit to more hours, instead of working part-time for me, part-time for the tax place, and picking up summer jobs in exotic locations whenever you get a chance. I don't know why you think you're looking for a serious relationship when you won't even commit to one full-time job. No more work for us today. I've got a hot date tonight." Her brother teased even as he spun a chair backward and plopped down across from her.

"I spent more time on that door earlier than you will on tonight's so-called relationship outside the bed." Practice helped her ignore his criticism of her lifestyle. Grabbing her lemonade, Zita gulped it. The sweet and tart liquid washed cold over her tongue but failed to grant the relief she sought. *I need rest, aspirin, and food, if that much sugar can't make me feel better. Tomorrow, if I'm up for it, I can scope out the Cairo apartment building in DC and work on my plans to creep out and spider up it some night.*

He shrugged and stole a bite of her bear claw. "Guilty as charged."

Unable to stand the claustrophobic feel of clammy fabric on her back another second, she pulled at her work coveralls, unzipping and stripping off the top half. Her head spun as she stood and let the clothing pool around her ankles. The air, thick with summer and burgers and exhaust, had to be only a few degrees cooler without the bulky clothes; nonetheless, she was elated as if escaping a fiery prison.

Without asking, Quentin washed down his bite with a gulp of her drink and held it out to her. "So, should I call one of my other friends, see if they're available this weekend?"

Stepping free of the coveralls, she bent and picked them up before answering. Her head swam, and she resolved to rest until the flu or whatever passed. "No. From Iggy's face, he was expecting someone more... more something not me anyway. What did you tell him?" After a brief battle to catch her breath, Zita fought to focus through the increasing pain. She rubbed damp hands on her cargo shorts.

Her brother shook his head, letting his fashionably shaggy black hair settle around his face. He puffed out a breath of air. "It's the hair. That's got to be the ugliest chingado hair on the planet. You should do a makeover. I know ladies who could work on you, ones who like a challenge. That's you all over and then some. As for Iggy, all I said was I had a cute little sister who picked up extra bucks working for my locksmith business when her accounting job was slow. Oh, and that you were a bit shy, but loved to have fun. Well, I might have added you were stacked, too." He smirked.

She stared at him. Her head was pounding her brain to jelly. The sun had disappeared behind the horizon, and the dusk should have been soothing, but the pain grew. "That's got to be the biggest pile of... prevarication I've ever heard. It's somehow true and a fat lie at the same time," she accused. There may have been some awe amid the disgust, but she would never admit it.

The bastard preened. "I know, I was proud of it," he admitted. "But if I'd described you as a hyperactive terrier training for a nonexistent Olympic event, who has had more failed and injured dates than anyone else ever, nobody'd go out with you. You'd be stuck with Miguel's picks since you don't look on your own. Nobody wants that, except him. Let's not forget the giant Technicolor tarantula on your head, either."

Zita pointed an accusing finger at him, but a wave of dizziness swept over her, and she forgot what she was saying. Her head ached. *Oh, right.* "My hair is fun! Why you got to be hating?" she scolded, her hands the punctuation.

He tsked, undeterred by her rebuke, but stopped. Quentin peered at her. "Hey, what's wrong?" Whatever he saw made him drop the chair and rush to her side.

She swayed. *Strange, I hadn't planned to do that.* Her vision shrank as the world faded. Zita fought it but felt herself falling, interrupted by a stabbing sensation on her forehead before the blackness won.

Chapter Two

Awareness nagged at her. Someone's phone beeped over and over. Was it hers? If it were, she would have something to say to whomever was bothering her. Her body felt slow and sore. Some jerk was pinching her arm, and... her brain registered the catheter and identified the pinch as an IV. *What if my cancer came out of remission? I'm not done yet.*

Zita's eyes shot open. She blinked, and once the ceiling had resolved into cream industrial drop ceiling tiles with tan water spots, attempted to sit up. Bonds on her arms yanked her back. *Tied down! Tied down!* Her breath came out uneven, harsh, and rapid, and the EKG monitor howled like an animal. A feral whine escaped her, and she forced herself to calm and to assess the situation.

The heart monitor began to slow to a more normal rate. She looked at her arms and chest; they belonged to a woman, not the just-pubescent child she'd been during cancer treatments. The infernal EKG beep rate dropped again as she controlled her breathing. Scooting her body as far to the right as possible, she twisted and reached down the side of the mattress. Her fingers had scrabbled for a moment before she reasserted control over herself. A disciplined search discovered leather restraints, not cloth, but the knot was in the same place as so long ago. *Helpless, my ass. I'll be loose faster than a raccoon can open a trashcan.*

With delight, she determined the years had not stolen her skill with knots, even at an awkward angle. Once one hand was free, freeing the other arm was easy. Restraints gone, Zita sat up and considered the catheter problem. She had no desire to risk damaging anything permanently down there by removing it herself. As she rubbed her wrists and arms, she checked: her range of movement was acceptable, and her ankle seemed fine. The sprain she'd taken in her last exercise session must not have been severe if a short rest had restored it. Her skin bore a distasteful layer of sweat as if she had skipped a few showers. Though she limited the motions she allowed herself, her muscles reacted as expected. *Strange. No one checked on me after the machine went wild?*

The undersized room was old: faded olive drab paint, cracked linoleum floor, and a whiff of dust and paper mingled with the usual hospital antiseptic scents. A translucent plastic film, peeled at the corners and waving in the minimal cool air coming from the air conditioner grumbling below it, obscured a double-hung window. Equipment appearing newer than anything else in the room surrounded her bed and crowded an empty bed against the window. Two minuscule tables arced over the beds. A clipboard adorned her table, a pen through the top part. Light came from institutional fluorescents; one had a dead cockroach in the discolored plastic cover. An empty IV bag dangled from a metal pole next to her, still attached to her arm. No television, telephone, call button, or any of the other expected accoutrements existed in the room. She snatched the pen and moved the IV pole into a better position for use as a weapon. The door remained shut.

Zita ran a hand over her head as she tried to figure out why she was here, and why her hair had been shaved in one spot near her temple. *Last thing I remember, Miguel's surprise blind date candidate almost got himself killed, and Quentin bought me a donut so he could make fun of my love life. Did I fall and hit my head? Enough thinking, I need to do something.*

"Well, better this than spending the rest of my existence incontinent because I couldn't wait," she growled. Wrapping the leather restraints around one fist like a boxing glove, she yanked the electrodes off her chest, flinching at the sting. The EKG went dead. Counting seconds in her head as if holding a difficult position, she hid her wrapped hand under the sheet and waited. And waited. She practiced polite ways to ask what was going on. At three minutes, she probed the shaved spot, finding only stubble and the tender line of a half-healed gash. At four minutes, she determined she couldn't understand her own medical chart. Around the five-minute mark, she began cautious abdominal crunches and arm curls with the restraints to pass time.

Someone in navy blue scrubs banged open the larger door around the ten-minute mark, glanced in, then turned to leave.

"Hey! You! I'm not dead! What do I got to do to get attention around here?" Zita bellowed, her practiced request forgotten.

The woman in the doorway flinched and turned. This time, she noticed her patient sitting up and twirling the electrodes with one hand. Her hand dove to a clunky, old walkie-talkie clipped to her belt, fingers fumbling and fussing over the buttons. It fell out of her belt and onto the floor, evading her grab for it. As she stared at Zita, brown eyes opened wide behind tiny circle glasses and her body tensed, shoulders drawn up tight. The woman shifted from foot to foot, leaving herself off balance.

Not a fighter, then, Zita decided.

Little tendrils of hair straggled out of a tight, short ponytail to cling to a face both pale and pinched. Parsimonious lips opened in a silent O. She crept forward and extended one arm toward her device.

Zita snorted. "Not going to stop you. Knock yourself out."

At her words, the other woman scuttled forward and snatched up the fallen walkie-talkie. Even as she snapped it back on her belt, she retreated toward the door. She had the sensible shoes and endurance gait of someone used to walking but lacked any other muscle tone on her spare frame.

Zita kept her sniping mental. *Wow, way to kill a patient. Did Q cheap out on our chingado health insurance when I wasn't looking? Maybe the cops figured out that I was the one who spidered up that building in March and had me committed to a psychiatric ward? Does that—not enough attitude to be a doctor—nurse have pepper spray next to her sad excuse for a walkie-talkie? It really looks like pepper spray. Being sprayed sucks and always reminds me of that one date.* She pasted an agreeable expression on her face. Aloud, she said, "Hi. I want to leave. Would you please tell the doctor I'm awake and remove the catheter for me, please? Oh, and why was my head shaved?" She was pleased she hadn't cursed aloud once.

The nurse, aide, or whatever her title, took a single step toward Zita, studying the Latina with an apprehensive expression. Her words had the deliberate enunciation most used with a dimwitted child. Without replying to any of Zita's requests, the nurse began asking questions in a soft, high voice. "Do you know your name? Is it okay if someone checks your pupils? On a scale of one to ten, how much pain are you in? Does anything feel strange to you?" Her hand skittered from the walkie-talkie and hid behind the pepper spray.

Weird. She's acting like I'm a mental defect serial killer. Maybe that's how they talk in creepy hospitals. Since she's missing a nametag, I think I'll call her... Nurse Mouse. Zita returned her suspicious look, and answered, "Yes, I do. Sure, you can. Whichever end of that scale is low. And, yes, the catheter. Please get rid of it and be careful. Adult diapers would mess with my lifestyle. You know what I mean?" She tacked on another smile, the one she used when convincing customers of her competence. Keeping her improvised boxing glove under the covers, she smoothed the surface of the sheet covering her with the other, the weave of the fabric rough under her fingers.

The nurse gave a slow shake of her head and took a step toward the door.

Zita blinked. Her original thought that the other woman had been scared of her had been facetious, but the nurse had paled as if Zita became a demon or whipped out Tupperware catalogs.

"I'm sorry, Miss, I can't change anything until after the doctor approves it. I'll go call him. Please don't move. Someone will be right back. Everything's fine." The words tumbled out of the nurse in a rush, and then she fled.

"Not like I have much of a choice," Zita grumbled. A thought struck her, and she shouted at the door, "Hey, can you bring food too? I'm starving!" The last half sounded forlorn, even to her.

A gleeful gurgle preceded a knock. A lanky blond poked her head in, then hurtled through the doorway, a stained lab coat flapping over a sky blue jumpsuit. Her nonchalant manner was at odds with her military-perfect posture and ground-eating strides. "Oh, so you're up now! Welcome to the Reed Quarantine Center and Toenail Polish Removing Station. I'm Dr. Trixie Turner. I know, what were my parents thinking? Better not to ask. Take it from someone who knew them. What's your name?" the doctor chirped, tramping over. Zita would have bet money she practiced a martial art. Her clothing concealed her figure to an extent, but given her pace and lack of exertion, the woman was in decent shape.

"Zita Garcia, but shouldn't you already know that?" Zita replied. "What—" she began, before the doctor cut her off.

"How are you, besides hungry? Do you have any weird urges to bend steel, breathe fire, or shoot lasers from your eyes or another orifice? You're one of the last to wake, you know, so I've been trying to get the others to take bets, but nobody likes to bet their Jell-O. People are so unreasonable. So, how's you? Tell me everything." The doctor plopped herself on the bed and opened her eyes wide, teeth biting her lower lip. She flicked her hair, the strands sliding back into place in the way that bespoke an expensive haircut.

Change creepy hospital to creepy mental hospital. Zita inched her hand closer to the pole. "I'm fine, but I'm tired of sitting still. No lasers or anything, sorry. What—" she started to say.

Trixie interrupted again. "Well, that sucks! I wasted great puppy dog eyes on nothing. No powers here either. I would totally abuse it, too, but in a superior way. Some people need a laser to their rears, in particular, if they don't use turn signals." She grabbed Zita's clipboard, snorting when she noted the pen missing. "It's thoughtful details like no pens that up the luxury factor here," she muttered. After reorganizing the papers, she flipped through the chart, and then turned it upside down. "Hmm. You've got a nasty case of chicken scratch, I see. Got a flashlight?"

A suspicion that had been niggling at Zita crystallized. "With my other belongings, but I don't know where they are," she answered. "What do you mean Quarantine Center?"

In a sudden move, the doctor grabbed something from her pocket and shoved it toward Zita's face.

Surprised, the Latina ducked her head to the side, striking Trixie's arm hard with one hand, and seizing the object with a fast twist of the other.

Trixie yelped and fell off the bed. Papers scattered across the floor.

Her heart pounding, Zita clutched the penlight in one hand, and held the IV pole in a defensive position, protecting her body. At the sound of cackling, she peered over the edge. *Pues. I guess the disarm drilling paid off, even if it was just a flashlight.*

The doctor stood and checked her arm. She waggled a finger at Zita, but from a distance. "For a girl who's slept a week, you're fast. Now you've bruised me and made me miss my dysfunctional friends, you should let me check your pupils for a concussion, brain damage, and dents. You know, anything you didn't have before you took your nap. At least, I'm assuming you didn't. No hitting this time, okay?" She scooped up the papers again, setting them to order before putting them on the table. Looking at Zita, she held out her hand for the penlight.

While Zita returned the light, she said, "You need to tell me what's going on, doctor."

The doctor raced through the test and tapped Zita's arm with the small light. "Let's do blood pressure and heart rate since we're short on nurses. Would you refrain from smacking me?"

Zita offered the arm without the IV.

Trixie performed the tests, her touch light and brisk, before secreting the penlight in a pocket. "Okay, good, no concussion. Since your reflexes are all kinds of ridiculous, you had a nonstandard awakening, normal for those here. Call me Trixie. Doctor sounds so... official. Boring. Do you have a brain-sucking squid attached to your head or is that blue and white substance supposed to be hair? Could go either way, there. Nice guns, by the way. If I could disarm someone and decorate their arm in early modern bruise without getting out of bed, I'd get to sleep in more." She reseated herself, this time, farther away, and grinned, displaying dimples.

Zita rolled her eyes and watched her in silence, lips pressed together, although she lowered the IV pole.

The blond blinked back at her for a few minutes, grimaced, then sniffed. "Oh, fine, party pooper. Quarantine, as in, you know, separating people who might be sick from the general population to ensure they don't spread cooties. In this case, super cooties. Literally. I'm guessing you're a non-presenter like the majority of us in quarantine. About a week ago, a whole lot of people dropped into comas worldwide. I mean, not many compared to the world population, but lots, possibly even a million. It screwed traffic."

Zita remained silent.

After a deep breath, Trixie continued, "In the US, the government ordered all the weird coma patients into internment—err, quarantine. Here in DC, that translated to this decommissioned military hospital housing a few hundred quarantined people. Most woke with none of the usual coma aftereffects, but forty or fifty here had wings, lasers, or other mutations. People outside quarantine who didn't do comas, or had short ones, got funky transformation cooties too. It's as if we lost a bet. So far, nobody equals the Seventies folks, like the vegetable lady who took over northeastern Cambodia or the knight with the flying pony. You know, I always wanted a pony, but not as much as a hippo. I hear they're fierce but cuddly. Come to think of it, that's how I like my men."

Zita dredged her mind for history. She had far preferred zoology, athletics, and lunch. *Mmm, lunch.* "Only fifteen people worldwide showed up with powers then, right? Aren't most of them missing or dead?" Remembering Pol Pot's grisly death at the hands... err, plants... of one of those people, she added, "Or people hope they're dead?"

Trixie tapped her nose and pointed at Zita. "You got it in one. Well, this time there's more, but most aren't as strong. The Seventies got Superman. We got the winged kid who fetches coffee for the Seventies folks. So far, the big one is a teenager in the Midwest who turned into a pink monster and stomped her town before a vet took her down with a bear dart. Oh, and a convict electrocuted other cons and flew off."

It didn't take a genius. "Okay, so I passed out... wait, a week? Can you hand me my phone? My family will be going nuts, and my Crock-Pots will burn down my building. What's with the shaved patch on my head, anyway?" Zita touched it.

Trixie shrugged. "No can do. All the phones and some other quarantined personal effects got stolen. You'll be allowed to use one of three specific landline phones in the building. Inmates get blocks of time to use those phones. The lines are long, and not in a porn-awesome way, either. The chart says you had a boo-boo, but you want me to check for a third eye?"

While Trixie was amusing, Zita was disinclined to allow her to monkey with any head injuries. "No, thanks, I think I'll wait for the real doctor. You know, the one Nurse Mouse scuttled off to get." Her voice was dry.

Trixie snickered. "Caught me, did you? I am a real doctor, just not one with any power. I happen to be a non-presenter too, lucky me. They let me help here on the medical floor because I already have the cooties. I begged, and that was one less person to let into the quarantine zone. We can't even get within a certain number of feet of the front door. Another coma patient woke up a couple hours ago, so the primary doctor is testing him."

The Latina exhaled, and ran her hand over her hair again, wincing when she touched the shaved spot. "Great. It's nice to know where my continued existence ranks. How many others are in comas?"

"Two here. A senator's daughter in a private room and one guy. Sensible people are scared of what'll happen if she dies because we can't have modern electronics. Are you in a medical profession?" Trixie confided, leaning across the bed.

The thought made Zita snicker. "Oh, no. I'm a tax preparer. Why can't we have modern electronics? Is that why nobody came when I pulled the electrodes? Are they afraid someone will watch porn? You'd think they'd want people to be occupied and happy if they have to be confined." She paused, and answered part of her own question, "Then again, you said this was the government. Happiness isn't in their mandate."

"As former military, I'd have to agree." The other woman chortled. She explained, "Lightning strikes and electromagnetic fluctuations messed up modern electronics the first three days. The result is we can't have anything fun in case it repeats, like the Internet or cell phones. The top three floors of this building are quarters for us non-presenters. Second floor is security. I have no idea what they hide in there other than steroids. First floor is medical, and the eerie basement is now a spooky obstacle course.

They'll test you there next. The lead doctor in the project, Singh, has all the records on paper and keeps his notes in this stupid leather-bound notebook. Between the Privacy Act and the paper I suspect he's writing, we've got adorable numbers instead of names on everything but his papers. Anyone else can only get aggregate data. On the bright side, security can't use standard surveillance gear, so we've more privacy, plus the ornamental bliss of brawny men cluttering up the place."

A sliver of excitement ran through Zita at the thought of a new obstacle course before the reminder of captivity quelled it.

The door opened, preventing further questions. Trixie sprang to her feet and scratched on Zita's chart with a pen from her pocket, all business. An elderly Indian man in a spotless lab coat, navy scrubs, and a matching turban, strode in, bearing a pen and a leather notebook; Nurse Mouse crept in behind him. His gaze glanced off Trixie and fixed on Zita.

She waved and tried to appear pleasant. "Hi, I'm alive. Can you please ask the nurse to remove my catheter? Without an audience would be preferable. Oh, and I need to make phone calls."

The doctor eyed her. Without turning his head, he said, "Dr. Turner, did you perform a preliminary exam?" If his nurse was a mouse, he was a badger.

"Yes, the standard assessment. She's a non-presenter with the usual abrupt awakening and lack of muscle loss," Trixie replied. Her pen poised over the chart, and her attention focused on his response like a border collie awaiting orders.

His eyes narrowed. "Probable non-presenter. Assumptions without data mock science. Set up the paperwork for an obstacle course run, please, and escort the other newly awakened patient to the fifth floor before writing your reports." The frown lines around his mouth deepened as he turned his attention to Zita.

Chapter Three

A few hours later, Trixie held open the stairwell door on the fifth floor with a flourish.

Zita stepped in, and immediately became the focus of a crowd of sky blue jumpsuit-clad strangers. The large common area boasted four couches, two old desks that may once have been nurses' stations, and one low table, where old paperback books competed in tumbling off the ends first. Halls extended to the right and left, showcasing more linoleum and fluorescents. The main attractions seemed to be a CRT television and a corded phone propped opposite each other on the desks. An old-fashioned clock hung on the wall above the phone, with a paper list on a clipboard hanging below it, pen dangling from a string. It was even odds whether the people loitering had been watching television or eavesdropping on an animated phone conversation. Two bulky guards stood by the elevator and across from the stairwell, batons at their side but missing any other armaments. *Serious weight-lifters, but I can't tell what else until I see them move.*

"Singh almost popped a coronary when you mouthed off on the obstacle course," Trixie continued their casual conversation.

Zita grumped, "It's not my fault he got excited. I work out all the time and could've done his course in my sleep. Blindfolds would have been an efficient and economical addition. You'd think people would appreciate my suggestions to improve the challenge." Stopping, Zita folded up the hems on her own jumpsuit again. She suspected the other four issued jumpsuits would also be oversized. At least the too-small bras would make decent sports bras if she tried not to bounce. The panties fit and stayed on without squishing anything she might use in the next ten years. She sniffed. "The clothing counts as a handicap as well."

Trixie gurgled another laugh and waved to people as she herded Zita down the lengthy hallway on the right. Their feet squeaked on the floor as they moved. "I must've missed that, probably good for my continued employment. I was referring to when you declined to participate in his study, then threatened him with the Civil Liberties Union and 'the most humongous lawsuit you've ever seen' if he went against your wishes. Writing your refusal on a sheet of paper and handing to him was a nice flourish," she answered. They passed close enough to read the Homeland Security patches on the bulging sleeves of the guards' black uniforms. Both women nodded as they passed.

The sentries did not reply or nod back, but that could have been a limitation of their neck movement range. Zita disapproved of their regimen. *What use is a man if he's so muscle-bound he can't maneuver well? That's no fun in or out of bed.*

With a shrug, Zita kept going. "It wasn't mean. Written notice of refusal is more legally binding. He had enough information to verify I'm healthy, and the government doesn't need more. What's with the schizoid personality switches, anyway? You're a person one minute, and Dr. All Business the next, right before you disappear."

Many doors stood open, and those within who noticed them waved, stared, or did both. The rooms were uniform: two beds, two tables, two trunks, all in aged industrial tones, with only the scents of habitation to differentiate them.

As she slowed near the end of the hallway, Trixie panted a little and sulked. "Why did I let you talk me into taking the stairs up? I never take them, ever. Singh has no sense of humor. If I demonstrate one, he'll stick me back up here and deprive me of

what pitiful entertainment I can get. As far as disappearing, I took
the other new person to his room. Wait until you meet him! He's
so pretty, half the women will fall for him, and the other half will
be jealous. I prefer friendly bears, myself, especially with picnic
baskets. He's next door to you, lucky girl. This'll be your room.
You've got a roomie like all us peons. Only Sleeping Beauty gets
her own place in case senator daddy complains." She knocked, a
staccato-quick shave and a haircut, on the open door. A woman
inside blinked, wire-rimmed glasses magnifying the curiosity in
calm hazel eyes as she unfolded from a lotus pose on an unmade
bed.

Trixie waved. "Wyn, this is Zita Garcia. Zita, this is Wyn.
You're roomies. Enjoy! I have to get back before they miss my
breathtaking alphabetization abilities. See you around." She
wiggled her fingers and made a swift retreat. Her hair bounced as
she left. Zita moved to the doorway, holding her belongings.

The roommate stood and floated over, one hand outstretched
in welcome. Her smile, echoed in her eyes, counteracted the
sterility of the sparsely furnished room. Based on her grace and
slim form, Zita guessed the woman had taken a few dance classes,
but the sylph before her lacked the toning of a serious athlete or
dancer. *She seems familiar, but I don't see her in martial arts movies
or nature documentaries, and I don't watch anything else. She could be
a model, but she looks too healthy. So, not malnourished, just needs
muscle tone. Ooh, maybe she'll let me design a workout regimen for
her.* The thought perked up her spirits. A low, sweet voice, further
gentled by a subtle Southern accent, interrupted Zita's musing.
"And here I thought I'd get a private room. I'm Ellynwyn Diamond,
but my friends call me Wyn. Blessings of the day to you! Wait...
your last name is Garcia? Do you have two brothers, Miguel and
Quentin?"

Zita gave her hand a brisk shake. "Yes... Have we met?" she
replied, dropping the other's hand and checking out her face. *I need*

to study faces before anything else and save figuring out their exercise habits as a treat for doing the boring bit first.

Wyn laughed. "Goddess, you haven't changed. You always did evaluate if a person would be any fun before you looked at their face, and you're even wearing your hair like those clown wigs after chemo! Don't you remember me from the cancer gene therapy group?" She spread elegant arms with a flourish, glanced downward through long lashes, and smiled. Something about the unsteady corners of that smile tickled her memory.

Zita frowned. *Chica needs to tone down the posing. I'm cutting my hair after I get out of here. The group didn't have a Wyn, but a skinny brown-haired white girl, hazel eyes, symmetrical face with a straight nose, and above-average height. It can't be.* As she watched, the woman nudged a tattered paperback book under her pillow with a familiar motion. Before it disappeared, Zita noticed the cover had a woman and a shirtless man embracing. *A romance?* She blinked, and her mouth fell open. "Dorrie? Dorcas McCurdy?"

Dorcas'—*no, Wyn's*—eyes widened, and she slapped a hand over Zita's mouth. She seemed oblivious to the aborted defensive move Zita had stopped at the last second. The scents of soap and old books rose from her hand. "Shh! Not so loud. If people hear that evil name, they might use it, and that would be awful! If anyone makes fun of it, you will be helping me wreak my vengeance," she hissed. Wyn dropped her hand and hesitated, then gave the Latina's shoulder a friendly squeeze. "It's fabulous to see you. Two of the others from the experimental group are here too, but you and Andy were my best friends."

Without hesitation, Zita hugged her, and blurted, "It is one of the worst names ever, but you know your parents were deranged. They needed strong meds the way the rest of us need air." She shook her head, remembering them. After a few seconds, she apologized, words scrambling out in haste, "But they were your parents and all, so I'm sorry. I hope they're..." *not incarcerated or in a mental hospital.* She struggled for a neutral phrase. "Well." She swore internally. *Smooth, Zita.*

One corner of the other woman's mouth curved up, then the other. Wyn threw back her head and laughed so hard tears shimmered at the corners of her eyes. She dabbed at her lashes with a tissue from a pocket. "No, tell me what you really think, Zita! Last I checked my parents were fine, other than the insanity. They think I'm going to Hell. I'm certain crabgrass will be their next reincarnation. They tossed me out on my eighteenth birthday. Now, I enjoy doing ninety-five percent of the things they warned me against, but with a better name. The bed and box by the window are yours. I'm not an early morning person, so enjoy the sun. Sit down, and we'll chat until the hordes show up to meet you. We're short on entertainment around here, so two new people is exciting news."

As she stowed her meager supplies in her decrepit footlocker, Zita watched her new roommate out of the corner of her eye. Adulthood had given her friend the warm, quiet beauty only suggested in the pretty teen... and a serenity that had been lacking. The way she moved bespoke self-confidence, except for now and again when her old timidity peeked out from behind the graciousness. Her body was loose and relaxed, so Wyn must have forgiven her gaffe. She wracked her brain to reply. "Wasn't that on your to-do list? Change your name, date lots, fall in love, and live a life of endless books and luxury?" she queried.

Zita tried to pay attention while Wyn enthused about her life, but her attention wandered to their shared room. It was similar where she had woken, except the paint in this one was a faded yellow, the ceiling fluorescents lacked insect life (or death), and a wooden door hid what she hoped was a bathroom behind flaking white paint. Tray tables arched over two small twin beds instead of hospital beds. A damp towel and two navy wool blankets lay in a tangle atop her bed, which bore military corners from whoever had made it. Each table had a towel draped over it like a tablecloth, and white flowers made of socks bloomed from a water glass on one. Wyn's bed was a rumpled swirl of sheets, with a pile of blue and white clothing in a heap beneath it. A solitary coffee cup stood on her table, half-filled with water. The smell of coffee and soap mingled with faint overtones of dust. After drifting to the window, she surreptitiously pried up more of the shedding translucent window film.

The fifth floor afforded Zita an excellent view of the surrounding buildings, all of which were old brick with ornate fretwork. If this building was similar, she could climb down, even without gear. The lack of decent shoes would be a problem, but she could wrap her feet to avoid damage. Guards stood at attention near the door of the neighboring building, and she could see men patrolling the length of a chain link fence. A shrubby garden sat abandoned and forlorn next to the fence, unrestrained weeds strangling stubborn roses. One fat squirrel peeked from the sanctuary of the overgrown bushes before bounding to another tangle of vegetation; Zita imagined herself doing the same and felt her mouth twist upward. While the fence wouldn't be a problem, she would have to be careful if she wanted to get around the guards. On her way up from the basement, she had noted three, all in Homeland Security drab, posted on the first and second floor entrances. The third floor boasted four, while the fourth and fifth floors had two each; outside, armed guards patrolled.

Mentally, she complained. *What war are they preparing for? I will go loca if I stay caged here. Most of the security guards I've snuck by before were observe-and-reports, not shoot-to-kills. Night will be my best chance, and it seems I have time to plan it. On the bright side, if that's a private bathroom, I can take the shower I've been having lurid fantasies about.* Zita interrupted her roommate with, "So are you married now or what?"

Wyn shook her head. "No, haven't found the right one. I am certain, however, the universe will send him when the time is right. I might cast a few spells to hurry it, though." She twinkled at Zita, who had turned away from the window at the mention of spells. With a chuckle, she tossed a ringlet over her shoulder, her rich chestnut locks struck through with golden hues and the perfection normally reserved for retouched pictures. "Oh, so you are listening. Here I thought you were tuning me out."

Caught, Zita gave her a sheepish grin. "Maybe I missed a little. Talking about clothing, makeup, girly sh—crap, and guys is boring." She paced beside her bed, unwinding the tangled blankets.

Wyn's eyebrows rose, but her hazel eyes crinkled at the corners. "I can see why the traditionally feminine arts might be an issue, but you find men boring?" Catlike, she lounged on her bed, curling her legs up.

Folding her blankets into neat squares and setting them on her trunk, Zita turned back and picked up the damp towel. "Not the worthwhile ones, but why dissect their every move? If someone's interested, he or she should say so to the person they like. It'll happen or it won't. Whatever. If a fine man wanders by, I might point him out so my friends can enjoy the eye candy, but that's about it for discussion."

Wyn stared at her nails for a moment before looking up with a smile. "Fair enough."

Did I insult her? I didn't mean to. Why is talking so much harder without sparring or climbing at the same time? Zita tried again. "You're not boring or anything, but I'm just not into fashion and social analysis-type stuff. If you want to tell me about your life instead, I can listen better."

Her old friend chuckled. "Right. The short version is I'm Wiccan. I'm not certain if my parents think that or dancing is worse, but I enjoy both. As far as the rest of my bucket list, I have a tiny house. I work as a liaison librarian at a state university, and a pair of cats graces my residence. They must be livid with me for such an extended absence, even if they like the neighbor I've got caring for them. I've revised my monetary expectations. Eidetic memory's not as lucrative as one would think, though finding books is faster when you remember every classification number you've ever seen. What about you? As I recall, you had a huge list of things to do. Did you ever go skydiving, BASE jumping, and so on? I check the Olympics lineup for you every time."

Her fingers smoothed the coarse terry fabric of the towel, and Zita shrugged. "As far as my list, I've been busy. The Olympics haven't happened yet. Floor gymnastics are unlikely with my figure, so I've been working on aerial acrobatics so I can be ready when it happens. One trainer had me thinking I might switch to judo instead of the aerial, but I love to fly too much." He had also labeled her a dilettante; part of her annoyance was her inability to deny the sting of truth in his words. In her opinion, his refusal to teach her until she gave up the aerial acrobatics was overkill. She continued talking, pushing away her disappointment. "That takes time, plus I play capoeira, rock climb, spar, and do any extreme sport possible. Skydiving is awesome when I can afford it! Oh, I work when I have to. People do seem to want to get paid," she admitted. Running a hand over her head, she winced when she touched the shaved spot. After prowling a few steps to the door, still holding the towel, Zita returned to the window and peeked outside again.

"Your figure is fine with the right clothing. These jumpsuits make us all look terrible," Wyn lied, probably trying to be nice. Although her outfit was identical, it appeared designer on her. Following the direction of Zita's gaze, she wafted to the window. "Looking at the machine guns? The men on our floors are bulkier than the ones on the grounds, but they're not so bad if you talk to them." She observed the strolling men without real interest, and then her gaze flicked back toward the pillow hiding the book.

I bet they were willing to talk to you, Zita thought wryly.

Wyn smiled.

With her own attention diverted to the window, Zita corrected her. "They're assault rifles, well, assault rifles alternating with shotguns, looks like. Machine guns are more elongated. They have batons and handguns too. If we're in quarantine, why is Homeland Security here and not the CDC? Plain black suits are lurking around too. And why are they carrying heavy weaponry outside? The guards on our floor just have saps."

With a shrug, Wyn twisted her curls up into a bun. "The guns all look gargantuan to me. As to why it's not the Center for Disease Control, government squabbling is likely at fault. Quarantine management has varied by location. New York lets quarantined people 'shelter in place,' and Los Angeles has a camp. Dr. Singh and his people only ask questions and take blood. They don't answer questions. One of the more loquacious guards suggested security was stricter because we're closer to major infrastructure. Rooms on the other side of the hall look out over the main parking lot, and you can see the media vans and picketers there." Grabbing a pair of pens, she anchored the coil of hair on her head and curled up on the bed.

"What are they protesting? The disregard for our civil rights that has us penned up in here, I hope?" Zita asked.

Her friend made a face. "Please. As if they're that unified," she said. Wyn counted groups on elegant fingertips. "The protesters are a few civil rights folks, crazies who think the coma is punishment for our sins, families who want more access, anti-government sorts, and one bum who has a sign offering to sleep for a week if they give him free food. Several looky-loos are loitering, but fewer show every day. Local news stations have interns camped out in vans, I think, in case any newsworthy events happen." She shrugged, and picked at a thread hanging from her pillowcase.

Deflated, Zita nodded. "Figures. What's the other building inside the fence?" She paced back to the window and focused there. It was almost identical in height, but the windows had blinds or shades in addition to the ubiquitous translucent paper. For the lack of another place to put it, she spread the towel over the air conditioner to dry. Once it was even, she paced to the doorway, then back to the window again, feeling like a jaguar in a cage she had seen once, back and forth and back and forth.

"That's where they put all the metamorphosed, with wings or what have you. A couple girls from this floor ended up over there. This one woman, turns out she was a prostitute, figured out she can make men give her all their cash. Another turned into a mermaid when she showered. I hear tell a teenage boy went there from the third floor, but I don't know what he did," Wyn answered.

Sympathy for the people trapped in the building warred with the hope security would be less stringent in this one. "Bizarre. Is there any way to find out if my things were among the stolen loot? And I need to use a phone still. Mamá and my brothers will be going crazy!" She ran a hand through her locks again.

Hazel eyes met brown, and Wyn pursed her lips. "Stolen? The guards gossiped about a security breach, but I heard nothing about thefts. You need to sign up days in advance for the phone if you want anything other than the obscene early hours of the morning. I've got a half hour tomorrow. You can have fifteen minutes." Her eyes flicked toward the hidden book again. She tapped her fingers on the tray table. "I'll keep an ear out for thefts, but so far our requests haven't netted us anything, other than one or two folks who got required medicines. The consensus is this is temporary, and we have to wait. People tell me things. I'll hear something soon, Zita." She gave a small smile.

Zita returned it. "Thanks. I need to let my family know I'm alive." She glanced at the bathroom door. "Trixie mentioned no modern electronics. Is hot water a problem?"

Her friend shook her head. "Oh, listen to me running on, you must be dying to bathe. I'll distract any guests until you're presentable. The water's fine." Scooping up her book and settling into the lotus position, Wyn flicked her fingers, dismissing Zita to cleanse. "Summon me if you need anything. Clean towels are under the sink. Lock both doors when you go in. The bathroom is shared with another room, but the room's empty, so it should be all ours."

Zita fished out her toiletries and headed into the bathroom, eager to wash. Unzipping the top half of her jumpsuit, she pulled open the door and rushed... straight into a man. Spanish vulgarities exploded in the air as they both threw out their hands to catch themselves. She felt her hands sliding over the warm, wet flesh of a toned chest even as unfamiliar hands grabbed her arms and... Her face warmed as she twisted away. Staggering from the impact, she hung onto the small sink and gaped at the strange man. His towel stayed on, but he backed up into the shower stall. The odor of soap and warm male filled the room.

Ay, Mamá, that is one papi chulo. He had the long, lean lines of a serious runner, with just enough muscle and hair on his chest to wake up her libido. The hair arrowed down a smooth stomach toward what the towel hid. She was suddenly aware of how much time had passed since she'd last touched a naked male chest. The man tightened the towel around his waist and eyed her. He had sexy, elongated fingers with a small shadow of hair on the back of his hands. His legs had the sort of definition that required serious dedication.

Her tongue darted out to wet her lips. She cleared her throat and brought her eyes up to his face. Black hair, brown eyes, and enough stubble to keep his caramel-kissed face from being too pretty to be masculine had just registered when Wyn burst in. Zita swore and dodged her roommate, ending up pressed against the sink. The black metal industrial shelves under the sink bit into the backs of her legs. The almost-naked man appeared bemused.

"Zita! What's going on?" Wyn took in the scene. "Oh, good gravy," she murmured, bringing a hand to her mouth and giggling.

"Ah, ladies, I appreciate the welcome, but... I prefer to meet people outside my bathroom," he said in a pleasant tenor, and added, "fully dressed." His hand tightened on the towel, but he smiled at Wyn. A lucky drop of water fell from the ends of his short black hair and traced a path down his shoulders toward the damp towel.

Realizing with a jolt she had been staring, Zita turned her head away and glimpsed herself in the mirror. Her brown eyes glared through the foliage of the blue and white dreadlocks (with black roots where hair had grown) obscuring most of her heart-shaped face, except for the shaved area with the jagged, healing cut above one temple. She closed her gaping mouth. The grungy jumpsuit looked terrible against her brown skin, but at least it went well with the dust smeared across her face from the obstacle course. The laxity of the fabric also made her seem twenty pounds heavier. Her jumpsuit was open to the waist and wet where his hands had touched, so everyone was getting an eyeful of her abundant assets straining the thin government-issued bra, and how delighted they were to see the man. *Someone shoot me now.* She folded her arms over her chest.

"Sorry, the bathroom is shared, and we didn't know you were here. You must be new. Come on by when you're decent, and we'll say our apologies," Wyn soothed. She grabbed Zita's items from the floor, waved, and dragged the Latina back into their room.

As the door was closing, Zita found her voice again. "Sorry." She put her back to the bathroom door and shut her eyes. *I'm sorry the towel didn't drop completely so I could have seen the whole package.* Out loud, she stated, "Well, that was awkward."

Wyn snickered. "You are so bad," she said, "Now zip up and put those things away before you poke someone's eye out. I guess your shower needs to wait."

***

The next night, Zita jogged in place in the common room, ignoring the television and the mass of people. A pair of men had located a checkers set and were playing in one corner. *Mamá was wrong. My hobbies won't kill me. Boredom from this quarantine might.* Wyn and two other members of the gene therapy group from her youth stood near, gossiping and exchanging exaggerated life stories. After the expected round of surprise at reuniting, in unspoken accord, they avoided revisiting their miserable shared past, probably due to all the others who had not survived.

Jerome, the sole male in the group, tossed out a story about one of his more interesting private detective cases. After a convoluted process, including rental of a goat, he had discovered that a suspected cheating husband rented hotel rooms periodically to watch television marathons without family interrupting. Despite being more than six feet tall and at least 250 well-muscled pounds, Jerome was swift on his feet and even faster with a joke. The corners of his brown eyes crinkled when he laughed, which was often.

The last member of the group, Aideen, began recounting one of her experiences, only tangentially related to Jerome's story. Based on the barbs she threw at him, Jerome had done something with computers resulting in big money before his private detective career. Perhaps the sturdy, black-haired policewoman resented the difference in their salaries or was used to being aggressive to be heard. The men in her family were all cops; Zita pitied her if they were all like Miguel. Then again, Aideen had little patience for any voice other than her own, and her smiles never quite reached her blue eyes. Wyn, in particular, could not seem to offer an opinion without interruption. *She's lucky Wyn is kinder than me. Girl has my sympathy with all that boredom and frustration she's oozing, but there's no reason to pick on—*

"Zita, would you please settle down? You're giving me a headache," Wyn complained. Brown ringlets swayed as she rubbed her forehead.

Zita glanced at her frowning friend. "Sorry. Do you want to go lie down? I was going to work out after my phone call, so you'll get peace and quiet," she answered. *Just a few more minutes, then hopefully big brother, FBI Special Agent Miguel, can give me some good news.*

"Again?" Wyn questioned.

Aideen jumped in with her opinion, probably crabby that they had abandoned the pretense of listening to her. "Most weight-loss plans require exercise. Civilians lack the dedication to equal the police or armed forces." She smirked and flicked her black bob of hair. "I'm sure you try, though."

Jerome chuckled. "Didn't I see you walking up and down the stairs on your hands earlier, Zita? Wasn't that enough of a workout? I admit, I miss the gym, but you were at it for a while. You ran through the obstacle course too, right?" Teeth flashed again in a smile brilliant against his dark face.

"I work out hours a day, every day." Zita cut herself off there, trying the whole patience thing.

The cop continued to smirk. "The weight will come off someday, Zita, with an exercise regimen and a diet. I'd give you tips, but I can't share the police training regimen with civilians, you know."

Screw patient. Condescend this, bitch. Eyes narrowed, Zita stared at Aideen for a moment, studying the other woman and replaying how she moved. Despite her large frame and strong, rectangular build, the cop had little excess weight, so she did do regular exercise. With her build, she would bulk up if she lifted, but Zita saw few signs of that. "You run a couple miles and do a few lighter weights or push-ups a couple times a week. You got baton and melee training at the academy, but you haven't kept it up. Unless you went to a strange academy, there's no reason you couldn't say what you learned. On the other hand, I've been training for the Olympics. With no equipment to use here, I'm improvising. Keeping my weight up so I don't lose muscle, not down, is a problem. We can't all have your boyish figure." She checked the clock. *Almost time to see if my brother has any news.*

Face turning red, Aideen glared at her, reprisals lurking in her eyes. After a moment of theatrical nostril flaring, she said, "You keep telling yourself that. I don't expect a civilian to understand.

The Olympics are a pipe dream for you, but perhaps you can eventually win a local competition."

Zita turned her head to look at the other woman full on. *Someone just volunteered to entertain me. Aideen might even choose a new target, and leave off hurting Wyn's feelings.* Chirping brightly, she asked, "If you think I'm that out of shape, you want to spar?" She bounced on her heels.

A surprised snigger escaped Aideen's mouth. "You're kidding, right? I'd crush you."

"Regular sparring is out then, given your weight class," Zita replied, her tone mild. "How about arm wrestling? You and me, right now?"

Wyn smothered a laugh with her hand. "Zita..."

Aideen snickered again. "Yeah, sure. You've been asking for it."

Metal howled against the floor. "Here's a spot you can use," someone shouted. A few in the group pulled sofas and one startled reader out of the way. Murmurs began in the bored crowd. Although they kept their faces straight, the guards by the elevator shifted to watch.

Zita snickered and lay down on the floor. She offered her hand and a grin. "Not too late to pull out."

"Fat chance." Aideen stretched out across from her.

Jerome lowered his body to kneel next to them. "I'm judging. First one to put the other's hand on the floor wins." No one argued with the big black man's qualifications, not with the way his jumpsuit strained to contain the breadth of his shoulders.

The women gripped hands, and Jerome steadied them as he delivered the rules. "I want a fair fight, and preferably a naked one. So, no spitting, hair pulling, or punching, but if your clothing is too confining, take it off." He grinned and let go.

Aideen began to press, all power and no finesse, counting on her greater size and weight. Their arms jerked an inch toward loss for Zita, but she used the opportunity to tug her arm toward herself and adjust her grip.

"Did you forget I have brothers?" Zita said. Twisting her wrist, she forced Aideen's hand back and destroyed the cop's leverage with another subtle grip shift. The struggle changed direction, and it was Aideen's turn to squirm. Biceps warmed and heat began to pool as Zita forced the cop's arm down. When their hands were only inches from the linoleum, another slight angle modification brought her shoulder muscles into play and finished it.

"Winner!" shouted Jerome. "The trophy goes to Zita!"

Aideen pulled herself up, rubbing her wrist. "Lucky." She turned on her heel and marched away.

Zita shrugged and waved at the departing woman's back. "Later! Thanks for the match." Something about the set of Aideen's back, as if she braced for something, stirred flickers of guilt.

Wyn hid a smile behind her hand. Pain etched small lines on her lovely face. "Try to be nicer next time, Zita. Nobody likes to be told they are second-rate." Her gentle tone belied the bite of her chiding.

"She could have said no or just not picked on people," she answered, rising to her feet. *I did play nice. Why don't people believe me?* She huffed, and Wyn's lips curved upward further.

Jerome laughed. "Do me next, little girl, I want to hear what my regime is." He folded his arms across his chest and smirked.

Letting go of her annoyance, Zita focused on the challenge and made a show of eyeing him before answering. Bulkier than she cared for, but not as bad as the gorillas by the elevators, Jerome was a heavyweight boxer: as dense and tall as a football player, but light on his feet. "It's easier to guess on people who spend real time in a gym like you. You're not a runner. My bet is strength-building exercises, weights, and boxing. If you do martial arts, it's a mixed bag, not a single discipline. You're fast for your size, and your footwork is probably sweet. Based on the ketchup bottle exhibition at lunch, you've fenced. You want to spar? You've come a long way from the kid who watched cartoons with Andy all the time." His size and strength guaranteed him the win, but she would enjoy making him earn it.

He grinned, straight white teeth proving his youthful orthodontia had been worth it. "Got it on all counts! You're on, hon. Oh, and it was anime, not cartoons. Anime is cooler."

"Sweet! Don't worry, I'll be gentle when I annihilate you," she teased.

Jerome scoffed. "Scary words from the featherweight."

"Hey! I could totally make bantamweight... depending on how the rules define it. It's my turn for the phone." Joyous, Zita moved over to claim her prize. The phone was still warm from the previous caller. She punched in Miguel's number as Jerome's laughter rang out behind her.

Her oldest brother picked up on the second ring. "Garcia. Talk to me," he said. His voice held the echoing sound of a speakerphone and the quiet trickle of water behind him. Metal on glass clinked as she drew in her breath to answer.

She smiled. Zita pictured him in his boring black work clothes with the sleeves rolled up while he washed his dishes with his favorite lemony soap. He would stare down his hawk-like nose at the dishes as if he could intimidate them into cleanliness. Every hair would be in place, except for that stubborn bit in the back he either didn't know about or had disowned years ago. Using the thick, fake Mexican accent that never failed to annoy him, she said, "Oye, hombre, you know where I can buy a poncho? I got nachos and a giant sombrero already." She snickered. Zita and Quentin had been using that accent to annoy Miguel for so long it felt natural. Once, she had kept it up for days.

Metal hit the sink on the other end of the line with a clunk. "Zita! You're awake! Drop the atrocious accent. Are you okay? Are you... changed? Why didn't you call sooner?" he exclaimed, ordered, and asked. Not an atypical reaction for her straight-laced brother.

Zita leaned against the wall, keeping an eye on the room. To ensure the local eavesdroppers would have to exert themselves, she lowered her voice as she answered. "That the fancy interrogation technique they teach you at work?" She made a face at the woman who leaned closer to catch her words. The other looked away. *I win. Go me.*

He interrupted. "Drop the accent, seriously."

She obliged but switched to rapid Spanish. Nearby strangers seemed disappointed. "If by *changed*, you mean *pissed*, then yes. Did you expect me to be happy, waking up in the Man's internment camp, where they're starving me, boring me, and refusing to answer questions like when can we go home? If you mean did I grow any appendages or learn to shoot fireballs, no change. Other people did, but they're in another building. Prison convicts get to go outside, but we don't. They only have three phones for a couple hundred people, so getting phone time is hard and timed. I figure they don't want to waste too many people listening in and recording our calls. Without a warrant, too, I bet. Let Quentin and Mamá know I'm surviving. I figured since you're a nosy bastard, you've been looking into it. When can I go home?"

Her brother was silent for a moment after her barrage, the splash of water from the faucet echoing in the silence between them. "Flattering description. It reflects money well spent by those college scholarships you earned. I'm glad you're well enough. Have you seen the news? Everything's in an uproar over all the... they don't even know what to call them yet. Changed. Superhumans. Parahumans. Mutants. Powered. It simplifies matters that you're not one, but the quarantine will continue until the government decides otherwise. Assume a minimum time of a few months, or more likely, a quarter of the year. My best guess is Homeland Security will open a new section to handle it, but they're not making friends. The CDC is furious."

Zita felt the sudden need to go work out, preferably on a punching bag or skilled partner, until sleep claimed her. Her voice was weak when she asked, "Months? Are you serious?" *I won't be able to go to the jungle this year! All the fun jobs will be taken by the time I get out of this place. Unless one of the adventure vacation places needs a last-minute translator and everyone else is busy, I'll have to scrounge jobs with Quentin to get money for bills.* She jogged in place, needing to move, even as she blinked, sniffed, and denied the reason why. *Dusty old building is giving me allergies.*

Sympathy radiated from his voice. "I'm sorry, Zita, but that's the latest. They said family members can send books and letters. Is there anything you want? They won't allow other items."

"Plenty of people outside the camp changed. Can't we at least be quarantined at home?" she queried. She avoided whining, but it was a near thing, averted only by vicious mental swearing.

Miguel sighed. "Zita, I've been asking. Nobody's giving on it yet. Try being patient for once."

She ran her hands through her hair, avoiding the shaved spot. "What about paying bills? Utilities and rent are on autopay, but if I don't have money coming in, that's a problem." Her foot started tapping.

Her brother exhaled. Metal squeaked, and the sound of water shut off. "Good point. Quentin has a key, right? I'll have him collect your bills and pay them out of your paycheck, and he can grant you a loan for the rest. You can pay it back when you're out or able to access a computer. Did you want a book?"

"Fine. Send me a one on intermediate Greek. I've been picking up the basics for kicks, and it might be hard enough to hold my attention," Zita answered. *If I can become fluent enough by Christmas, that restaurant owner will throw me extra translation work and free dinners.*

Her brother seemed to feel otherwise, his voice gaining cheer as he spoke. "You know, being there could be beneficial. It gives you time to decide what to do with your life."

¡Ni madre! Not this again. Why is he bringing this up now? Her desire to smack something gained a specific, fraternal, target. "There's nothing wrong with my life."

Miguel continued, undeterred. "You'll be thirty in a few years. Have you saved anything for retirement? You can't keep bouncing from job to job and giving half your attention to anything other than those dangerous hobbies of yours. Just pick one job and stay with it. If you develop a five-year plan, I'll help you polish it when you get out."

"Four years until thirty," she said. "Four. Putting more in a 401K won't solve anything and I—"

Raising his voice, he overrode her, having found his stride and his happy place in well-meaning harassment. "Zita, take it from someone older and wiser. In time, you'll be physically unable to continue. No one wants to see you alone and crippled or in an early grave."

Zita almost said the last words in unison with him. *Anyone who says a man can't nag has never had one care about them. I need a diversionary topic.* Swallowing her annoyance, she continued, "Can you at least find out if the possessions stolen from quarantine victims included my stuff? I was wearing Papa's Saint Jude medal, and I want it back."

Miguel's voice sharpened. "How did you hear something like that? Who told you?"

Oh, Trixie, you naughty girl. What doors have you been eavesdropping at? We need to talk. Putting her back against the wall, she gave a vague answer as she surveyed the room. "Oh, someone must've mentioned it. I guess it's true then." Jerome and Wyn continued to chat nearby. The excitement of the arm wrestling over, everyone else there worked on their mastery of loitering.

Miguel exhaled sharply. "I can't say either way. If it were true, I would be looking into that medal for us—you. Who is spreading that rumor? Because you could be withholding information on what would be an active investigation."

His disapproving tone made her homesick. Zita used as much truth as possible. "People have little to do here but gossip. Even if I remembered, they were repeating something someone else said."

"Don't repeat rumors to anyone but me or another investigator, you understand? You don't want to spread misinformation," Miguel ordered as if he expected her to listen.

Inwardly, she snorted. He probably waved a sponge at the phone, too.

Her reply was forgotten when the elevator dinged, and a platoon in black suits and earpieces poured out. While it was only four more guards, they took up so much space, it seemed like more. The room hushed. At the elevator, the usual sentries sneered at the newcomers, then stood at attention. Either oblivious or not acknowledging the insult, the new guards spread out and searched the room for threats. Gazes lingered on Jerome before one barked into his walkie-talkie. "Clear." The elevator doors closed.

"Something's happening. Extra guards are pouring in," Zita whispered into the phone in Spanish.

When the doors chimed again, everyone was watching the elevator. Her hopes were for an official announcing the end of the quarantine. She clutched the phone. Miguel was shouting, but she ignored it, a familiar and comforting habit. He was probably splattering the wall by his sink with water, too.

"Vampires are now real," boomed a reporter on the evening newscast. Someone slapped the television off.

As the elevator doors opened again, Zita had to crane her neck to see what was happening through the gathering crowd.

Guards all but saluted when a slim woman stepped out. The room seemed to hold its collective breath. From what was visible to Zita, the other woman did aerobics and jogging, with ballet classes and gymnastics in her past to explain the walk. *The boobs are probably fakes.*

"Hey, now, how are all of you doing?" the new woman drawled, lashes sweeping down over her azure eyes and up again. She flashed a brilliant politician's smile and tossed perfect golden hair over her shoulder as if filming a shampoo commercial.

Zita froze. Murmurs began circulating through the quarantined, and she caught the words "Olympic gold medalist," "famous," and "celebrity." Scattered cheers began. *Oh no, it can't be. My life hasn't been nearly bad enough to deserve this.* She scowled.

One of the extra guards spotted the phone in her hand, perhaps hearing Miguel's frantic commands for her to report. "You! Hang up the phone now!" He advanced on her.

The blond celebrity and everyone else turned their attention to Zita, allowing the Latina to see the other woman without obstructions. Two people hung back behind the newcomer.

I would recognize that clueless tool anywhere. The boobs are definitely fake. I'm in Hell. Is Trixie hiding behind her with that man? "Miguel, they're making me hang up the phone because Caroline Gyllen is here. I'll call back when I can. Get me out! Send help! Send lawyers and an exorcist, especially the exorcist!" Zita managed to hiss that much into the phone before the rude guard snatched it away and disconnected her call.

"Hey, I had several minutes left on my time," she snarled, grabbing for it.

He held it out of her reach—simple, given the differences in their heights—and told her, "You can make your call later."

Zita glared at him and calculated the consequences of scaling him for the phone. With reluctance, she had decided against it when a woman behind her spoke. Turning, she faced the one person she had hoped to never see again.

"I'm sorry for the inconvenience, Miss. They're a little jumpy about security here. I'm sure you can finish your phone call soon. Don't let it ruffle your feathers," Caroline placated her, having snuck up through the adoring swarm. A simpering fan asked a question, and she turned to answer. Others among the quarantined thronged around her, crowding Zita and her friends away from the celebrity.

She doesn't even recognize me. Spoiled bitch. Zita glowered, bitterness filling her mouth before something else caught her eyes.

Wyn was white, and rubbing her forehead.

"Wyn? You okay?" Zita asked, forgetting about the guard and Caroline.

"Migraine. Don't worry," Wyn whispered. Her voice was weak, and her body slumped.

Was Wyn sloping to the side? Zita touched her friend's shoulder in alarm as Wyn's eyes slid shut, and she dropped. After catching her, Zita dragged her to a sofa, shoving the guard away when he came too close. "Trixie! Get over here!" she bellowed, then ordered, "Jerome, keep these idiots back."

Caroline said something that Zita missed.

Trixie shouldered her aside, taking Wyn's pulse.

Zita joined Jerome in trying to give the doctor space; wound up by a celebrity and the drama, people kept pushing forward like a flock of sheep. Behind her, the doctor muttered to herself.

Wyn murmured, and her eyes fluttered open. Trixie whispered quiet questions, to which she only whispered, "Migraine. Dizzy."

"A fainting spell. We'll take her downstairs for observation overnight. She'll be back up and around tomorrow," Trixie announced. "Can we get help getting her to medical?"

Zita stepped forward, but Caroline spoke a few words to one of her bodyguards first. The suited man brushed Zita aside and scooped up Wyn.

Caroline retreated to the elevator. "I'll stop by again soon. Take care," she said as her guards surrounded her, one carrying Wyn. The noise rose to a mild roar as people chattered about the excitement.

Jerome stood next to her, hands on his hips. "Poor Wyn," he said. His brown eyes were soulful with his concern.

Zita kicked a chair leg. An opportunist had grabbed the phone too. Near Trixie, who was scanning the crowd, a short, dark-haired man stuck his hands in his pockets, hunching his shoulders like a perching bird. His face appeared troubled as he observed the room.

Trixie's eyes met Zita's, and she lit up. Seizing the man's arm, she dragged him over. "Here I was about to cry because you left, and you're right next to me," she said.

"Me? Will Wyn be okay?" Zita queried. Watching him trail behind the doctor, she assessed Trixie's companion. *Martial artist, accomplished.* Zita decided, as she watched his lean, graceful form move. Nagging familiarity tickled her memory. *Black hair in a long braid, brown eyes, Italian or Hispanic, and cute if you like the type. Native blood might be mixed in. Why did he try to draw on a mustache and goatee? It's worse than a bad toupee.*

The doctor waved her hand. "Probably a migraine with vertigo. They'll run tests, but a night of peace and quiet in a dark room should fix her up. Zita Garcia, this is Andrew Cristovano. Drew will be rooming with Remus, next door to you. He woke up an hour ago, so will you show him to his room? Drew, this is Zita. That's Jerome next to her."

He coughed and stuck his hands in his jumpsuit pockets. "Actually, people call me Andy." After a moment, he nodded to Zita and Jerome.

Zita put her hands on her hips as she processed the presence of another member of the gene therapy group. "Andy? Do you remember me? We had that wheelchair race on the roof. And you remember Jerome Saint George, I'm sure, from the cartoons at the hospital," she inquired. *Out of all the hundreds in the cancer treatment group, two of my surviving best friends show up here plus a few others I recognize? Bizarre.*

Jerome turned to her. "I told you, girl, it was anime, not cartoons," he said with a shake of his head. Rotating toward the other male, he said, "Andy, man, how you doing?"

They exchanged brief handshakes and nodded at each other. Male ritual completed.

"Zita? Really? How could I forget? You know how much trouble I got in for that? Hey, Jerome." Andy grinned, and his face lightened.

She gave him a hug, slapping him on the back and beaming. *Sí, he works out. Bet he'll spar with me too. Life here is looking up.* "Hey, those races were worth it! Good to see you again. Though, as a friend, the mustache and goatee thing? It's not convincing."

Andy flushed and rubbed the back of his neck. "I had the luck to pass out on a university bench near a frat house. I'm hoping it'll fade soon," he explained, shoving his hands in his pockets.

Her peripheral vision caught Trixie withdrawing from the crowd and moving toward the stairs. *After whining about her hatred of stairs, she uses them tonight? If I can find out where she got the information about the stolen items, it might help if I need to escape.* "What a bunch of fu- losers," she commiserated, moderating her language at the last minute. As the doctor slipped out the stairwell door, she added, "Aideen is here too. We should spar, er, talk, and stuff. Listen, Jerome, will you introduce Andy to Remus? I want to catch Trixie and ask her a couple questions about Wyn."

Jerome nodded. "Sure thing."

Andy threw her a questioning look but remained silent.

"Hasta, guys," Zita tossed over her shoulder, already halfway out the metal stairwell door. She closed it with as little noise as possible. While her eyes adjusted to the light, she listened for the doctor. Footsteps sounded... from above? The only thing up there was the entrance to the roof. After removing her flapping shoes, she padded up the stairs without sound, eyes wide in the dim light.

Trixie squatted at the top of the stairs, messing with the combination lock and chain on the roof access door. Her back muscles were tense, but her feet had the wrong placement for combat.

Zita let the doctor poke at it for a few more minutes before leaning against the wall and flicking a pebble at her back.

Trixie jumped. She turned around, holding two bread knives at ready.

Based on those holds, the doctor can throw a knife. Zita wiggled her fingers. "Hi, there. Is this when you tell me they're so cheap you have to scrape penicillin off moldy bread?" she asked in a soft voice.

The doctor straightened, and brushed her jumpsuit, pocketing the knives. "I like that one. I'll have to remember it. This isn't what it looks like. I have a fresh air addiction," Trixie began.

Pushing off against the wall, Zita walked a couple steps nearer and tapped the door. "So, you're not trying to get onto the roof to do something you don't want people to know about, like planning an escape? You have to do it at night because guards watch the rooftops during the day." She left out her own rooftop excursion earlier, ended when she spotted movement on another building. Jerome had nearly caught her coming down the stairs. The lock was new since then. She weighed her options: trust or not?

"Okay, maybe it is what it looks like," Trixie whispered back. "You're awfully well-informed about their security measures for someone who woke up yesterday."

"I pay attention when someone around me has guns," Zita answered. She regarded Trixie then surrendered. When in doubt, she went with her instincts. "You owe me—if bad things are coming down, tell me. An option to escape would be awesome, but I won't hold you to that. Neither one of us has to mention anything about this to anyone, either." She tilted her head and studied Trixie's response.

"Deal," the other woman whispered. She held out her hand, a pinky extended. "Pinky swear."

After solemnities concluded with finger oaths, she set her shoes beside the door to have both hands available. Taking the lock in her hand, Zita studied it, pulled, and turned the knob a few times. She snorted and opened the lock. *I don't even need to be a locksmith for this one. High school kids can pick this.* "An ass picked the combination numbers. The combination is 36-24-36."

"What accountancy school did you attend? I like it. Thanks." Trixie smirked, shoved the roof door open and stepped onto the roof.

Zita slipped out behind her and drew a deep breath of oxygen that had not been recycled. The air was sultry, and the river rocks forming the gravel of the roof radiated the heat from the day up through the soles of her feet. Tar warred with the scents of distant cooking. Air vents and little stovepipe things speckled the rooftop, all dwarfed by the roof entrance shelter. It was otherwise bare of anything other than herself, pigeon crap, and the doctor. No one had bothered to install lights up here, so the entire roof was dark, lit only by ambient light from elsewhere. She tilted her face up and soaked in the freedom, false as it was. Her shoulders relaxed, and she purred. *I'd go home if it were possible. I would leap off the roof and fly like that hawk I spotted earlier.* The thought was both wistful and heartfelt.

Trixie interrupted the picture of home so distinct she could almost touch it. "Ahem."

"What?" Zita said, her concentration broken. After looking around, she located the other woman.

Arms crossed over her chest, Trixie stood near a group of three vents.

Ambient illumination is enough to do a fair amount without turning on lights because that frown wouldn't be visible otherwise. Good to know, Zita thought.

Trixie's voice had chilled when she stated, "I like my fresh air alone. It's sort of a ritual. I might have to get naked for it. You're not my type." The blond doctor scanned the roof as if searching for the source of Zita's voice.

"Oh, fine. Enjoy your happy fun naked time, then." *Guess my night vision is better than hers if she can't see me. I'll come up here later and find out what she's hiding. Unless... if she really can't see me...* Zita walked to the door, each step as loud as she could make it, and shut it with a bang. Then she ducked behind the corner, crouching low, inhaling in short, shallow breaths, and trying to make her bare feet as silent as a cat on the stalk. After a moment, a penlight clicked on, aimed her direction. Zita prowled around behind the roof entrance, circling it as Trixie came over and checked to see if she was gone. If there had been other cover, she would have taken it.

After panning the roof with her light, Trixie finally clicked it off. Both waited. It was probably ten minutes before Trixie headed back to the three vents.

Zita peeked out from her hiding place, her eyes well-adjusted to the dark after the wait.

Reaching the vents, the doctor poked at them. One responded, as Trixie retrieved a bread knife from her pocket and removed the grill. From inside, she drew out a coil of metallic cord, and something else hidden from view by her body. The penlight clicked on again, and paper rustled. The other woman turned off the light, stowed the paper in her pocket, and hid the items away again.

Ay, I'd like a look at that love note. Later tonight, I will sneak back to see the whole cache. But if she locks the chain behind her now, I'm hosed! Zita used the sounds of the grate being returned to its position to glide back in through the roof access door. Shoving shoes on her aching feet, she ran downstairs.

Chapter Four

Three weeks later, Zita put the last load in the dryer and turned it on. She paced and exhaled deeply.

Wyn's migraines had grown more frequent, but the medical staff could not rule out brain tumors. When cornered, Trixie admitted the quarantine building lacked the right equipment. *Brain scanners should be higher priority given Wyn's history of cancer. If it were Caroline—the tool—they'd beg, borrow, or steal the necessary machines. Maybe a ploy to pressure people into the research group? Study participants get extra privileges, but denying medical services seems extreme. I convinced others to refuse participation in Singh's study. Was it wrong to do so? Would the cost be so high? Wyn insists the omphaloskepsis, whatever that is, and her visualization exercises to wall off the pain are helping. It all looks like New Age meditation to me. Dios, a sign would be helpful.* She growled and glanced at the clock above the ancient washing machine and dryer. If the cycle finished soon, she would have time to work off frustration before the minimal breakfast they served became available. Her stomach grumbled at the thought of food.

Dreaming of chilaquiles, fuba cake, and bacon, she put the soap away and started folding clothes from the last batch, separating them by owner. She shook out one of Jerome's jumpsuits with more force than necessary; somehow, he had talked her into washing his garments in exchange for his participation in their peaceful protest. Her mouth twisted in reluctant amusement. At least, he had brought his new lawyer girlfriend into the group, an expert on business and civil liberties law. Andy, who had lived on the Navajo reservation, and Wyn, who preferred holistic medicine, had required little persuasion. Aideen was participating in the research project. The prickly cop had even laughed and implied Zita paranoid for resisting, straining the détente they had arrived at due to their shared past. *You'd think a cop from a cop family would have less faith in the system by now, being a part of it and all.*

The old dryer coughed and rattled, and Zita smacked it. Just as the sting of her flesh on the metal registered, the room went dark, and the dryer stopped. "Seriously? You have got to be kidding me," she said. When the lights remained stubbornly off after a count of ten, she fumbled her way to the dryer. She pulled out the wet clothes and dropped them on top of the dry things in the laundry basket. "Guess it will all air dry or mold, whichever happens first." She was still grumbling when she stepped into the hallway with her basket. After a moment to orient, she headed toward her room. The diffused glow of the city outside provided the only illumination, leaking through the windows at the end of the hall. *It must be a localized problem if the streetlights are still on. If the outage is an extended one, we'll all develop eyesight like a cat or an owl. Probably more like a cat, at least it's mammalian.*

The fifth-floor hallway was empty, but stirring whispered behind some of the doors as Zita passed. Hefting the basket, she strode down the hall. When cloth rustling warned her of another moving in the common area, she slowed. A small circle of light, a penlight, bobbed at a rapid clip toward her, held by a dark shape. As it drew closer, she recognized a familiar face.

"Oye! Be careful where you're going!" Zita exclaimed as she dodged. Wet clothing, probably her underwear, slopped out of the basket and hit the floor.

Trixie gasped and shuffled back a step. "Zita? What are you doing wandering around?"

Zita threw a hand in front of her eyes when the light lifted toward her face. "Could you not wreck my night vision?" She snorted and scooped up the clammy clothing, dumping it back into the basket. "I was doing laundry until the power died. Us rebels only get into the laundry room after dark and before dawn, remember? What's your excuse?"

Trixie took a step toward the stair exit. Her voice was shrill and tense. "I was getting in a quick phone call. The guards are usually gone for a couple minutes about now when the shifts change, but they seem to be running late getting back." She crossed her hands over her chest, rubbing her arms.

Oh, a phone call without an audience would be awesome. My brothers will survive if I wake them up. It's not as though Quentin and his conquests hesitated to wake me when I lived on his couch in college. Still, I won't be grabby. "Are you done with the phone?"

"It went dead seconds before the lights went out."

A chill fluttered through Zita. "The guards are missing, the phones are dead, and the power's out?"

"Sounds right, Captain Obvious." Trixie's mouth was a thin, tight line.

A muffled, hollow sound detonated below several times. The wash became airborne. Both women dived to the floor that smelled of feet and cheese curls. Their gazes met. Trixie's eyes were wide and feral; Zita assumed her own matched.

"Gunfire!" they said at once.

Trixie rose to a crouch. "Jinx. Assault rifle," she identified. Her hand went to her side, then her back.

Zita nodded and added, "We are so chingado." She got to her feet, stooping low, her mind whirling. *I can't help everyone; I have to get my friends to safety! Start with Wyn and Andy, get to Jerome if possible since he's at the other end of the floor. Aideen too, I guess, she used to be okay.*

While she was thinking, Trixie scurried toward the stair exit, penlight flickering with her movements.

The sharp claws of memory pricked Zita. "Hey, Trixie? If you use your rope to get out, please leave it up so we can try to use it too. And good luck."

Trixie paused, a hand on the door. "Aren't you a clever one? I will, but you're on your own with it. It's not meant for a crowd, though I'd bet that was a planned contingency." She giggled, a high, strained sound with little real mirth in it. "Good luck to you too," she called, switching off the penlight and slinking through the door.

Adrenaline pouring through every fiber, Zita sprinted to her room, leaving her slippers and the scattered laundry behind. As she went, she pounded on random doors and shouted. "Wake up! Guns!" *At least they won't be asleep when whatever it is happens.*

In her room, she pulled a sleeping Wyn onto the floor. "Wake up!" Zita hissed, then added, "Keep down."

Wyn let out a shocked yelp as her body contacted the cool linoleum. "Wha? Zita?" Indignant hazel eyes peered out of the tangle of woman and blanket. An arm flailed in a punch that would have been vicious had its owner hefted more dumbbells and fewer books. "It's not even dawn yet." Her words slurred with sleep, menace, and the South coloring her voice.

"Get dressed, but stay low. Someone's got guns, and they're using them," Zita said. She threw open the bathroom door and banged on the one that connected to Andy and Remus' room. "Get up and get dressed! Guns!" Upon returning to her room, she crept to the window and peeked into the predawn. Several nights' effort in removing the film had resulted in a wide-angle view. Most of the time, she watched the local birds squabbling and calculated escape routes.

Zita squinted, trying to decipher the feverish activity below. A handful of white vans parked haphazardly on the remains of the chain link fence. Brake lights glowed red in the darkened morning, and the low rumble of motors was audible this close to the window.

Dark figures moved around, but in irregular patterns that failed to follow standard patrol routes. Her stomach roiled at dark, immobile blotches on the ground of a size and shape to have been men.

"Coffee," Wyn muttered, "Tall skinny mocha, extra foam." Blankets rustled. "What time is it?"

Zita glanced at her roommate, who propped herself up on one arm, rubbing her eyes with the other. "Before dawn. Get up and dressed. Keep low. Somebody isn't playing, and we don't want to meet them." Elsewhere on the floor, someone shouted. Gunfire spat again, and she flinched, banging her knee on the air conditioning unit.

Wyn inhaled sharply, and a hand flew to cover her mouth. She got to her feet and grabbed clothing. Another flood of gunfire, this time, closer, elicited a whimper and increased speed. "Hide where? These rooms don't even have dressers."

"Excellent question." Zita scanned the sparse room and dashed to the door. After cracking it open, she checked the hall. Flashlights moved and lit the halls enough to show the outlines of men with guns. One light headed their direction, so she eased the door shut, leaned against it, and planned.

Words became intelligible in the shouting. "Stay in your rooms! Remain in your rooms, and you will be safe!" The command repeated, growing louder, then fading away.

The women gazed at each other. Zita spoke first. "I bet they got a bridge for sale, too. You gonna trust the gunmen in the hall or you want to hide with me?"

Wyn hesitated. "Is there a way to do both? If that's Homeland Security, I don't want to be arrested. This is bad enough." She struggled into her jumpsuit, wincing when the zipper caught on her skin. Done, she smoothed the clothing.

One hand raked through her hair as her brain raced. Zita pulled out her emergency stash: a purloined roll of duct tape and a sharpened bread knife. Her mind drifted back to the Brazil debacle and another friend. Swallowing to free her throat from a lump, she took a deep breath and pushed all that away. *Deal with now. The past is gone, and I won't let anyone die through inaction again.* She forced a smile. "Here's the plan. We use the beds to get up to the ceiling and put the tiles back in place behind us. Stay still and stick to the wall once we're up, since the ceiling won't hold our weight. If we're lucky, they won't check up there, and the bad lighting will hide any marks we leave." She pushed Wyn's bed into position by one wall, followed by her own near another. Shoving the Greek texts aside, she angled a table to arch over the head of each bed for extra height, though they seemed too unstable to help. Her friend gaped at her. Something loud thudded nearby.

"I don't know if I can get up there," Wyn said. Her steps slow, she walked over and stared at the ceiling as if memorizing the water spots.

"Can you free climb a building?" Zita asked, knowing the answer. If Wyn had been able to, they would have gone out the window already, despite her guilt at leaving the other quarantined people to their own devices. Gunmen reaching the fifth floor that fast required more haste than care. Someone barked a command in a nearby room.

Wyn shook her head and chewed her lip.

"Right, and they're in the halls, so we're stuck in the room. That leaves under the beds or up in the ceiling. Which of those sounds best? If you've got a better idea, princess, let's get on it."

The other woman clambered onto her bed. Stepping on the table, Wyn moved aside the panel and tried to pull herself up. Her hands groped at the edge and slipped off. A fine white dust drifted down from the open hole. The table teetered underfoot. Another clunk sounded, closer.

Zita hurried over to help. After climbing on the bed, she steadied Wyn. Her toes sank into the bedding. "Forget the table. I'll heft you up. Step into my hands and try again. You can do this. Let's go," she said, lacing her fingers together.

Her friend nodded, took a deep breath, and did as she'd asked. Grunting with effort, Zita heaved her friend up.

This time, Wyn managed enough of a hold to start dragging herself into the ceiling.

Most of Wyn was in the ceiling when the door to the room flew open. A bright white beam of light speared the dark, blinding bright after the predawn murk. The ceiling groaned. A stream of dust poured down on Zita's head.

Coughing and sputtering, she hopped off the bed and away from the opening, hoping to draw his attention.

The man holding the light snickered. "What do we have here? Is little chicken running from coop?" A Russian accent tripped through the sounds in his query. An assault rifle swayed from one hand, while the flashlight in his other hand lowered as he laughed. She could make out a crew cut and dark clothes, but the flashlight beam prevented her from seeing more.

Another man, similarly dressed, nudged the Russian. In an American accent, he ordered, "Let me see her." The light blazed into Zita's face again. She raised a hand to cover her eyes in protest. "Skin's too dark. Where's the second one? All the rooms on this floor have two occupants."

Zita shrugged and brushed off dust. "It's just me in here. My roommate got hauled off to the other building yesterday," she lied. Silently, she prayed they missed the dust cascading down from the gap, and that Wyn would not move.

The light flicked up to the ceiling, where the hole yawned. "She was under that hole when I come in. Perhaps other one is in ceiling, and this one lies." The Russian pointed the beam back at Zita.

The American nodded, and said, "Easy enough to find out. We don't need this girl. Whoever is hiding, come out now, or the girl with the ugly hair dies. You have ten seconds. I have a schedule."

The Russian chuckled. "Ah, is good, the others will be more pliant if little one is made example."

"Aww, come on. I can't help it if they took my roommate away. Don't shoot me!" Zita tried. She palmed the knife she'd set down earlier and prayed Wyn would stay hidden. *Come on, trust the harmless little woman and move on. If I throw the knife, it may distract them enough to miss us in the darkness. This close is bad for accuracy, anyway.*

"Five seconds left," the American announced in a bored tone. The Russian raised his weapon.

"Stop! I'll come down. Don't shoot! Just give me a second," Wyn's voice drifted down. Scrabbling sounds came from above, and the circle of light moved to the ceiling. The tile fell. First, the lower half of Wyn's body appeared, then the top half. Something gave way as she attempted to get down, and she landed on the bed hard. She coughed and sat up.

The Russian cackled. His American counterpart groaned. "Shine it on the new one," he ordered.

The light focused on Wyn, creeping up and down her body as she slid off the bed, brushing at the dust.

The Russian made a suggestion, "Do we have room for extra? That one should be worthwhile one way or another." He panned the light over Wyn again. Zita could have smacked him.

"Yeah, grab her when we've finished searching for the targets. I'll keep going with Johan. You watch her," the American concurred. He touched the slick radio at his side. "Command, we're bringing an extra for bonus bucks. We got the space, right?"

"Yes, granted," a man's voice crackled over the radio. The Russian laughed. His partner spun and walked away.

Beside her, Wyn shivered in the beam of light. Zita scowled.

The American shouted down the hall, "Two females, no blonds." He paraded out of sight. A loud thud sounded next door. After a pause, the American's voice called out again. "Two males, white."

Zita's mind corrected them automatically. *Andy is mixed, and Remus is that lovely caramel all over... unless his towel was hiding...*

The radio popped. "Primary target acquired. Secondary target secured and out. Tertiary target Saint George located. Make examples as necessary. Begin withdrawal."

They wanted a blond woman and Jerome? Zita wondered.

A burst of gunfire echoed from down the hall, followed by a scream. An American voice shouted, "Stay in your rooms!"

The Russian made a brusque gesture. "Pretty girl, you come with me. Cause trouble, I shoot your friend. If you are sweet to me, it will be better for you." He strode forward grabbing for Wyn, who was shaking her head and backing away.

Panic rising in her face, Wyn clutched at her temples and squeezed her eyes shut.

Helpless, Zita watched the goon advance on her friend, her fury increasing with each step he took. A rushing sound filled her ears. *I can't let them take her. Once he passes me, I'll surprise him with the knife, and Wyn can hide in Andy and Remus' room. If I survive, I'll climb out the window.* She moved into a better position, muscles tightening.

Her voice silken steel, save for a quiver at the end, Wyn said, "Zita, don't."

A loud sound, like a jet screaming airborne, sounded from next door. *Andy and Remus!*

"Little chicken, you will stand aside and not interfere," ordered the Russian. He stalked Wyn, who had backed herself into a corner.

Zita's thoughts tumbled over themselves, indignation fueling her as she poised to spring on the man. *Chicken? I'll show him a chingado chicken. The past few years have been sparring without hurting people, but my teachers played rough and dirty before that.*

The world darkened, even as it exploded into colors, fluorescent violet and plum shadows where none had been before. Fabric smothered her, turning the world black. The whispering rub of the cloth and sounds of breathing were loud. Instinct whispered, and she stilled. Fury warred with concern.

The man's voice boomed overhead as if he had switched on a loudspeaker. "What? Where did the little one go?" Something poked her, and light outlined an opening.

Zita screeched and exploded out of the pile of her clothing, right at the confused gunman. Feathers flew, and the flashlight soared across the room to clatter on the wall as the Russian threw up his arms to protect his face. Furious, she flapped her wings and pecked at his face and any exposed skin she could reach. A sweep of his arms almost hit her, and she perched on the edge of the bed between the man and Wyn, a low warning cluck escaping her.

Wait. What did I just do? ¡Carajo! Ruffling her feathers, Zita angled her head to better survey the man with one eye, then the other, as she sorted out impressions. Colors she had never seen before kept distracting her and the room appeared so much darker. She stretched one wing, then the other, and shifted on her perch. At the realization she was clucking again, she stopped. *Other people get to shoot lasers, and I turn into a chicken? Mamá said we'd reap what we sow; I must have been in a planting frenzy.*

The Russian retrieved the flashlight, and the beam soon centered on her.

Zita snapped at him, wings flapping, but stayed out of reach.

He roared with laughter. "A chicken? The others will believe I have been drinking. Now, girl," he gestured to Wyn, "you come with me, and we will leave the poultry here."

"Goddess! Zita, are you okay?" Wyn asked from behind her.

The goon's laughter stopped when he came within reach, and Zita pecked him hard enough to draw blood. He swore in a language she didn't speak, vile tones dripping with annoyance.

Zita shook her head to rid herself of an odd buzz in her ears.

"Perhaps I will break her feathered neck before we go. Stupid bird. Do you think I cannot catch hens?" He secured his gun on his shoulder, and set down the flashlight, flexing his hands.

Zita gave him an intimidating stare out of her beady little eyes. It worked about as well as it would have in human form. Not at all.

To her horror, he seized her, and held her spindly legs tight in one hand, with the other arm pinning her wings. "This joke ends now," the big Russian growled, fumbling for her neck, a process slowed by her vicious bites.

Wyn shrieked. "No!"

Oh, ni madre. No way. Zita threw her whole body into bucking and squirming, like the greased pig she had seen as a child at a fair. She and the Russian were both flabbergasted when the mental comparison became reality. His grip slackened in surprise, and he screamed as the weight of seventy pounds of distressed piglet landed on his boot. Zita scrambled to all four feet, instinct telling her how to move, retreating until she sensed Wyn behind her. Colors had lessened, but her overall vision improved, and scents were so rich she could have taken hours to sort them all out. The floor still smelled like feet and cheese curls. However, she needed to do something about the hopping, swearing man with the gun. Instinct suggested a solution.

With a loud squeal, more through accident than design, Zita lowered her heavy head and charged.

Her Russian nemesis fell with a shriek and a cacophony of cursing. As he rose to his feet, he fired a shot that embedded itself in the ceiling while he fought to bring her into his sights.

Zita dodged, and clattered for the door, grunting. *Yes, chase me. Forget about Wyn! If I'm lucky, I can get up enough speed to knock him down and break his gun arm.* As she careened out the door, she gave a triumphant squeal.

In the dim hall, a flashlight lay abandoned near a dark shape on the floor, and her nose identified carrion. Multiple sources of it. *The boys.* Squashing her fears, Zita ventured near enough to the body to recognize it as a stranger in dark garb, his chest and head a bloody ruin. The same stench farther down told her another body lay in the hall closer to the elevators. Despite her stomach roiling, she swallowed and turned back to their room. Her hooves rattled on the hallway floor. *Wyn needs me.*

Snarling caught her attention. The Russian hobbled to the doorway, clutching Wyn with one hand, sweeping the assault rifle around with the other. Her plan dissolved; she could not trample him while he held her friend.

Wyn's reply was comprehensible. "I won't let you hurt her, and you can't have me either! Let go! I'm not for sale!" She slapped him with her free hand.

A corner of Zita's mind judged the performance. *Girly slap, open-handed. If we survive, I need to teach her the right ways and places to punch someone.*

The man stiffened, his breath rattled, and he fell.

Wyn stood unmoving in the doorway, staring at him.

Then again, maybe she should stick with what works for her. Nonplussed, Zita trotted over, picking a delicate path around the dead Russian, nudging her friend's knee with her snout. *If I had hands, I could grab his gun and flashlight, and we'd have a much better chance.* She blinked, and found herself on her hands and knees at Wyn's feet. The floor was chilly and fetid, but at least the scent of death had receded. As Zita stood, she assessed herself. She hugged Wyn. "I'm me," she said with jubilation.

"Zita?" Andy asked, emerging from his room. In the light of the flashlight, his face was pale and sweaty, and the arms of his jumpsuit dripped. He blinked. "Do I want to know why you're naked?"

Oh, right. "Are you and Remus okay? Long story, nothing important," Zita said in haste. No one needed to know she had transformed into a—"cluck." She fussed, flapping her wings. *No, no, no! We need to grab the flashlight at least and reach the roof before anyone sees.*

His eyes rounded. "Oh. I guess that makes sense then. Remus ran. Fast."

Wyn bit her lip. "I got it, Zita," she murmured, fetching the flashlight as if she could speak chicken. The emerging dawn gave the hall just enough light to see her averting her gaze from the downed Russian.

Feathers ruffled, and Zita shook her head. *Thanks, Wyn.* The words came out a cluck.

"You're welcome. Why do we need to get to the roof?" Wyn asked. The brunette massaged her forehead. "Goddess, why is everyone so deafening?"

Andy crammed his hands in his pockets. "Roof? I don't know, you're the only one who mentioned the roof?" His eyes also fell on the Russian. When he winced and turned away, his attention stopped at the man with the crushed head. "Sec," he said, dashing into his room.

Chickens must have superb hearing because it sounds as if he's vomiting right next to me. Most of the loud voices are coming from below, but whispering is audible on this floor too. As for loud... normally, I'd say it was too crazy ass to be true, but I'm a fucking chicken right now. It might explain a few things. She fought the urge to lose her own stomach contents. Zita waddled into her room and pecked at her pile of clothing. As she tilted her head sideways, she chose her thoughts carefully. *Wyn, I need clothes or Andy will fall off the roof trying to look elsewhere. Could you carry some for me?*

"Poor Andy, he's disconsolate about that other cretin's death. He didn't mean to shove that hard, mercenary or not," Wyn said, following Zita in and picking up the clothing. She paused. "I'll get you one of those hospital gowns they gave us for nighties too, so you can throw it on faster if need be. I'll carry a spare one too." After she had dug out a gown from her own trunk, she set it atop the other items, smoothing it with exaggerated care.

Now trailing behind her friend, Zita clucked. *Awesome idea. By the way, you're reading minds. Telekinetic or whatever. Andy accidentally killed someone? We need to get out of here, so you're not sold, he's not murdered, and I'm not on Colonel Sanders' menu.* Everything around them was bigger and darker as a chicken; she stayed close to Wyn to keep from losing her in the chaotic gloom.

Wyn's lips firmed into a line as she stopped and looked at the hen tailing her. "Telekinetics is moving things psychically. Telepathy is reading minds. I can't do either. The best I can do is cast a few spells to encourage serendipity. You know, encourage the good karma outcomes."

Wings fluttering, Zita hopped after her friend. As she tilted her head up and surveyed Wyn out of one eye, she fluffed her feathers. *How are we talking if you're not reading my mind? I'm a chingado chicken. All I can do is fucking cluck.* Her head twisted to allow her to glare from her other eye. A disgusted squawk escaped her.

Hands on her hips, Wyn rounded on her and paused. "Ah. I'm superb at reading body language?" She folded the clothing into a neat pile, a certain sign of stress in the woman who usually draped her things around the room and claimed it as art.

Zita tried to laugh. It ended up as a cackle. *Of a chicken?*

Andy opened the connecting door as Wyn rubbed her forehead again. "That does explain a bit."

Told you so. Score one for team Latina! Zita crowed. She blinked, returning to her own human form.

Andy squeaked and closed himself in the bathroom. His muffled demand came through the door. "Naked bad! Clothing good!"

Grabbing the hospital gown, Zita threw it on, tying it as tight as possible. "I'm decent, prude," she called to the bathroom.

Andy emerged.

Zita continued, "Even if more armed men don't come after us, the government will move us to the other building, so I'm escaping. You should come too. Here's the plan. We go to the roof, scope out the situation and hide. If we can get out by the stairs, we go that way. If we can't, then, we get to a neighboring building with no gun dudes and sneak out of that one. I'm not staying here to live the revenge section of a fight film or end up a research subject."

Her friends looked at each other and nodded.

Chapter Five

The gunfire came again, rapid assault rifle chatter with the belching exclamation of shotguns as the three escapees hid on the roof. They huddled by the fan vents until the sounds paused. Zita wrapped the chain from the door around one hand and pried the vents open with her knife. *Gone. Let's hope it's safe and ready for us despite the bombardment below.*

Wyn gestured from the north side, where she peeked down the edge of the building. "This side has news vans, cops, and four vans of ill intent," she called out.

"Same, without the news vans, and one less villain van," Andy answered from the east. While pale beneath the olive of his skin, his color had improved when he stepped outside. He had done that as a teen too—every now and again, his time living in the open spaces on the reservation showed.

Zita hurried to one of the other sides to evaluate the situation there. Bursts of light and noise revealed men firing another brief salvo before they ducked down again. As dawn broke, she spotted three of the plain white vans she had seen from her room, encircled by a rushed cordon of marked cop cars and unmarked American cars. Suits and uniforms crouched or slumped behind doors and vehicles, blocking the streets but not the sidewalks in an incomplete wall. The building next door, housing the people who had morphed after their comas, had a huge hole in the side of it, with smoke whirling out in the wind. A few motionless forms lay below. One had blue-feathered wings shivering in the warm June breeze. Zita's stomach clenched. A helicopter was on the other building's roof, blades idly twirling while men with guns ran around. She scanned again, preparing to run to the remaining side when she spotted it. Affixed to one corner of their building, a black cord, almost invisible in the dawn, stretched to the roof of a lower building. *¡Gracias a Dios!*

Zita scuttled over to it, gesturing the others over while she examined the setup. A five-sixteenth-inch cable anchored solidly to the cement. *Trixie knows zip lines.* She ran her fingers over the line and checked the give again with a strong tug. While she would have connected it a few feet over by a yellow paint splatter, the line would work. Wyn and Andy would need to pull their feet up before the ledge on the other side, and Zita would have to improvise something, as they had no gloves or pulley.

"Trixie knows what?" Wyn asked. She clutched the sad pile of their meager belongings so tight that her knuckles were colorless.

Zita pointed to the rope. "Zip line from this building to that. She used the part you hang onto to go across. We'll use the chain from the door, though that will only work once. Decision time. Will you hide on the roof that will be burning hot by noon, ride out on the zip line, or try to sneak out below? If you choose hiding or sneaking, tell me your ninja training stories someday. I vote to use the line because it avoids the gunfire, and really, free zip line. Andy, you're extra strong and all now, so you should carry Wyn across if we go the cool way. In case you were curious, zip line is spelled z-i-p-awesome."

Gunfire sounded again from below. "No pressure," Zita added, "just hurry faster."

Andy's head shook in sharp negation. "No. I'll try the zip line, but I'm not carrying her. Look what I did to the door," he answered, pursing his lips and jerking his head toward the door. They all gazed at the mangled door wedged and duct-taped into the stairwell opening, great chunks gone from the doorframe where the hinges had been.

Although her lips pressed together into a line, Wyn's words were gentle, even soothing as she turned back to their friend. "Don't worry, I don't need to be carried. I can do the zip line thing. Stealth is not among my accomplishments."

Running a hand through her hair, Zita reworked the scenario. "Wyn, we're six stories up here. Weight training isn't your thing, so we don't know how well you can hold your own weight at speed for several seconds. Plus, one chain means one trip. Andy can hold the chain to cross, and you can ride him piggyback. Pull up your legs before you hit that ledge, Andy. You can put our clothes between you." Internally, she crowed at avoiding direct references to Wyn's sad, wimpy arms.

The pretty brunette folded her arms across her chest. "You know, I can hear you thinking about my sad, wimpy arms."

Zita rolled her eyes. *No privacy.* "Ay, then stop listening. I tried. So, consensus is the zip line wins? Andy, loop it like this around the rope, and then Wyn will need to climb on your back. Push off once she's secure. Fique tranquilo, you got this." She demonstrated with the chain, picturing each step in her head, including the slide across and landing.

Wyn nodded first, showing she had been eavesdropping again.

Andy contemplated the zip line and copied Zita's motion with the chain. "What about you?" he asked at last. "If we use the chain, how will you get across?" His brown eyes met her own.

The fire alarm went off below their feet. Indistinct shouting began in the stairwell. Zita swore in English and Spanish. When those seemed insufficient, she swore in Chinese. "I'll swing across after you. I do midair rope stuff all the time." *If I can maintain human shape all the way across, it won't be too hard. If I can't, well, the cops will have an interesting time figuring out how a farmyard animal got up here.*

With a sharp inhale, the other woman said Zita's name. Any other utterance was lost with the crack of a gun nearby. All three escapees ducked and hunted for the source.

"There. On the other building," Andy said, nodding at the other quarantine building, chain forgotten in his hands. The women followed his gaze.

Helicopter blades revved in a furious whir of sound as gunmen boarded the vehicle, pushing a blond woman in a blue jumpsuit ahead of them. A man in a dark suit struggled to his feet at the base of the vehicle. As it lifted, one attacker leaned out and stopped the wounded man's efforts with a quick burst of gunfire. Gunfire ignited below again at the shots. The shooter hanging out of the helicopter fired at the ground—*suppressing fire*—then his head turned toward the three huddled on the roof. His weapon followed that line of sight as the helicopter proceeded north, passing over them. It hovered next to the building, the gunman facing the roof.

Zita grabbed Andy and pressed the chain into his hands. "Go, go, go," she ordered. He draped the chain over the line and crouched.

After a second of hesitation, Wyn climbed on. "Perhaps," she began, clinging like a barnacle.

Zita felt her form begin to shimmer, even as the gunman raised his weapon. *Not now! I need to be human.* "Later," she shouted, pushing them off the ledge.

Wyn screamed.

A line of bullets spat around her, and Zita twisted and turned desperately trying to avoid them. She gripped the building edge in stunned disbelief that they had missed.

Andy flinched as the bullet spray continued to him. Jagged lines of rips appeared on his clothing, and bullets ricocheted. Blood stained his chest. One or more struck the building opposite, and the cable shook as the cement around the anchor began crumbling.

The ledge broke, and the wire holding her friends disappeared just as they were about to reach the other side. Zita inhaled sharply.

Wyn went silent.

"They can't be dead. No lo creo. I won't believe it." Zita shook her head.

A low thrum began, joined by the rumble of falling stone and shattering brick. Thunder cracked. Her position did not allow her to see to the street below, so Zita dropped to her hands and knees, steeling herself to look. The whole world shook around her, and she shuddered, digging her nails into the surface of the roof so hard her callused hands complained. Wyn's shriek reverberated in her head. *Wait, that actually sounds like her.* Pushing away the terrible dread, Zita forced herself to peer over the edge.

She reared back, twisting and returning to her hands and feet, scuttling away from the edge. A colossal bird struggled up from between the buildings. *That would be a golden eagle, if you fed one mutant nuclear steroids to make its eyes glow, increased size to equal a jet, and added an aura to blur details. Considerate of it to not demolish those buildings, even if it's more work that way; cities thrive so much better if giant creatures avoid smashing them to bits.*

Color changed, and the world warped again. As she obeyed wordless instincts, Zita launched off the rooftop, gliding on a warm updraft. Her blue hospital gown fell away to the rooftop when she stretched her own, normal-sized, golden eagle wings. Flying was even better than she had dreamed; it required so much delightful work, even if instinct handled part of it. Veering out of the way of the larger bird, she circled the rooftop.

When the gigantic creature was free of the buildings, it winged upward, the back draft hurling Zita's winged form downward.

She yelped again as she rolled along the rooftop, losing feathers and plummeting off an edge. Her wings flapped frantically to stop her fall. The keen eyes of her current form picked out legs in a blue jumpsuit and a blur of long brown hair hanging from one claw before the other avian disappeared with a sonic boom. For her not to have felt it, the creature had to have gotten very high up. She hadn't paid enough attention in school to figure out the distance.

As she fluffed and settled her feathers into a better flight configuration, she hopped toward the edge of the building again. Hope for the impossible bloomed, as she reminded herself about Andy and Wyn.

Something exploded behind her, then boomed again, louder and more resonant. With a yelp, she rose higher, following half-felt instincts to dip, roll, and avoid the pieces thrown by the explosion over the rooftop. While some of the wreckage rattled like metal as it struck the roof surface, other pieces burned. Zita's wings furiously struck at the air, carrying her over to land on the paint-splattered ledge of the building opposite. Her mind refused to dwell on one smoldering chunk of debris, shaped like a leg in a flaming boot, even though it landed on her discarded hospital gown.

A woman in high heels and an artistically tattered bikini hovered in midair on the other side of the building where Zita had seen the helicopter last. While one hand was upraised, the other hand held a limp man as if he were a handbag. A leg was bent, toes touching the opposite knee, while the other pointed downward like a ballerina pirouetting. She turned her head, and Zita's eagle vision cataloged the flying woman's face. *Dramatic closing presentation. The glowing golden nimbus shouting out her position only makes her an easier target at a distance. How did she escape an explosion without getting dirty?* As Zita absently preened her flight feathers into a better position, her mind finished identification.

Seriously? Caroline? Zita yelped, a disgusted, high-pitched sound.

Oblivious to, or uncaring about, the dismayed eagle, Caroline flew higher, then dove downward, behind the building.

In disgust, another feeble yip escaped Zita. The pounding thrum of helicopters monopolized her attention for a moment; a few more helicopters approached, but her sharp vision picked out the media logos on the sides of the vehicles. *No help from them. At least they are focusing more on Caroline's side of the building. Ay, I have more important things to do than watch her perform.* Zita made herself look down, praying, "Por fa, don't let Wyn and Andy be dead."

No splatter marks, she noted, confirming a suspicion. Relief welled. *I'm not the only shape changer, then.*

Evil black smoke curled from a few windows of the building that had held her captive for so long, and a quartet of dark-clothed men burst out the side door. Two people in blue jumpsuits stumbled between them; after a second, she identified Jerome and his girlfriend. One invader stopped and wrapped chain around the handles of the door.

Her stomach curdled at the idea of locking people in a building streaming smoke. She launched herself and looped closer.

The gunmen hauled their prisoners toward a white vehicle, where a driver waved from a window. A few men crouched beside the vans, their guns pointed at the remains of the police perimeter as they argued. The words eluded her hearing.

Zita took a deep breath and waited for the gunmen to get close enough that the van would provide her cover. *Think fast, Jerome. You're going to get as much assistance as I can give. If we're lucky, you can help those people inside.* After tucking her wings in tight, she dove at the men and their hostages. She raked one invader and snapped at another, frantically beating her wings to bring herself higher again. Hands battered her before she gained enough altitude to reassess. When she soared out of their reach, she cheered, although her avian lungs translated it into a weak peeping sound.

"Go," Jerome bellowed to his girlfriend. He threw a furious haymaker at the man holding her, and his opponent went down in a spray of blood.

The woman ran, her legs eating up the distance.

One of the remaining men shot at Zita, his aim wild. After peppering the air with invectives, the invaders separated. "Fuck! Shoot the pigeon!" ordered the one who held a hand to his face where blood dripped from talon marks.

Bloody Face, she dubbed him. If her bird form could have snorted, she would have at the poor avian identification.

The shooter, blood dripping from the arm she had bitten, turned and aimed at the fleeing woman. "Let's cut our losses and take off without the bonus," he snarled. The two remaining men, including Bloody Face, went for Jerome.

Jerome tackled one.

The invaders by the vehicles shot at the police line, giving them cover.

Zita stooped, aiming for the shooter with the injured arm. She hit him hard, clawing his shoulder.

The Kevlar vest he wore prevented any serious injury, but her strike diverted the majority of the bullets and sent him sprawling. As the gun fired again, the woman shrieked and split into three identical women, one of whom went down under the bullets. The other two clones continued in opposite directions, dodged the invader's vehicles, and disappeared behind the police lines. More gunfire mingled with the sound of big dogs barking as Zita tried to gain altitude again. *Carajo.* She fell as feathers turned to fur in midair.

Pain jolted through her as she hit the ground at a run that straggled off when one canine paw failed to cooperate. She struggled to remain standing and turned to look. Her vision had diminished, colors fading and blurring to dulled shades of brown and gray, with bites of blue and yellow. However, her nose burned with the acrid sweetness of gunmetal, carbon, fire, and blood overriding a glorious myriad of other scents. Sounds amplified in her large, sensitive ears, the continuing gunfire a painful punch with each shot. She flicked her ears; people shouting inside the building were now perceptible. The corpse of the lawyer woman's clone was gone, without even any blood left behind. Jerome was rising from his tackle victim, who smelled like carrion. The shooter, Torn Kevlar Man, got to his feet, and another attacker, Bloody Face, seemed to be waiting for a shot. Zita growled, a deep resonance drawing the invaders' attention before they could assault Jerome again.

"Sky rats and now a German Shepherd? What's next, police horses or flying monkeys?" Bloody Face exclaimed. Torn Kevlar raised his weapon in her direction.

A protesting whine escaped, as a change built within her, but she remained in the big dog form. She slunk to the side, shadowing them, as her mind whirled and searched for an angle that would afford her as much cover as possible.

A pinging sound came from each of the black-clad men. Bloody Face glanced at his watch and pushed a button. "Five minutes to operation time limit. Retreat," he ordered. Both invaders backed away.

His substantial shoulders moving up and down as he panted, Jerome made a move to follow them.

All the way up the side of the building that had housed her for the quarantine, stairwell windows deepened to black. *Shit.* Nearly falling when she put her weight on one of her front paws, Zita limped to her friend. She barked, ran in front of Jerome, and raced toward the chained door.

The hulking man snarled. "Stop it, Lassie!" he ordered, striding after the fleeing men.

She repeated the action, barking as loudly as possible.

Torn Kevlar paused, then ran for the middle van.

Come on, Jerome, if you can make mad money, you can figure out people will die in that fire. Her barking increased in madness and urgency until he focused on her as she ran past. The sting in her nose intensified. When he stilled, and his lips parted, she knew he had spotted the windows and the smoke.

Once he figured it out, Jerome swore and ran toward the door.

Her tail wagged, an autonomic function. Determined to be a distraction, if nothing else, Zita shambled toward the white vans. When Torn Kevlar raised his gun at Jerome after reaching the safety of one vehicle, she lunged at him. While she had intended to make it a feint, he fell back a few steps and aimed at her. His aim was terrible, though, since her hobbling dodges avoided all the bullets.

She charged and bit Torn Kevlar, knocking him off balance. Struggling to free his arm from her, he fell hard against the van, his head banging the metal with a clunk. He slumped. Shallow breathing declared him unconscious rather than dead, and she released his arm. The man with the gory face had climbed inside and locked the van doors. Zita snarled at him while assessing other targets interested in Jerome's activities.

The van engine roared to life, and the driver slammed it into reverse, trying to back over her. Zita lunged out of the way, putting another vehicle between herself and the vindictive man. He hit the brakes and swerved, but collided with the other van. Imprecations in multiple languages colored the air.

Did you not notice running over your buddy's leg when you made a try for me? Bro, you aren't keeping any friends that way. She circled farther away from the vans.

The collision had distracted two vehicles loaded with invaders, but the diversion could not last much longer. She flicked her ears and kept a wary eye on them as she retreated.

Most of the gunfire had died down, and people, alive and dead, littered the ground by the cop cars. Three patrol cars and random black suit men versus three white panel vans with at least four scum, each with assault weapons... *The poor cops.* Bloody Face put his vehicle in reverse to disengage it from the other one.

Zita pricked an ear at a strident shriek from within the building and glanced over a shoulder when Jerome cursed. He reversed direction, sprinting full out from the still-chained door, which had an odd brownish-black stain growing in the center as the edges warped.

Then the world exploded. The door and Jerome shot into the air like rockets. Zita yelped as the edges of the blast of force and heat hit and smashed her into the pavement. Metal and glass projectiles spewed out in a rush of tiny, stinging bites.

The pungency of the explosion burned her nose, blurring scents into a mix of colossal stench, other than the strongest, which her canine instincts identified as singed dog hair. Zita's ears felt odd, and the constant noise she had tried to ignore was muffled. A dull pain traveled down her throat and into her chest with every inhalation, while the back of her head shrieked with pain. *So not doing this lying down.* She staggered to her feet, coughing black phlegm and shaking with effort.

A vaguely human shape, where fiery eyes burned dark in a face and body of flame, emerged from the doorway. Shoulders hunched, fists clenched, the figure strode forward, attention riveted on something in front of it.

Zita followed the being's gaze and regretted it.

Bloody Face's van had been in a direct line with the doorway and had partially melted. The driver was... probably the black and white meaty char hanging out the window with the liquefied metal covering half of him. The grisly skull seemed to be screaming. Her stomach churned, and she gagged. Zita's chest protested the violent movement, and she fought the urge to be sick or fall.

The remaining invaders near the cars had noticed the flamboyant exit. A few of them, including the one who had been aiming for her, raised their guns. On the farthest end from her, one clever soul drove away on the sidewalk, scraping the side of the van on a tree to escape, leaving behind two swearing gunmen in his wake. Being neither flameproof nor bulletproof, Zita lurched out of the line of fire, limping around small smoldering heaps, searching for Jerome.

Flames flared higher as the fiery person screamed unintelligible words and pointed.

Some of the invaders opened fire.

Her stomach roiling, Zita turned away when three gunmen spontaneously combusted. The other invaders scrambled into the remaining van and sped away, leaving their injured or dead behind. She forced herself to breathe deeper and disregard the odors or what the pain accompanying the inhalation meant. *Jerome, I have to help him before I escape. Dios, am I steering all of my friends in the wrong directions today?* Her tail crept between her legs of its own accord. She wheezed, glancing frequently at the flaming being to ensure no further fire was incoming. *What is that thing?*

The creature put its hands on its hips, an oddly feminine gesture from the robust, androgynous shape. Like an almost-naked avenging spirit, Aideen emerged from the coruscating flames, fury painting her face. The woman shook out her shoulders, and the flames settled down, sinking into her skin with one or two last caresses. Most of her pale skin was visible as only her standard-issue bra and panties had survived.

Bet it's even flashier without dog vision. Does she know Caroline's already running around in her undies, and that the golden girl has better lingerie?

Aideen scanned the area, anger fading from her face. She strode past three piles of twitching, smoking corpses without paying them any particular attention and sank to her knees by a shape near a police car. Rising with a gun in her hand, she climbed inside the vehicle. Her words inaudible, Aideen spoke into something, maybe a radio, before pulling on a police jacket. As she leaned out of the vehicle, she cupped her hands around her mouth and shouted before taking a ready pose, brandishing a handgun. Someone near the cars was moaning, crying, or both.

A loud wheeze caught Zita's attention; once she recognized it was not her own breathing, she realized a large shape on the ground was a person, half under the remains of the metal door. She shambled over as fast as possible. Horror made her mind stutter and freeze. Although the heated metal made her vision darken with pain, she shouldered it off the person underneath. Jerome was face down on the pavement, arms and legs spread wide. Raw lumps of seared flesh alternated with smoother black and white charred areas over his entire back. His jumpsuit was singed, missing, or melted onto him. Bone shone in intermittent bursts along the length of his spine, and below the neck, his body seemed to be either oozing or fried. He gasped for air again, loud enough for even her damaged ears to recognize it. His head was unmarked, with healthy hair and skin visible in stark contrast to the ruin of his back. Zita stared at him, biting back nausea. The invaders were gone. She had to get help for him.

Zita barked.

Shock on her face, Aideen turned and gazed at her, then at the smoldering meat near Zita's paws. Pity filled her face, but she instead headed to the cops.

Hope blossoming, Zita barked again and danced by Jerome, ignoring her own pain until another coughing fit made her stumble to the ground.

Aideen threw her hands up and dug out the car radio. She hesitated after using it, then hauled a medical kit to one of the injured officers. Fumbling through it, she pulled out bandages.

Hang on, amigo. I hope you're first on the EMT list when they get here. Don't die—oye, wasn't bone showing there a second ago? Zita blinked. The awful gasping breaths of her friend were no longer audible. None of his spine was visible, and some of the black charred areas had turned red. His hand twitched. She stared like a ninny. *That's far more useful than uncontrolled animal shapes or a showy nimbus, but disturbing to watch. Still, nice work if you can get it.* While her brain could not make sense of the information, fleshy things extended and grew inside him, although his overall body barely trembled. Crisped—organs, she guessed—plumped and changed colors beneath bone, while muscle crawled in to fill gaps. The contortion in his body eased as his body restored itself and tension eased.

Near the cars, one of the fallen cops moaned as Aideen handled him, appearing to focus on splints and amateur bandaging.

Caroline soared overhead. Despite radiating light and wearing only underwear, she had obtained a head microphone unit somewhere. She spoke into it as she passed, but staccato gunfire spat once from one of the other sides of the building, and she altered her course to zoom that way.

No one seemed to be paying attention to the dog or the man near her.

Zita's friend groaned. She glanced down at Jerome, then at the open stairwell. He remained unconscious, but his body convulsed as it healed. She whined, low and unhappy. *What if someone's in there?*

She hobbled over and peeked in the stairwell, careful not to touch the melted edges of the still-steaming doorway. Soot covered the area. Burnt rubber, hot metal, and acrid chemicals clawed at her nose, and she coughed, eyes tearing, chest throbbing. The interior door would never open again. Liquefied substances ran and twisted in puddles and piles like children's drip sandcastles at the beach. Dark slashes, scorch marks, were every place she looked, and the stairs themselves were barely identifiable. One set of footprints, bare ones, led to the door. *Oye, nobody here needs my help. If anyone's dead, they're unrecognizable. I hope everyone else got out through the other stairwell exit. While I'm still mobile, I should make my escape.*

With every intention of limping off to lick her wounds—not literally—she turned and almost collided with a gigantic black wolf. Blood dripping from its muzzle, it slunk toward Jerome, head lowered, legs bent, and ears pricked. *Is that someone who transformed like me or a real, mutant beast? The body is all timber wolf, but I don't know of any wolf breeds that reach... three hundred pounds, give or take a few.* She blinked, feeling her body shift again, this time to a mirror of the animal in front of her, though less than a third of the size of the other canine. The wide eyes of the huge animal, intent on Jerome, showed no sign of human intelligence, only feral aggression, and hunger.

Oh, hell no. Zita hustled back and stood between Jerome and the approaching wolf. She yawned and licked her nose. Her attempt to shoo came out as a whine.

The massive creature snarled at her, showing teeth. His ruff rose.

I think I was bigger as the German Shepherd. Her perspective shifted slightly, and she gained a few pounds. Before she could figure out what to do next, her instincts laid back her ears and drew up her back into a painful hunch. *I can work with that. Scare him off.* She indulged in an explosion of mad barking and snarling.

The other animal crouched, as if to lunge, then... turned tail and ran.

Zita straightened. Her ears perked up. *Sí, sí, who the—*

It took her a moment to decipher the words that came from behind her. "Yeah, you better run, mutt." Zita looked.

Aideen floated, aflame again and smirking. She tossed a fireball from hand to hand. When the black wolf had gone, the flames died down. Nonchalantly picking up the jacket she had tossed on the ground, she donned it and returned to tending the injured policemen.

Right. She is. Zita grumped to herself before focusing attention on Jerome.

He was twitching now, but his body had filled out again. Smooth, dark skin stretched over exposed muscles. He swore, or at least that's what his tone indicated, and curled into a ball, presenting his derriere to her. Everything around her still sounded as if she were listening underwater.

Zita blinked. Philosophically, she decided on an action. *I'll get him a blanket so he can cover that fine dark chocolate ass.*

Her injuries grew more painful as adrenaline subsided, but she wobbled to the cop cars. She averted her eyes from the gruesome remains in and on the white van. Aideen had left the car trunks open, and Zita poked her head in one. Spotting a blanket, she seized it between her teeth. A few hard, if agonizing, pulls brought the blanket crumpling to the ground.

Overhead, a sonic boom echoed, and something simultaneously passed overhead, obscuring the sun for a moment. *What now? This has to be the most chingado...* She gave a hoarse growl. A few seconds later, the reverberating boom of thunder followed a piercing avian chirp, and a downpour erupted. *Rain. Because obviously we were having too much fun here.* The noisy hum of the circling helicopters broke rhythm, and their sound receded. She shook herself and dragged the blanket toward Jerome.

"Zita! Oh, Goddess, where are you?" Wyn yelled.

Caught by surprise at the volume and clarity, Zita tripped and almost fell. She shook her head and scanned the area, but didn't see Wyn. Zita barked once, then barked out the shave and a haircut sequence in case her friend lurked nearby. To her damaged ears, her barks came out muffled, but Aideen stopped splinting, grabbed her sidearm, and looked around. *Oh, right, people are scared of big dogs, even adorable half-dead ones.*

Wyn's voice sounded again, this time at a normal volume rather than a shriek. "You're a dog now?"

After a moment, Zita wagged her tail.

Aideen did a quick reconnoiter of the area by the police vehicles, darting around objects and any place providing cover in textbook style. Finding nothing and struggling with her medical kit, she returned to ministering to the downed officers.

A wheeze escaped her abused lungs as Zita towed the blanket to Jerome. The now-sodden material pooled at her feet, and she noted the impressive swelling on her own injured foot. *Oye. Recovery is going to suck. Wyn, where are you? I don't see you.*

As she reached him, Jerome sat up. He rubbed his head and made a face, not looking at her. "I should sue that truck," he mumbled. His voice sounded wrong, but if she concentrated, she could make out the words.

With a laugh she could not voice, she dropped the clammy fabric in his lap.

Jerome yelped and swore, yanking the blanket away from his waist.

Gritting her teeth, Zita sat, tail thumping as weight came off her injured paw. She offered Jerome an innocent expression, letting her tongue drop out the side of her mouth. *The rain and wet dog smell just add to my charm.*

He snorted and stood. "Good boy," he muttered at her. In a practiced move, he tied the sodden blanket like a toga around his waist, then surveyed the area.

Wyn's voice held more questions than she answered. *I'm talking in your head. Andy and I are on the roof of the building that's not on fire. You know, the one without any holes yet? What happened? It looks like a bomb exploded down there.*

Zita took a moment to think about Wyn's comments. Slanting her head up, she scrutinized the nearby structures and waited to work up the will to move again. Two dark heads poked over the edge of one building. *Ah, there you are.* Hesitating, she summarized. *Those creeps had Jerome and his woman hostage. What's her name, the lawyer with the kid? The cops and the bad guys had a firefight, and she got away. The police lost. Aideen exploded over the whole mess, worse than usual. Jerome was hit, and the bad guys either ran or died. Jerome got better. Now Aideen is playing EMT. Oh, and Caroline Gyllen blew up a helicopter and is flying around like a porno lightning bug.*

"Aideen, what's going on?" Jerome called out. Zita's hearing was improving; his voice was distorted, but intelligible without effort.

Aideen pointed at him, surprise written across her face. "Where did you—never mind. Get over here and help with the injured," she ordered, "The EMTs can't get through until they clear out the last pockets of attackers. What were you doing, taking a nap?" The rain lessened to a steady fall, now that it had soaked those reeling from the sudden battle.

"Man can't get any respect around here, boy. You got my back, right? Us against them," Jerome confided to Zita as he headed Aideen's directions. Smooth, perfect skin again covered muscles gliding in untroubled movement.

I don't know whether to laugh at his cluelessness about animals or bite him.

Wyn's mental reply interrupted her deliberations. *We'll need the detailed version of that later, but we have to move...now. The cops have an outer perimeter, and they're pushing inward. You could run. They'd never guess a human hid under the dog fur.*

Please, and leave you two? I'm the one who almost got you killed. We all get out together or not at all. Not to mention, I'm not up to a run. Zita hobbled toward the building Wyn had described and considered the front façade.

Concern laced Wyn's words. *We'll be right down. Andy's, ah, opening the door now.*

Zita crawled over by the main entrance, around the corner, and under the shelter of a bush and column. *I'll just lie here behind this big pillar. Have a little nap, maybe.* Her brain went fuzzy. The next thing she knew, hands smoothed over her back. *Pain!* She yipped.

Andy greeted her. "Hey, Zita. Probably Zita, anyway." His lips pressed tight.

"It's her," Wyn said. "Goddess, you're a mess." She lifted her hands and sat back on her heels.

Praying it would work, Zita pictured herself, her normal human form. Encouraged by the rough scrape of the ground and prickling branches on bare skin, she crawled out from under the bush. Even in human form, the caustic reek of the area made her nose crinkle in rejection.

"Uh, yup, Zita," Andy mumbled, averting his eyes and backpedaling.

With a mirthless smile, Wyn wiggled the fingers of one hand at her. Dark blood spotted a makeshift sling, the same blue as her wet jumpsuit, on the other arm. Diamond raindrops formed a sparkling net on windblown hair, with more accenting her hazel eyes like dramatic makeup. Her glasses and the arms of her jumpsuit were missing. Otherwise, she seemed uninjured.

Andy was untouched by anything, completely bare, save for red dust puddling at his feet and...

"Are you wearing a diaper? A blue diaper?" Zita croaked. *Is it National Clothing Malfunction Day already?*

"It's a kilt. My clothing ripped, not that you can criticize, since you're naked yet again. Your hospital gown was too small for me, and everything else got dropped," Andy said, fidgeting. He peered around the corner at the police and others there. His olive skin was tinted red, including the tips of his ears. Water dripped off his nose and dribbled from long strands of hair, now free of the ever-present braid. The rain lightened from a shower of silken torment to a sticky mist.

Zita ran her good hand over her head. Small pieces of glass or pavement adhered to her soggy dreadlocks. She glanced down at herself. Black streaked her body and small flakes stuck in patches that she suspected were a combination of blood, ash, and sweat. Soot ran in midnight rivers down her body, streaked by the rain, and undecipherable debris fell as she watched. None of it sufficed to hide her nudity. *Genial. I continue to be the class act around here.* "Well, I don't want your man-skirt back now, that's for sure. Wyn, how badly hurt are you?" she said, seizing Wyn and hugging her, avoiding injuries as much as possible. When she had Wyn, she grabbed Andy, pulling him in too. They returned the squeeze, though Andy kept his head turned away.

"It's of no consequence. How serious are your injuries?" Wyn asked. She whimpered when someone bumped her bad arm. They separated.

Zita tried the stoic shtick. "You know me, more agile than a turtle," she joked, an impulse regretted when another shift took her. Her friends waited while she struggled to return to human form. She cleared her throat. "Lousy shot, I guess. The back blast from the fire caught me." She stopped to cough. "If you had any doubts, smoke inhalation sucks."

Gaze carefully averted from Zita, Andy stared up into the sky. His chin jerked to the west. "We have problems. How do we explain all this?"

Zita eyed the rapid approach of helicopters and police lights. She swore and closed her eyes. *Mamá will kill me if I'm nude on television. Miguel will have a coronary or ten since he's always been an overachiever. I really don't want to become a research subject and disappear forever into the bowels of the government, but I can't hide my problem.* "Maybe Wyn can talk you both past the police. They won't hear about you from me." She exhaled, opening her eyes again. *Unless they torture me. Everyone breaks eventually. I can't run in this condition. Claro que sí, if they give me enough time to heal before they lock me down too hard, I might be able to escape.*

Wyn drew in a sharp breath and frowned.

"Stop eavesdropping, then." Zita would have laughed if her throat permitted it.

"I can't help it. You and Andy have distinct brain patterns, and if I focus on one of you, it's easier to ignore the rest of the world. It hurts if I listen to all and sundry for any significant period of time." Wyn's mournful words trailed off.

Andy offered with no enthusiasm, "I could try the bird thing again, I guess, but I'm not certain how. We could end up anywhere. It, being that, was like it wasn't me." He rubbed his hands against his outer thighs and his shoulders twitched.

Shouting issued from nearby, and the rag-tag trio peered around the corner. The area swarmed with men in several variations of official uniforms, running around with handguns, shotguns, and assault rifles at ready positions. Jerome took one look, dropped to his knees, and put his hands in the air. Caroline flew high above the destroyed parking lot, carrying an ambulance over her head, which she set on the ground near Aideen.

"Cars aren't built to be carried that way. She shouldn't be able to do that. The physics..." Andy muttered, sounding personally offended.

Someone must have given a command. A few seconds later, the blazing lights and sirens of multiple ambulances filled the air. The three escapees pressed close against their building in mute agreement. As the vehicles disgorged EMTs, the flash of scrubs mingled with the darker police uniforms. Aideen still wore the jacket and pointed a lot. Jerome, surrounded by cops, shrugged in whatever story he was telling them. A pair of policemen lifted one still form, carrying it to a dark panel van parked by a corner of the battered hospital. Zita's stomach churned. The hum of helicopters increased as black specks at a distance became recognizable as distinctive forms of the aircraft. Caroline flew in and out of view between the buildings, picking up things and carrying them away, but did not approach the three refugees.

Wyn voiced what they were all thinking. "They'll notice us soon."

Andy followed Caroline's progress, as multiple emotions chased themselves across his face and disappeared just as fast. "I don't think I can go back in there again, or wherever they move people," he said, his voice scarcely audible.

Zita rubbed his bicep. "We'll figure it out." *I hope.*

Wyn touched an uninjured spot on Zita's shoulder. "We will," she promised. "You could turn into something and escape."

Zita glared at her. "I'm not leaving you behind." *Even if I could.*

Their time ran out. A man in a suit gestured in their direction. All of them swore, and three pairs of frantic eyes met. With one hand on Andy's arm, Zita squared her shoulders as Wyn clung to her other arm. Zita yearned for her apartment.

"Oh, Goddess help us," Wyn murmured, her physical voice not as certain as her mental one had been. Her fingers tightened on Zita's shoulder, sending pain streaking through as she touched a burn.

Then the world changed around them again.

Chapter Six

"Well, I guess I can postpone that panic attack until the occupant here comes after us," Wyn said, looking around, her hazel eyes wide. Her intact hand dropped from Zita's shoulder and rubbed above the makeshift bandage on her own injured arm. Despite her words, fear trembled in her voice.

Andy pressed his lips together and folded both arms over his chest.

Once the warm tangerine paint registered, the color racing down the hall toward the two bedrooms and bathrooms, she knew where they were. "It's my place, so little chance of that," Zita said, although each word made her throat burn. Her apartment had that empty, shut-up smell, and she hurried to open windows. Wyn and Andy seemed to need recovery time, so she granted it while she struggled to open the windows one-handed. The nubby taupe carpet was a welcome change from the rough rooftop surface on her tender feet. Something still reeked. Opening the balcony door, she stepped outside, gliding between the vertical blinds without opening them. The morning sun gave the metal panniers and metallic paint of her motorcycle an impressive sparkle, glinting through gaps in the reserved parking carport. When she returned inside, she slid the screen door shut behind her. Coughing stole a moment, and dizziness claimed another. *Not good.*

When she recovered, her friends had moved to stand by her side. Andy half-carried her to a white chair in the dining room while Wyn kept pace alongside.

"Zita? You're more hurt than you said," Andy reprimanded.

Her reply was terse but honest. "I'll survive." Tension dissipated as Zita surveyed her place from where she sat. With more color and verve than money, her apartment suited her far better than captivity had. Her wallet, keys, utility knife, and phone were scattered across the dinette table. "Sweet! Quentin brought most of my belongings home, so I didn't lose my wallet or phone." She scooped up the phone, checked the battery, and plugged it in to charge. Forcing herself to act casual, she moved the other items with a finger. When her father's Saint Jude medal did not appear, she bit her lip. *Things to do, Zita, keep moving. Set your friends up so they can run before you have to turn yourself in for medical help.*

Wyn appeared distracted. "What does that even mean? You're barely mobile," she said.

With a sigh, Zita marshaled her thoughts. "It means escaping took precedence over me whining." Consumed with the need to do something, she dragged herself from the chair, retrieved a water bottle from a cupboard, and filled it at the kitchen sink. Her hands trembled, and her stomach executed a sick loop again as images of the past intruded. Cold water splashed her as the bottle overflowed, recalling her thoughts to the present.

Stress leaked from Andy's posture as he approached the patio doors, near the tropical plants in the jungle animal pots. He peered out. "It's very colorful." *Reminds me of Arizona. I don't think I've seen anything like it since that restaurant near the res.* In his reflection, his lips didn't move.

Zita decided that was a compliment. The colors were cozy, cheerful, and not boring. "Yes, I painted it myself when I was recovering from a minor injury," she answered. *It's sweet, right?*

His head inclined, but his attention was outside.

Hey, dude, are you telepathetic now like Wyn? This head talk stuff reminds me of one of those playground phones.

Turning from the door, he blinked at Zita and looked away again. His voice echoed as his thoughts mirrored his words. "No, at least, I don't think so. Maybe it's you? Why are you still standing up?" Andy's hands reached for his pockets, but his man skirt-kilt thing offered nowhere to put them. He rubbed the sides of his legs for a minute then fell still.

"Because I'm not sitting." Zita made a face at him, sticking out her tongue. She jiggled her water, relieved when her returning hearing picked up the softer sound of the splash of liquid against the bottle.

Wyn's voice held a tinge of self-derision. "Telepathic, not telepathetic. As much as I hate to admit it, it's not you, it's me. I was trying to tune out your neighbors by focusing here without reading you. It worked, but I tied us all together. Give me a few moments to rectify it. I am trying."

"How did we get here? Zita, please sit down," Andy said. "We'll deal, Wyn."

"Oh, the mind stuff is like a mental party line. Super. I'm so not responsible for anything you overhear that way." Zita shrugged and sipped her water. Although the cold helped, her abraded throat protested even the gentle slide of liquid. "Andy, you're asking the wrong girl. Wyn might know how we got here." Dirt tracked in small footprints from the kitchen to the balcony. A glance at the others' feet revealed the culprit: herself. Zita scowled, annoyed. Cleaning it would have to wait.

Wyn stared at her own bare feet. Her voice was soft as she offered, "He might be asking the right girl. It's not my doing. Andy hasn't been here before, and he had other things on his mind." She bit her lip and her eyes focused on him.

From the corner of one eye, Zita glimpsed Andy turning red.

Wyn continued, "I caught a flare of the apartment colors in your mind right before we appeared here. The colors are, ah, distinctive. Andy's right, you should rest." In Zita's mind, Wyn's voice was rueful. *I am trying to stay out. It's harder when you become emotional.*

Me? I got us here? Zita pondered that for a moment before setting the whole issue of how they got there aside for later. Perhaps she could use it to escape the hospital. Fatigue nagged at her. She tried another sip, then screwed the cap back on the bottle. *I'll handle that another time. We have to plan.*

What's a party line? Is that like one of those charge-per-minute dating numbers? Andy wondered.

Wyn responded with a flurry of images and information that had the other two blinking at her as they tried to assimilate the information. "What?" she said aloud, "Photographic memory, remember? I'm surprised Zita knew the definition."

Andy pondered. "So it's a shared phone circuit that connects to a central exchange. In this instance, Wyn would be the exchange, and our thoughts are bouncing around as if we're sharing a phone?"

Guilt on her face, Wyn nodded.

He patted her arm. "We'll deal. Keep working on it."

"You watch too many old movies, based on that crap ton of info. I stayed at a campground with one," Zita murmured, coughed, and leaned hard against the sink. When she recovered, she could have slapped herself. *Why didn't I run for the medical kit first? Where is my brain? This is not the first time I've seen violence.* "Your arm! We should clean that while we have the chance. What happened to it anyway?"

"A bullet ricocheted off my skin and got her," Andy contributed. Misery and regret dripped from his voice. Now hovering nearby, he must have edged closer during her coughing fit.

At the same time, Wyn shrugged. "I don't know... Oh, that explanation seems plausible. Don't feel guilty, Andy. You cannot claim responsibility for others' actions. Zita, we should help you first."

Since talking irritated her throat, Zita's reply was mental. *Yeah, don't be a dumbass, Andy. Since you didn't fire the gun, drowning in guilt is stupid. Seriously, you should be doing a victory boogie and working a swagger. You get to be immune to bullets and turn into a sweet eagle, even if the size is overkill.* She swore as her form changed to an eagle. *Listen, I'll get my medical kit, and we will clean Wyn's arm. You two can run for it before I go to a doctor. My injuries need more than we have. If I pretend not to speak English, perhaps they'll assume I'm an illegal, and I can escape before the government catches on.* She flapped her wings for a moment before managing to find human form again.

Wordless, Andy blocked the entry to the hall.

After a second, Wyn stepped up next to him. "Why don't you sit? Andy will retrieve it, and then we can all talk."

He nodded, his eyes somber.

We're wasting time. Zita fumed. Her friends remained in her way. She threw her hands up in exasperation and planted herself on a kitchen chair. When even that small motion caused her bad wrist to throb, she mourned the time she would lose to physical therapy. *Fine, then, it's in the equipment closet. Go straight down the hall to the blue exercise room. Look for the two white doors. You want the one closest to the silks hanging from the ceiling track. It's the purple bag with the white cross.*

Andy grunted and left.

"It's for your own good, Zita," Wyn said. She tilted her head. "Do you have a bathrobe or something I can get you?"

Zita scowled. *My robe is on the back of the first door on the right. When you two are done overreacting, can we start cleaning your arm and planning?*

Neither of her friends bothered to reply. Andy returned first, carrying Zita's duffel. He set it on the counter by the sink. Wyn swept back a moment later and laid the bathrobe on table. "This is all I could find," she said, sounding apologetic.

After Zita rose from her chair, she slid into the old purple robe and belted it. "That's the one. Let's hose your arm out over the sink," she ordered. After a quick scrub of her hands, she rummaged through the bag, cautious of her aching wrist. She tossed a few sealed packages and soap on the counter. The astringent scent of cleanser stung her nose as she gestured to her friend.

Wyn and Andy drifted closer, but Wyn stopped out of arm's reach. Her face was pale and glowed with sweat. "That whole thing is your medical bag?" she asked, wrapping her unhurt arm around her stomach.

Zita placed a magnifying glass on the counter. "That's the portable one, why?"

"The portable one?" Wyn's voice rose in pitch.

Andy chimed in. "That's the biggest one I've ever seen."

Despite her concern with the bag, Wyn snickered and teased Andy, "I usually only hear that in a romance novel."

Andy smirked, but his ears went red. "I've heard it a few times before."

Ignoring the joke, Zita moved to start unwrapping Wyn's arm. *If I keep moving, maybe I can ignore my injuries more easily.* "Sí, I like to be prepared for an emergency. The wound equipment is easiest to find in this bag. Doesn't everyone have one? Let's clean up your arm," she rasped.

"That bag is preparation for a zombie apocalypse. Many labelers died to tell us what everything is," Andy mused. Zita could not decide if his expression was amused or awed or both.

"You said it, not me. That duffel is enormous. What are you expecting to find when you finish removing my bandage?" Wyn proffered a smile, but the line between her eyes that appeared during her migraines was visible. "Sit down before you collapse. No insult intended, but you're near to filthy, even if you did cleanse your hands. I'll take off the bandage myself and give it a wash, get out any debris. Ointment and a bandage will be fine. I don't want to explain how I got shot or have to sweet-talk people into not calling Animal Control." Wyn eased Zita's hands away from the sticky, makeshift bandages.

At that, Zita stopped and nodded. She ran a hand back and forth over her sodden locks. When her hand stuck in something, she made a face. After sniffing, she realized the source of the stench. "You're right. I think I passed filthy and gave it the finger."

Wyn's discomfort at the conversation rose through their mental link, even as the witch worked on undoing the makeshift bandage. *I don't like hospitals or even doctor's offices much anymore*, her mental voice whispered. With a moan, she removed the bandage and dropped it in the trash. A wide gash stretched down her arm, trickling blood.

Andy inhaled sharply. "It might not be as bad as it looks," he said. His sentiments mirrored hers. He reached for the bag, but stopped and withdrew his hands.

Zita grimaced at her friend's wound. "The bag has aspirin and cream or spray. If that graze requires stitches, we need the ER. My stitches never come out even, and I'm down a hand." She stopped to wheeze and returned to the chair before her friends could fuss again. *I'd get Andy to do it, but he has poor control of his strength based on the door thing.* The thought slipped out.

Andy turned away, his shoulders slumping.

Distress showed on Wyn's face, and she winced. "Oh, Zita."

Before the others could say or do anything more, Zita spoke aloud. "At least let me finish the thought before you get all pissy." When she felt her throat clench, she switched back to mental communication. *You have no control yet. I've all the control of a wiener dog in a butcher shop.* When the change in her perspective registered, she twisted to verify the transformation. Scents almost overwhelmed her wet black nose. The kitchen was all about the food. Andy radiated a surprisingly complex scent of desert and wind and asphalt. Wyn's aroma was much like before, save the addition of a breath of air and rain, and the strong tang of blood. With a toss of her floppy ears, her toenails clicked on the chair seat as she marshaled her thoughts. A low woof escaped. Her two friends eyed her. *Wyn's listening in on the entire state, and apparently making us hear each other's thoughts, despite you and I lacking any telepathy.*

Wyn gave a sharp nod. "Sorry."

We all need to practice control of our respective abilities. I want to be human again. The kitchen tile was cool but hard under Zita's hands and bare knees as she struggled to stand again. Part of her mourned the loss of the wealth of scents.

Andy pointed to the hall. "I'll be there," he said and escaped.

Since Zita could neither stop him or call after him to see if he had taken her message to heart, she let the matter drop. Rinsing Wyn's injury was... unpleasant. By the time Andy rejoined them, Zita (redressed in the bathrobe) and Wyn were arguing about the now-clean gouge in her friend's arm. If he noticed Wyn's red, puffy eyes, he said nothing.

"Can you please tell Wyn that her arm needs a person with actual medical skill?" Zita said through gritted teeth, before she collapsed into her glittery, white wooden chair, tugging her bathrobe shut as it drooped open.

Andy's eyes widened, and he turned back toward the bathroom. His bare feet shuffled on the beige carpet, and he shifted his shoulders. "Uh," he began. Tension returned to his stance.

"Technically, that should be 'Will you please tell Wyn,' and it doesn't matter what he thinks," Wyn said before he could offer an opinion. Her soft voice held steel beneath its usual sweetness. She waved her uninjured hand in the air. "You and Andy are lovely, but it is my arm. We cleaned it, and now I will cast a healing incantation. I'll bandage it again after that. If that doesn't take and infection sets in, then I'll consider going to a doctor."

Andy let out a relieved breath. "It is her arm. Seeing a doctor if it gets infected seems like a fair compromise," he said. *If nothing else, my sisters have taught me that the most dangerous place in the world is between two women arguing,* he thought.

"Really? Worse than being on the wrong end of a bazooka?" Wyn asked. She set one elegant hand on her hip and narrowed her eyes at Andy.

He winced.

Worse than a bunch of makeover-crazed twelve-year-olds? Both of the others turned and studied Zita. She huffed. "What? They're relentless, vicious, and armed with strange pink instruments of torture. Bazookas run out of ammo after a shot or two." Her good hand compensating for the other, she packed up the medical supplies and tucked them back into the labeled compartments.

"The phrasing is all Zita, but the last bit is true." Wyn's attention returned to Andy.

Andy's eyes went wide. "Aww, man. What a lousy time for party line to come back." *Maybe they'll lose interest if I stay quiet and refrain from moving.* He almost achieved a blank facial expression, but he swallowed a few times under the heat of their glares. He grimaced.

Wyn muttered under her breath. "Sorry, I thought I had it figured out, but Zita's neighbors are copulating. I really didn't want eavesdrop on that. Give me a second," she said aloud.

Zita blinked. "One of my neighbors? Who? All the other residents on this floor are over sixty. They do more than power walking, gossiping, and baking cookies?" A coughing fit took her breath and attention for a minute. *When I'm their age, hope I'm still at it. Pues, I'd like to be at it before I hit their ages.* With all sincerity, she continued, "Good for them! I hope nobody breaks a hip."

Wyn straightened, her eyes brightening and cheeks flushing with a becoming color as she shook her head. "I don't know who they are, because it turns out people don't think things like 'I, George Smith, will now eat beanie weenies. Now I, George Smith, will enjoy congress with my wife of twenty-three years, Angie Smith, here in Apartment 2B.' Thanks to the telepathy, I'm becoming an expert on cogitation. I could listen in, but why would I? You might want the visual, but I don't."

Andy snickered.

Zita choked. "Enjoy congress? And you said copulating earlier. If you call it that on dates, I may have to grant you membership in the club for sex-deprived women. I'm President so I can abuse my power like that for a friend." She thumped her own chest with her good fist and laughed until tears stung her eyes and coughing seemed to tear her lungs apart. "Oye, you can both join the club. No hay bronca, I mean, no worries."

"Hey!" Andy protested. "Still male here. Zita, sit down."

Wyn's mouth curled up into a small smirk as she examined her fingernails. She said, "The eligibility requirements likely require celibacy, and I don't abstain, especially if you count the whole Winter Solstice indiscretion. Never trust homemade wine." She winced. If her smile had strained edges, no one mentioned it. Brightening, she gave Zita a mischievous look. "It explains a few things about your exercise schedule, though," she teased, though the deep line in her forehead spoke of continuing pain.

Andy turned and set his forehead against the refrigerator, putting his arms over his face. Muffled sputtering or laughing drifted out from beneath his arm.

After waving a warning finger at Wyn, Zita staggered after him. She punched his arm with her good hand. "Hey, you okay?"

A strangled-sounding voice answered her. "I'm fine. Let me know when the girl talk ends."

"What, like machos don't talk about getting a little action? I've got two brothers, even if Miguel has a stick up his—anyway, we're done," Zita replied.

Wyn mumbled. Her friend radiated innocence, save where amusement danced in her eyes. She set a white candle and matches on the table. "I will cast that healing spell as soon as you join me."

Zita sat.

Satisfied, Wyn placed Zita's water bottle in front of the Latina. "Later, I'll do it again properly with better supplies and so on, but it can't hurt to nudge the healing in the right direction. Do you have any incense or sage?" After crossing to the counter, she gave Zita's spice rack a spin, the little holder rattling and buzzing. One bottle popped free and spun across the counter. After glancing at the label, Wyn left it there.

Zita had to ask. "Why? Sage is in the spice rack. No incense." Her eyes strayed to the fallen bottle.

"For cleansing," Andy commented, as he turned back around. His face was too neutral. "Pretty standard equipment, back home," he said.

Setting aside a few spices, Wyn inclined her head. "Pen?" she asked, shaking a bay leaf out of a bottle. She stepped to and opened the fridge, then drew away after a quick perusal, shutting it behind her with a frown. "You need to go shopping. Store displays have fuller fridges." After selecting a pair of leaves, Wyn gathered up the other spice bottles and took them to the table. The bay leaf bottle sat on the counter near the other abandoned spice.

Mystified, Zita rose, unearthed a pen from a drawer under the counter, and handed it to Wyn. "It shouldn't be that bad." *Quentin should have cleaned out the perishables, but the longer-term food should still be there.* Unable to resist the urge, she tucked away the two rejected containers. After slipping by Andy, she opened the refrigerator and glanced inside. Her mouth dropped open. The white shelves mocked her; a green jar of jalapeños moped alone in the lower half. The appliance beeped complaints at her for holding it open. Zita growled back at it. "He even took my bottled water," she murmured with disbelief. "No lo creo. I do not believe it." Slamming the fridge door shut, she yanked open the freezer. It had fared better than the main compartment, but not by much. Her brother had, from what she could tell, taken all the meat and fruit, and left only the vegetables and other miscellany. Fratricide and disappointing her mother were both sins, she reminded herself.

Wyn's voice broke into her appalled contemplation. "Much obliged," she said as she labored to write on a leaf, her touch delicate. She nibbled on her bottom lip in concentration.

Andy drifted over, careful not to bump into Zita, and gazed over her head into the fridge. "Geez, Mother Hubbard," he commented.

Zita closed the freezer door with more care than she had the other compartment and rummaged through the cupboards to see what other supplies were missing. Her uninjured hand flew, driven by trepidation that her friends would lack food in their escape from another government camp or from whomever had attacked the hospital.

When tiny script decorated the leaf, Wyn set down the pen. "Right, improvise," she mumbled. "Please don't interrupt me while I'm casting." She tapped a finger against her lips. Then she absently wound her hair up into a bun, anchoring it with the pen. After arranging the small stack of supplies, she sat at the white table and lit the candle. By folding her legs, she perched in a lotus position on the chair, her breath slowing and deepening. Her gaze locked on the candle. One hand lifted into the air.

Bizarre. I don't know how I feel about this casting spells stuff, especially since it's wasting one of my emergency candles. If she finishes soon, we can plan how to get the two of them to safety and start being useful. Zita closed the pantry door, a bag of mixed beans in her hand as she watched Wyn. Andy stood beside her, also staring at their friend, his body tensed as if to run.

"No negativity during my casting, please," Wyn said, without turning her head.

"Then stop listening," they replied in unison.

"Jinx," Andy crowed.

"What?" Zita asked.

"Goddess. Please, I need to concentrate here. Just try to be quiet." Wyn exclaimed, twisting around to glare at them. Her hand dropped. With a flounce, she turned back to her candle. Straightening her shoulders, she restarted her deep breathing. The hand rose again.

Two pairs of brown eyes met behind Wyn's head. Zita rolled her eyes, and Andy grinned. Without ripping the bag, Zita ran the beans through her fingers like rosary beads as they watched, but the food fell to the ground with a thud when a silvery green radiance ignited around Wyn's upraised hand. Zita moved closer to see, Andy beside her.

Wyn's eyes focused on the candle, and she slowly touched the glowing hand to the bandage covering her wound. A trail of incandescent glitter floated behind the hand. The shimmering glow spread to the injured arm, and the telltale line of pain between her eyebrows smoothed.

Oh, a light show. On any other day, that would be bizarre, but today it barely merits unusual, considering I was a... The world went dark, and Zita fought her way out of the bathrobe with a series of irritated clucks. Tilting her head one way, then the other, she eyed the bag of beans she had dropped earlier. This close, the amount of detail was both arresting and hunger-inducing. She pictured herself human again. When she blinked and registered the change in vision, she folded her arms across her chest. *I have to get that under control.*

Next to her, Andy turned away, too obviously avoiding all the bare skin.

As she put her robe back on, her mind wandered again. *Is magic glitter better or worse than normal glitter? Will it be like the normal kind and stick in my carpet forever? I should have had Wyn sit in the chair I use when decorating thrift shop finds; the glitter is already permanent there. Will the spellcasting end soon?*

"Hey, we should see what's on the TV about the hospital so we can figure out what they're saying about our escape. You have one, right? Where's the clicker?" Andy asked, facing the refrigerator.

After tying the belt on her bathrobe, Zita set the beans on the beige counter with a rattle. To fortify her throat since the party line seemed to be down again, she drank more water before replying. "I'm dressed. I have two televisions. I sprang for a big thirty-two-inch flat screen in the exercise room. The other television is over there, but I haven't bothered to get a remote for it." She gestured to where a hefty white armoire hid a smaller television, across from a matching stool masquerading as a coffee table.

Andy headed straight to the living room, scrutinizing the blue and yellow birds painted on the armoire, and shook his head. "How can you not? Oh, never mind. Let's go see the other one so we don't break Wyn's concentration."

Without interrupting her stare at the candle or stopping the glow, Wyn said, "Thank you. Go." She waved them away.

What did Wyn just do? Zita's mind finished processing what she had seen. "Your arm!" She rushed to the witch to check the injury. She stopped and swayed as vertigo, pain, and nausea assailed her from the rapid movement.

Andy gasped and wrapped a steadying arm around Zita.

She shook him off. "Thanks. I'm better already," she said, her voice gruff.

The glitter show stopped. "It's as though the ricochet never happened," Wyn replied, exultation obvious in her voice. She showed off the arm, slim and unmarred. "It looks like my magic got a real boost in addition to the telepathy. Most of the time, the spell aids the natural process, but it doesn't happen this fast." She admired her own handiwork, wiggling her fingers and giggling.

Zita poked at the arm. The flesh beneath her prodding finger was warm and real. It needed muscle tone, but it matched the other arm. *Talk about a project.* "Sweet! Now you don't have to stop for more than a few minutes if you get hurt while exercising. If the magic works on anybody else, you could help so many others, but we should keep it on the down-low, though, so you don't get hauled off to be someone's personal medic or a government research subject." She took another pull of cold water to soothe her throat after the speech. The back part of her brain calculated the weights her friend could handle.

Wyn shot her a look. "I suppose. You can stop measuring me for weights," she murmured.

"Not responsible for what you overhear that way," Zita returned in a whisper.

Andy rubbed his eyes and his forehead, started to speak, and closed his mouth with a snap. After a pause, he offered, "Guess that explains the green glow."

Zita nodded.

"You saw it? My hand always does that, well, in my mind. It's a visualization exercise to aid concentration in sending healing energy to the wound," Wyn said. She touched a finger to her lips and tilted her head. "I'm sorry, I must have been broadcasting what I was picturing when I worked the spell. Zita, hold still and let me do you!"

Zita grimaced. "You're not my type. Totally about the whole penis thing."

"Ridiculous woman. I assure you, your heterosexuality is not in question," Wyn answered, seizing Zita's arm and dragging her to the table. "Now keep still and let me see if you can avoid the doctor." The witch closed her eyes, and chanted, one hand on Zita's arm.

Andy started to make a hand gesture but rubbed his eyes again and moved away toward the exercise room. His face was troubled.

Hope warred with hesitation, and Zita took a deep breath, losing the air in a barrage of coughs as her abused throat protested. *Is it any weirder than turning into animals?* She stole a glance at the other woman and the serenity stealing over Wyn's face. *It's important to my friend. If nothing else, it will help her feel better about leaving me behind. How can I refuse that?* As she decided, a cool sensation and light the color of new leaves backlit by sun emanated from Wyn's hands and twined over Zita's body, blooming over her chest and spreading. Zita inhaled again, this time releasing the air in an extended, pain-free exhale. Her headache receded, and her stomach calmed. Flexing her wrist and wiggling her fingers, a full-fledged smile burst free as one of her concerns disappeared. "Thanks! Now we can all go on the run together if necessary."

Wyn opened her eyes, satisfaction apparent. "You're welcome. I still hope running is avoidable. Where's Andy?"

"This way," Zita answered, going to the exercise room. She flapped a hand toward her bedroom and a bathroom as they passed. "My bedroom. This is the main bathroom. This is my exercise room. Applause is unnecessary. I know, it's awesome."

After marching into the exercise room, she stepped aside so Wyn could appreciate the place that made Zita's blood sing with the need for movement. Mirrors plastered one wall, floor to ceiling, and reflected most of the room. Silk plants in vibrant greens tumbled down from a shelf running the width of the wall, above the irregular patchwork of mirrors. Her weights and exercise equipment stood in formation the length of the longest wall. A sizable window had white vertical blinds tilted to let in light, but keep out the rest of the world. The remainder of the room was empty to allow for floor exercises. Their faces reflected at her, Wyn's curious, Andy's guarded, and her own beaming.

Wyn spoke first. "Goodness gracious, now I see why you were so cranky about the lack of workout equipment at the hospital." She blinked from her location in the niche where the larger television captained regimented racks of martial arts movies and exercise DVDs, guarded by a basket storing chalk, wraps, and hand care items. The brunette gave a perfunctory scan of the room, and patted her hair in the mirror with first one hand, then another. She took the remote from the basket and tossed it from hand to hand.

Andy drifted around her sanctuary. Zita approved. It was what she would have done, but with happy noises and touching. He made no sound at all, really, other than the shuffle of his feet on the soft, thick mats covering the floor. One worn piece of equipment, almost hidden in a corner, stopped his slow revolution around the room. His hand reached out, but quickly returned to his side.

Wyn joined him. "You have a cat? I didn't see one. That's an enormous scratching post," she asked, an expectant smile flirting with her mouth.

Zita answered, "Animals are wonderful and all, but it would be cruel to have a pet given how much I'm gone." She flexed her healed wrist again and rubbed her hair with the hand.

"Is this a martial arts dummy? I've always wanted one of those," Andy said. He eyed the jaunty pirate hat that sat atop it, then Zita. The feather in the hat drooped, more bedraggled than dashing, but at least the color was a pink so bright it almost vibrated.

Zita nodded, gave the dummy a fond pat, and straightened the feather. *Live the present. No guarantees on tomorrows. It is a cool dummy.* She grinned, and Andy favored her with a pleased smile. "Yes, a friend made it from scavenged wood to pay back a favor. Isn't it sweet? Oh, and look, Wyn healed me!"

Andy gave her a sidelong glance and nodded. His shoulder twitched.

Wyn focused between them, and animation left her face. "You're uncomfortable with the witchcraft. I'm sorry, I should have asked..." She pretended interest in the weights, a shout of mismatched colors ordered from smallest to largest, on a rack that sagged under their weight. A pair of medicine balls snuggled against the legs of the rack.

His body still poised to flee, Andy shuffled his feet and raised his head. "It's not personal, and I'll deal. My people are okay with it, but I lived among the Diné for years, and they're not fans of witches."

Wyn considered her own reflection in a mirror for a moment, and Zita could almost see her paging through her scary perfect memory. She also noticed when her witchy friend reached the pertinent information about the Navajo, or Diné, as Andy had called them. Her eyes went wide. "Oh, I'm so sorry," she began again.

"No big," Zita said, waving her hand dismissively. "Don't go changing us into flying monkeys or any creepy sh—stuff and we'll be fine. Takes an adjustment, is all." Cocking her head to the side, she smiled at her friends.

Andy nodded, his posture relaxing. "What are a few lights between friends? It's better than the party line of perpetual oversharing, and Zita, we're both so proud of you for making a movie reference, even it was a little wrong," he added.

Zita smiled and bounced on the mats as the tension between her friends ended.

Andy's shoulders straightened, and he nodded. The smile died as he looked away and at the ceiling and walls again. He coughed and spoke aloud, "Zita? Since you're home and all, could you put on clothes? Your robe has a, uh, gap in the front. If you have men's clothes, can I borrow some? This is drafty." He gestured at the hospital gown tied around his own waist. *Please let there be clothing. This is like a nightmarish flashback to my sisters barging into the bathroom.* His earnest plea made it obvious the party line functioned again.

Zita checked herself in a mirror. "Right, I forgot."

With an apologetic expression, Wyn made an offer. "Words are inadequate to explicate your lack of cleanliness, too. Clothes would be good after a bath. Additionally, I propose we eschew any mention of fauna before Andy develops vertigo from his repeated revolutions."

Zita nodded. "There's that common sense again, but hidden under the big words. Make yourselves comfortable. I'll give you the full tour when I get out... with clothes on, so you can look at me again, Andy. Quentin probably left something here you can borrow." Squaring her shoulders, she ran through a list of items to secure. In her equipment closet, she checked the contents of her emergency go bag, pulling out steel scissors. The door to the closet hung open so she could hear her friends. *Andy needs clothing, or he'll attract attention in his skirt. We will probably need to crash after all the excitement, as soon as we stop moving.*

"Kilt," Andy corrected. He hesitated, then added, "Not that I wouldn't prefer pants and a shirt. Perhaps even a complete outfit with shoes and socks and underwear."

She grinned. "So you're dying to get into another man's underwear? Wyn, you going to take down that party line?"

"Zita, you know better than that," Andy answered, exasperation leaking into his tone.

"Working on it. I'm just hoping we can all go home and nobody's after us," Wyn offered. "No offense meant, Zita, you have a lovely home. It's just not my place, and I miss my life. My poor cats have probably wasted away and gone feral. Poor babies." Her voice exuded yearning.

Four paws were easy to adapt to once the clothing was out of the way, Zita discovered. She swished a fluffy black plume in irritation, then wrapped the tail around her.

Andy snorted. "It's been all of a month."

Watching her tail was interesting. Zita could flick her own nose with it, then checked to see if she could reach her ears. The dangling laces on one of her pairs of hiking boots were fascinating. She punched down that instinct and concentrated on her human form. Just as she changed, Wyn spoke again.

Wyn's rejoinder held coolness. "They're cats."

It was childish, really. Her tail lashed the air in frustration. *I know they are, but what am I?* Zita thought, trying to shift again.

"Sorry," Wyn said. "I forgot about your problem."

Straightening the hiking boots that had gotten crooked somehow, Zita dressed again with speed and seized the scissors. After closing the equipment closet, she headed to the hall closet housing her miniscule laundry machines. "Wyn, we all want our lives back. If we're lucky, we'll make a phone call, you can go home, and we can plan a celebratory dinner later. I'd love a pizza almost as much as a decent workout." Her thoughts wandered. *Ay, and if that workout was with a hot dude, and he and I could have pizza between rounds... During would be fine too. I'm not picky.*

In the exercise room, Andy groaned loudly and Wyn giggled.

Opening the double doors to the alcove, Zita delved into the bulky white dryer. "Score! You're in luck, Andy," she called out, "That cheapskate Quentin left most of a load here. I'll grab clothes, and you can dress in the bathroom." She took a selection to him.

Andy met her at the door. "You folded it for the three steps between here and the dryer?" he asked, mirth in his voice.

She shrugged and surrendered the tidy pile.

His movement to take it was ginger, tentative motions that were painful to see. He entered the bathroom, then stared at the door.

Zita reached over and closed the door until it was ajar just enough for him to open it without using the handle and headed into her bedroom. *I'll help you get your mojo back, buddy.*

A mental grunt was his only reply.

Opening her chest of drawers, she grabbed the first clothing items she touched. *Oh, hey, I can put on a bra that fits right again! Hallelujah, I'm so tired of the chafing, especially—*

"I heard that. Oh, God, why do I have to hear that? If you go to the toilet, please don't think about that too," Andy complained loudly.

"Hombre, you guys are the ones who are listening in. I'm not doing anything," Zita retorted. She was uncertain how Wyn could clear her throat over a mental link, but the witch did it.

Andy returned to the exercise room. Both hands found his pockets. Quentin's clothing hung on his slighter frame, the shorts coming to his knees. "So, ah, if this is the uh, larger TV, why don't we turn it on and see what's going on within the quarantine zone. You think they've identified whoever attacked yet?" He cast a covetous look at the remote in Wyn's hand. Within a few clicks, Wyn found a channel playing news.

Zita headed toward the master bathroom and closed the door behind her. Stepping into the shower stall, she snapped the vibrant rainforest curtain shut, closed her eyes, and savored the relative solitude as she switched on the hot water. When the bathroom filled with the scent of the vanilla soap Quentin had given her, instead of the stink of fire and pain, she opened her eyes again. Rivulets of water, at first black, then clear, ran down the tan stone tiles. The rock soothed her and promised hope of the wilder places she loved. Of course, if she left for too long, her brother would be insolvent from bartering for luxury shower tiles instead of insisting on cash. Reminded of mundane practicalities, she ended the shower, dried, and dressed. The soft, familiar fabrics in cheerful orange and lime green pleased her.

Zita stopped in front of the sink. She stared at herself, then picked up a pair of scissors and began snipping. When she set them back on the counter, she cleaned up the mess and leveled the towels. A glance in the mirror verified her dreadlocks were gone. Her head felt lighter, but odd, given that she had cultivated the hair since... *That's the past. This is the present,* she reminded herself. *All the different lengths of hair are almost punk, and it will be easier to clean or hide under a wig. It's less recognizable too, which works better on the run.*

The what? Wait, on the run? Wyn asked in her head.

Short, wet hair clinging to her head, Zita stepped out of the bathroom, releasing a puff of scented steam when she opened the door to the exercise room.

Andy's voice was resigned. "She did something to her hair. If you talk about boys next, I'm leaving. Start on the topic of feminine supplies, and I'm shooting myself."

Curiosity compelled Zita to ask. "Wouldn't the bullets just bounce? If we talk boys, Andy, I might be the one who leaves."

The other two stood, watching television in her exercise room. Wyn shivered while newscasters blathered, and smoke oozed out of the building that had housed them for a month. When the first newscast segued to the fiery obliteration of an Icelandic mental hospital, Wyn pushed buttons on the remote until she found another station covering the quarantine.

"Bad day for medical facilities," Zita remarked. The others nodded, but the screen riveted their attention. Image after image focused on the devastated hospital, the frenetic activity of the rescue and investigation squads, and the celebrity who flew through so many of the shots. Despite or due to his size, the few images of Andy's bird form were blurred and incomplete.

"Well, the cameras missed most of us," Wyn offered.

Glumly, Andy pointed out, "Except for me. And your hair, Wyn."

Zita snorted. "You were a gigantic golden eagle with glowing eyes, like the stylized thunderbirds you see on motorcycles. Nobody will recognize you. They appear more distracted by the flying tool, even if she doesn't seem that interesting to me. It's lucky for us, though." She was grateful that at least the inevitable change had been to a normal eagle rather than a giant one. Andy's version would not have fit well in her apartment. Zita put her clothing back on as fast as possible.

Andy and Wyn gave her identical looks; people always had that expression before they spoke to her as if to a child.

He said, "Caroline's a hot blond flying around half-naked and taking out terrorists by herself, not an oversized bird that vandalized two buildings and flew away." His attention returned to the screen as Zita managed to return to human and began dressing again.

Wyn pinched the bridge of her nose. "Plus, she's the rich celebrity daughter of a politician in DC."

Zita gaped at her friends before glowering at her decrepit treadmill. "Seriously? She's boring. No skills, no personality, some flight."

"You're talking about a bulletproof blond, fighting on the side of justice with super-strength. She's Supergirl—no, Powergirl. In lingerie," Andy interrupted, his eyes glued to the newscast.

"Who?" Zita asked.

Wyn reminded them both, her own gaze on the television. "Rich celebrity with a senator daddy."

Scowling, she followed their gazes. Swaddled in a policeman's coat, Caroline held court in a circle of reporters. Other than a fetching smudge on one cheekbone, she had the tousled appearance of a just-awakened television ingénue wearing her boyfriend's shirt. The blond flashed perfect white teeth at the cameras, downplayed her role with demure, downcast eyes and clasped hands. Zita sniffed; the other woman may claim the credit belonged elsewhere, but the gratuitous lifting of a car to allow an emergency vehicle through proved otherwise. *Publicity hound.* "First, if she respected the government as she claims, she would not be flirting with the reporters when she is supposed to be quarantined. Second, fine, she's strong and flies, whatever. You shouldn't be a jet-sized footnote, especially in DC. Third, and most important, what about everyone else? We escaped, but what about the other four hundred people in those buildings? Saying some died, and survivors are being treated elsewhere is an asshole way to alarm their families. I know Jerome, Jerome's girlfriend, and Aideen got out, but what about the rest? Did you see anyone else?"

They shook their heads simultaneously.

Wyn touched a delicate hand to her forehead. "No, it was too far away for details. The hospital roof had all these awful lumps all over it, and one was on a hospital gown. We assumed you were dead until you answered me. Once you thought about being canine, I deduced the dog was you, and told Andy while he was tying on his kilt."

Andy appeared intensely uncomfortable. "Things are fuzzy from when I was... I was flying. If we had known you were alive, I would have tried to land closer."

Waving her hand, Zita dismissed their apologies. "No problem. It's almost time to harass Miguel and find out if we need to skip town to avoid Uncle Sam. Leave that news station on in case they report something more useful than how Caroline's farts smell like roses."

The others rolled their eyes. Andy opened his mouth but closed it when Wyn put a hand on his arm and spoke first.

"What's our cover story for how we escaped? The truth won't do if we want to stay free," Wyn said.

Andy made a face and agreed.

They exchanged glances. Zita ran her hand over her half-dry hair, back and forth, as she thought. Andy rubbed the sides of his borrowed shorts while Wyn toyed with a strand of hair that had fallen free to tickle the side of her face.

Zita offered, "The closer we stick to the truth, the less likely we are to mess it up or contradict evidence." She curled her toes into the springy floor mat.

Shutting his eyes to concentrate, Andy began. "The men came to your room and threatened Wyn... Remus ran off from my room when one guy threatened us with a gun. Something happened in the hallway, and they died. We ran to the roof because..." He opened his eyes and contorted his face.

"Because we heard assault rifles," Zita added.

Distracted for a moment, Wyn turned her focus to the shorter woman. "How can you recognize guns like that? What have you been doing besides butchering your hair?" She wrapped the distracting strand of hair around her finger and bit her lip. "While we were on the roof... the helicopter with Caroline flew overhead, and the avian creature picked us up and sped off. That'll cover anyone who saw us on the roof... or anyone who noticed my hair."

"What? Lots of people can identify basic gun types, especially rapid-fire ones." Zita shrugged. "Not bad, and as close to the truth as we want to get."

Her face thoughtful, Wyn inclined her head. She tapped the remote against her leg. "It flew off and set us back down near here. Since this was the closest place, Zita used her hidden key. Guns are guns. There are big ones, bigger ones, and tanks. All guns can make you dead. It's just an issue of splatter after a certain point."

Zita nodded. "That'll have to do. Say it was a park. This area has bunches. Hopefully, nobody will ask where I keep my key."

Andy's tone was wary. "Why?"

"I keep the spare buried in a pot on my balcony. Miguel would flip if he thought I was climbing to my balcony, even if I have done it before, lots of times. And Wyn? Size matters, but your skill and the ammo you use in it are more important details."

Wyn giggled. "Oh, that's true for guns too? Good to know. Valuable information."

"So not here," Andy grumped.

Zita snickered. Her stomach growled. "Right, I'll go scrounge up a meal before we do anything else."

By mutual consent, they ate the stir-fry she served on mismatched plates with minimal conversation and watched the smaller television set to the news.

Chapter Seven

Her stomach full for the first time in weeks, Zita set her fork down by the sole piece of broccoli remaining from her third serving. Wyn nibbled at her first plate of food. Andy, wearing a conflicted expression, was pushing around the ruins of his second helping, with a small pile of bent forks and broken plates beside him. If they didn't have to run, local thrift shop owners would make money replacing Zita's tableware.

Zita planned aloud as she began washing up. "Now, we need to be ready to run after Mamá gets the latest. Miguel will be all up in everyone's faces trying to find out what's going on, and he'll tell her. He will report us as alive, but escaped. Everyone hit the toilets. The closet in the exercise room has empty gym bags you can use. Andy, pick out a couple of Quentin's things to wear. Wyn, you can try my clothes, but not much will fit you. My bedroom's the first door on the right if you want to attempt it anyway. While my panic bag has basic gear, if we want my tent or anything else, we'll need to grab it. It's only a one-person tent, so we might be better off raiding my blankets. Take only what you can carry."

"Why?" Wyn asked.

"I only have a motorcycle. The buses run nearby, and the metro's a quick hike, a mile or two away. We can get lost in public transit while we figure out where to go. Hopefully, I can remain human for the duration. It's that or wait for Andy to get turned on by birdseed and carry us off." Zita winked at him and grinned.

"Hey, that's unfair! Probably," he protested. He set his dish with exaggerated care on the counter. After poking at a clump of rice with her fork, Wyn emulated his action.

Zita glanced at the clock. "We could've walked here by now from the park. I can't put off calling my mother any longer. Are you ready to run for it if we need to?" The other two nodded.

Andy said, "Wait, your mom? I thought you were calling Miguel?"

Zita walked over and muted the television. "No. Harassing a sibling directly is for fun. Involving your mother means the situation is serious. Plus, nobody knows when it's time to cut and run like Mamá."

Turning her back on them, she pressed the shortcut button on her phone. Andy gave an anxious laugh behind her; he had sisters, after all. Given Wyn's parents, she was lucky to exist; siblings would have been too much to ask. *Wyn's parents probably had accidental sex while blinded with pepper spray during one of their endless pickets.*

"No soliciting," were the accented words that greeted her.

She grinned. *Some things never change.* In Spanish, she said, "Mamá, it's Zita. I'm safe for the moment." For the illusion of privacy, she padded to the exercise room.

Her mother squealed. "¡Mija!" she said, "I am so pleased! We just got back from lighting the candles to pray for you. Were you hurt? Where are you?" Sound muffled as her mother put something over the mouthpiece and spoke in English. Although audible, the phone garbled her husband's pleased-sounding reply.

"For now, I'm home, but I'm not going back into another government camp. Would you please talk to Miguel and get the latest news so I know how far and how fast to run?"

"Of course," her mother replied. "Your go bag is ready, yes? And you have an escape route planned?"

Zita exhaled and leaned against a wall. "Yes, but I'll have to take a less optimal route since I have a couple friends with me. Remember Dorcas and Andy from the hospital?"

"My name is Wyn now," came a shout from the other room. *So much for privacy. Wyn doesn't speak Spanish, so she must've recognized her old name.* If Zita's guess was right, her bookshelves were enduring intense scrutiny while Wyn snooped. Andy was probably staring out the sliding glass door again.

"Of course, I will always remember the children. Such a sweet girl to have such crazy parents. Andy, I never knew such a skinny little boy could hold so much vomit. I thought I would never be done with the cleaning that day. I will pray for them as well." Fondness gentled her mother's tones.

"Dorrie goes by Wyn now, umm, Wyn Diamond, but yes, that's them. They escaped with me. We got really lucky because none of us are hurt, but I need to put together go bags for them." She was certain her mother could smell a lie, but the physical distance was hopefully enough to hide any omissions. Idly, she tidied up her videos and set the remote back into its usual position. The phone line was silent a moment. Zita reminded herself holding her breath was a tell, and she needed her mother's support.

"Praise God! We were both so worried. I will use a text to tell you when to answer the phone or if you must run. Miguel will listen to me. It will be easier for him if we do not speak of your friends to him right away. He chases another of those nasty serial killers, and now this, so he will be unhappy, my poor boy." After a slight pause, her mother intimated, "I don't suppose you and Andy..."

Seriously? Now? Doesn't she ever give up? One of my brothers had better distract her with grandchildren soon since I'm pretty certain I can't have any. Zita exhaled. "Ay, no. Way to put me off my food, not that I had much left. Quentin emptied out everything in the apartment, almost."

"Him, I will speak to as well. Now, you prepare for the running. I will see what your brothers can tell their poor old mother, who may not live to see her children married, let alone long enough to hold her grandbabies." Somehow, Mamá managed both imperious and pathetic. Zita's stepfather laughed in the background, and she imagined her mother swatting at him.

"I love you, Mamá. Thanks, and I'll watch my texts." A hard knot settled in her stomach at the thought of living on the run, and what that would mean.

"Yes, I will. I love you too. You will be in my prayers. Try not to die." With her customary farewell, her mother hung up.

Setting the phone down, Zita froze, thinking, for a moment. With an abrupt turn, she strode over and removed the jaunty pirate hat from the martial arts dummy. Her hands flew out in a comforting pattern and hit the dummy enough times to bring up her heart rate and center her thoughts. After retrieving her stash of emergency cash from the small secret compartment in the plant shelf, she went to assist the others with their bags.

***

Zita tried to nap but conceded defeat when her phone rang several times with both brothers' ringtones. An hour later, she had taped a pair of maps up on the patio doors and was arguing with Andy about the direction to go when her phone beeped with a text. Her bag and his crowded together near the door. Wyn poked at the duffle Zita had packed for her, a frown clearing at the text alert. "Please tell me that says we can go home and resume our normal lives. I have cats to support, and they have a pricey salmon habit."

The too-familiar sensation overtook her while Wyn was speaking, and Zita barely had time to pull dainty black paws out of her clothing before the second transformation began. She gasped for air, her mouth opening and closing as her tail flailed against the heap of clothing, propelling her onto the carpet. As she flopped onto her scaled side, her heart and mind raced in her aquatic form.

"Goddess! Zita, I'm so sorry! Andy, get a bucket of water, quick!" Wyn wailed.

Seriously? Air, I need air so badly. I need to be human again with perfectly lovely lungs and arms to strangle my friend. This time, she did not fight the change when it happened and found herself crouching on the floor as Andy raced back in the room carrying a large bucket, sloshing water everywhere. He made an eep sound and marched back to the bathroom. Zita shot Wyn a dirty look as she tossed her clothing back on and scooped up the phone again. Reading the text message, Zita shook her head. "Miguel's worked out a deal. Quentin will replace my groceries, too. That alone qualifies as a minor miracle."

"Call him!" Wyn and Andy demanded in sync.

Her face open and innocent, Zita baited them. "I'll have to take inventory and make a grocery list before I call Quentin." At the dirty looks the others gave her, she snickered. *Suckers.*

Wyn took a step toward her.

Zita held up a hand to forestall any actions. "Sí, sí, have patience, I'm going." Flipping her cell phone open, she dialed.

Andy blinked. "They still make flip phones?" he asked.

Zita raised her eyebrows at him as she brought the phone to her ear.

"Yeah, yeah," he said to her unspoken comment as he wandered over to the patio doors and pretended not to listen. Wyn made no such pretense and leaned closer.

Miguel answered on the third ring. "Garcia—Zita, is that you? How are you? Where are you? Tell me what happened," he demanded. A buzz of conversation came behind him. *He's not home, then.*

With a quick switch to Spanish, she brushed aside his questions. "That's my name, last I checked. So how are things? Weather's been interesting lately, don't you think? If it stays this humid, mosquitoes won't need puddles to breed. Speaking of procreation, have you found a serious girlfriend yet?" She stuck out her tongue at Wyn. *She could at least pretend she's not listening, like Andy. Since she doesn't speak Spanish, let's see if I can do a two-for-one annoyance special.*

"Where are you? Are you injured?" he tried again, dropping into Spanish as well.

Zita gave an exaggerated sigh. "Well, you wouldn't be this uptight if you were getting it regular, so I'm guessing not. That's a shame, as Mamá isn't getting any younger. She'd love grandbabies. As the responsible one in the family, I think you should find a boring Catholic girl and pump out nieces and nephews. Well, not pumping out, that might be counterproductive, but you get the idea. If not, Quentin can give you tips or instructional videos." With interest, she noted he could growl and grind his teeth at the same time. She grinned.

Miguel complained, "Oh, God, not you too. Can't you ever be serious? Quit fooling around and answer."

"I'm fine, thanks. So are the others."

"I don't speak Spanish," Wyn interrupted in a quiet response, "but you and Andy do. The meaning comes through. If that is your typical mode of interaction, I can see why your mother has to mediate."

"Who is with you? Are they a danger? Do you need the police? Where are you?"

She made another face at her friend, and plopped down, swinging both legs over the chair arm. Zita let her head fall backward to stare at the ceiling. *Of course, you can. How could I forget about the mental eavesdropping thing? Do you think I should paint my ceiling or leave it the boring white color?* "Lighten up, Miguel. I told you I'm fine. They're not a threat. If they'd been a hazard, Mamá would have had you send a SWAT team. So, what's the deal with the quarantine? We're not going back to see whether they can bore or starve us to death before more gun-toting apes shoot us." Seams ripped as her form shifted again. Looking down in frustration, she cradled the cell phone in large, elongated hands, and wiggled black toes. Her chair creaked under her, and she hopped to her feet, her clothing falling to the floor in tatters around her. *Seriously? A gorilla? This has to get under control soon.*

Andy shook his head and turned his back on her again.

Ignorant of her change, Miguel's voice rattled out of the phone. Moving it awkwardly to accommodate her new hand dimensions, Zita held it closer to make out his words. "- didn't tell me you had company. How many are there? Why did you go haring off?"

Her form shimmered again, and the phone fell into the pile of fabric as Zita shrunk. She drummed a foot on the floor in frustration and swore mentally.

"Aww, you make a really adorable little potty-mouthed brown bunny," Wyn whispered. "Can I boop your cute little snoot?"

Shut up. Leave my nose alone or I'll bite you. Her nose twitched and wiggled. Zita hopped over to the phone where Miguel was still issuing commands disguised as questions. *My plants smell delicious. Wyn, can you help with him?*

Wyn walked over and picked up the phone. "Hang on, Miguel, Zita's traumatized by the lack of sufficient nourishment in quarantine, and is having a nibble." She stepped delicately over Zita, holding the phone away from her head at the verbal explosion the comment had caused.

Zita glared.

When you are human again, I'll give you the phone and fetch clothing so poor Andy doesn't have to stare out that door forever. Wyn's voice held suppressed mirth as she spoke into the phone. "I agree, she can be foolhardy, but we share her concerns about our safety, both individually and collectively, in quarantine. Oh, this is Ellynwyn Diamond, but you can call me Wyn. The other person here is Andy Cristovano." She turned her back on Zita as she listened to the phone.

The more details you give him about who is here, the more easily they can track us. Zita scowled at Wyn, though it translated as an ear wiggle and sniffing in her hare form. *Now how do I change back?*

That stupid Caroline doesn't have to deal with this sort of thing. She can fly and blind people with her bleached teeth while life bounces off her, and her perfect hair shines in the fucking breeze. Her form shimmered again, and she relaxed for a moment, finding herself human again. When she brushed a hair from her face and realized what the light color and light skin meant, she yelped in involuntary protest. Gagging, she fought not to reject her meal.

Andy and Wyn spun to look at her. His mouth dropped open, and his face was scarlet. He presented his back to her again. "Oh, God," he prayed.

Her female friend's eyes were wide, but she brought a hand up to her mouth. "Honestly, it's nothing, Miguel. Zita bit herself, that's all," Wyn giggled into the phone.

Shoving a strand of blond hair out of her face again with a perfect peaches-and-cream hand, Zita glared at Wyn as she rose on unfamiliar feet. *Not a word if you value your life. Doesn't the girl ever work out? You'd think a gold medalist would do better. Her arms are almost as bad as Wyn's.* When her friend pouted, Zita's spirits rose at catching her. *All you have to do is not listen, Wyn, like everyone else. Except maybe priests and the NSA.*

Easy for you to say, Wyn answered mentally.

As Zita moved toward the hall, swaying to adjust for the change in balance, she mentally spat. She crossed her arms over her chest and stalked into the bedroom to shove on intact clothing, a job made more difficult with a taller, less curved frame. *My body is way better. I'm fitter, and my boobs are real.* Glaring at her sock drawer, she felt herself change again, and her balance told her what she needed to know, even before she looked down. "Yes, yes, yes!" she shouted, punching the air in triumph.

Lalala, Andy sent, *so not listening.*

As she padded back into the living room in another outfit, Wyn's voice was quizzical, though she smirked at Zita's questioning look. "None of us were participating in Dr. Singh's study, so it doesn't matter what he thinks. Zita had us all document

our refusals to participate. Did you know she was leading the
opposition to his study? Plenty of people can act as witnesses to
that." She laughed at a comment and grinned at Zita. "Ah, so true!
Here's your sister back."

"So what," she began, but her brother cut her off with a rapid
spate of Spanish.

"Zita, are you certain you're safe with these people?"

She let her head droop. *This again. Someday, my brother will
realize I'm a grown woman.* As there was no point to using Spanish,
she switched back to English. "Pretty certain. Wyn's a librarian and
Andy's a physics graduate student. We were friends before Brazil."

Suspicion flavored his voice, but he followed her lead and used
English. "Which time?"

"The first one. So what's the deal? If you didn't have an
agreement, Mamá wouldn't have had me call you." With a wink at
Wyn, she stage-whispered, "Plus I think I can take both of them in
a fight." She heard a masculine snort from the direction of the patio
doors. Her other friend nodded from where she had enthroned
herself with colorful pillows on the futon, her attention on the
sparkling lights between her hands.

Unaware of her companions' responses, her brother
harrumphed. "Given who you and Quentin associate with
normally, is it any surprise I have concerns?" Miguel complained,
and in her mind's eye, she saw him rubbing his forehead. "They
sound acceptable," he grudgingly admitted. "Here's the deal. Other
patients also complained about conditions, and there's pressure
higher up to resolve this. Anyone not required to have medical
supervision will quarantine in place. Where are you three?"

Zita perked up, bouncing on her heels. *¡Gracias a Dios!* Her
shoulders relaxed, losing tension she had been unaware of until
then. "That shouldn't be a problem. We're at my place. I'll drop the
others off at their homes, and we'll all play at house arrest like well-
behaved children."

Wyn beamed and hugged herself as she rose to her feet.

Andy turned, a smile trembling on his lips, his thick eyebrows arching with a question. His voice was eager. "Thank God! I can go home, get on my computer, and talk to my girlfriend in privacy."

Miguel shattered her illusions. "Actually, Zita, you can't drive them home."

Her eyes narrowed before she came up with a solution. "What? Fine, they can send a sealed van and take them home then without spreading germs," she replied, waving a dismissive hand in the air. Wyn and Andy hovered nearby, the joy flickering on their faces. "It's the government mucking things up, no worries," she reassured them, or maybe herself.

The phone was ominously silent for a few seconds. "I'm sorry, Zita, but you all have to stay in your apartment. Shelter in place is exactly that. I'll verify, but you should plan on houseguests until this is resolved. You can't leave or interact with anyone else. Although you can open your door to receive packages and such if the deliveryman has already left."

"Seriously? Whose crazy ass idea is that?" she snarled. The need to run, spar, or move rose. Glimpsing the others—Wyn fluttering shiny lashes rapidly and Andy turning away again to the patio door—Zita tried a different tack. "How much harm can it do to let them go home? It's not as if the government hasn't had to move everyone else around. Heck, if the authorities are more paranoid than usual, they can drop off a sealed van. My friends can jog on down in the middle of the night and drive themselves home. Official types can bug bomb or fumigate or whatever when they take the fucking van back." Her arm flew out in an arc, and she paced back and forth across her small living room.

Wyn turned her face toward the red futon cushion, and Andy opened the patio door, pulling it off the tracks. His shoulders slumped as he stepped through to the balcony, brushing by the grabbiest of her plants to stare over the parking lot to the trees beyond. Her screen door tilted behind him.

Zita itched to do something, or better yet, punch something shaped like the government.

Her brother spoke in that annoying tone she hated, the reasonable one that invariably made a well-thought-out argument meant to destroy her opposition. "The alternative is a central quarantine location for all quarantined people who do not live alone. Many of the survivors from your building are already in one. Senator Gyllen has been pushing for quarantining at home since his daughter... fell ill. It seems the powers that be are listening now." A touch of acid dripped in his voice, as he continued, "Apparently, the fine men and women of our armed forces are inadequate to protect her. So, she will be quarantined off-site with whatever private security her father feels is acceptable."

Crossing the living room in a few short strides, Zita growled into the phone. "Like I care about that piece of—" she stopped, and took a deep breath. "Give me a second." Zita yanked the tipsy screen door off and put it back on again with more force than necessary. The moment of respite gave her an idea. In all likelihood, it would not work, but it would annoy her brother. That counted as at least a partial win. "Oh, Miguel, so sorry, Wyn and Andy already left. I can't stop them without breaking quarantine. You can report on your paperwork that they're in their homes." She made little motorcycle noises like one revving and driving off. Her friends both looked at her.

"Zita! ¡Basta! That's enough."

She paused. "Vroom rumble rumble vroom?"

A grunt preceded Miguel's quiet answer. "Zita, just, no. I can't do that. I won't do it. Please don't put me in that position, and please stop making that, that, sound! They only told me that much as a professional courtesy. The best I can do is tell them where you are, and ensure they know you don't require retrieval. You didn't interact with anyone outside quarantine, did you?"

This is why I didn't want to give him any information; he has too much integrity to falsify a report. Zita exhaled. "No, we saw no one except for the ones who busted into our respective rooms."

Regret tinged Wyn's mental voice, as she whispered, *I didn't know. I'm sorry.*

Zita's response was immediate. *No te preocupes. You didn't know. If I have to share my place with anyone other than a beefcake who is into me and working out, at least it's you two. I mostly like you.*

Andy's only comment was gruff. "Thanks. Ditto and stuff."

"I'm glad it's you too, though I call dibs on Zita's bed," Wyn said.

Zita grunted. *That's enough mushiness. We'll deal with the practicalities once I'm off the phone.*

Miguel's next words were all business, but relief and warmth sounded in his tone. "That works. While I'm certain it's an interesting story, don't talk about it with anyone until you have permission. That includes your friends, who should also not talk about it. Someone will want witness statements about today, but nobody knows when, as an alphabet soup of agencies has to finish fighting jurisdictional wars first. My clearance won't get me anything more. As it is, my agency is displeased with me for interfering with this when they've got a killer strewing dead bodies across state borders."

Zita paced and made a derisive sound. "See no one, talk to no one, and starve quietly while they make us bankrupt. Got it."

"Zita... Half the world delivers, and Quentin will run you supplies."

She controlled her breathing and the urge to whine. "I understand, mano, nothing you can do. It's better than another institution. Go catch the murderer. Expect a call in a few days. Love you."

"Love you too. Try not to get into trouble." His voice cheered up. "You could use this as an opportunity to hunt online for a full-time job or apply to schools."

Snorting, Zita answered. "No. I'm going to fritter away my house arrest working out and perhaps planning a new hobby to drive you nuts. Bye." With a click of the button, she ended the call and eyed her new roommates.

Wyn spoke first. "Well, this is unfortunate, but I'm certain we can make it work amicably."

"It sucks big hairy—" Zita cut herself off before she could finish. She took a deep breath. "We should make the best of things. Wyn, why don't you call a friend to bring things over? Andy, you want to use my computer and email your girl? I can't promise privacy with the party line bopping in and out of our brains, but it's the best I can offer. You can use the phone when Wyn's done. When you've finished, we'll make a grocery list and figure it all out."

A smile crept onto Andy's face. "Really? You don't mind?" he said. "I haven't logged on since before the coma and it was really hard to reach my girlfriend during the limited phone time allotted. She's been preoccupied with a breakthrough for her dissertation."

"Fine with me," Zita said. "It's in my bedroom." She led the way into the room, this one a vibrant green. Crossing the area in a few steps, she pulled back the jungle print blackout curtains. Light danced inside through the sheer curtains with the tiny green and blue birds embroidered on them. She scanned the rest of the room with a critical eye to see if Quentin had meddled with it. Her queen-sized bed was as she had left it: a pair of fluffy pillows nestled together, purple tie-dyed sheets straight, and a deep green blanket folded at the end. The bed took up most of the space in the room. Sometime when the others were occupied, she would need to verify her emergency knives and the box of self-defense gifts from Miguel were in their hiding places. A diminutive brown wicker nightstand had been crammed between the bed and the window. An alarm clock blinked the wrong time against a tiny yellow lamp. On the other side, a second, almost-matching nightstand brushed the closet. It held a lamp, this one shaped like a turtle. White closet doors hid her dresser and a small assortment of dresses, suits, and coats. The window took up most of the far wall while a photograph of the view from her room in her aunt's Brazilian home pretended to be a window opposite the bed. When Andy stepped in, she waved her hand at the wooden desk next to the faux window.

He stopped, and Wyn ran into him with a slight exhalation of air. Andy gaped at the dusty beige tower leaning drunkenly against the old desk and the chunky little monitor. "How old is that thing? Does it even have a web browser? You aren't on a modem that uses dial-up, are you?"

Zita looked at him. "What? It worked fine last time I used it a few months ago. The monitor's only five years old. I don't know how old the other part is. Did you change your mind?" She marched over, positioned a black folding chair, and dropped it in front of the desk with a metallic clatter, softened by the cheap beige carpet. A pile of maps slid toward the edge of the desk, jolted into losing the war with the monitor, a clip-on light, and a cup of pens for desk real estate. Snatching the maps, Zita dropped them into the correct desk drawer. *All the fun jobs will be taken by the time quarantine ends. Guess I won't be leaving the States this year.*

He faced the computer, hovering over the seat for a moment before dropping into it. "No, no, it's fine. I'm sure it'll be great. I just... umm, won't be playing any games on it. Do you keep a fire extinguisher nearby?"

"Seriously?" Zita cocked her head and gave him a dirty look. Her brows lowered as she considered. *Should I have an extinguisher in here for the computer? Was that a legitimate question?*

"I have a telephone call to make." Wyn retreated.

Andy flushed. "I feel foolish for pointing out your machine's obsolescence." Turning toward the computer, pleasure grew on his face. His eyes danced. "I can't wait to get online." Leaning down, he punched the power button with a finger. Something cracked deep inside, and small plastic bits tumbled out as he removed his finger. "Aww, man."

Chapter Eight

"I hate you," Wyn **groaned** a month later. "If you're going to torment me, at least wear your own countenance when doing it." She lowered her arms and propped her hands on her slender hips as she stood.

Blinking hazel eyes at her, Zita unfolded from the yoga position. She mirrored her friend, placing her own hands on her hips. A glance in the mirror showed identical Wyns, save for the clothing. She far preferred her sensible white sports bra and stretchy orange pants as opposed to the librarian's leotard and filmy skirt. The latter particularly puzzled her; neither concealing nor protective, the useless accessory got in the way every time Wyn's attention wandered, such as when speaking. "What? You told me you were physically incapable of taking that position. That's what you said about the weights, and you've moved up on those from a month ago. If I can do it wearing your form and off balance because our bodies are different, you can do it. So, put on big girl panties or something." Zita squirmed; the nine-inch height difference made her underwear uncomfortable. "It's only a little more complex than the yoga poses you do every other day. Do you want me to show you how to take the pose again?"

Wyn scowled at her, eyes narrowing. "No."

"Pues, someday you'll be thanking me when you're all bendy and flexible. Your future boyfriends will be so impressed. They will shower both of us with flowers and chocolate. Oh, once you get in the position, you should do one of your magic tricks so you can practice two things at once." Just in case, Zita flowed into the yoga pose, careful to move at a pace the other woman could copy.

Through practice, she had learned she could stay in another form until she wanted a change. She slept as a cat every night, thanks to having to share a bed with her friend. Wyn had a fondness for cats that extended to imitating one while she slept; she would sprawl out so her slim form claimed possession of most of the sleeping area. Sharing the bed required Zita to ignore flopping limbs and pretend to be part of the mattress, or to be a cat herself, in which case Wyn unconsciously ceded territory and allowed peaceful coexistence. What Zita had spent most of the past month doing was practicing the hard part—stopping a shift when she thought of an animal. People's forms were complex. She had to concentrate to take a human form other than her own and only had to stop herself from shifting when she got emotional about a person. Andy and Wyn would shout out random animals at all hours of the day and night; as annoying as it could be, she had asked them to do so for the practice. In comparison, controlling her teleportation had been simplicity itself.

Wyn cast her eyes upward in a dramatic fashion. "They're not tricks. They're spells and illusions and... fine, I'll try it just to shut you up. At least, I haven't had to do eight million crazy exercises like poor Andy." She bent and eased into position. Once she achieved the pose, a wicked grin crossed her lips. A pale shimmer passed over her, and when it disappeared, the woman posing looked like Zita, uneven hair, outfit and all. Her illusory top even included a stain on the front where sauce had dripped at dinner.

Stung, Zita frowned at her friend. "Your left hand goes more straight than that. Those drills are helping. And for your information, Andy is doing worlds better. I haven't had to replace any doorknobs this week at all, and he's almost ready to move to a new medium. In fact, if he's careful, he can even use his laptop."

Andy's voice interrupted from the doorway. His brown eyes lit up as he considered them. "Really? It'll be great to do something other than move, stack, and balance ice cubes. It feels like I'm stuck in an Eighties adventure game because I missed combining a cracker crumb with a sardine tin lid or boot. What's the next medium? Weights? Lemurs? Can I use my laptop more? I've been stealing cautious computer time, but never enough to get comfortable." While his tone was light, his face wore the same sorrowful lines it had held for the past few days, and his body was tight, tensed for a fight.

Zita shook her head and shifted back to her own form. Andy's attention switched to her when she spoke. "Water-filled balloons. Some will be lubricated."

While holding the yoga pose and the illusion of Zita, Wyn turned her head. "Lubricated balloons? Sounds prophylactic." She and Andy shared a snicker.

Zita shrugged. "Most of them will be. I have more novelty condoms than balloons around here, so someone might as well use them. Quentin is always giving me boxes, so it'll be a relief to reduce the stockpile. Did you know they expire? You can start with the expired ones." Picking a pose, she bent, and twisted, and breathed until she was upside down in a more complex pose.

Nonplussed, Andy blinked. "Umm, you're kidding me, right?" He turned red.

Zita beamed. "You know, we get to spar again after you've practiced with the condoms."

"Thank you for not wearing my form to say that!" Wyn lost the battle to control her laughter. As her glee rang out, she slipped out of the yoga pose and crumpled into a graceful heap. Dancing brown eyes gleamed as she added, "Oh, and I'm not trying that pose." She flicked her neck with a hand; it took a second for Zita to realize she was brushing at hair hidden by the illusion and not swatting at an insect.

Moving to a pose that required more strength, Zita shook her head. "Nope, got to make use of what we've got at hand. Besides, do you really want to explain to Quentin why we want balloons and lube? He'll come up with a perverted explanation, and we will never hear the end of it. Wyn, I don't expect you to. You need more upper body strength to do this one." *Even I can't fix wimpy arms in one month.* When Wyn didn't react, Zita all but rubbed her hands together in glee. *Excellent. Her migraines have been disappearing as her control improves. Does she realize that?*

"I'm not sure I want to progress then," Andy muttered, making a face. As the color faded, the hangdog expression returned. He shifted from foot to foot, and added, "Oh, I had something to show you, Zita. To help with your shapes practice."

Zita perked up and flipped to her feet. *A new exercise? Sweet!* "Really?" Practice had given them all better control of their new abilities, but the confined space restricted their activities. She had been unable to practice any large forms or explore their capabilities. Andy had not turned into a giant bird since the hospital, and instead spent most of his waking time on the balcony, practicing handling things without breaking them. After a spell to encourage plant growth had left the tiny balcony more like a jungle than not, Wyn was judicious about what spells she attempted. Mostly, she had been practicing controlling her telepathy and healing the numerous small injuries they (mostly Zita) incurred. In defense of their friendships, Andy and Zita had both learned how to close their minds to keep from leaking every thought. While they had made progress, the more emotionally laden ones slipped through when Wyn had the party line up.

Letting her illusion drop, Wyn's lips curved in a conspiratorial smirk. "It's done, then?"

Her friend's question gave her pause. Zita considered the pair with suspicion, remembering how they helped her practice teleportation last time they had a surprise for her. "Look, I'm all about delicious food, but if this is a ploy to get me to teleport to the

Eiffel Tower for more pastries, you're out of luck. The Pisa trip used the rest of our cash, though, and I'm not teleporting in front of anyone else unless I have no choice. Plus, we're pretending to be quarantined."

Wyn shook her head. "No deception, though I could go for fresh croissants for tomorrow's breakfast. Ooh, or éclairs."

Her friends smiled. Andy said, "Yes, it's ready. Follow me. I think you'll like this, even if no food is involved." With Wyn following behind, he led her into the bedroom. "So you're thinking you have shifting under control, right?" he asked.

Zita nodded, running her hand back and forth over her short, uneven strands of soft hair. "Yes, I can write chicken on the grocery list without tempting Colonel Sanders to use his herbs and spices." Having seen similar gloating on her brothers before, Zita narrowed her eyes and looked back and forth at the other two. "Should I be worried?"

The cheap laptop that had replaced her ancient computer sat open and humming on her desk. Andy paused by the stool in front of it, the chair gone after one of his failed attempts to control his strength. "No, you'll like this, I swear. You've been so good about devising tort—tests for us that we have the ultimate trial for you. Sit down, and watch these feeds," he said in a soothing tone that did nothing to alleviate her qualms.

Confused, Zita complied, twisting to watch them. "Wait, now you're saying there's food? Where's the food?" she said, looking around. Her stomach rumbled at the idea of a snack. The other two snickered. "What? Dinner was a while ago," she said, her tone defensive.

Wyn giggled. "The dinner we ate early because you were hungry? When Andy said feeds, he meant the cameras. Try to pay attention to the computer, Zita." Her eyes twinkled as she confirmed with Andy, "You did set it to the small ones, right?"

Andy nodded, a smile on his lips, though it did not extend to his eyes. Catching Zita's gaze on him, he jerked his chin and mouth toward the computer, his version of pointing.

Zita shrugged and turned her attention to the screen. She concentrated. "Otter cam at the National Zoo?" she asked, leaning forward to get a better perspective. Choosing to allow the transformation, the now-familiar change in viewpoint was no surprise.

Andy stepped forward and glanced at the screen. "You don't look quite like the ones on the cam. We figured you could use the cams to check out various animals for practice."

In one flowing motion, Zita exited her clothing and leapt up onto the desk. *I don't?* Bringing her pointy little nose close to the monitor, she squinted. The only otter visible was at the edge of the screen, next to the water. *Ay, I guess not. These are different from my mental image. The claws are shorter, and it is smaller than me.* She barely noticed the adjustment to her form, so absorbed in her comparisons of herself and the real otter. *The fur is a little different too, change it like so. This would be easier to see if I were there. What is he*—instinct told her it was a male—*staring at? Is something among the rocks?*

Warm water enveloped her, and Zita sputtered and flailed. With the hard-won practice of the past month, she released control to her instincts. Her movements smoothed as she righted herself and paddled to solid ground. *I need to practice the teleportation more. I thought I could only go to places I can see, landmarks, or home. Looks like the zoo cam was my ticket for a trip to see the animals.* She darted onto the land and took a moment to evaluate her new surroundings. Motors humming and chemically clean water branded the creek as artificial. A tall Plexiglas wall hemmed the creek in on one side while a tumble of stones bounded the other side. The zoo resident watched her curiously, rising to his hind legs, a rock in one paw. An older female otter, followed by a bevy of others, charged toward them.

Zita backpedaled. She sat on her haunches and tried to appear respectful and repentant. Experience had taught her to recognize an old tía about to ream her for something that had made sense at the time.

The older female stopped a few feet away, tilted her head, and made a chirruping sound. The otters around her bobbed up and down.

Clueless, Zita nodded and sank down to all fours. If necessary, she would shift and flee as a bird; it was preferable to harming zoo animals or being maimed and must have been the right thing to do as she found herself surrounded by myriad furry forms as they tumbled around her. Her nose was overwhelmed, and she counted, trying to keep them all straight. The otters numbered ten, possibly eleven total. After a few minutes of tumbling around her, one of the younger ones pounced on another otter and the group splashed in the water.

Zita shook herself dry from splattered water. Standing and settling onto her haunches, she scanned the enclosure. The original male dove into the water and swam nearby, popping out of the water to sniff her. Then he was back in the water again, chattering at her before diving under again.

Seems I have one more skill to practice if I can go somewhere other than where I can see, landmarks, and my apartment. Ay, I will save a bundle on airfare if I can use webcams. It'll be so fast, and I'll get to do more fun things and spend less time sitting around for hours, breathing stale air, and hoping nobody farts. Her whole body quivered with joy. The real otter did convoluted loops in the water. Within a second, Zita leapt in to duplicate it. *While I'm here, I may as well enjoy practicing.*

The otters seemed rhapsodic to have a new playmate, and they enjoyed a few rounds of acrobatics before Wyn's voice sounded in her mind. *Zita? Where are you?* Andy's presence was a warm glow in the background.

Otter pen at the zoo, Zita replied. *It's fun, to tell the truth, though I'll get out of here soon before the zookeepers count and realize they have an extra. I never realized I could use a webcam to go places.*

Andy's mental voice was matter-of-fact. *Told you she was goofing off in there.*

Wyn sounded relieved. *Don't worry about it. I'm glad you're okay. Are you coming back?*

Floating on her back in the water, Zita scratched her furry belly. *Sure. While I'm here, I may as well study the animals. Ooh, I've always wanted to try the O line, so I'll do that once witnesses are gone. After I do that, then I'll fly or teleport back after dark.*

The what? The others chorused.

Zita blinked, slipped beneath the water for a moment, then resurfaced. Her otter friend had already wandered away. *The O line is an elevated line the orangutans use to travel between two buildings. I've always wanted to view it from closer... and maybe to try it.*

Andy's amusement beat Wyn's by a few seconds. *Typical,* Wyn sent. *Here I was hoping for something more prurient, like a strip club near the Zoo.*

By the way, Wyn, excellent job getting the party line going over the distance, Zita sent. The male otter returned with a gift. "Yeah, dude, nice rock," she said. It came out as a series of chattering noises. It pleased the animal so much, he ran off and returned with another otter and pebble.

Wyn said primly. *You're welcome. Don't scare me again like that.*

Andy sent a brief farewell. *Fine. We'll let you get back to playing with substrate and whatever.*

Hasta, she sent, flipping a paw at the camera. No reply returned. Zita snorted, or made a growly sound anyway, while surfing down a small waterfall to a lower area, following the other otters. She flipped out of the pool. A bunch of the furry creatures crowded around, showing each other stones. *Oh, more rocks. It's rock exhibition time. Oye, here's granite-y piece, friend.* She proffered one to an otter, but he did not take it from her. "Right, show and tell only," she vocalized, aware that it must have sounded like a series of chirping noises. A pair of otters sniffed around her, then dashed into the water. "Geez, even the otters are critics. My rock is way more interesting than your dumbass ones," she grumbled. Zita hunted around the enclosure, assessing the camera emplacements for handy gaps.

When she thought she was unobserved, she shifted to a crow and scoped out the zoo. Spotting orangutans crossing between buildings, she flew close enough to study how they traveled, and how they held their hands.

***

Practicing at the zoo rocked. Zita could get closer to all the animals than she could as a visitor, and better observe the nuances, like their specific grips when climbing a rope. Her mental list of activities to try as assorted animals grew exponentially. While it was well after closing by the time she used the elevated line, she enjoyed every moment. After taking the line across, she practiced new grips as a chimpanzee in a tree near the zoology education building—a bronze plaque proclaimed it the Think Tank. Idly, she deliberated if she wanted to return to the confinement of her apartment or continue practicing nocturnal forms here. Even though full dark enfolded the zoo, nighttime lighting and animal eyesight allowed her to function. A muffled foul exclamation broke into her internal debate. She tracked the sound to three men attempting to skulk nearby.

Automated sprinklers spewed water on two men lurking in the bushes bordering the sidewalk between the Think Tank and the parking lot. One seemed morose, the other angry, and both were getting soaked. Each side of the path had water sprinklers going, with only the center of the sidewalk left dry. The third man stood in shadow on the walkway, on the periphery of the water, though a black splotch on one leg suggested he had moved. The nearest light was out.

"This is idiotic. Why do we have to do it this way and here? This is too public," one man muttered, his tone angry. His scrawny, too-skinny build and jittering energy suggested his vices came in pill or needle form. A scent of sweat and sickness rose from the dark sweatshirt and sagging jeans that hung off him. Jeans, growing sodden from the water, revealed a small gun in his waistband. His constant motion left the bamboo reeds rustling and swaying in the small stand, throwing shadows over a skull dissipated to a sullen leanness and shaved close. A tangle of dark plastic yarn hung from his waist. Zita squinted and stopped to eavesdrop. *Why is he wearing a sweatshirt in this heat?*

A second man, darker, with a heavy unibrow and thick frame, shook his head. Light caught on the gray at his temples. "Shut up and do the job." He shifted, leaning against the tree he'd chosen for cover. His clothes, though also dark, fit well enough for Zita to see the way the fabric stretched over his chest and arms. *Strong pectorals and biceps, overdeveloped compared to the legs... weight lifting for strength and looks, rather than what develops naturally from a physical job.* The muggy air carried less of his sweat than the first man's, and his clothing only bore stains under his arms and where the water hit. Unlike the first man, he wore gloves and moved with an economy of motion. His eyes checked the surroundings in the habitual scan of a cop or the criminals they chased.

With the annoyed tones of a person repeating himself, the last man, the smallest of the group, whispered. "Stick to the plan and get the package. I'll wait in the car so we can exit quickly and pick up a paycheck tonight."

It took Zita a moment to parse his words, as his thick accent veered oddly between American, bad German, and even worse Russian. She craned her neck. Separated from the other two, he had avoided the sprinklers on the sidewalk. His shoes reflected shards of light as he moved, and his self-conscious swagger shouted more of image than threat.

The last man tossed his head, forcing uneven bangs to swing away from his eyes. Foul smoke curled up from the cigarette hanging from his lip. "You lack vision. This is why I'm management and you're not. Follow my commands." Fuzz ran from his lower lip to his chin in a jagged stripe that stood out against a soft face richer in indulgence than years. Jamming a ball cap on his head, he turned on his heel and strode into the parking lot. The man never left the pavement, though he veered from one darkened area to the next. Despite his precautions, the lamps still showed the creases in the dark slacks, the glint of gold at his waist and wrists, and the silky mesh of his shirt. He paused by a black SUV, lit another cigarette, and slid into the car.

Ah, charming, drug dealing at the National Zoo. If a pen and paper are lying around, I can leave a note for security. I can't walk up and tell them in this form. If I returned to my usual form, they'd get all weird and distracted by my nudity. People are strange.

A growl came from the first man, who swore. "Damn Boris and his attitude. You know he's going to sit in the AC while we do all the work. Let's do it our way. I don't see why we have to follow the orders of some..." Sweat ran down his face and neck, onto his clothing. One of his hands dipped into his pocket and emerged empty. He shifted in place again, unable to keep still.

Jitters, Zita decided. *I'll call him Jitters. The thick shirt probably hides track marks and helps him deal with withdrawal chills. He'll be real cold by the time the sprinklers quit, though.*

The calmer man cut him off. "The kid's a mouthpiece. Do as he says. If we can't get the pickup within the hour, we go again another night. I have to get back to handle deliveries at Danz Mizer soon, or Boris will screw it up trying to manage things. This isn't the first package, and it won't be the last. Kid let it slip that the boss is looking to get his hands on a whole file of packages soon from that doctor, with leads on another list. The way he messes up, the kid won't stay a favorite. Do you want the boss' attention? If Sobek gets mad, he can take it out on Boris, his right-hand fucking man, instead of me. I'll take the cash and keep my skin in one piece. Besides, the boss was always hard on people... even before he got freaky powers."

A reluctant nod accompanied the reply. "You got a point."

"Of course, I do. Remember the boundary line for the cameras is that tree over there. If you get on video, I don't know you. You don't know the boss, and you say nothing or you know what he'll do." When he turned to gesture at a tree, his shirt pulled tight against a bulge at his lower back.

I had better mention they're armed in my note, Zita thought. *This one doesn't seem like an idiot. I guess he can be Brains.*

Jitters picked at a nasty sore on his face and nodded. "Yeah. Yeah. I got it." Bamboo whispered with each tremor shivering through his form. A rivulet of sweat ran down his neck, joining the dark river of perspiration already on his shirt.

Cruelty touched the second man's lips as they curved upward, and he leaned into the shadows of his tree. "Yeah. Now shut up and do the job before I forget you're related and smack you."

Shifting to an owl—Zita hoped no ornithologist noticed a South American great horned owl in DC, but it was the first one that came to mind—she took flight, circling up with a beat of her wings. Most of her flight practice had been as small birds in her apartment, save for the brief time as a golden eagle. Soaring freely on the sultry night winds was almost joy enough to distract her from her self-appointed mission. A discarded pen was her first prey, and she flew with it in an awkward clutch, searching for paper. At this hour, few people stirred as zoo employees and security staff went about their business. If she stayed above the lights illuminating the paths of the zoo, evading their eyes would be simple.

Spotting something white as she returned to the Think Tank area, Zita was stooping to get it when a scream sounded in her mind, throwing off her concentration. The female voice, an unknown, spoke a senseless garble that would have been unintelligible had the terror running through it not delivered the message.

Falling out of the dive, Zita flapped sideways, trying to avoid gravity's harsh call and return to the balance of instinct and intellect that allowed flight.

From inside the building, a screeching cacophony erupted as if every ape, macaque, and other animal inside chose that moment to shriek.

Zita flinched and fell. Pain bloomed as tree branches slowed her descent, and she landed with a jarring thud and a squelch in a trash can.

A woman shrieked again; it took a moment for Zita to realize her ears had registered the noise rather than her mind. The Latina marshaled her thoughts, trying not to contemplate where she had landed that smelled so awful. A wrapper fell from her body as she struggled out of the can and shook her feathers into order, launching back into the air find the source of the sound. Her right shoulder, the one she seemed to injure every few years, throbbed from pain with every flap, and something... pungent... smeared her body. An assortment of trash adhered to her, a receipt fluttering to the ground as she circled.

The source of the noise became apparent. The skulking men from earlier had accosted two women, one of whom, a curvy redhead, lay unmoving in a fetal curl on the ground. All four were on the dim sidewalk, with little or no illumination reaching into the foliage framing the path. His knife wavering, the shaky man menaced a tall brunette in a lab coat. Jitters panted and shivered, the sounds warring for dominance with the involuntary half-sobs escaping the brunette clutching her purse to her chest. Brains snapped another cartridge into a boxy gun: a Taser, Zita surmised. Both men had balaclavas over their faces, and water drenched their lower halves from the sprinklers that tossed water in the air like confetti. In the distance, light bobbed down a path.

Landing nearby on a thick tree branch, she was grateful for the near-silence of owl flight. Zita swore in a few different languages mentally as Brains finished reloading his weapon and raised it at the brunette. "Cuff the freak for travel." Jitters scrabbled at the tangle of plastic hanging off his belt, which she realized were zip tie cuffs.

No time to plan. She shifted back to herself, the area growing dimmer as her vision changed. Her shoulder throbbed; the other sore spots seemed negligible in comparison. Crouching, she bent her legs, preparing to spring on the man with the Taser. The branch cracked under her increased weight but did not break.

"What was that?" Jitters asked, his knife wavering as he turned her direction, then away, trying to locate the source of the disturbance, the knife following his eyes.

Brains glanced around to identify the noise but turned back to the woman in front of him.

Zita took advantage of their distraction to leap out and knock the Taser from Brains' hand, sending it into the bushes as she continued onward. He swung, but she was well below his fist.

"Was that a naked chick?" Jitters gaped and gestured where she had been. Despite his carelessness with his knife, he did not to cut himself, but his actions diverted attention to her last location.

Good thing I'm no longer there. Moving fast, Zita spun to the knife-wielder, moving up into a low, fast cartwheel interrupted first by one kick to Jitters' knee, then by a strike using the other foot to kick the knife from his hand as he collapsed with a shriek. When she finished the aú batido move, her foot skidded in the muddy earth. She slid under a nearby bush, her abused shoulder slamming on the ground. Pinpoints of pain sprang up as the branches raked her.

Brains pulled a gun. "What the?" His eyes narrowed while he scanned where she had been. He raised his gun in the general direction.

Zita shrank back, hoping the tree would hide her. If his vision equaled most people's, he would discern the others on the path, but not her petite form, hidden in the decorative shrubs and small trees that lined the path.

Jitters sobbed and held his knee.

"Get up. Nobody move," Brains ordered.

Struggling to his feet again, Jitters leaned on a sapling near the path.

Zita looked down at herself. *Oh right, I don't have any clothing or a mask. I'm next to that tree where he said the cameras stopped.* She shuddered as she crawled away from the camera zone and deeper into the underbrush, heedless of the scratches she was gathering or the detritus sticking to her. Mud squelched against her body, cooler than the air on her skin. *I so need a shower. When I come back to practice animal things, I'm going to hide clothing so the naked thing isn't a problem.*

"What's going on here? The zoo is closed. This is the National Zoological Park Police, and you need to raise your hands in the air," another male voice barked. The black of a bulletproof vest, gaping open, presumably because of the heat, blended into the trademark green pants, and stood out against the light khaki of his uniform shirt.

Brains pointed his gun at the newcomer.

Zita sprang to stop him from hurting the zoo cop.

The cop clicked on a flashlight, blinding Zita and making her miss her target.

The brunette gasped and raised her hands to her chest. They jerked out as Zita blinked to restore her night vision and find Brains. Hissing filled the air as the can in the other woman's hand went off.

Fire burned along Zita's eyes and face, and she choked, even as she collided with Brains, who was also swearing and staggering. They both fell. Moving blind, she crawled back into what she assumed were the bushes. Her nose and eyes held a contest to see which could run more as she curled in a ball. One hand landed on a sprinkler, and she thrust her face into the water. The sounds of a scuffle ensued while she scrubbed bleary eyes. What she now recognized as pepper spray hissed again. Profanity and a woman sobbing grew louder. While Zita worked to focus on the moving figures, the darkness and watering eyes did not aid her attempt.

"All of you are under arrest," someone said. Something buzzed, and his voice continued. "Request backup, two or three armed assailants."

The woman sobbed. "Help us!"

"Shit! My eyes!"

A car horn honked.

"Everyone, shut up! I swear I'll shoot the next person who complains or moves. This fucking hurts!" Jitters shouted.

Zita exhaled, controlling her breathing as she let the water wash her face clean. After a moment of thought, she shifted. Rising to all four paws, she prayed that men stupid enough to wear guns in their waistband were poor shots. She growled. The babble of threats, pleas, and warnings paused, but only momentarily. Her nose felt as if it were on fire. Her tail lashed, whipping against nearby tall grasses. While her eyes still smarted, the path and the blurry forms of those on it were visible. The white lab coat shouted the presence of the woman. Jitters' stench identified him, but the other two men blurred together. She snarled again and prowled through the underbrush to another location. One of her front legs pulsed with pain, making each step a torment. This time, the low, inhuman sound cut through the conversation, leaving silence.

"What was that?" Jitters asked. Panic and pain ran through his voice.

The lab coat inched toward the black and khaki blur, which stood frozen, light still pouring from one hand.

After a first failed attempt to retrieve something from the ground, a bulky form picked up an object, then the now-twitching lady from the ground with a grunt. "You are all going to stay put, and we're leaving. We won't hesitate to shoot you, but we don't have to if you behave. Come on, let's go."

Ignoring the instincts that told her to be silent, Zita roared. Apes inside the Think Tank exploded with noise. She stepped out onto the path, her tail flicking, crouching low to pounce or jump. Her eyes finally cleared when she blinked rapidly.

"Tiger," Jitters wailed. "Tiger!" The gun shook in his hand as he hobbled to aim at her. His fear permeated her senses. A feline part of her mind marked him as prey. His fetor marked him as inedible, while his stupidity in mistaking a jaguar for a tiger marked him as ignorant.

Brains waved his weapon in her direction but stepped away from Zita. The wavering point of his gun proved his vision had not completely returned either. His fear was salty on her tongue but tempered. "Shut up. Don't make it mad." He inched toward the parking lot.

The park police officer drew a revolver and shoved the brunette behind him. Zita salivated, scenting a chilidog spill on his shirt and in his breath. "Run," he ordered while brushing his radio with one hand. "Jaguar loose. Bring the tranqs."

Her voice shaky, the lab-coated woman said, "N-n-no. Back away slowly, try to look it in the eyes, and make noises. Look as big as you can. Feeding time wasn't long ago, so if we don't trigger its hunting instincts, we should be okay." She suited actions to words, stepping away toward the Think Tank, her eyes staring as she made a series of unidentifiable noises. When she opened her lab coat and flapped it, the scent of fear, pepper spray, and hospital astringency spread.

The same horn beeped twice in the parking lot. Something in Jitters broke. "It's a tiger, you fucking fucker! Tiger! I am not going to be eaten by a fucking tiger," he shouted. He fired, his arms flailing upward. Wrestling the gun back down, he fired again.

A bullet cracked, and a nearby tree sported a new hole. The second shot did not hit her, and no one else had fallen, so she didn't worry about where it had landed. Crouching low, Zita darted to a new spot nearby with another snarl and an internal sniff at the idea of consuming something so disgusting. *Cheetah or leopard would be understandable, but tiger? How many brain cells had to die to make that mistake?*

The woman in the lab coat froze in mid-flap. Her mouth opened and closed without sound.

The policeman aimed his revolver, shifting his aim between Zita and Jitters. "This is your last warning! Drop the weapon and back away."

"Stop before you kill me, moron! Fucking aim first!" Brains shifted the now-struggling redhead to his shoulder and tried to get a better grip on his own weapon. He took another step off the path.

Ay, I will regret this later. Zita charged Jitters as he brought the gun down for a third try. To evade any future shots, she zigzagged any way that avoided putting people between herself and the maddened man. As Zita barreled past him to stop Jitters before he could kill someone, the combination of 200 pounds of jaguar, the mud beneath the assailant's shoes, and the woman thrashing in his arms, knocked Brains off his feet again. He swore as he crashed into the mud, but managed to hang onto his gun. The redhead dropped to the ground again, this time with a squeal.

Zita lowered her head like a bull and charged, mouth closed to keep her teeth covered. When the top of her skull met his form, she threw the rest of her body to the side so he would not get the full impact. Jitters screamed at the contact, a shrill sound that cut off with a crack when he hurtled into a tree despite her attempt to soften the blow.

She stopped, jaw falling open. Closing it again, she darted to his side to see if he breathed. *Dios, don't let him be dead. I didn't mean to kill him.* Zita leaned close to sniff, opening her mouth to better scent him. The car horn sounded again, three times, startling and annoying her.

"It's eating him!" the park officer shouted. "Run while it's distracted, I'll cover you." Heels and a softer shoe pounded on the sidewalk, growing fainter.

Jitters moaned and curled into a ball. The leg she had kicked refused to curl. The scent of blood saturated the air, overriding even the chemicals and filth that comprised his natural odor.

Horror laced the cop's voice. "He's alive! It's eating him alive!"

Instinct sent a shiver that caused the fur on her back to stand on end, and she spotted the cop aiming at her. She turned, stumbling through the darkness of the brush to evade any bullets. The brunette in the lab coat and Brains had fled: the earlier running sounds, she reasoned.

The red-haired woman moaned and stirred as Zita slunk by practically on her furry belly She froze. Feline eyes met human as the other woman gazed at the jaguar.

Risking a glance back, Zita noticed the cop had lowered his gun but held it in a ready position. He advanced toward her—no, toward the redhead on the ground, they happened to be close together—scanning for enemies with a jerky motion that showed his tension.

The redhead spoke again in her mind, the words unintelligible, but a sense of calm and friendship came through. "Shhh, beauty, calm yourself. Let me help you," the other woman crooned aloud. Had it not been for the fear pouring off her scent, Zita might have thought her unafraid.

Zita blinked. She looked behind herself, then back. She tried replying, "Thanks, but it's him who needs to chill." Unfortunately, her words emerged as a grunt.

This close, she could see the confused wrinkle appear between the brows of the other woman. "Why can't I hear you?" the redhead inquired.

The cop doubled his pace toward them. A door slammed in the parking lot, echoing in the otherwise relative silence.

Zita leapt and bounded through the trees that direction and the park beyond, landing with a stagger.

As she burst out of the treed area and into the circles of shadows in the lot, a dark SUV careened toward the exit. She sprinted after it, stopping at the entrance to shift to an owl when she realized the panic a jaguar would cause in the city.

Her launch into the air to follow the vehicle failed when she crashed to the ground immediately. Her abused shoulder gave way, unable to support the five-foot wingspan of a South American great horned owl. Managing to wobble up into the air, Zita tried again. At the entrance to the zoo, she struggled to ride the air currents higher while searching for the fleeing car. The flare of headlights and shop signs showed multiple SUVs in both directions. Stymied, she swore in silence.

A pack of zoo cops and men with tranquilizer rifles exploded from the dark brush of the zoo. Gliding to spare her shoulder, she abandoned the chase and retreated to the trees of a neighboring park. Zita perched on a low branch and tried to smooth her feathers. Once darkness enshrouded her, she took a deep breath and shivered, weariness settling across her. Her shoulder shouted with pain, and her hip complained. Coupled with other small injuries, she needed medical attention. Adding insult to injury, her stomach growled. *So much for a leisurely flight home.* Hunching her shoulders and fluffing her feathers, she contemplated her options.

When she caught herself visually stalking a rabbit below and inching down the branch to keep it in view, she knew she had to get home. *Rabbit dinner is plan B. I'll teletravel, no, teleport back.* Zita pictured her apartment.

Andy fell off the couch, dropping what looked like a brownie, when Zita appeared in the middle of the living room. She ducked in reflex as lasers zapped and spaceships exploded on the television screen. "What happened? Did an otter beat you up?" he asked.

Her eyes narrowed, and Zita changed back to human. The promise of chocolate scented the air. Andy made a strangled sound, but she was already crossing the carpet toward the Promised Land. "You got brownies in here? You been holding out on me. Why didn't you say so? I would've been back sooner. Did you hook me up with the otter webcam to hide them from me?" A half-eaten pan of brownies was cooling on the stove, a used knife discarded in the empty half. Realizing the amount of grime on her hands, she stopped and washed first. The handle of the knife emitted a gentle heat as she cut a generous slice, placing it onto a napkin. *Lord be praised, pain be damned, they were warm.*

From the direction of the couch came the first complaint. "Can you at least put clothes on? We were going to save you a few but couldn't wait, so we had a couple first." Andy carped further, but his words were incomprehensible.

Zita took a bite, closing her eyes and letting the decadent chocolate flavor melt on her tongue. A woman moaned; she realized it was her. "Dude, I'm so hungry. You could have told me."

"And you could wear clothing."

Another bite of warm brownie crumbled in her mouth. Zita purred around it. "I'll get to it. Don't look if it bothers you."

Andy folded his arms over his chest. "Would you at least stop moaning? You sound like you're enjoying that brownie too much."

Zita refused to dignify his comment with any response other than to push another large bite into her mouth.

"Oh, hey, do my ears deceive me or are those the dulcet tones of our wandering friend? I made brownies—ah, I see you found them. Goddess, what happened? Did yesterday's rain start a small mudslide?" Wyn smiled as she entered the room, her teeth white against a mysterious green sludge that garnished most of her face except for her mouth and eyes. The glop smelled like avocadoes and lemons. Worn purple cloth, plastered with happy golden faces all over, hung from one arm, and her hair was up in a towel. She set the cloth down by Zita.

Finishing the snack and licking her fingers, one at a time, Zita turned her attention to where Andy was steadfastly not looking.

She sniffed. "See? At least she told me right off. Not exactly, Wyn. I'd be better if you'd use that handy healing spell on me. Wait... is the gook on your face contagious?" Her eyes on Wyn, she grabbed, unfolded, and pulled the bathrobe tight over herself.

"No, it's a facial mask for better skin. You know, like putting on lotion. Even you use lotion occasionally, right?" Wyn walked over. Setting an elegant hand on Zita's shoulder, she murmured an invocation under her breath, and the now-familiar shimmer of the healing spell appeared around her.

Zita released a deep breath as pain eased, releasing tension from her shoulders. "Things got weird," she admitted.

The healing took more time than it had to fix the minor scrapes of practicing, but she elected not to complain. When the process was done, the glow disappeared, and her friend lowered her hand. Then she jabbed Zita's shoulder. "Stop getting hurt. Weird how? I'm relieved you're back. The news broke into my show, you know, the vampire one you all refuse to watch. They announced an escaped jaguar at the zoo and an attempted kidnapping. Did you see it happen? I came out to let Andy know and was about to contact you. She's dressed, Andy." The witchy brunette took a second to rinse the creepy sludge off her skin.

"Finally," he muttered.

With a wistful glance at the fridge that housed the leftovers from dinner, Zita headed to the TV armoire. She changed stations until she found news. "Exit the otter, enter the jaguar," she joked. Both of her friends gave her blank expressions. "Seriously? You say I have no culture? How could you not know one of the best Bruceploitation films of all time? You're lucky to be somewhere with it on the playlist." She detoured to grab another hunk of brownie and stood next to the futon; her bathrobe was more washable than the cushion.

Wyn sat by Andy, face gleaming with dampness, and avocado still lingering in her scent. "Don't worry. You were here all night with us, Zita, no matter what they caught on film. You worked out and complained about our viewing preferences," Wyn said.

Andy nodded. "And you ate most of the brownies," he added. Zita narrowed her eyes at him and continued to munch.

On-screen commentators concluded their discussion of a panic in Detroit and discussed the National Zoo incident. Other than the oddity of a naked woman and a jaguar, they had little information. Zita wiped sweat off her forehead.

Andy got up and switched the channel to whatever he had been watching, just as a massive round object exploded on the screen. "Crap! I missed the best part. Seems the police haven't announced if they got you on tape, Zita." He collapsed back onto the futon and folded his arms over his chest while glaring at a youth in a spacecraft.

With a sympathetic glance at Andy, Wyn rose and patted Zita's shoulder. "It does seem as if they don't know what's going on. Give us the full story in the morning, and we can make plans from there. I'm heading off to bed. Night, you two."

"Night."

"Sleep tight. I'll be in after a snack and a shower," Zita said.

With a final thoughtful scrutiny of Andy, Wyn disappeared into the bedroom, leaving them alone in front of the TV.

Staring at her friend on the sofa, Zita shifted uncomfortably from foot to foot.

Andy watched the show, a sullen expression on his face. "What?" he barked.

Zita twitched. "You're bitchy and have been watching space shows for many days straight. Is there a problem, or what? Do you just want another brownie? I left some. We can slither out and go punch rocks or whatever. Quentin can leave beer for you if you want."

"Why don't you ask Wyn? She saw it in my head and couldn't come up with anything helpful or a magic spell," he said, his tone sour.

A pit began to form in her stomach. "If that's what you want. You know she's working to control that," she said.

Andy swiped a hand at the air. "No, I don't want. I know she is. It's not about her or even the creepy witchy stuff. She's lucky. I don't need a beer. I don't want to talk about it. I especially don't want to chat about my feelings."

Panic rose in Zita at the last sentence. She sucked at the kinds of conversation heralded by those words, holding out a hand to pause the torrent of his words. "Oye, mano, I didn't ask—"

Once unleashed, Andy seemed unable to stop talking. "I don't want to be trapped here, inside all the time. I don't want to have to think about every little move I make. And I don't want to break up with my girlfriend and never have another one, but I don't have a choice about any of that, do I?" he exploded, his pitch rising with each sentence. He stared ahead, his eyes on the wall rather than on the small screen.

"Uh." Her stomach twisted.

"Yeah." He glared.

Zita took a deep breath and calmed herself. All of the things he had mentioned were fixable. She would solve his problems, and he would be happy again. Then they'd return to not talking. A twitch escaped her. "We aren't trapped. We've been choosing to comply with the stupid quarantine. I'm totally in if you want to skip out, even if it's to go sit on the roof. If we can figure out a safe place, we can teleport. You know I'm going to practice that webcam thing, too. Why don't you find some deserted spot and go with me? No talkies." *Ever.*

His eyes strayed to the television, where a woman in white was handing out medals to a bunch of men and a giant hairball, but he nodded and closed his mouth.

Zita considered his next point. "You're already working on the thinking-about-every-move thing. The point of the practice is to make it a habit so you won't have to think about it. Come on, dude, you were a backup for the Olympic Judo team. You know how practice works, and I'm an awesome coach. Not only have you improved since we left the hospital, but you haven't had problems with the mindless actions. For example, you have yet to break the handle on my toilet or my toilet seat. Maybe you just think about it too much? As much as I hate to bring her up, that tool, Caroline, lifted the ambulance without breaking it. You both got super strong, but you told me you'd break my treadmill if you moved it."

"Pat your own back much?" he replied, but his shoulders loosened more. "I hadn't thought about the toilet or Caroline like that. Technically, the ambulance should have broken, unless you accept Farnswaggle's Thirteenth Theorem, which nobody does."

"My rep is deserved. Anyway, stop overthinking it." Giddy with her success, she made one last attempt to avoid his last problem. "As far as dating, you've never done that anyway. No need to worry. Want a brownie?"

His mouth firmed. "Bite me."

Sighing internally, Zita continued on to the last point, even though it made her feel as if she were dying a million lame, girly deaths. Externally, she may have twitched... multiple times. "So, for real on the dating thing, your girl has a problem with you? Are you certain she is a real girl? You're not bad, I guess. Plenty of girls might go for you. Quentin could hook you up. You want brownies?"

His lips twisted into a frown, and his shoulders tensed again. "No, things have been going well when she's not immersed in her project. I can't... We can't even play World of Warcraft together with the status quo. What's the point of a romantic relationship, or any other, if it'll never progress beyond online chatting and an occasional phone call? I don't want to imagine what an accident of strength would do to a girl if we held hands or were... close." Andy blinked rapidly and returned his focus to the credits scrolling up the screen.

Pues, I should have quit while I was ahead. At least he doesn't want to bang Wyn or me. That would up the gross factor by a million bazillion. "Uh, listen, I already covered that. You will keep practicing and get the habit going. You will get laid again, though it'll have to wait. You two could stick to cowgirl at first too. It's all theoretical now anyway, so unless she has been suggesting the two of you get together and sex things up, you should be fine." *Don't make me say it. I have been avoiding that quite well and on purpose.* Zita ran her hand back and forth over her head.

He glared at her. "Easy for you to say. You don't have the same problem."

She punched his shoulder. "Buey, have you missed everything that's happened? It'd be fatal if I turned into a hippo on top of a dude. Almost worse, if he wanted me to shift to an animal while banging, I'd have to dump his ass because that's disgusting! We both got to stick to our practice schedules. I love practicing as much as the next girl—"

"Way more. Way, way more," he interrupted, but his shoulders relaxed. "So, you think I can stay with my girl? I never considered your shifting like that."

She snorted. "I sure as hell have. Yes, if you like her that much, hang onto her. Are we cool now?"

Andy studied her and gave a nod. "Yeah, we're cool. Fetch me a brownie, will you?"

Sensing the danger had passed, she exhaled and said a silent prayer of gratitude. Zita punched his arm. "Sure thing, mano." *For this, I get another brownie on my way to the shower.*

Chapter Nine

Two days later, the news had little else to add, other than speculation and wild rumor.

Wyn laughed the fifth time she checked the broadcast. "Ah, the famous accuracy of eye witness testimony! You're a tattooed runaway teenage nudist gang member, Zita. How does it feel to have such accurate media coverage?" She relaxed in a pile of pillows on the futon, fluttering a dismissive hand at the television.

Zita rolled her eyes. "I resent the implication that a girl can't be a medium-to-dark-skinned teenage nudist with tattoos without being in a gang. Maybe a girl likes body art. Even I've thought about getting a little cross tattoo, but the pull to commit hasn't been there. I mean, Wyn, you have ink, and that's not a gang sign." She bit down on a carrot stick and went back to putting together a sandwich.

Wyn blushed. "No, it was just a... thing."

Zita snickered and waved a bread knife. "Other than that, I don't mind since it means I'm not a suspect."

In a better mood since their talk, Andy nodded from his chair. They had climbed up on the roof the day previous, and he had been his usual contented self, a real relief. One heartfelt feelings discussion a year was more than enough. "Shouldn't even a nudist gang give a girl a scarf to wear to show colors? Hey, is that Remus?" He jerked his chin at the television, where the female news anchor interviewed the handsome Puerto Rican via video conference. A ticker at the bottom of the screen noted Remus as the man known for running to California from DC in seconds.

Remus leaned into the camera, his face alight, as he announced the creation of a group supporting small businesses operated by people with special abilities. His future business would be delivery of documents, available for cross-country delivery within an hour of receipt.

The news anchor nodded, toying with a strand of her hair. "Your new organization already has a list of small businesses signed up to join, including one owned by Dr. Linnea Bagley. Are you familiar with Dr. Bagley? Have you spoken to her about her attempted kidnapping at the National Zoo?" Her eyes intent, the TV commentator inched toward Remus' monitor again.

"The motivation behind the free publicity they're giving his organization reveals itself," Wyn murmured. Andy grunted.

Zita assented around a mouthful of sandwich. "Plus he's total eye candy. It's a shame they can't get his whole body on-screen. Shirtless. Female viewership would be crazy good. Do you think he can wear pants when he runs? I can't when I shift, and if he's going that fast, his clothes might rip off." She shivered with delight, not entirely to incite laughs. *Ay, now there's a happy thought.*

Andy groaned. Wyn appeared thoughtful.

Zita grinned wider and raised a hand. "Just keeping it real." She took another bite of her lunch as Wyn giggled.

On the television, Remus' eyebrows drew together. "We've spoken a few times via email, but not beyond that, sorry." He was silent for a few seconds, then continued, "I hope she's recovering well. It must have been a terrifying experience for Dr. Bagley and the others involved."

The reporter nodded. "Yes, we wish the best for everyone involved in the incident. While your website does not list her, do you know if Caroline Gyllen will be a part of your organization? For our viewers who may be unfamiliar with her, she is the daughter of Senator Theopold Gyllen. A former gold medalist in gymnastics, Caroline was a familiar sight on the social circuit prior to the quarantine. During the terrorist attack on the DC quarantine buildings, she heroically defended first responders." The television switched to familiar footage from the hospital attack starring Caroline.

"Tool." Zita grumbled into her sandwich.

"Yes, we hate her," Andy and Wyn chorused. They exchanged a glance.

Zita narrowed her eyes at them.

On-screen, Remus shrugged after a pause at the question. "No, we haven't approached Ms. Gyllen about participating, but anyone who wants to open a legitimate business that utilizes a special ability is welcome."

The phone rang. Wyn answered. "Random check-in time," she announced. "Oh, the authorities want to interview us about the hospital incident and quarantine." She blinked multiple times and hung up. "They will be here for the debriefing in ten minutes." One hand smoothed her hair in a gesture that seemed automatic.

Zita almost choked on her sandwich. "Ten minutes? They invite themselves into my home and fail to give me time to hide my questionable possessions? How rude!" Finishing her mouthful, she scanned the room to figure out what she wanted to hide most. Besides herself.

"Nobody expects the Homeland Security inquisition," Andy intoned.

Wyn snickered.

Zita shot him a puzzled look, which made the others laugh harder.

Wiping her eyes with a hand, Wyn got herself under control. "What's problematic with your place? The only thing I've found hidden around here is a Best of Cesar Millan DVD that was behind a bunch of other ones. I was meaning to ask. Why do you have one of those, anyway?"

Andy asked, "Did you have a dog?"

"Uh. No dog." While Zita considered non-incriminating answers, Wyn turned pink and gasped.

"What?" Andy said.

Zita sat up straight and attempted a dignified pose. *Might as well own it.* "I enjoy watching a calm, self-confident man who is knowledgeable in his chosen field. Stop eavesdropping on my thoughts."

Wyn snickered. "You certainly do. Shouldn't that be listening in on your libido? Sorry, I guess my curiosity led me astray. Don't worry, I didn't dig into the thought about things you wouldn't want them to see."

She sniffed and flicked her fingers. "You should try watching him. I make no apologies. He is a sexy beast even without a serious exercise program." Zita took a large bite of her sandwich and savored the flavors as she prioritized objects to hide. *It is an interview, not an inspection, so just the obvious items need to be out of sight.*

"Oh, God, things I really didn't need to know." Andy cringed.

Are they still thinking about that? "Stop busting my ass about my healthy interest in an attractive guy and help me hide these books. My brothers' books on forensics and bombs would raise bad questions, so they need to be concealed," Zita said, pulling some of the questionable hardbacks from the shelves. "Wyn, can you shut all the doors, except the bathroom?"

Wyn sobered. "Yes, let's not give them a motive to prolong our incarceration. Zita, you should refrain from speaking to them." She cleaned the plates and the table, leaving the food on the counter as she hurried to comply.

When Zita's arms were full, she surveyed the apartment for a place to hide the books. After she dumped them on top of the washer, Andy followed with the rest. By the time a knock came, the empty section of the white bookshelves was camouflaged by pictures and interesting souvenirs.

Party line to keep our stories straight? Wyn asked mentally as she answered the door. Her voice held a sweet lilt as she greeted whoever was there.

Posed at the counter with the remnants of their lunches and Wyn's discarded plate, Zita and Andy exchanged looks. *Sounds like a plan to me.* "Make sure you check their badges," Zita called.

Andy grunted. *Fine, don't keep them waiting or they'll suspect we're talking about some forbidden topic. Well, not talking, but you know.* He and Zita bumped fists.

With a smile plastered on her beautiful face, Wyn stepped aside to allow three men entry. The first was tall and beefy; he had the confidence and movement of someone who knew how to start or end a fight, and he bulleted into the room as if expecting one. Both of his hands showed scrapes and bruises, and the baggy sport coat he wore revealed glimpses of a shoulder holster as he moved. After a pause and a thoughtful assessment of the three occupants he exhaled, and his body untensed. His eyes stayed flat and unfriendly. "Clear," he said as he approached a wall and stood at parade rest while the others entered.

Military, or I'll eat my hat, Zita thought.

If you eat one of your hats, could it be the rainbow glitter monstrosity? Wyn spoke first, waving a hand toward the dinette set. "Please, why don't you have a seat? Can I get you a Coke?"

The bulk and speed of the first man had hidden the other two. As the second one entered, he scrutinized the situation. The sturdy middle-aged man had the steady stride and eyes of a cop, but his gait had a hitch as though his ribs hurt. He lacked the fit menace of the first, but he displayed the cynical distrust of a survivor, despite the injuries. His battered briefcase had a piece of paper pinched in the seam.

Justin, from the disastrous blind date that had preceded the coma, was the third man. The young analyst had a massive black eye and an arm in a sling. This time, no gun bounced at his belt, although his suit was the same or identical to the one he had worn when they had met. All his attention was on Wyn, though he fussed with a clipboard in his uninjured hand.

Her words blurted out before Zita realized it. "Justin? What happened this time? Did you lose your gun again? Weren't you FBI, not Homeland Security?"

The other two men eyed Justin, even as his attention shifted from Wyn to Zita. He went pink, then white, then flushed pink again after catching the smirk from the oversized military man. He refocused on his clipboard, and at Zita again and groaned. "Right. Z. Garcia. I'm attached to DMS now."

A mugger attacked him and the older gentleman. In addition to their wallets, the muggers took the original list of quarantined off-site individuals, so these three have to redo days of interviews. How do you know him? Wyn nodded as if acknowledging Justin's comment.

"DMS?" Zita sent a quick reply to Wyn. *Bad blind date.*

Weren't you trying to give people their privacy? Andy interjected.

Wyn sniffed. *If they dislike us, they can imprison us or recommend we stay here forever. A little eavesdropping is acceptable. I'm not digging through their brains for information.*

Your flexible morality is inspiring. Zita shrugged at Justin, waiting for the answer.

"Division of Metanormal Services, for now," Justin mumbled. He glared.

With a quelling glance at Justin, the older man showed Zita a badge for the same organization. "After the attack on the hospital, a special division was formed from select Homeland Security, FBI, and Department of Corrections personnel. I'm Special Agent Soper." He nodded at big man. "That's Specialist Miller. Apparently, you know Dr. Smith."

"Unfortunately," Justin muttered.

Zita offered the government men her best company manners. "Seats? Drinks?" With a glance at Justin and the older man, she added, "Ice pack? Aspirin?" *Reminder how I saved your ass?*

Soper shifted position, favoring one side. He lifted an eyebrow at Justin. "Is history going to be a problem?" He paused. "Dr. Smith?"

The look Justin gave was anything but amiable. "No, no problem, sir."

Wyn, snooping in heads again, added commentary as if Zita cared. *He despises you. Thanks to whatever happened with you and a jewelry store, Justin has to pass a gun safety course before he can carry again. Due to the mugging, he was unhappy even before he discovered you here.*

Zita laughed and tried to aid the floundering doctor. "Don't worry. It's only fifteen to twenty minutes of history, most of it not very memorable."

Stop helping! Wyn added as Justin's cheeks and ears turned rosy again, and the burly specialist snickered.

Turning aside to give an unconvincing cough, Andy covered his mouth. *Seriously, Zita, are you trying to piss him off? Let Wyn charm the nice government agents while we sit by in silence, and by we, I mean you.* He gave her a squinty-eyed look.

The older man nodded. "No food, thanks," he said, easing himself into a seat at the end of the table. Soper motioned to the seat next to him. The young doctor sat, again fiddling with his clipboard.

Zita opened her mouth, then closed it again. *Would it help if I mentioned that he didn't score?*

Wyn choked, and tears came to her eyes.

Justin leapt to pat her back.

Andy rubbed his eyes. He turned to get himself a drink from the fridge. His shoulders shook with unvoiced laughter. *That's even worse. Please remain silent.*

"Thank you, I must've swallowed the wrong way," Wyn said. *Listen to Andy's sage advice.*

The older man waited until Justin had reseated himself and the specialist—whatever that was—had resumed his lean against the dining room wall. "If you're better, Miss, we should start these interviews. We will speak to each of you individually, and you will need to segregate in your rooms for the interim. We will come for you when it's your turn."

Andy gave a cough. "This is my room. I mean, I sleep on the futon. The girls share the bed in Zita's room." Her futon, a model that folded out to a double bed, had a red frame and white pillows. A blue and yellow lamp next to it threw light across a rainbow of interesting pillows clumped at one end. He gestured at the untidy jumble of bags beneath it.

Miller and Justin looked to Wyn, then Zita. The specialist smirked. Justin turned pink again. The older man seemed nonplussed.

Ah, great, the younger two are perverts. Soper just wants to avoid litigation or extra paperwork. Wyn complained.

Andy stuck his hands in pockets. "It's tight quarters, that's all I meant. Since someone lacks decent cable, our biggest excitement is watching the cops break up Bingo at the church across the street when it gets too feisty on Tuesday nights. I never knew the game could be so hazardous."

Zita rubbed her hands over the uneven scrub of hair on her head and reveled in the fact that she was not a telepath, only a telepath's favorite target. She focused on the Talavera knobs in the kitchen while she schooled her face to pleasantry. "I call dibs on the treadmill. You can take the computer. That should keep us separate."

Andy smiled. "I'd be happy to take the computer."

Wyn gave them a beatific smile and inclined her head.

Seizing on Zita's words, Soper nodded. "That works. Now, we will take Mr. Cristovano first, then Miss Garcia. Miss Diamond, you'll be last. Please close the doors behind you when you go in the other rooms."

Zita escaped to the exercise room. Flipping on the TV, she settled in for a light workout. Andy shared the brunt of the questions with them but did not give the women a word-for-word exchange. She suspected Wyn might be using her telepathy to listen in. *I can do this. I'll be calm and collected, and win them all over with my charm. I got this.*

When her turn came, she grabbed more carrot sticks and gnawed those between questions. For the events at the hospital, she stuck to their story, adding only what seemed relevant. The older man, Soper, questioned her regarding the attack on the hospital; Justin probed life before and during the quarantine. Miller continued leaning against a wall. Based on the evidence, a Specialist did not talk much, though her identification of the gun types used by the attackers drew him into brief conversation. Justin grudgingly confirmed Miguel's military service when she mentioned her brothers had taught her guns. When Justin pried into her personal life, she discarded her good intentions.

Soper and Miller seemed pleased with her version of events. Justin needed a smack upside his head, perhaps with his own clipboard. Zita held onto her temper when he asked if she had any depression, anger management issues, or if she heard voices. She abandoned hope of winning him over as he continued to press, repeating previous questions.

"Seriously? How do I feel about the quarantine again? You're supposed to be a prodigy, but you can't remember the answer to a question you asked five minutes ago? Like I said before, cranky. The government confines us in a worthless quarantine so a politician can tell reassuring lies. We've got bills piling up, but no way to pay them because we're here and not at our jobs, and I haven't had a challenging workout in a while." Zita narrowed her eyes and looked at Special Agent Soper. She tapped her fingertips on the table. "Speaking of bills, where is the reimbursement for all the unpaid time off work we've had to take for the quarantine?"

Justin immersed himself in his clipboard. Specialist Miller hid a smile behind a fake cough. Soper gave her a flat, unblinking stare and stayed motionless. His words held the echoes of an oft-repeated line. "Remuneration for fiscal hardship is under discussion, but is handled by a different department, so I can't speak as to the exact status. Doctor, please finish up."

After shuffling papers, Justin complied. "Have you noticed anything different about yourself or the others quarantined here? Do any of you require special accommodations now?"

Zita pursed her lips. "No. Again." Her brow furrowed, and she carefully formed the words she wanted the others to hear. *Justin keeps rewording the same questions. Was it this bad with you? Did they keep at you this long, Andy?*

No, he sent, *but I didn't piss off the shrink.*

Justin stared at her; his eyes were bulbous evil in his youthful face. "Are you certain none of you have exhibited any new powers or other changes?"

Zita reminded herself that he wasn't worth the penance her priest would give her if she gave in to her urges. "We're closeted here all day, every day. One of us would have noticed anything strange. Are your ears having problems? I've answered that before." She maintained her civil tone, even if her words sharpened at the end of the sentence. Biting off half a carrot stick, she narrowed her eyes at him.

When it's my turn, I'll smooth things over. Miller voted you the second best interview, though, Wyn laughed over party line.

Competitive instincts prompted her to ask. *Second best? Who got first?*

Trust me, it's unimportant. Wyn was cagey.

"How do you feel—" Justin began.

Soper held up a hand, cutting off Justin. "We're done, Doctor. Miss Garcia, the government issues full apologies for the inconvenience of the quarantine. Should you have any repercussions from your illness, the government offers free medical care and counseling for the next year. If you would sign the documents verifying our discussion and your acceptance, we will depart." He dumped forms from his briefcase. Digging through the mess, he selected a few forms and proffered a pen.

A hasty mental conference when he had made the same offer to Andy had told her what her answer would be. Zita folded her arms across her chest and bit off another bite of carrot with a snap. Bright flavor flooded her mouth as she considered her next words. She swallowed. "I'll sign a paper confirming this debriefing. No thanks on the medical care or counseling. The only government help I want is an end to the quarantine and a check for my lost income." Taking his papers, she sorted out the ones she wanted. While reading every word, she ignored the way the agents fidgeted, glared, or seemed to nap respectively.

"Are you certain? Anything the doctors or counselors find is confidential. Your brother won't know," Justin tried. He scribbled on his clipboard.

Like I want to be a guinea pig for The Man. Zita glared at him, and bit off another large chunk of carrot. Her tone was flippant. "Positive. I'm healthy and have insurance. Why deal with the extra paperwork of a government health program if I don't have to?" She scribbled her signature on the debriefing acknowledgement and drew lines through any references to the health program.

Soper shrugged, though his eyes were watchful. "If she doesn't want free health care, then it's her loss. Please get Miss Diamond."

She rose, setting her empty plate by the sink. "So when you leave, is the quarantine over?" she asked. Andy had asked the same thing, but she had to try.

Soper shook his head. "No, Miss. We will inform you when that happens. These interviews should hasten the end, however." Justin was straightening his tie and smoothing his hair with his hands. Miller straightened up and tugged his shirt down. Soper shuffled the forms into his briefcase and brought out a new set.

Zita rolled her eyes and tapped on the door to the exercise room. "Wyn, they want you."

Many do. Few succeed. Wyn opened the door and stepped out. She gave a saucy grin and waved the remote control. As she sauntered toward the kitchen, she called over her shoulder. "Your brother's on TV, Zita."

Stepping inside, Zita closed the door. She shook her head as the camera changed focus from Miguel to a smiling reporter. *Teeth shouldn't be that white. Perhaps the reporter was part shark?* Unaware of her speculation, the reporter concluded his story. "Special Agent Miguel Garcia assures us the FBI is following all available avenues in the search for the serial killer terrorizing the DC area. They will release more information as the investigation progresses. Our sources tell us the male victims participated in the illegal drug trade, with the female victims either related to or involved with the male victims. So perhaps the real question is— Are these torture murders the work of a deranged vigilante or part of a bloody drug war?" The cameras returned to the news anchors at their desks, wearing their best sober looks. After the female anchor thanked the reporter, her saccharine partner picked up papers and began speaking.

"In other news tonight, a fatal car crash claimed the life of an executive member of the DC region quarantine, Dr. Amun Singh, and an assistant. After a distinguished career in infectious disease research, Dr. Singh's studies were crucial to learning about the coma sickness and the second emergence of individuals with superhuman abilities. A spokesperson for the Division of Metanormal Services says that they both will be missed, and progress on the research will be set back by this tragic loss." A picture of the doctor and Nurse Mouse flashed on the screen while he spoke.

Zita concentrated. *Dr. Singh died, and so did that nurse who followed him around.*

That must have just happened. Ooh, Soper has a phone call so important he has to take it outside. Justin is trying small talk, and the other gentleman hasn't said a word, Wyn commented.

Andy was apparently resigned. *So you're going to listen in? It's probably his wife wanting him to pick up milk and bread or something.*

Or tampons. Zita chuckled. At Andy's mental groan, she added more. *Just keeping it real.* Sick of news, she slipped in a classic movie and started the treadmill. As the first fight scene of *The 36th Chamber of Shaolin* played, her muscles began to relax.

Wyn ruined the brief respite. *Oh no.* After a moment, her mental voice returned, more composed. *Soper and Miller are going to Singh's tomorrow to seize his notebook and computer. The doctor and nurse were transcribing important details from the notebook, and the government is salivating to cross-correlate names and medical files with the most extreme divergences from normal. They want to isolate anyone with major deviations, but the hospital fire destroyed most of the records, so his notebook is their best chance.*

Zita blinked and slowed. *I don't know about you, but Andy and I fall into that category since we were the last to wake. Singh also mentioned irregularities with my blood work when he was trying to convince me to join his study.*

My migraines gave him extra data on me, Wyn fretted.

Andy's mental voice held concern. *Maybe I should move back to Canada. Mom's nation would keep me safe, but I'd also have to give up physics unless they need a teacher.*

Before Zita starts packing duffel bags for everyone again, let me get rid of these gentlemen. We can discuss it in depth then, Wyn sent, and then ended the mental link.

Once the agents had departed, the friends gathered in the living room. Zita shared her idea first. "I'm going to Singh's tonight after they leave. Andy, can you find his address?"

"Let me try. Singh is a common last name, but with luck, I can get his township and full name from the news reports. Oh, and you are not going alone. That's a statement, not a question." His face was somber.

After a round of mental swearing, Zita considered the practical aspects. "Any ideas?"

From the futon, Wyn added in her opinion and proved she was still eavesdropping on her friends' minds. "Your brain has a terrible potty mouth, even if you hide it in multiple languages. What can we do anyway, even if we locate his abode? Andy is right. You aren't in this on your own."

Zita gazed out the patio door, not really paying attention to the view. Alternatives stampeded through her mind, but she could see only one workable solution. She didn't want to bring her friends into it, but suspected from their expressions that they would insist. "We take the notebook and the computer and destroy them. I don't like stealing, but I don't see any other peaceful way to avoid attention. We also need a list of quarantined people so we can warn them of the government's interest. And Wyn? Remember that concept of privacy?"

Andy's answer was troubled. "Do we have a choice?"

Zita spun on her heels and paced. Movement always helped her think. "Always, but none of the other choices will have better results. Do you want to be locked up for study? This way protects us and the other people with powers they've overlooked."

"What, Zita?" Wyn added, her tone worried.

Zita tried hard to keep Aideen's flaming form or the grisly sight of Jerome's back from her mind. "Don't poke your nose in, Wyn. It's not our business, and they're no threat to us." *I hope.*

Wyn pursed her lips, but gave no indication if she had complied with Zita's request.

Zita stopped, faced the others, and put her hands on her hips. "Let's grab masks and go get Singh's computer and notebook after dark. We need to beat The Man to that information."

"Sounds like a terrible plan," Andy replied. "I'm in."

Chapter Ten

With Zita clutched in his massive talons, Andy flew that night, landing in a park near Dr. Singh's home. For whatever reason, the circuitous route he took to avoid DC required them to soar over the Mississippi and back again.

An hour and a walk from a nearby park later, Zita jimmied open an upstairs window and slid into the cooled air of the two-story Colonial. Below her, dense evergreens gave Singh's small back yard privacy and disguised the closeness of the houses in the neighborhood. The trees also hid Andy, now in human form, from streetlights and occasional cars. Indirect light gave Zita enough illumination to see, but not well, and her movement through the house was slow as a result. An alarm panel glowed in the foyer, and she sped to it. *Gracias a Dios for cheap security systems.* One gloved hand danced over the box, while she dug in her small tool bag with the other. Trepidation and excitement warred in her stomach, almost making her regret the loaded pizza she'd eaten for dinner.

I don't know how you talked me into this, Wyn complained from her safe spot at home.

Andy's response was reasonable. *Someone has to answer the phone on the random check-ins and bail us out if necessary. Look on the bright side, you aren't doing any breaking, entering, or stealing.*

The thought slipped out. Zita couldn't help it. *You're also the least stealthy, and these giant houses are right on top of each other.*

The witch's tone was grudging. *Thanks, Zita, for your tact, as always.*

Zita tapped her headlamp to get a better angle, readjusting again. Her ski mask, inverted to hide the pink pattern and pompom on the black knit fabric, preventing the light from staying in position. "Clear," she whispered. "Let's get this party started." The air was redolent with rich seasonings and beans, with an undertone of char, which she traced to a Crock-Pot on a speckled counter. An ordered army of spices stood guard. Sympathy made her pause and unplug it. She ghosted to the patio door and unlocked it. "Patio's the only safe entry. Anything else will set off alarms. Hurry!"

Andy slipped in, closing the door behind him. The white half-mask he wore gleamed in the poor light. When he flicked his flashlight on, she pulled drapes shut. Their beams played over one of those fancy kitchens with the double wall ovens and an immaculate supersized refrigerator. Her light stopped there while Andy turned to investigate elsewhere.

"You sure he was single?" she whispered, eyeing it. She took a step closer to the monolithic food storage of her dreams. *Mi amor. You are perfect.*

Andy whispered, "We don't have time for snacking! I didn't check his personal life." She glanced over to see him open the white French doors to another room. His flashlight played over it. "No cars in the garage when we looked, though. Oh, hey now, here's his study, and I see a laptop." As he raced inside, the light and his step acquired a bounce. Curtains scraped shut.

"I wasn't going to." Zita sniffed, giving the Promised Land one last, longing glance. A closed door hid a well-stocked pantry. At the hum and beep of a computer starting up, she abandoned her explorations to enter the study. This room held the faint smell of antiseptic, brass, and dust. Andy leaned over a hefty desk, his gloved hands fussing with a laptop. A stone fireplace, bare of ashes, was behind him. A smaller chair and table were located at the side. *Perhaps where Nurse Mouse had worked?* An open book, in an ornate holder, lay in front of the lone window, and a portrait loomed over the desk. Had they not been in Singh's house, she wouldn't have recognized the doctor as the smiling young man in wedding finery who stood with a young woman and two older people. Every other wall was pregnant with books.

Shaking her head, Zita approached the bookcase with the most volumes and began searching. *The man was serious about his books. He had a bazillion.*

Andy meandered to a different one, mumbling and reaching toward one hardbound work in particular. "Did you know he had the second edition of *Farnswaggle's Physics*? His work's hardcore." Fascination laced his words.

In revenge for his earlier comment, Zita issued a command, more amused than forceful. "No physics. Don't get distracted. Let's get this done and get out."

He caught her looking. "Laptop's booting," he said.

Is it time to taunt the librarian with books she can't see? The notebook was bound in coffee-colored leather with gold Copperplate lettering, if that helps. It had a red and blue silk bookmark. Despite the complaint, Wyn's long distance input helped speed the search.

Zita shook her head. After perusing the row of books, she considered the painted image of the smiling family. *The spotless room has only one picture, and it is crooked.* With gentle hands, she lifted a corner and peeked behind it. *The gold goes to Zita Garcia!* After a fist pump, she whispered, "Think Singh would store the notebook in a safe? Help me with this sucker."

The painting had just touched the ground when a low rustle came from the kitchen. She stopped and looked in that direction. Keeping her voice low, she asked, "Oye, did you hear that?"

"What?" Andy raised his head.

Her pulse was racing. Zita padded toward the French doors as Andy moved the portrait. "I thought I heard something," she whispered. The muscles in her shoulders tensed.

When no sound came from the other room, Andy shrugged. "I don't hear anything." Zita returned in time to see his hands fisted on his hips. "I could force it, but that goes against my idea of sneaky."

Snorting as she examined it, she said, "I got this. I'd need a drill for anything better. Since I don't have the right tools, it will take a few." To let Wyn know their progress, she sent an update, trusting the telepath would be listening. *We found a safe. If I can't finesse it, Andy can pry it open.*

Teeth showed in Andy's grin. "You do doors, alarms, *and* safes. You're either going to jail or will make some criminal very happy someday. You know that, right?"

She elbowed him. "Go do your computer crap. Dick."

"Tyrant," he muttered, settling into the chair again.

Digging through the limited tools she had brought with her, she almost missed the slight scraping sound from the kitchen. Armed with a sharp pick, she dropped everything else and hurried in, her LED headlamp beam bouncing off walls in the empty room. Nothing stirred, except the curtain over the sliding door, disturbed by her rapid entrance. Since the door was ajar, she closed it and frowned. *Possible it was the wind, but I could have sworn something moved.*

I sense no one else in the house. Paranoia is a sign of mental illness, Wyn suggested.

"Paranoia is the name the less-prepared use for good planning," Zita grumped, both out loud and mentally. After returning to the study, her actions to unlock the safe were slow to avoid leaving marks.

Andy swore, "The laptop's password protected. I can't tell if this is the right one or not. After I shut this down, I'll check the rest of the house for another. If you see anything that looks like a password in that safe, grab it. We may have to take the stupid thing." After a moment, he transmitted the information to Wyn.

Zita mumbled agreement, her attention still focused on the safe.

I suppose it was too much to ask that it be simple, Wyn sent.

Andy chuckled, his footsteps receding as he left the room. *It is our first felony.*

As part of a team, Zita added.

***

A loud bang, followed by the house alarm, shattered Zita's concentration several minutes later. "Seriously? I almost had it," she muttered. Setting down her locksmith tools, she hurried to silence the alarm. A yowl like an enraged feline with a sore throat, a squeal, and a series of thumps echoed from the foyer. The girly yelp belonged to a familiar voice. Her fists clenched with apprehension, and she sprinted in that direction.

When she burst in, her headlamp and the ambient light revealed a dark form leaning over Andy. The front door gaped open, splintered wood hanging on the doorframe.

"Are you dead? Life just became difficult for me if you're dead, even if it's your fault for dodging the wrong way. You should have watched where you were falling," a woman's voice said, petulance dripping from the tones.

Andy grumbled and started to push himself up.

The woman looked as if she were about to kick him in the head.

Without planning it, Zita threw herself into a cartwheel and booted the other woman in the chest, reversing the move to avoid landing on her friend.

With a surprised mew, the other woman flew backward but did not lose her feet. She hissed and attacked. Using his head as a vault, she leapt over Andy and swung wildly at Zita. The intruder missed.

Wyn's mental voice came across as puzzled. *What's going on?*

Zita spared a second to broadcast. *Burglar smackdown, talk later.*
The two women circled each other with Zita falling into a capoeira

ginga out of habit. The alarm continued blaring, but she doubted the other woman would consent to pausing combat so Zita could silence it.

Andy scrambled out of the way and shuffled up against a wall.

In a flurry of movement, the intruder attacked with a series of punches and kicks.

Zita eluded or blocked the blows, which showed more speed than skill by her opponent.

"Two others in here. I got it, though," the newcomer called out in a loud snarl.

Awesome, she brought backup too. Countering with a few strikes of her own, Zita evaluated her opponent. When she threw in a quick takedown move, the other escaped by virtue of preternatural flexibility.

Lighting made assessment difficult, but the other woman had a few inches and pounds on Zita. When her opponent flipped unnecessarily to try to deliver a boot to Zita's head, she revealed a lithe, acrobatic form, a lengthy tail, and the fact that she was already panting. *I'll call her Kitty.*

Pride flared at the ease with which she suppressed the urge to shift. Zita initiated a sweeping kick to knock down her opponent, but Kitty bounced off a wall and landed on her feet.

Relief broke free inside Zita as her opponent unloaded another torrent of kicks and punches. She laughed, fierce exhilaration sweeping through her as she evaded again and returned with a combination kick and cartwheel that punted the other onto the stairs. *No stamina, but Kitty's agile enough to be a challenge. I've needed one of those lately.*

At her obvious enjoyment, the attacker hissed again, even as she twisted impossibly in the air to land on her feet. Fabric tore. "Are you laughing at me?" Her tail cut the air, and furry pointed ears perked, then flattened to lie smooth against her head.

"You're too close together, and she's got powers," Andy called out, apology in his tones as he retrieved his flashlight and pressed against a wall.

"You think?" Zita replied with no shortage of sarcasm. *Watch for her backup. She's tiring fast.*

Will do, Andy promised.

The catlike girl tried to pounce on her, leaping farther than she ought to be able from the stairs. Although Zita evaded the brunt of the attack, sudden pain shooting down her leg and a ripping sound exposed what Kitty had been holding back.

"Kitty has claws. Real ones." Some of her enjoyment fled. As the other darted around her, Zita feinted left, then seized the trailing tail. It felt like that of a real cat, bone and cartilage beneath fur, and her grip gentled. With it as leverage, she hauled Kitty closer and kicked her ribs.

The resulting screech lured in Kitty's helper. A light flared in the doorway, blinding Zita for a precious second. The tail slipped away.

With a final slash that caught on and tore Zita's shirt, the other girl bolted to Andy. She dove between his legs, then spun to kick him in the back. He crashed into Zita. They collapsed onto the hard tile in a jumble.

"Distraction now! I'm bored," Kitty hissed, darting out of the door.

Andy was a dead weight on top of her. "Move!" Zita ordered, shoving him off.

"Sorry. Get the alarm?" he shouted, rising and running outside.

Moving fast, Zita peeled open the alarm panel. "Remind me why we're chasing a burglar instead of getting what we came for?" she asked no one.

Andy's voice exclaimed in surprise at the same instant a bass voice growled.

The deep voice rumbled again outside, and an enormous crash thundered in the dining room. Dread gripped Zita, and she turned back, steeling herself to look. An uninjured Andy rose from a shining pile of glass shards and plastic atop the former dining room table. He shook off the broken bits, glowering and batting at his head as he bumped it on the chandelier that had hung low over the table. Small shreds of cloth fluttered to the ground from his body. "You could have killed me! You can't just throw people through windows," he shouted out the hole where a bay window had been, and ran past, glass pieces trickling from his clothing as he sprinted.

Right, he's tough. I think the flinching makes me forget. The debacle this had turned into seemed a valid reason to swear, so she did so in multiple languages as she shut off the obnoxious alarm. A small bang sounded from the study, not quite like a gunshot. When she went to investigate, Zita reached the kitchen before a particularly meaty thump and Andy's yelp came from outside. With a last glance toward the study, she seized the Crock-Pot and ran out the front door to see Andy assaulting a fifteen-foot-tall black man. Lights flooded the windows of all the nearby houses that had been dark and silent earlier. Andy ranted about windows, both verbally and mentally; Wyn mused about whether it was truly defenestration if one was thrown into a building rather than out. Zita zoned both of them out.

The giant had the muscles of a physical laborer, and wore a domino mask. His pants were too long for his legs, an odd sight considering, but the rest of his sensible black clothing fit well. The one time his blows connected, he snapped a sapling when he kicked Andy into it; most of his strikes missed the slighter man. Despite that, he fought relying on his unnatural strength, instead of skill. Andy was holding back, but the giant winced when one of Andy's strikes landed. A corner of Zita's mind noted this was excellent practice for Andy. Kitty was nowhere in sight.

Watching the combat, she waited for an opening. She sent a thought to Andy. *I'll distract him if you do a takedown. The alarm's off, but we don't have much time. We have to get the safe open before the cops show. In a neighborhood like this, that's another five minutes, tops.*

Andy kept his answer short and sweet. *Go for it.* He loosened his shoulders and emerged from the collapsed tree.

As Zita was preparing to join in, a whisper of movement and the whiff of sweets warned her. She dodged low, and Kitty's pounce passed so close that Zita could smell spicy perfume and candy. One claw caught in Zita's ski mask as she passed overhead, yanking it up and almost off.

The world went dark around her, but Zita grabbed the mask before her identity could be revealed. It ripped. Her headlamp clattered to the ground. Frantic to avoid another attack, she retreated to the location where she remembered the wall to be. She crouched and struggled with the mask, her back to the house siding.

Grunts, smacking sounds, and the occasional crunch came from where the men fought. Kitty must have been close because her sniggering comment was audible. "Quit playing and let's blow!"

Just as Zita's vision returned, something came at her head fast. When she ducked, she swept one leg out, keeping low, hoping the feline girl had thrown herself off balance with the amateurish move. The kick connected.

Falling sideways when Zita's kick caught her, Kitty twisted to land on all fours. She narrowed her eyes and stared at Zita for a moment, tail lashing. With a forced laugh, the cat girl ran off into the darkness, tail swishing behind her. "Time to go!"

Andy wielded the downed sapling like a bat and swung at the colossal man, eliciting a pained grunt when he hit.

Zita picked up the Crock-Pot. The lid had shattered on the ground, but most of the food still steamed within.

The giant snatched the tree, and she took her opportunity.

"Now!" she shouted. Zita ran toward the men, swinging up and onto the tree around the middle. While the it was suspended, she moved with all the speed her tightrope training had given her and kicked the giant in the nose. It was oddly spongy underfoot, and she doubted she did any damage.

The surprise served to make the giant release the tree. His mouth opened.

Zita threw the Crock-Pot and hot contents in his face. She flipped off the log and rolled to a landing. "All yours!"

The giant sneezed and pawed at his face, beans dripping down him in a fragrant, steaming cascade.

Andy dodged to the side and did a hard punch to the back of the giant's knee.

The behemoth, already off balance from Zita's attack, fell and hit his head on the pavement. His eyes closed, and his form shivered, losing inches until the same man, now only four feet tall, lay unconscious in the street amid the remains of the Crock-Pot. Andy checked his pulse, then scooped him up and moved him to the grass.

"Alive," he said.

As if on cue, sirens rang out. The former giant moaned. Lights strobed at the end of the block. Zita and Andy raced to the house, hoping to reach the study and be gone before the police arrived.

He stopped at the office doorway, and she almost plowed into him, having paused to retrieve her headlamp. "Shit," he said.

She could only concur. The computer had vanished, and the safe hung open. Acrid smoke hung in the air. Seizing her tools, she stuffed them back in her bag. "Vámonos. I don't think we want to explain."

Andy nodded. She grabbed his arm and teleported them home.

Chapter Eleven

The travesty of a quarantine lasted another two boring weeks. Once Wyn finished squealing and hopping around like the girliest of girls, she and Andy packed their belongings in record speed. They departed within the hour though not without reunion promises and hugging. Once they left, Zita filled up the rest of the next two days with necessary errands and hoped-for workouts. Her exercise routines would be simpler than she liked; her trapeze partner had gotten a job in Las Vegas so she had to delay the aerial work until she found another catcher. On the other hand, Miguel remained in town, still chasing that serial killer. Zita's brothers were treating her to lunch tomorrow to celebrate her emancipated status.

By the time she steered her motorcycle into the complex, it was eight thirty. Perhaps to reduce lawsuits by the inhabitants, most of whom had left fifty behind decades ago, the sidewalks by resident parking were well lit. To make up the shortfall and discourage late-night guests, visitor parking had only a few far-spaced lamps and the glare of passing cars on the nearby road to illuminate it. The headlights on a vehicle in the visitor section were the only sign of life in her corner of the lot. Zita pulled into her assigned spot under the resident carport. As she shut down the engine, she took off her pink dinosaur helmet, letting the night roll over her senses. Warm asphalt, green trees, and dinner scents mingled in the humid air. The rumble of a vehicle in the lot neared, and a car door opening broke the usual evening sounds of overloud televisions, traffic, and insects. About to set down her helmet and open the pannier holding her work clothes, she paused.

Rapid footsteps raised paranoia. Her peripheral vision showed a burly man reaching for her. The open door of an SUV spilled darkness behind him, with no interior lights to give away any secrets.

Reflexively, Zita smashed him in the face with her helmet, throwing her weight behind it. *Screw that.*

Something snapped under the impact, and he covered his nose with his hands.

Her helmet was slippery in her hands with his blood, but she hurried away until another large man blocked her path.

With a mental curse, Zita threw her slimy helmet at him, hard. When he caught it, she kneed him in the crotch.

Wheezing, he bent over.

She struck him again, under the chin, in an upward strike with as much leg force in it as possible. For the second time that evening, something fractured under her blow.

He gave a choking wail as he doubled over.

With their height advantage, they're probably faster, but if I can get enough of a lead, I can outlast them. She darted past him, sliding across the long hood of a neighbor's Oldsmobile. The metal was warm from the day's heat beneath her butt.

The first man chased her, uttering a torrent of curses.

Her feet moved on automatic, and she vaulted up from the Oldsmobile, catching the edge of the carport roof. As she flipped up, belated recognition struck. *Was that Brains from the zoo?* A glance below as she ran divulged that a dark SUV shadowed her, and cursing warned her that one of the men followed close while the other lagged behind. *Can't teleport. Someone might be waiting in my apartment.* Oblivious to her dilemma, cars passed on the road by the complex, and the church across the street glowed in innocence. *Wait, is it Tuesday? Hallelujah! I know where I'm going.*

At the end of the roof, she leapt onto the top of the SUV pacing her. Slapping her hands down to keep her balance, Zita rolled onto the hood. With a jaunty wave at the wide-eyed thug behind the wheel, she hopped onto the ground on the opposite side of the SUV from her pursuers. She dashed through the parked cars in the lot, somersaulting off hoods and keeping herself a moving target. They didn't fire, though she caught glimpses of both men and the SUV in pursuit. When she reached the street, she sprinted full tilt across between passing cars. Horns blared at her, but she made it. Her feet smacked the pavement hard as she raced up the path to the gathering hall of the church. A glance over her shoulder revealed one man at the edge of the road, leaping out of the lane from a car speeding by.

Panting, and no doubt wild-eyed, Zita skidded into a room full of people. The cops by the door stared at her; no one else even glanced up from their boards.

"Geez, lady, it's just Bingo," one policeman said.

"Men tried to kidnap me," she answered, followed by, "Help!"

The announcers stopped speaking. Now, people stared at her, and a low snarl began in the crowd, most of whom had surrounded themselves with moats of Bingo boards.

Did I escape kidnapping to have an angry mob of devout Bingo worshippers tear me apart? She raked a hand through her hair, stopping when she realized her hand was sticky. Zita stared at the blood of the second attacker—who was definitely Brains from the zoo—on her hand. Her own mind felt slow and stupid. *Someone tried to kidnap me. Dios, have they realized I was the jaguar? How? I can't tell the cops.* "I think I injured a couple of them when I got away."

The cops followed her gaze to the blood, and the older one snapped out of his indolent pose. "Call it in. Attempted kidnapping, backup requested." His orders were the first of many. It began a long night of alternating between maddening questions, restless boredom, and blurry exhaustion before the police released her.

***

What little sleep she managed was on Quentin's couch, and occurred sometime after one in the morning. Even though her calls and texts went unanswered, she assumed he would not mind. Unable to sleep past sunrise, she grabbed an early workout on the silks at the aerialist gym before wasting the rest of the morning at the police station answering repetitive questions. Now, she snacked on a soft pretzel as she ran up and down the steps of the nondescript building where Miguel's task force was based. Watching for her brothers and any loitering kidnappers kept her mind busy. Straps on her backpack rubbed at one spot on her side as it bounced, and her oversized T-shirt stuck to her skin in places in the heat.

Finally, Miguel descended the stairs, marching, his head down like a guard dog on patrol. His shoes shined, his pants held a crease, and his tie flapped in the breeze with the cadence of his gait. One arm held a coat, but the other was unrestricted in case he needed to draw his gun. From experience, she knew he would leave that hand free as long as possible. Zita had the utmost faith he would spot a bomber but miss an attractive woman's interest. *A part of the war lingers.* "About time," she muttered and checked her phone. Quentin still hadn't returned her calls or texts.

"Miguel!" She hopped up on a railing and waved both arms over her head to get his attention.

Her brother tried to seem disapproving, but the expression dissolved as she sprang down and hurtled toward him. Miguel caught her up in a hug and winced when he noticed her head. "What did you do to your hair?"

She returned the hug and pounded on his back, taking comfort, for a moment, in his familiar piquant aftershave and warmth. Zita stepped back, running a hand over her hair defensively. "I'm fine, thanks for asking. Nothing's wrong with my hair. I cut it. Is your case done? Will you be in town for a while or are you back to Bumble soon?" As she washed down the last bite of pretzel with water, she craned her neck to see if Quentin had arrived.

"Did you give your statement officially about last night?" he countered. Miguel scanned the street, eying it with the same suspicious scrutiny he subjected everything to since he returned from the Middle East. He leaned against the rail.

Zita growled. "Yes, I did. I even spent quality time looking at mug shots though none of the pictures matched any of the three guys. A science chick took samples of blood off my hands and my helmet last night. The cops might be able to catch the guys from that. Since Quentin and I installed the cameras in the lot, I can tell you they're not high definition. It's possible the cops can get a license plate, but I wouldn't bet on it." She shrugged.

His eyes were thoughtful as they returned to her. "I thought only two attacked you?"

Zita nodded. "Yes, the third was driving the SUV. I can identify him and the one whose jaw I probably busted. Given the circumstances, I paid attention to what they looked like. Sketch artist was out sick." Her leg vibrated with the need to move. While Miguel stood there, she had to stay close enough to hear.

Her brother kept pestering her. "Did you come up with any reasons why someone would try to kidnap you?" He was a dog with a bone. The night before, she had hung up on him to get him to stop.

Zita's foot tapped faster. She adjusted the straps on her backpack and unclipped her water bottle from the side. "No, I don't know why anyone would try to kidnap me. I've been in quarantine, remember? Stop hounding me, Miguel. The cops wasted most of the morning asking the same questions and flashing mug shots at me. The only one I recognized was a former blind date. If he had been one of the men last night, I could have walked. If you're curious, I'm not a fan of the prison gorilla style." In the hope of distracting him from her lies, she narrowed her eyes and glared at him. "Or the pug dog look, especially if they don't need to shave yet. I'm not convinced the coma wasn't stored-up boredom from listening to Justin drone on."

He declined the bait. "You should stay with me until this is all sorted out. The hotel can supply a cot." Miguel shifted his weight and checked over his shoulders.

She shuddered at the idea. "We talked about this last night. Let's not test sibling love like that, hermano. I like being on friendly terms with you. Besides, you'll wrap up your case soon and go back to Bumble or wherever until the next one. No hay bronca, I'll check in with you once a day."

"Four times a day," Miguel snapped.

"Twice."

"Three times. I don't like it, Zita. On your second day out of quarantine, someone tries to grab you?" he growled.

She shook her head and tapped her foot. "Two's all you're getting, Miguel. I got a life to live, and you can't be answering personal calls all day. You have criminals to put in jail."

His exhale was loud. He started to speak but stopped. Miguel drummed his fingers on the rail. "I spoke to the lead detective on your case. He has a larger-than-average number of missing persons right now, a high percentage of which were quarantined."

Zita almost choked at that little nugget. "Wait, folks from quarantine have gone missing?"

Her brother paused while a group passed. Once they were out of earshot, he continued. "Some have disappeared. That's not for public dissemination. They may have chosen to run off."

She considered that. "I can't blame them if they did before the quarantine ended, but they should be back if that's the case. You do know I'm warning my friends." *If quarantined people are disappearing, the kidnappers have not identified me from the zoo. That would be a relief, but I need to tell the others, whether Captain Law and Order likes it or not.*

Miguel had that expression, the one where he looked pained, constipated, and resigned to those conditions. "Please ask them to keep it quiet."

"Look, I'll stay with Quentin while the cops investigate. If it seems more serious than that, well, I can crash with friends until I find something south and poorly documented to do."

His brown eyes crinkled with concern. "What about your so-called real job? You work less in the summer, but you spend half the week there. I thought your boss loved you or at least loved having you bring in business with the translations?"

Zita snorted. Shoving down resentment at the memory, she ran in place. "Oh, the same boss who took a half hour to ask if I'd changed... so she could accommodate my new special needs? No, she claimed she had no phone translation jobs during the quarantine. Yesterday, I had to meet her at a diner near work, probably so she could verify I hadn't sprouted horns or anything that might frighten a customer. If I had, she'd either fire me or pimp me out so she could show how her office cares about special needs, right before she cut my hours to almost nonexistent." *She wants to climb the corporate ladder using my linguistic abilities, fine, but that conversation was disturbing. Just to get a reaction, I'm half-tempted to tell her I'm the naked zoo jaguar gang member teen. With my luck, though, she'd believe me and I do need the job. Still, imagining the reaction is hilarious.*

Her brother snarled. "Zita, you need to take this seriously. Someone tried to hurt you. Even Quentin's flaked about it."

"Pues, I was there. I kind of kicked their asses." Zita chuckled, as much at her own pride as at her win. "You know, before the running and screaming for help bit. Quentin contacted you? Did he say why he's been dodging me? Is he having trouble in the bathroom or what?"

Miguel stiffened. "What do you mean? Didn't you tell him what happened?" His forehead furrowed, and his lips pressed together.

She shook her head. "No, he's said nada since we parted ways yesterday. His place was set up for his date, but they must've gone to her house. Since he didn't reply to any of my texts or calls, I assume they got busy. He wouldn't ditch us, though, so you yell at him whenever he shows up, smelling of sex and old cologne." Her stomach turned over at an unpleasant notion that she pushed away as soon as she could. In defiance, Zita clambered back on the rail and balanced.

The furrow deepened. "It's unlike him to not call back in the morning, or right away."

"True. I'll check with his answering service and see if he had a busy schedule today." After a step or two on the rail, Zita caught Miguel's expression. She acquiesced and hopped down. *His office is probably a hot mess since I haven't been around to remind him to take money and not just barter.* After dialing Quentin's answering service, she went through the usual steps. Taking a gulp of her water, she nearly spat it on Miguel as the computerized voice announced the number of messages. "I need paper and something to write with," she muttered.

Miguel pulled a small notebook and pen from a suit pocket and handed it to her. His eyes looked pained as he said, "You shouldn't delete anything... in case..." His words trailed off, and he turned his head away.

She nodded, taking the items from him, and wrote. When she leaned the book against a massive stone pillar to write, one of her legs began bouncing again. When she finished, she snapped the phone shut and fumbled once before tucking it away. Her troubled gaze held Miguel's. "Quentin never picked up any messages from last night." She licked her lips and took controlled breaths. As her stomach clenched, Zita forced the words out. "Fifteen of the urgent messages and two of the non-urgent ones were from his date's dad.

Apparently, the girl he was with last night hasn't come home either, and she requires medication."

Miguel swore. "Quentin's missing and so is his date?" His color washed out.

Zita closed her eyes and tried to remember the woman. "He met her when we filed a report for my missing personal effects. Fit but not athletic shape, I'd guess his date plays tennis and is about thirty. Her name's Jean... no, Jen Stone. Quentin said she was just his type: unattached, fun, and not looking for more than a sexy weekend and done." She handed the notebook and pen back to Miguel.

She could see him pulling back, switching to focus on work as he recorded notes. "That's something at least. Can you give me a better description than the sports she plays?"

Her brother was missing, and she had a sinking feeling she would spend the rest of the day at another police station. "Sí, sí, get picky. She is a white girl, about five feet eight, 140 pounds, medium build, brown hair, and eyes. The hair was shoulder length, I think. He said they were going to do dinner, then dance at a new place where he'd received a VIP invite, and Vitamin Q if it worked out. You know him. Never met a pair of panties he didn't want into." *You had better be fine, Quentin, you dumbass.* A lump rose in her throat, and she fought back the impulse to pace.

Miguel's pen raced over the notebook, and he flipped pages. "Who called Quentin about her? What medication?" His face was somber, the same expression he used for taxes, work, and asking out women.

"Her dad... he sounded upset. His number's the circled one. He didn't say what she took, just that it was daily. Maybe diabetes?"

With a grunt, Miguel flipped back to the page with messages and copied the number. Dark hair tumbled into solemn eyes as he looked up from the page. "Given your misadventure, we can assume he was kidnapped. We need to file a report. You spoke to him and met her so you need to come too."

She let her head roll back and closed her eyes for a moment. *I refuse to be caged in your hotel room or office, so that had better not be in your plans, hermano. If Quentin's been taken, I can't sit around.* When her eyes opened again, her brother was watching her, his features so similar to Quentin's, she felt a pang. "Yeah, whatever."

Miguel opened his mouth, and the lines around his eyes eased before expression left his face.

A voice behind her greeted them. "Why, Agent Garcia, this must be your charming sister." Footsteps sounded on pavement.

When she turned to see the speaker, she recoiled. The man walked a step ahead of two other men and a woman. He had a beefy body crammed into an expensive suit and perched on stubby legs. While his steps were slow and his fingers blunt, his hand gestures had an unexpected deftness. The foolish might have discounted him as a chunky white man with a head shaved to hide incipient baldness, but she recognized a predator. His two male companions shouted bodyguard to her instincts. The taller one, a couple inches over six feet tall, had the gun-flashing swagger of a thug who enjoyed being a threat and the uncoordinated movement of someone who relied on size to win. She would have bet the other bodyguard, a blond an inch or two shorter, could have taken him in a fight. While the first one was a junkyard dog, the second was a stalking rattler; grace coiled and waiting for the moment to spring, content to hide until then. Both of them, however, lacked the rabid gleam of their boss' eyes. *Nice of them to stick together so people can see examples of men to avoid all in one spot.* The last member of the group was a woman, whose suit and briefcase suggested a lawyer. Of moderate height and immoderate weight, she brought up the rear of the group and stayed as far from her client as possible while remaining with them. Nothing in her movement bespoke physical skill, but Zita gave her survival instincts points for distancing herself from the men.

Miguel straightened, his eyes all cop. "Tracy Jones. What are you doing here?" His voice was flat, and his eyes flicked to Zita and back. Zita narrowed hers, recognizing brotherly protectiveness kicking in.

A smile with entirely too many teeth met his question.

Proving her wish for survival was less than her professional ambitions, the lawyer spoke first. "Mr. Jones is reporting voluntarily to assist in the investigation, as requested by the lead investigators."

Jones crossed thick arms over his chest and gave his lawyer a quelling expression that made her drop her eyes to her feet. "Again. I don't know why your office insists on calling me in, but I am a man who believes in doing my civic duty. Agent Garcia, you are positively brimming with welcome today. May I assume this is your adorable sister, Zita? I've heard so much about you, but reality exceeds rumor." Cold little eyes fastened on her, and Jones made a move as if to capture her hand in one of his. As he neared, bringing with him the scent of exhaust and dead fish, she sidestepped, touching Miguel's arm to avoid him. His bicep was a rock under her fingers; her brother's instincts must have been screaming as well.

Zita's eyebrows rose. The words escaped her before she could stop them. "I doubt that."

Miguel stepped between them, possibly to stop her from hitting Jones if he attempted to touch her again. Her brother's posture mirrored every bit of the soldier he had been. Miguel's poker face fell into place, but not before his annoyance leaked. Someday, she would mention his habit of pressing his lips together gave away his displeasure, but not until he swore off playing cards with her. "My family is of no interest to you and has no pertinence in the investigation."

The odious man smirked at her brother; she wanted to punch his teeth in. "Don't be ridiculous, Agent Garcia. It's only natural I'd be curious about the man harassing my friends, family, and presumed associates, especially when he asks about me, but does not speak to me." His gaze fell on Zita again. "I do like a feisty girl," he murmured, licking his lips.

His lawyer coughed, her face set in resigned lines.

The blond bodyguard stepped forward and muttered in Jones' ear. He nodded.

"I do not harass. I investigate," Miguel answered. "I eliminate the innocent from the suspect list and arrest the guilty. If I ask questions that seem to pertain to you, it would be in pursuit of those duties."

"Then I eagerly anticipate your apology for the time you've wasted. Excuse us, Agent Garcia, we have an appointment, as my associate reminds me. I'm sure a man like you despises tardiness." Jones swept up the steps, his blond bodyguard falling back and speaking to the lawyer.

His counsel nodded, lips pinched, and continued following. Her knuckles were white on the handle of her briefcase.

The blond man took out a cigarette, lit it, and began to smoke. Although he focused on nothing and no one with the disinterested gaze of a smoker, she suspected he watched them, or more specifically, her brother.

Said sibling sighed and put his suit coat back on. Miguel checked his tie to ensure it was straight, his lips pressed together. Zita knew what that meant. He fumed but kept the sound down. "Nobody told me he was coming in. He isn't supposed to be aware he's a person of interest. I don't like that he recognizes you. Look, I'm sorry, but I think you should come inside."

The bodyguard inhaled a few more times, stubbed out his cigarette, and entered the building.

Returning attention to her brother, Zita shifted her shoulders, loosening the muscles. *Miguel has to be close to solving the case if the bodyguard is keeping an eye on him.* "How could I miss Take Your Sister to Work Day?" Zita answered.

Chapter Twelve

Miguel meant to keep her imprisoned forever, locked in a succession of miniscule conference rooms pungent with burnt coffee and stinky feet. Zita lacked the clearance to hang out anywhere she might see anything of interest; apparently, she also lacked the authorization to sit in chairs that worked. Careful experimentation had determined that the furniture in every room had been scavenged and replaced with defective ones that leaned, tilted, or slumped like drunks at closing time. *Not that I want to sit. I want to do something, anything.* Since they'd reported Quentin missing the previous evening, Miguel had remained by her side or kept her corralled by other cops. The only respite from utter boredom had been the few minutes she'd spent retrieving Quentin's messages and forwarding jobs to his apprentice and other locksmiths. Out of desperation, she tested the watchfulness of her guard dogs, slipping in and out of rooms in the building. She could escape them, but the problem was exiting the building through security.

The only reason she was outside now was that her brother could not finagle their way out of attending the press conference. Zita inhaled what might be her last breaths of fresh air, or at least DC city air, and thought furiously. Miguel squashed her between himself and a pillar, her body partially shielded from the press cameras by his larger form and the fluttering black suits of his associates. Annoyance brought out a frown. As relatives of one of the missing, she and Miguel were supposed to stand in the background.

Midday sunlight glinted off silver hair and worry grooved care lines deeper into the face of Quentin's date's father. Sympathy plucked at Zita, tempered by the knowledge he, at least, could do something. Even now, the distraught man offered outrageous rewards for his daughter's safe return and lesser rewards for information leading to it.

Miguel must have felt it too. He shifted, sliding an arm around her shoulders as if she were a delicate flower requiring support. "Poor man," he murmured.

His words were a catalyst, and Zita knew what she had to do— what Quentin needed—and Miguel could not be involved with it. *It's better for him if he doesn't know. I can't explain I recognized one would-be kidnapper from the zoo incident.* "I need out," she whispered.

He blinked. His eyes were wary, and he whispered so the cameras would not pick up their conversation. "Zita, I don't have time to argue this with you."

"Yeah, I got that. Nobody needs me to help. I've been going crazy, and you wouldn't be keeping me so close if you weren't afraid of a leak. Staying here isn't the safest place. Your killer tortures both captives but starts with the female. If your killer has Quentin, but not me, our brother continues breathing." She withdrew from under his arm.

Miguel interrupted, hissing his words. "Who told you that? Jennifer Stone is missing so he may not wait for you."

"Our brother barely knows her, and it was your teammate, Parzarri, earlier today. He came by to question me and insinuate Quentin is dirty." She continued, ignoring the fury that intimation ignited, "I'll take any chance that'll extend Quentin's life. The best place for me is off the official grid. Pues, I can do that. No hay bronca. I'll check in with you. If you've got a problem on your team, they won't see me leave." Zita willed the Miguel of her childhood, who could occasionally be teased into joining her on her escapades, to help her out.

"This is—" he began.

With a glance at cameras more interested in the emotional pleas of Jen's father than a pair lost in the herd of background agents, she interrupted, "Sensible. It makes sense, hermano. I'll call you later so you know I'm safe. You leave a message as soon as you find Quentin. I'd rather you concentrated on getting him back." She punched his arm and drew away.

"Absolutely not. You will stay here." Miguel had his business face on, but the tic in his cheek was twitching overtime, and his fingers clenched as he pulled her closer again.

She narrowed her eyes, studying his face. *Poor guy, it's better if he can honestly say he tried to stop me.* Zita looked away and swore in Spanish, hating the subterfuge.

Her brother accepted that as capitulation and squeezed her shoulders. "It's for your safety." One hand ruffled her hair.

"Got it," she grumbled, pushing away, her mind spinning with plans.

The agent in charge stepped forward to spin the reward and missing person information in the Bureau's favor. Her chance came when he signaled Miguel to come forward to answer questions. Lights flashed their direction as an astute cameraman caught the motion.

"Watch her," Miguel growled at one of his coworkers, handing Zita's arm to the other man. Striding through the crowd, he stepped in front of the group. His words rang out, strong, reassuring, and lacking any useful information. The cameras turned to him.

Seriously? I'm not waiting. "Ow, not so hard," Zita complained to his coworker.

He loosened his grip on her arm. "Sorry about that," the poor sap whispered.

She nodded. "I'll deal. Nothing personal," Zita apologized, hitting the pressure point in his hand to make his fingers loosen further.

He yelped.

In the seconds that afforded her, she slipped free, squeezing past the pillar thanks to her small size, and darting into the crowd. From behind her, the throng stirred but made no major outcry. Jaywalking across the street, she darted around the corner. Victory was sweet, and only a little bitter when she slowed later to find she had lost any pursuit, if any had existed. *Since my duffel is in Miguel's office, I'll stop by my place and get things. It will have to wait until later though, so I can surprise anyone waiting there. I'll want a phone to call my friends and one to call the cops if I find something. Time to do something.* At the first park she passed, she shifted to wear the face and hair of a woman no one in this hemisphere should recognize.

***

Hours later, Zita did a pop vault to scale Jerome's wall and stopped at the top to survey the tiny, ornate garden within. A minute waterfall burbled in the center of a rectangular koi pond, where flashes of orange and white hinted at fish. Gray stone cobbles poured down the center from the patio, splitting to go around the water. Topiary animals and stranger creatures grew from substantial pots, providing the only real cover in the yard and framing the stonework. She contemplated the cameras. Every emplacement had blind spots; she just had to find them to minimize her exposure. Satisfied, she flipped down from the wall.

From her angle, his immaculate kitchen and dining room had the picture-perfect appearance of a home décor magazine, saved by sunglasses and other junk on the table and a crooked sweatshirt draped on a chair. She knocked on the patio door, pulling out a paper she had cadged earlier from a college artist and written on.

Jerome charged out of a room off the kitchen, a saber in his hand. His surprised expression was worth the wait. Whatever words he exclaimed were lost by the door separating them, but the tone and volume were audible.

She lifted the paper higher as he disabled his alarms and approached.

He slid the door open. "That's an interesting note. You have thirty seconds to explain since I have an appointment—". His doorbell rang. Jerome exhaled. "Now. If it's him, it may take a few. And if it's important, you can sit on the patio. Don't touch anything and leave my fish alone."

She bobbed her head.

He paused, and walked away, depositing his sword in the kitchen as he went.

She huffed at his back. The gap he had left in the door was enough for her to pick up his heavy footfalls and a murmured exchange of greetings. *Had he eaten Thai food last night?* Zita sniffed the air. *I could eat. Throw a girl a steak with some of that peanut sauce.*

Jerome's voice boomed out. "Yeah, have a seat. You want a beer? I've been running around all morning and could use one myself. Oh, and I have a great new microbrew you'll love." Leather creaked as a familiar voice murmured assent.

Moving quickly, Jerome returned to the kitchen and pulled out a couple of glass bottles from the fridge. As he yanked off the caps, he approached the patio door again and opened his mouth to speak. The doorbell rang before he could say anything. Still holding the beers, he called over his shoulder. "Can you grab the door, man? If it's a curvy woman with glasses and crazy eyes, don't let her in!"

A clicking came from the other room, and the other man exclaimed. "Hey, what do you think you're doing? Stop! Jerome, watch out!" Something fell.

Jerome sighed. He complained, "Some people don't understand what the words *restraining order* mean. Give me a sec." He mostly closed the door. Carrying the bottles by their necks, Jerome turned his back to Zita and strolled into the living room.

Guilt lanced through her for all of a second as she eased the door open and eavesdropped.

"Well, shit." Setting the bottles down with exaggerated ease on something, Jerome strode out of sight. "Things just got serious. Why don't you all run on home now and leave me be?"

Zita pushed the door further open. A muffled curse followed a noisy click. She recoiled, as something crashed, followed by a painful sounding series of thuds, breaking glass, and a hard object rolling across the hardwood floors.

A harsh male voice hissed, "Cuff him while he's down. You, take the other one." Zita heard another click, this one followed by a dull clunk and a crack like a whip.

An unfamiliar voice said, "What the?"

She retreated a few steps, hopefully into a camera blind spot, as she shoved off clothing. When Zita shifted to jaguar and launched herself toward the house, her claws tangled in fabric. As she tore her leg free, the clothing became airborne as she sprang forward to squeeze through the patio door. Her paws were silent on the carpet, and she held her form low, in stalking position, while easing into the living room. Jerome lay on the ground, with the remains of a glass object, a shattered side table, and two beer bottles bleeding alcohol around him. Three others stood around him. Two held Tasers, and the third held a stun gun and plastic zip ties. The last looked hesitant to approach. Hops and yeast perfumed the air.

Closer to the door, Remus faced a fourth man. "Don't make me hurt you," he begged. His face was pale beneath the luscious caramel of his skin.

The man facing him—six feet and 225 pounds, she judged, more genetic and pizza than effort—held a Taser in one hand. He tossed it and pulled a real gun. "We don't need you alive. Try to hit this away."

Jerome's eyes opened and widened... and his muscles tensed.

Her tail lashed the air, and she yowled. Several sets of eyes turned to her. Zita waved a paw.

Using the shock of her appearance, Jerome surged to his feet and gave the man trying to cuff him a powerful uppercut. He followed with a quick jab that disarmed the man of his stun gun. His opponent reeled back, hit the wall, and slid down to the floor, cuffs falling from his hand.

Zita pounced on one of the surprised men holding Tasers, pushing him into the back of a leather sofa. He tripped and fell with a whimper. Lithe and sinuous, she regained her feet as a Taser cartridge clattered to the ground.

With another whip-like crack of sound, Remus was suddenly next to Jerome. His arms crossed over his chest. "Please, I don't want to hurt anyone." The runner's scent was acrid with sweat and emotion.

"Mind the leather!" Jerome barked. He cracked his knuckles and advanced on the remaining male by him who stood holding an exhausted electroshock weapon. An odor she could only label as annoyance sang in his scent as he loomed over the man.

The guy with the gun stood in the doorway. "Why won't you people surrender?" he shouted.

Jerome's knockdown victim sobbed a little and held his jaw.

Zita crawled up the sofa and snarled at the man with the gun. Her tail whipped the air. *Please run away or be sidetracked. I don't want to kill anyone.*

The thug she had knocked down raised his Taser to aim, then yelped, dropping the weapon when the air snapped.

Remus stood next to the other sofa. "I really am sorry about your hand," he said, tipping the furniture over on the thug.

The last one on Jerome threw a wild hook at her friend's head, which the black man avoided and countered with a jab that left his enemy gasping. While his assailant was still distracted, Jerome seized his attacker and spun him around, propelling him into the gunman.

Zita pounced on the gunman's arm, sending the weapon rattling across the floor. The tiled foyer was cool under her paws as she leapt away and raced to the gun.

A series of cracks sounded and the pistol disappeared before she reached it.

She bounded up a step or two to prepare to spring again. Wrinkling her muzzle and lowering her chin, she let air rush in her mouth, as much to show her teeth as to gather scents.

The attackers on the floor had disentangled themselves. Their gazes stopped at her, poised on the stairs, moved to Jerome, and ended on Remus next to a heap of Tasers, plastic restraints, and a pistol. The moans and sobs of their disabled teammates were a soft chorus of misery.

"I told you to stop," Remus said, his voice quiet. The Puerto Rican held a gun clenched in one white-knuckled hand. His legs, so sexy in tight spandex, tensed as if he were ready to run.

Zita sucked in an audible breath, air whistling past her teeth as she inhaled again. Her felid senses recognized fear and anger in the jumble of smells and identified each of the individuals in the room. Her tail cut through the air.

The last two thugs scrambled to their feet and raced for their car. Jerome started to follow, but the one under the sofa shoved it off. The big black man booted the furniture away with a swift kick. "You want another round?"

Cradling his right hand, the man on the floor shook his head.

With a graceful leap to reach him, Zita perched by the man holding his jaw. His sobbing had died down... his eyes met hers, and he whimpered. "Please, don't let it eat me."

Jerome snorted. "You think I could or would want to stop it? I'm not even certain it's on our side."

She chuffed. Outside, tires squealed, accompanied by a whiff of nauseating burnt rubber. *Not that I would ever condone eating a human, but a steak would alleviate the poor kitty cat's hunger.* With what she hoped was a soulful look, she waited until she had

Jerome's attention and looked toward the kitchen then back at him. Zita made a chirping sound.

Oblivious, or pretending to be so, her friend made no move to fetch food. "Remus?" Jerome asked. "Would you use their restraints to tie up our new friends until the police get here?"

Between one blink and another, plastic zip ties hampered both intruders at the wrists and ankles, and her ears stung from the repeated snaps of Remus' rapid movements. Finished with his task, Remus dusted off his hands in the foyer. "I got the license number of the van. Now, what?" He waved a piece of paper. His eyes were glued to Zita's jaguar form. "You never mentioned a pet."

Zita narrowed her eyes at him, and her ears lay flat on her head. A growl escaped. *Sexy legs or not, I'm nobody's possession.*

"It's not mine." Jerome kept a wary eye on her, and Remus tensed.

She inclined her head. With as much dignity as she could muster, Zita minced her way out of the room, stepping carefully to avoid shards of glass. In the backyard, she dragged her clothes to what she hoped was a blind spot for the cameras, and changed to human form, again using the disguised face and hair she had chosen earlier. Color sprang up around her even as her senses of smell and sound decreased. When she went to retrieve her clothing, she noted with dismay that her pants and shoes had fallen into the pond. She tugged at her shirt; it barely covered her butt. *Guess I should be glad not to have much culo,* she thought as she fished out her sodden items, dropping them on the flagstones with a squelch. An extensive rip rendered the pants incapable of staying up as well. *Since the kidnappers attacked already, my warning might be superfluous.*

When Zita reentered the house, she snatched the gray sweatshirt from the back of the chair. She pulled it over her head, tugging the hood as far as it would go over her face. It hung to her knees like a dress. The process finished by rolling up the sleeves and zipping the hoodie shut before padding in bare feet back into the living room.

Jerome and Remus were standing by the righted sofa, having a hushed discussion, when she returned. Two captives shivered in a pile in the foyer. Despite everything that had happened, other than the shattered mess by the entry to the kitchen and the pervasive beer aroma, most of the room was untouched.

Using a thick Mexican accent, she said, "I guess I am late to tell you that quarantine people are being kidnapped." The voice of this form, an octave lower than her normal one, sounded odd. She tilted her face down to let the oversized hood further hide her, even though a part of her fretted over the obscured visibility.

"No shit," Jerome answered. "Thanks for the assist." Appearing aggravated, he turned the bottle in his hands around.

"No problem. I was hoping they would run if they saw a jaguar. The police probably prefer you not clean up," Zita answered. "Are you both okay?"

He shook his head. "You misread me. I'm not picking up. I'm mourning the loss of a beer and a day that had a promising start at the early hour of noon and a date with my girl later. Yeah, I took a dive when they shot at me with the stun gun, so I'm fine and grateful they missed."

Remus licked his lips and smiled. His eyes crinkled at the corners with pleasure. "I am fine, thanks."

Zita forgot her plan to advise Jerome on the difference about stun guns and Tasers. *Ay, yes, you are.*

Unaware of her internal drooling, he continued. "I hired Jerome because people have been disappearing from my group for business people with powers. Now you say, quarantined people?" Although he clutched the other empty bottle, his color was back, and the question suggested his mind was recovering.

"My super detective powers, ratified by a secret agent ring I got in my cereal and a fan letter from Bruce Wayne, tell me they're after people. To be specific, they want ones with powers and those who got all the great coma, but none of the great abilities." Jerome still seemed suspicious. "Is that my Batman sweatshirt?"

Zita bit her lip. "Sorry about that. My clothes got messed up. I'll return it later."

Something danced in Remus' eyes. He set his bottle down by the stack of weapons and restraints. "It looks better on you than on him. I'm Remus, and so sorry for implying you were Jerome's pet. If he had an animal, it would probably starve within a week. You have a name?" Her throat closed up when he gave her the eye. The eye. On her. The one that meant he liked what he saw.

Yanking the hood further over her face, she opened and closed her mouth a couple times before replying. *He's looking. He must be a leg man since the sweatshirt hides everything else.* "Sí, I'm, umm..." For safety's sake, she angled her face away more.

Jerome choked on a laugh. He turned until his face was under control.

Remus displayed that inviting smile again. He switched into Spanish. "Well then. Give me a call and we'll have dinner, lunch, or whatever?" He picked up a card off the table and handed it to her. "My cell's the second number. Use that one."

She opened her mouth, but no sound emerged. Numb, she took the card. "Thanks, I will," she forced out in the same language. *Did I just join in a fight and get asked out by someone I'm actually attracted to? The rest of the day has sucked but this, this half hour is epic.*

Control restored, Jerome put his brawny hands on his hips. "Did you break into my house to mack on him? Damn, I was worried you were one of my exes. Well, if you're done with flirting and delivering warnings..." He cocked an eyebrow at her.

"No, stay, the police will want to talk to you too," Remus pleaded. His expression implied the police were not the only ones with questions.

Oh, I so don't need to talk to the cops right now. But the man has lines. She inclined her head, her eyes on the handsome Puerto Rican. "Oh, sí, I have places I need to... to go, and you know, people to do... I mean, things to do," she stammered, pointing over her shoulder at the back of the house. "Right. I'm leaving. Bye." Zita turned, narrowly avoided a collision with the doorframe, and escaped into the backyard. She smacked herself in the head before remembering the cameras. "Ah, fuck me. I needed to talk to Jerome." Resisting the urge to look up, she wheeled around and went back inside. She scratched her head. *No way around it. Just be cool and pretend not to be an idiot.*

Jerome slouched on a sofa, his shoulders shaking with laughter that did not abate when he spotted her. He swung his feet up on the armrest. "What? You moving in now?"

Zita shook her head, bit her lip, and glanced toward Remus nervously. "I need a favor."

Remus looked up at her, a phone at his ear. A smile came to his lips, and he waved. Curiosity shone on his face and in every line of the tight body she was trying to ignore. While she pretended otherwise outwardly, she did not lie to herself about her interest. *I'm going to have so much to say next time I go to confession.* When a voice rose in query from his phone, Remus spun away to answer, apparently needing to concentrate on that conversation.

Jerome rose, glanced toward Remus, and strode toward her. Taking her arm, he steered her into the back room, an office packed with leather furniture, paper, and giant televisions. After Jerome seated himself in front of a keyboard, she realized they were huge computer monitors. His oversized leather chair creaked under his large form. One screen showed multiple zones, displaying camera feeds around his house and yard. The others held text or a pixilated forest. In chaotic piles, assorted computer accessories mingled with papers and empty takeout bags on every surface of the room except for his chair. Shelves held toys, spaced apart to best display each one. "Step into my office. You didn't eat Ken or Ryu, did you?"

"What? Who? No..." She hoped. "Who are they?"

"My fish." Jerome waved his phone at her. Her panty-clad rear end wiggled at her from the screen from when she had dragged her clothes out of the water.

She pushed the oversized glasses further up her nose and studied the wall. "Oh. No, I was careful with your pond and fish."

"Reflecting pool. It's a reflecting pool. You should be more careful with your clothes too." He laughed. "I'm guessing you're the Zoo Streaker. Guess I got the bragging rights to say I chased you off my lawn. Well, then, let's talk."

"Right, I need a couple things. First, the address and phone number of a club. The name is like Dance Mister or Dan's Misery or something like that."

He nodded, and his hands danced over the keys. She felt a moment of envy for speedy typists who could use more than a couple fingers at a time. "I should be able to find that in two seconds... are you sure you got the name right?" His brow furrowed and fingers stilled.

"No." Spotting a plastic figure with a large head, wearing a yellow gi, Zita went over to examine it.

He grunted a laugh. "Yeah, right."

"I kind of like the koi pond. It's all meditative and shit," Zita said. She touched her finger to the afro on the toy, and it wiggled at her. "Is this Jim Kelly from *Enter the Dragon*?"

He nodded at her. "Sharp eye. Try not to break my bobblehead. It's custom."

She withdrew her finger and just watched the plastic toy bounce. "Dude was robbed. His character should have ripped Han a new one, and instead, they killed him. It was just wrong." It kept nodding as if it agreed. Smart toy. Zita tilted her head. "Shouldn't you be typing?"

Jerome grunted. "Damn straight. Thanks for the compliment. Now, what do you want other than to admire my home, toys, and handsome face? You got a name?" He pressed a few more keys and propped his chin on a meaty fist while web pages and almost-

English text scrolled by on most of the monitors. The exception held an armored green woman with tusks, who wielded an axe against monsters. While Zita marshaled her thoughts, one corner of her mind puzzled over how a woman muscled like a male bodybuilder and wearing a thong bikini could fight so acrobatically.

She stared at the Jim Kelly bobblehead, then gave it a vicious flick. "Not that I can give you," she answered. The plastic toy bobbed violently, and she forced her gaze away to focus on Jerome again. Paper under the figurine caught her attention. "Wait..." She nudged a flyer out from under the toy. "This is the place. Danz Mizer."

A web page appeared on one monitor. Paper spat out of a printer. "Here's your address. What's your interest in the club?"

She hesitated. "It might be the last place two of the kidnap victims were seen before they disappeared. Can I keep this?"

Jerome grunted, and slid the paper, a VIP invite, from her hand. "No, but I'll tell the cops what you said about the club so they look there too. I printed you the address and directions from Rock Creek Park. Did you need anything else?"

She raised her hands in the air. "That's it. Thank you."

He dismissed her debt with a wave. "Why didn't you just call with your warning?"

"I don't have an unregistered cell phone or your number. If you've got a spare cell, I won't say no to it." She rubbed the back of her neck. Out of the corner of her eye, Jim Kelly nodded at her in approval.

"What makes you think I've got an unregistered cell phone?" His query sounded aggravated.

She blinked. "You're a private detective and a computer hacker. Isn't it a requirement?"

"Not everyone who works with computers is a hacker. You knowing my address, but not my phone number, is a little creepy, though." A smile belied his words.

"No? Oh, well, you're still a PI." She shrugged. "Sorry, computers aren't really my thing."

White teeth gleamed. "Of course, denying it doesn't mean one isn't a hacker either. Yeah, I can hook you up with one, even if you're a Luddite. Is that all? Did you want to make time with Remus until the cops get here? They should arrive soon, it being a respectable neighborhood and all, despite your presence." After opening a drawer, he drew something out and handed it to her. "Here's my business card, so no more stalking unless it's necessary." From another drawer, he extracted a pair of cell phones and set those near her.

"Comprendo. I didn't stalk you. It was all Google." Cars pulled up outside, and Zita heard Remus speak. Seizing the phones, she nodded at Jerome. "And that's my exit cue. You'll get your sweatshirt back eventually." She bolted out the back door, snatching her shoes and ruined pants as she passed. Her head low and half-blind from the hoodie, she ran across the backyard and vaulted back over the wall.

***

Two hours later, she was pacing back and forth in the diminutive kitchen of Wyn's cottage. A washing machine chugged away with her clothing and Jerome's sweatshirt. A pair of Siamese cats stared at her, tails flailing back and forth, while her friend made a liquid that smelled like flowers and not like the tea she purported it to be.

"Isn't this a case for the authorities?" Wyn tried, fussing with little floral teacups.

Zita's words stampeded like horses from a wildfire, and her arms jabbed at the air as she gestured. "Right, I can go to the cops and say, hey, this dude tried to kidnap someone, but I can't tell you how I know. It might connect to my brother's kidnapping, or it might waste your time. Alternatively, I could hope that whoever took Quentin finds me and snatches me too. Did I mention they think a sadistic torture-loving monster has him? I can't play helpless and do nothing." She rolled up the sleeves on the borrowed bathrobe she wore and scowled.

Sympathy shone in Wyn's hazel eyes, and Zita both appreciated and hated it. "Still..."

Her spine stiffened. *Quentin does not need pity. He needs action.* Zita calmed herself down and planned her appeal to her friend. *She likes rational. I'll be so rational her head explodes from the mad logic.* "All we're doing is following a lead. We find him, get him where you can concentrate, then ask questions. You listen to his brain, and if he knows something, you get the info."

After pouring into the miniature cups, Wyn set them on the table next to equally tiny flowery plates with miniscule cookies. *Mice are weeping somewhere at the loss of their cookies.* "Sit, Zita," she said. "It's Quentin. Of course, I want to assist, but the moral ramifications of abducting a person and searching his brain troubles me." She seated herself at one chair and gestured to the other.

"It's not right to kidnap, torture, and murder them either, especially Quentin!" Zita answered although she fidgeted in one of the white wicker chairs when she did it. She frowned at the girly cups in their almost-matching saucers on the gauzy lace tablecloth. The cats paraded around the table, and took up seats on opposite ends of the table, between the two women. *The cats are almost as creepy as the fancy tea party. Who keeps a lace tablecloth on their kitchen table every day?*

The witch took a sip of her tea. "I prefer a certain level of formality to remind me of the niceties of life," she answered.

"How is it wrong to get a few answers out of his head when you're constantly peeking into mine?" Zita consumed an entire cookie with one unsatisfying crunch.

Wyn picked a treat up and nibbled at it. "That's different. You're familiar and easier to read than a stranger. Even if I can't help overhearing you, I don't go digging to find out all your secrets, though." She giggled. "Not like you have any."

Her mouth filled with the taste of flowers after a perfunctory sip of tea, Zita sprang to her feet, unable to remain seated. She set the cup back down. "I have secrets." Her voice had a guilty tone as she took to pacing again. Stopping by her plate, she snatched up the other cookie and munched.

"Your vibrator is in the drawer next to your bed," Wyn murmured. One of the cats washed itself. The other stared at Zita.

She flipped off her friend with no real animosity. "My relationship with Bruce Ee is none of your business. If you think the location of a vibrator counts as a secret, you've been way sheltered. I'm not asking you to hurt anyone or do brain surgery. We get the kidnapper out of the club and ask him questions. You listen in on whatever he thinks for an answer. If it pans out, the cops get a tip, and they rescue my brother. We go disguised so he can't link it back to us. That's it. You don't have to do anything else."

"Bruce Ee. Really?" Wyn brought her teacup up to her mouth and giggled before swallowing.

Zita snapped her fingers under the other woman's nose. "He's fast and knows what he's doing. Focus. You're getting distracted. Are you going to help me or not? If not, I'd ask you to at least not tell anyone about this conversation since I'll have to go to plan B."

Wyn took a sip. "Is B for Bruce? Never mind, don't answer that. It's like reading a Darwin's List book; I don't want to read it, but I can't seem to stop. You can count on my discretion. It's doubtful I want to repeat this discussion or remember it." She toyed with her cookies.

"I'm the one with problems when you're obsessed by what I call my vibrator? Are you in or out?" Realizing that might not have been the best way to phrase it, Zita tried again. "Are you coming or not?" *Not any better.*

Her friend snickered. "Fine, I'll help you. If I don't, you'll devise an even worse plan." She took a deep breath. Wyn gazed at Zita wide-eyed, blinking rapidly. "Are we calling in Andy for backup?"

"You got a problem with your eyes?" Zita resumed pacing. "No. He didn't answer his phone, maybe because I had to use a number he didn't know. We shouldn't need him anyway." The uncanny cats stayed out of her way.

Dropping the weird eyelash batting, Wyn picked up her cookie, setting it down again uneaten a second later. "My eyes are fine. Disguised?" Her clever fingers crumbled the morsel to bits. A part of Zita mourned the waste of a cookie, even one almost too small to qualify. "That's probably smart."

"Hey, I'm all about protecting our identities. I might need to borrow clothes to wear, though." Since she had left her bag at the FBI office, she had to sponge clothing from Wyn. Given the way her friend had *winnowed* her wardrobe as a *favor*, she owed Zita some clothes, anyway.

"How will we find him? Did you liberate a file from your brother? Sneak out a thumb drive with case data... do you even know what a thumb drive is?"

"Sure," Zita lied.

One cat stopped grooming and turned to stare at her.

It was Wyn's turn for exasperation. "Right. So what do you have?" She stroked the head of the nearest cat. It almost looked smug.

"He's in charge of some kidnappers and is the favorite of a scary murderer named Sobek. I have his first name. He's one of the guys I saw at the zoo. You can do your telepathy thing and see his face that way. What the cops know is anyone's guess."

Wyn drummed her fingers on the table. "So how do we find him with only his first name?"

Without pausing, Zita explained. "At the zoo, they mentioned him managing a club, Danz Mizer. I got Jerome to find it, and I called and verified he's working tonight while you were at work. If they had spelled the club name right, it would have been faster."

"Boris? Does he have an assistant manager Natasha or a thing against moose and squirrels?" Wyn groaned. "I sound like Andy."

Puzzled, Zita stopped in her revolutions around the kitchen to consider her friend. "Do you know him? I didn't ask about other employees."

Putting a hand to her mouth again, Wyn hid a smile. "Never mind. So we're going clubbing?"

"You're going in a disguise so you can charm him into stepping out back with you. I'll be in the alley behind the place." Feet itching to move, Zita started another loop around the kitchen.

Wyn thought about it. "It would be easier to scan him without needing to go too deeply if we weren't in a crowded environment. Why don't I ask him to coffee and question him? It would be a congenial endeavor rather than one that strays too close to abduction." She sat up straight.

As much as she hated to stop the cheer that was spreading across her friend's face, Zita snorted. "He looked like a wannabe player, and we know he participates in kidnappings. I don't think he'd stick around to think of the right answers if he can walk away from questions about his crimes. I want to be there to make certain it's the right Boris..." *And kick his ass if he won't take no for an answer from you.*

Long lashes swept down over hazel eyes and glimmered wet. "Much obliged," Wyn said softly. "I had not thought of that, and I would prefer not to... have that difficulty with him." The cats leapt from their chairs in unison and twined around her legs. One purred when a hand crept down to stroke it.

Zita blinked at the other woman. "What? I wouldn't let him paw an unwilling stranger, let alone my friend. You're eavesdropping again, by the way."

Wyn rose and halted Zita's movement with a gentle hug.

Everyone is hugging me today. As a rule, I like hugs, but these make me feel useless.

One cat jumped onto Wyn's chair and investigated the liquid flowers in the cup. Understandably, it curled its lip and began grooming. The other feline meowed disapproval. "And that's part of why you're my friend."

Ay, crap, mush. With an awkward pat on Wyn's back, Zita nodded and replied, "Cool."

The twinkle returned to Wyn's eyes, although this time it had a sadistic glint to it. "Let's go see what I can find in my wardrobe to fit a pocket Venus." She literally rubbed her hands together.

"Uh, I got to try to call Aideen and Trixie again to warn them about the kidnappers targeting quarantine folks. Can I use your kitchen to make a snack? Food is a necessity if we're running all over. It might take a while. Why don't you pick clothes without me?" Zita tried.

Wyn arched an elegant eyebrow and shook her head.

Busted. "Right, be there in a sec."

Chapter Thirteen

Next time she kidnapped a person, she would resolve the logistics issues first. Normally, she planned better, but this differed from her usual plans for trips or stunts... or illegal climbing. Zita grimaced. Maybe her excuse was weaker than she had originally thought.

She huddled beside Wyn, or rather, Wyn's illusory guise, and peered at the club across the street. A flashing neon sign, a billboard atop the club, and a strobe light nearby that made the streetlamps seem anemic, provided illumination enough. Farther down the block, similar clubs were closer together and better lit. Opportunistic cabbies perched like vultures between clubs, available signs beacons in the shadows. People in clothing too short and too tight for comfort came and went at a steady pace. Her friend assured her the club was nowhere near capacity or the bouncer would have been choosier, rather than just collecting phone numbers and cover charges.

"Can you tell if he's in there? He was supposed to be on shift from ten," Zita whispered, though the pulsing bass that leaked out each time the door opened made it unnecessary. Her shoulders twitched; her current voice still seemed alien. To minimize the risk of failed athletic moves, she had chosen to shift only her hair, face, and voice to match the ones she had used at Jerome's home. She had even given herself pointy ears to avoid identification; Wyn, who had spent quality time with Miguel's forensics book during quarantine, had suggested it. The thigh-length hair was distraction enough, though she liked it. *If nothing else, it would keep prudes like Andy from squealing if she ripped her clothing again. Well, Wyn's clothing.* Zita grimaced. A nine-inch height difference and different body shapes had made clothing selection a torment. They had given up on shoes completely and just painted her rainbow leopard print slippers black.

Her friend shot her an exasperated look and coiled hair around a finger. "No. Unless he suddenly starts ruminating on why his parents hated him enough to name him Boris, I cannot differentiate him from rest of the crowd. The only minds I can identify are you and the terrifying man in the white vehicle down the street." Even whispering, the soft soprano voice was musical.

Zita craned her neck and looked at the pickup to see if the truck contents had changed. "The sleeping guy? He looks cuddly if you like your men big and furry."

Wyn sniffed. "He's faking. The sleeping is subterfuge while he waits for someone. His mind is almost incoherent with rage about a girl, and he intends to beat his prey until they tell him something. I'm endeavoring not to listen."

"He's snoring." Zita stared at the nondescript truck and the giant pretending to sleep within. "Seriously?" The heavy braid of hair down her back shifted, and she shoved it back into position.

"Bloodcurdlingly so."

She shuddered. "Is he waiting for our target? If the angry guy is connected to one of his previous victims, he could be after Boris too."

Wyn shrugged, silvery hair sliding over the almost-nonexistent shoulders of the fluttering scrap of a dress she wore. Illusory green gems were woven through her hair and matched the dress and high-heeled shoes. She had refused to wear a black dress instead of the emerald and silver thing she had on. When Zita had suggested something less noticeable, she had claimed that a honey trap dressed to distract, and she would do so. Wyn bit her lip every time her gaze touched the truck.

Plucking at her borrowed clothes to separate the sweaty fabric from her skin, Zita tugged the strained neckline up again on the borrowed, long-sleeved black top. Her conscience nagged. *It seems wrong to leave a feral man waiting for prey.* "Oye, can you make his appearance reality? He can sleep off the hissy fit, whoever he's after will be safe, and everyone else will be too. A nap might even sweeten his temper." Self-preservation stopped her from mentioning how homicidal Wyn got when awakened for anything less than an invasion of gunmen. When Zita tilted her head, sparkling glitter and minute blue feather tufts shed everywhere from the mask she had borrowed, the only usable one in the closet.

Amethyst eyes wide, Wyn whirled around. She hissed, "How am I supposed to do that? I don't want to be in proximity to him. He'll go ballistic at the next opportunity!"

Glitter flaked when Zita shrugged. "You could sing a lullaby in his head? Or use the shiny woo-woo stuff, like when you heal."

"It's magic. Can't you call it that?" Wyn snarled. "Snapping my fingers doesn't constitute a spell, not to mention, a major tenet of my magic is that it harms no one."

Zita raised both hands in the air. "Are you asking me or having a panic attack out loud? I know shit about magic. You wave your hand to heal and chant words to turn a two-inch chili pepper into a giant bush that's even now sitting on my balcony. It can't hurt to try snapping your fingers for a solution that doesn't hurt anyone... can it?"

Lips in a moue, Wyn shivered despite the heat of the night as her attention returned to the white truck. "I suppose. Sleeping spells aren't that uncommon, and it would be for the greater benefit." Her gaze turned thoughtful, and her pout smoothed. "Give me a couple minutes."

Punching down impatience, Zita waved her hand, keeping her tone casual to pacify her ruffled friend. "Sure, I have nothing better to do. Help him sleep off his mad."

It took ten minutes, but a pink cloud twined itself around the ursine man and soon his snores rang out in a counterpoint to the throbbing bass beat. Wyn beamed.

"He must have amazing lung capacity to get that loud. Before, you had to walk by his open window to hear him," Zita murmured, impressed.

Wyn turned her head, eyes narrow and tone sharp. "I put someone to sleep with an improvised sleep spell, and you're awed by the volume of his snoring?"

Zita slapped her friend on the back. "Claro que sí, I knew you could do it. The snoring was a surprise. If he can belch that loud, he probably walks into bars, belches, and all the other dudes buy drinks for the king." At her friend's annoyed expression, Zita tacked on, "Good work! Okay, so you go on inside, and once you're in safe, I'll pussyfoot around behind the place, and we'll look for Boris. If he goes out the back with you, we'll talk to him there. If you go out the front with him, haul him over here, and I'll meet you."

Still muttering complaints under her breath, Wyn slung a handbag over her shoulder and sauntered across the street, veering wide to avoid the white pickup. The snoring did not change in cadence or volume. Within a minute, her friend set a hand on the muscle-bound bouncer's arm and smiled up at him. He escorted her inside. A snippy mental comment from within verified Wyn was in the VIP section, and without a cover charge.

Right girl for the job. Zita gloated. Satisfied, she crept through the alley, darted across the street, and moved toward the back of the club from a couple shadowy alleys down. She adjusted her mask, now damp from sweat and the humidity of the hot night, more firmly over her face. Part of a feather drifted down during her rapid march to the nightspot, as she avoided lights and cameras as much as possible. When she neared the right alley, she slowed. *The number of cigarettes Boris smoked at the zoo makes me suspect he'll be heading out back on a regular basis. Wyn may miss him inside, but I'll catch him out here—momentito, what's that?*

With a quick step behind the cover of the dumpster for another shop, she peered toward the door. Fragments of music and pulsing bass rose and fell. Uniform navy paint, interrupted only by a crooked Employee Only sign, covered the entire rear wall of the club, making it hard to ascertain the door from a distance. Burger and pizza aromas warred with the harsher odors of alcohol, cigarettes, urine, and trash. The bulb over the door was out. A billboard facing away from the alley threw light from atop a neighboring building, but only where a yellow glow escaped the corners of the advertisement. Each time an overhead strobe turned the right direction, flickers of illumination flared, then failed to overcome the dimness, only fading black to gray. While the loading dock and dumpster for the club were on another side of the building, old liquor boxes and other assorted refuse warred with massive pots holding dead greenery. Deeper shadows pooled in the gloom thrown by the containers. Those shadows made Zita press deeper under the cover of the dumpster. *Depressing. Even a cat would have trouble seeing in this light.* Zita slapped control over her shape before she could shift. *I didn't take all that time to pick out a form to wear to lose it over a passing thought.*

Still, her momentary distraction proved useful; the world brightened, and scents grew richer, darker, and more pungent. Her enhanced eyesight picked out the paint's age and dinginess and allowed identification of the trash on the ground. *Oh, gross. Thanks to the cat visual and olfactory senses, I can play count the condoms and what's that smell while I wait.* The darkness beneath one pot resolved into a man's form in a crouch, a long gun cradled in his arms like a lover. Her eyes widened, and she followed the point of the gun to the door. *Shotgun on a sling.* Zita's mind whirled. *Sobek* must be cutting Boris loose. *If that's the case, Quentin and Jen may not have much longer.*

Wyn! Can you hear me? Zita pretended to shout in her head. Wyn had claimed that she had stopped listening to everything, so unless Zita thought loudly—whatever that meant—she had privacy in her own mind again. She eased back farther into the dark until her back almost touched the grimy wall of a building.

The reply carried irritable undertones. *Yes, stop shouting! I said we were linked. Try to point the thought at me instead of whatever you're doing. What is it? I'm chatting him up. The VIP area is decadent.*

Zita narrowed her eyes. *This mind crap is a pain. How do you point a thought?* She tried stage whispering in her head; her lips moved, but it was the best she could do. *A masked man with a gun is hiding out back. What if he's partners with Sleepy in the truck? Could Sobek be taking out Boris because the cops are onto him? Can you put the gunman to sleep?* Glitter flaked off into her fingernails when she scratched the itchy top of the mask, and she grimaced. She wiped her hand on her pants.

Much better. No, I have to see him to cast the sleep spell. Just keep away from him. I almost have Boris willing to leave. Irritation did not accompany her friend's words, so she must have adjusted the volume to Wyn's satisfaction.

She eased her shirt away from her skin to allow respite from the sticky fabric. *I got this.* Zita's mental tone was indignant. *No time. Find Boris and take him out the front to somewhere safe to question him. Let me know where and I'll join you when I finish distracting this guy. Quentin's location is more important than ever.* She crept closer, ignoring the part of her brain berating her for getting closer to a man with a shotgun. Her feline instincts rumbled with delight in the stalk as did a more human part of her. Taking her time and full advantage of the shadows, she inched closer. *If I can get to that pot, I can jump him.*

His black clothing was cut close enough to his body to reveal where padding—*maybe bulletproof vest plates*—blurred a honed figure, an unyielding weapon of little excess fat or anything else, simply muscle and intent. He was immobile in the manner of a predator, all coiled strength poised to strike when vulnerable prey came into position. A corner of her mind purred admiration ... *my taste in men may be off.* She yanked her thoughts away from the analysis of his physique and studied his gear. Nothing identified him as a cop of any kind. Besides the handgun strapped in a hip carry on one side, his belt hung heavy with gear, including handcuffs, a coil of rope, and an odd, boxy gun. *Ay, is that a grapple gun? I've always wanted one of those. If he weren't planning to murder the key to Quentin's location, I'd ask his regimen or the shop that sells the neat toys. Who am I kidding? I wouldn't have the cojones.* Gloves covered his hands, though the glimmer of skin at his wrists was pale. A square of black darker than the shadows was almost lost on the edge of a pot. *Ah, a coat to hide the guns and war gear.* A mask and goggles concealed his face and hair. Her mind whirled, planning angles. *Right, so if I can jump SWAT Ninja Man before he sees me, I should be able to—*

"Close enough. What do you want?" a deep voice ground out. Her improved hearing picked out a slight electronic buzz to it. With a deceptively casual movement, SWAT Ninja Man aimed his handgun at her with his left hand. The shotgun hung in his other hand. His lean form tilted away from her.

So much for my crazy cat stealth. Zita straightened and angled her own body sideways to reduce the size of the target she made. *He holds those guns as if he were born with them, despite having two out at once. What now?* She let her mouth run away with her while she schemed. With a heavy Mexican accent, she replied, "Peace on earth, good will toward men, and cinnamon brownies. You seen my cat? His name is Chalupa." Her stomach growled, ruining the line. She offered him a bright smile, anyway.

Although his goggles hid his eyes, she thought he blinked. She gave him an innocent look, remembering her mask only when she ran her hand over the top of her head, forward and back. Her stomach growled again, the noise loud in the alley. Neither of them spoke.

Just then, the back door to the club opened, and a blast of electronic music poured out. Boris stepped out with the slow swagger of a man on the prowl, the silver moonlight of Wyn's pale hair gleaming behind him. "No, baby, it is my club. No one would dare—" he boasted with that awful accent that slid between German and Russian and back again.

The gunman braced his shotgun against his shoulder and fired faster than Zita would have believed possible. He gave a low grunt at the recoil.

Boris squealed and fell back into the club, writhing and whining. The tang of ozone hung in the air.

Too late to stop SWAT Ninja Man, Zita was already in motion. Although he managed the one shot at Boris, she knocked the handgun from his hand with a fast, spinning kick while his attention was split. She danced out of his reach, performing a quick bandeira, before rolling into another strike with her foot in an attempt to rid him of his shotgun.

He dodged, reloaded, and tried a brutal strike back that narrowly missed her, but prevented her from connecting.

Zita circled away to find a better opening.

He fired.

Leaping and twisting, she evaded the shot. *Get his ass to safety and find out where my brother is,* Zita shouted mentally to Wyn.

On it. He's dazed. You? Her friend sent back.

He reloaded again.

She dropped into a careful ginga, moving away. *Perfecto. Save Quentin. Busy here.*

Raspy, low, and electronic, his soft voice held notes of derision and thoughtfulness. "What are you trying to accomplish? Is that...

a capoeira move?" This time, he tracked her movements, bringing up his other hand to aim the shotgun.

As she danced to the side, she narrowed her eyes, and continued to move, putting as many things between them as possible. *Keep moving before he gets a clean shot.* "Stop you." Her answer came in gasps. "Stop, not kill. Holding back. I'm not homicidal like your boss, Sobek."

Zita sprinted to the closest pot and jumped into it. Without pausing, she used her momentum to bounce off the wall and flip onto the roof of the building next to the alley. She ran the edge of the rooftop, peering over to follow his progress. He tracked her with his gun but retreated to the pot that held the rest of his gear. As she ducked behind cover, she softened her footfalls and thought furiously. *The more time I can buy Wyn, the better, but I can't get his gun from here. If I teleport away, he'll go after Boris again. Quentin, I love your dumb ass, mano.*

Zita scoped out the rooftop. It held a lit billboard, the advertisement facing away from her, and the revolving spotlight that had made the lighting so odd in the alley below. Other than a few large exhaust fans, it was bare of anything... save dark asphalt tiles and bird poop. Tile shards lay scattered across the roof in plentiful abandon. A stairwell entrance was the largest object after the sign and the light. The day's heat radiated from the rooftop to her feet, and it smelled of warmed tar and exhaust, a welcome change from the alley. An extension cord for the spotlight almost tripped her in her attempts to sneak and monitor the gunman. Roofing shifted underfoot, and she dropped to a crouch in case the gunman took a shot. She peeked over again. His goggles stared back from where he waited. Her hand landed on a broken piece of tile; the gloves Wyn had ridiculed stopped it from piercing her skin. Scooping up the one that had assaulted her hand, she hefted it to check the balance. With a deep breath, she leaned down and threw it at the gunman.

It hit, but his armored vest prevented it from penetrating. She ducked back. *The balance is awful. I was going for his arm.* With quiet steps, she moved to a new position, scooped up another, and threw again. This time, she did not wait to see if it hit before crouching low.

Right, hope that keeps you wondering about my next shot. I know I'm worried about yours. Zita halted and tracked the extension cord over to the revolving spotlight. As she considered options, she collected more tiles. The bright cylinder continued to turn and wink. After chucking another missile at the gunman, she ran over to it. Although she averted her eyes from the light itself, her shadow loomed in giant relief when it turned toward her. She bent down, below the beam, and studied it. *Accuracy is difficult if you can't see your target.* As soon as she spotted the power switch, she turned it off. Following the cord, she found a set of toggles by the stairs and the socket for the power cords. With a smile, she turned off and unplugged everything. The billboard faded, then went out. *Maybe I can tie him up with the spotlight extension cord.* Sounds distracted her before she could finish planning.

A soft thunk, followed by a whirring hum, came from behind her. As she turned, he leapt nimbly onto the roof, gun in hand. *Grapple gun confirmed. I want one of those so bad.*

She threw another piece of tile, this one away from herself to distract, and she vaulted over a fan. *Why do rooftops in the movies always have more hiding places than the ones where I end up?*

With a deep breath, she peeked out. He was taking cover, handgun at the ready, shotgun on back. His head was tilted her direction. Zita threw another piece of tile in the same direction as the last and somersaulted behind the stairs. Teleporting to the opposite side of the roof, behind the looming billboard, she scaled the access ladder, black with the loss of the strobe. More importantly, it hid her from SWAT Ninja Man. She crouched in front of the sign and listened for movement.

Zita? Are you okay? Wyn asked mentally.

Busy. You away? Zita sent back. Easing forward, almost on all fours, she edged along the billboard.

Wyn's reply was slow as if she had considered and discarded answers. *Yes, we're out.*

Get the info. Can't talk. Zita considered her options. The last thing she needed was Boris to get away, so she had to escape and help Wyn if she could do it without being shot or leaving evidence. The billboard and the dark would hide her, but neither would provide protection if he shot her. Her first priority had to be to get rid of the handgun since the sling made disarming the shotgun problematic. *The fewer guns he can shoot me with, the better.* As she focused on a plan, she calculated angles. *If he is still in his last position, I can knock him down and disarm him. It'll combine aerial work and capoeira. I should try the combination again when lives are not at risk; it will be a sweet move.* She chanced a quick peek out. He was there, body sideways to reduce his silhouette to where she had been previously. Since his head faced her last hiding spot, his chest made an excellent target. Bending down, he picked up something and began to straighten, slow and steady. *Perfecto.*

She swung off the edge of the billboard and used her momentum to add force and speed to her kick. Despite his crouch, she hit him in the chest, knocking him down while she regained her feet. Zita struck his gun arm hard, kicking the weapon away while he gasped for air. It spun across the rooftop.

Up again in a second, he twisted with enviable agility. SWAT Ninja Man attacked in a flurry of arm strikes, varied by a few vicious kicks.

Zita's arms ached where she had intercepted those punches and returned a few of her own. *He has mad skills. Krav Maga, I think. I can't play too much with Quentin at risk, though.* She felt her mouth curl up in a smile when he blocked. "Glad I didn't kick you too hard."

His only reply was, "What do you know about Sobek?"

Spinning away in a flurry of cartwheels and movements that would have made her instructors proud, she ran for the gun. He was fast, but she had seen where it had gone while he had to look. She pounced upon it, and spun around, assuming a shooting stance. *Miguel is never finding out he was right about the position being automatic when you've practiced enough.* "Don't make me find out what the kick is on this baby or if you've messed with the safety. Hands away from the shotgun," she warned him. Belatedly, she realized she was still using the cheesy Mexican accent. "Gringo." *Go me, camouflage and comedy in one obnoxious stereotype.*

He stopped advancing and balanced on the balls of his feet. Light reflected on his goggles as he tilted his head at her. Not a word escaped him, but at least his breathing had roughened with the exertion, like hers. Immobile, he watched her with his head tilted and magnificent body sloped away.

Zita backed toward the extension cord in cautious steps, never taking her eyes from him. *If I can get to that side street, the buildings will provide cover. I can teleport away to join Wyn while he searches in the wrong direction.* With his gun and her eyes still trained on the man, she felt with one hand for the extension cord. Grabbing it, she moved to the edge of the building. Other than swiveling to face her, he remained in place.

She grinned at him and jumped backward off the edge. Using the cord like a rope, she twisted around and swung down toward the street. The gloves protected her hands, and the building was low enough she bet she could reach the ground before the cord broke or the light toppled. Instinct blared warnings, but she was too focused on landing safely to dodge. A shotgun boomed, and the shell hit while she was in midair. The gun dropped from her hand, sliding down into the street storm drain. Zita could have sworn he cursed. Her muscles seized, and she fell into the agony.

When she could produce a coherent thought again, she was on the ground, and hands searched her with a cold efficiency. Based on the coated plastic feel, the extension cord restrained her arms behind her. Her shoulders hunched up almost to her ears, her teeth chattered, and she wheezed.

SWAT Ninja Man shook his head when he unfolded the plastic bag she had pocketed to hold her clothes if she had to shift.

At the time she had chosen it, the smiley face and Have a Nice Day message had seemed cheerful; now, it mocked her.

He let it fall at her side. The search continued, slow and methodical, pausing again only when he ripped off the bagged homemade protein bars taped to her calves. He might have sniffed them before resealing the bags and dropping them on the taunting happy face. All sensation muted but the hurt, he loomed closer, a large utility knife skating toward her neck.

Unbidden, a tear leaked from an eye, and she felt anger ignite. "N-n-no," she forced out. *Don't touch me.* Zita ordered her legs to kick at him, but the disobedient appendages just lay there. The searing pain began to subside.

Instead of the slice she expected, black-clad fingers curled around the edges of her mask, and the knife freed it from her face. Glitter and feather tufts drifted downward and clung to his pant leg. He jammed it into one of his pockets. "No weapons? Go home, amateur. This isn't a game. You may have cost someone her life. Don't lose yours too," the stranger rasped. He stepped away, and looked down at her, then back at the club. As he walked away, settling his coat over his arsenal, he paused. "My path goes past cameras if you decide to be more foolish." Even electronically altered, the disdain in his voice stung.

"Morality... from Sobek's man?" she managed a derisive whisper. Her teeth wanted to chatter despite the heat, and every muscle hurt. A whimper escaped. Now that the agony had receded to extremely sore, she attempted to get her body to move. One of her toes twitched.

The man turned and considered her. "I'm freelance," he stated, striding back to her side. One gloved hand grabbed her head by the thick hair of her long braid. It might have hurt if her entire body had not already felt like a large stick had pummeled it. "Where does he keep prisoners?"

Her eyelids slid to half-mast. "I don't know... yet," she answered in slurred Spanish. The worst of the pain subsiding, she drew up one leg, then the other.

He released her even as she braced for a blow and stepped back, out of range of her feet, and out of her line of sight.

By the time she regained sufficient motor control to raise herself up on an elbow and check for him, he was gone. Zita grumbled and felt for the ties at her wrists. Smooth plastic greeted her fingers, coiled in a knot with sharp metal threads at the ends. *He knows how to tie a girl up, but not show her a good time. Skilled enough to do all that, and he doesn't even give me credit for disarming him.* She worked to release herself, griping internally. It was not happening with her arms behind her, so she curled up tight, and brought her arms down. With a grunt of effort and a little more pain, she brought her arms over her feet so they were in front of her. The severed end of the extension cord waved at her from the tie. If he had used a better material, she would have had more trouble twisting out of it and getting the complicated knot undone.

Rubbing her wrists, she checked the side street. It was deserted, the reason she had wanted to escape down it. Her clothes bag laughed at her, looking up at her from where he had dropped it at her side. She snatched up her protein bars from where they lay piled like a toupee on the happy face, wincing as her ribs protested. Most of her body felt as though she were one enormous bruise. The raw spots on her legs where the street had abraded her skin were only a minor annoyance in comparison. Zita withdrew behind a dumpster, trying not to dwell on the stench. One of her legs and her ribs passed agony back and forth, so she endeavored to ignore that too; she must have landed badly or bounced when he shot her.

I should go to meet—no, what if someone innocent gets that gun? What if it washes out and kids play with it? She grimaced. Guilt rose. Am I so lazy that I can accept the chance? I suppose it couldn't hurt to have a way to identify that superior pendejo if we cross paths again too. I'll take one moment first. Zita leaned against the wall and closed her eyes, marshaling her will against the pain. Her own breathing sounded too loud and fast; she forced it into a more regular pattern. One arm wound itself around her middle. The torture in her ribs at deeper breaths informed her that her fall had been worse than she'd first guessed. *Bad time for adrenaline to wear off.*

"Are you all right?" A voice interrupted her self-absorption, coming from the street.

Zita forced her eyes open. She caught a brief impression of light hair and shimmery fabric as someone touched her arm. Her breath hissed through her teeth as the Wyn turned her around. Pain escalated. "Fine. Ribs got a bump."

Cool hands grasped her wrist, fingers centered over where her pulse throbbed. "Were you shot? You need a thesaurus. Try broken or fractured. Thank the Goddess, I came back."

Zita blinked, and turned to the other woman, but the movement put additional stress on her sides. She gasped as purple eyes, surrounded by curling silver tendrils, met hers. "Wyn?" slipped out before she could stop herself. "What are you doing here?"

Her friend lifted a shoulder. "I disliked the content of your communication, and once he stopped vomiting from his seizure, Boris declined to speak to an undercover agent." Green light began to emanate from her hand, sending a cooling frisson across Zita's abused body.

Air broke from her throat in a gasp as she inhaled without accompanying discomfort. "Seizure? That was a stun bullet. They're new and amazing if you enjoy agony. Why did he think you were a spy? You're..." Her instincts shied from saying it aloud. *You're a research librarian at a university.*

"I'm gorgeous and alleged that he kidnapped people, according to him. Additionally, when he asked if I worked for the government, I didn't deny it." Wyn's eyes gleamed. *Stop interrupting. The university is a state school; therefore, the government pays me. Back to Boris, his group took Quentin and a woman two nights ago. He sent the flyer to lure them here and called the others when your brother arrived. Sobek's bodyguards hauled them off, though, rather than sending them down the usual channels. More of Sobek's people would have been here tonight, but they took a female cop earlier, and the others are dropping her off.* She frowned. *Aideen invited me clubbing tonight, but I turned her down for this. I hope he didn't mean her.*

Zita winced, remembering the living flame eating up the hospital pavement with every step. "Thanks for the healing. Can you keep watch on the street for a minute?" Standing, she tried an experimental stretch. Her muscles were warm, but nothing hurt.

Wyn nodded and scurried to the street. "I got an address where he dropped off his kidnap victims. Can you try getting hurt less? It's hard on your friends."

Once she verified passersby and cameras could not see her, Zita took off her clothing, folded it, and set it in her bag. After shifting to a relatively small yellow anaconda, she slithered over to the storm drain and dropped inside before she could consider her actions too much more. *It sucks for me too. I haven't had so many injuries so close together since the cancer. Wait... how'd you heal me without candles or your other paraphernalia?*

Sheer desperation? I guess all I need is a few hand gestures and the intent to make the spell work, perhaps because of all the practice you've been giving me. Wyn stepped away from the street as a car passed.

I prefer less painful practicing. Zita asked the next question as she glided through sewer detritus. *People are animals. So how'd you get all this information so fast?*

If you ask a question, the truth floats to mind first. Wyn must have been practicing her telepathy at work again to know that. *I asked many questions in rapid succession.*

A few minutes later, Zita reemerged, carefully coiling to get the gun and her body out of the drain. She was grateful it had been a dry week, so the filth had been minimal, at least to her and the serpentine instincts she borrowed. *Did you find out anything else?*

"Sobek and his newest pet, one of his bodyguards, are freaks like us," Wyn answered. She shifted from foot to foot.

Zita hissed. *We're not freaks. We're awesome. What can they do?* She moved the gun toward her bag.

Although her friend faced the street, Wyn tilted a shoulder in a shrug. "Sobek can do something with water."

Zita's answer was wry. *He must be sorry none of that exists here on the East Coast, near a giant estuary.*

Wyn choked on her laugh.

A college girl with big hair, a miniscule shirt, and no pants stumbled out of the bar, leaning on a man. She giggled. "I'm so..." she began, as her reddened eyes caught sight of the snake. She stopped, teetering. Her brows lowered as she struggled to comprehend what she'd seen.

Don't let me stop you getting laid, lady. It's not as if I've gotten any lately. This back exit is way busy. Zita flicked her tongue, a low hiss escaping.

When her eyes focused on the anaconda, the drunken woman shrieked and fled, almost running Wyn down. Despite the stripper heels and inebriation, she had an impressive sprint. Without even looking to see what had frightened his companion, her suitor staggered after her, clumsy even in his more sensible shoes. *Ay, no stamina. You're better off without that one, blondie.* Zita enjoyed the heckling while gliding back to the dumpster. In an instant, she shifted back to her disguise form.

Wyn turned around before Zita could dress. Grumbling, she said, "You should try keeping your clothes on for the entire day. That or charge for the shows."

"Sounds like a boring-ass day," Zita replied. After pulling on her borrowed clothing, she put the gun into her bag. She grinned, ripped open the plastic bag, and tore off half a protein bar in one ravenous bite. The pair headed for the street.

Wyn shook her head, but her lips curved up, and the little worry line between her brows disappeared. As they passed under a lamp by the alley entrance, she tittered. "Where's your mask? Do you know you have a rip in the rear of those pants?"

"What?" Zita twisted and tried to see.

A hand rose to hover over rosebud lips. "Nice puppy panties. You know, you can keep those capris," Wyn said.

Zita mumbled a profanity and walked forward again. The ground stung her feet through the thin soles of her shoes. She kicked trash out of the way and chewed. "I guess it's good I don't have much of an ass or it would be falling out of these pants."

Bell-like laughter trickled out from the woman jogging to catch up. They peered out at the street in front of the club.

"Looks like your buddy got woken up. Hope he chilled out after his nap," Zita said.

"Where's Boris?" Wyn queried. She poked her head out further. "I left him hiding by the white truck. I couldn't talk him into answering questions, but he was going to take my advice to run. He refused to do so without going back for a hidden stash of money, but he said he'd wait for me to scout for the assassin first." Wyn rushed across the street and dodged into another alley.

Plastic bag banging against her leg, Zita followed. "Why are we wigging out? I mean, if it's time to panic and all, cool, but I'd like to know why?"

"Wait here." Wyn hustled toward the bouncer. Light haloed her face as she consulted with him. When she returned, she sank down on the curb and lowered her head in her hands. "He woke up. The door guard told me Boris and another man got into the pickup truck." Lowering her voice, she moaned, "Boris is going to be beaten to death because my spell was inadequate."

Zita patted her back a tentative time or two. The lights of occasional cars glowed in the distance, but this area was awash with the gaudy neon from the strip of bars and clubs. "Your spell was fine. Maybe a nap mellowed him or SWAT Ninja Man woke him." Warm pavement and lavender began to seep through the dissipating cigarette smoke and exhaust.

"Who?" The other woman looked up at her.

"The hot gunman in the alley." At the other woman's incredulous look, Zita blathered. "His clothing was all leather and bulletproof. He had to be melting. His ass was the best I've seen in a while, though. Right. I'll see what I can do." She strode back toward the alley, her eyes scanning for cameras. Hooking her thumbs in her waistband, she began to shuck her clothing before Wyn rushed up and grabbed her arm.

Stepping in front of her, Wyn asked, "What are you doing? They have minutes on us, and even an old car goes faster than a bird if they hit a highway. Even if you catch up, what will you do?"

Zita's mind raced. She had neglected to consider that. "Traffic could have delayed them. I'll follow and let you know where they're going." *Genius.*

Exasperation tinged Wyn's voice. "And then what? You're going to watch while they pound on Boris or worse? Do you think you can take that giant ball of fury?"

Her fingers stilled. "In a fair fight, no, he'd beat me any time. Fair fights are for show or for dead people. He might retreat from a jaguar or bear." Zita took a deep breath. She hated it when her friend was logical in her counterpoints, emphasizing how ill-conceived Zita's plans were in contrast.

"Great, assume he's frightened by exotic wildlife. What about the gun-toting assassin who has already beaten you once?" Releasing Zita's arm, Wyn folded her arms across her chest.

"No, I, no, we beat him. We rescued Boris from him and got what we wanted. He only caught Boris after the moron refused our help. So go us!" She did a lame fist pump in the air.

Wyn shook her head. "Perhaps, but he has what he wanted. How badly did you hurt him?"

Zita looked away. "I bruised him, and he's down one gun."

"Right, and I healed far more serious injuries than that on you." Wyn pointed a finger at Zita.

Zita put her clothes back on. "It's not about who beat up who worse. We achieved our goal first. Therefore, we won." She lifted her chin.

Wyn shook her head. "You couldn't stop them, even if you found them. At worst, you'd lose your life trying to help a slime who kidnaps people. That old dog won't hunt."

Tilting her head, Zita asked, "What dog?" She tucked the plastic bag with the gun under an arm to disguise the distinctive shape of a weapon.

Pink tinged her friend's face. Wyn rushed toward the mouth of the alley again. "Never you mind. How would your death help Quentin? Shouldn't we inform the authorities? What happened to just reporting our results?" The illusion her friend wore stood by the entrance to a closed business under a light, pale and shining and alone as she waited. Her eyes were dark and bottomless.

Zita gritted her teeth. "Have a seat. I'm going to call the missing persons cop to tell them that Boris knows something about the kidnap victims. Would you hand it to me?"

Wyn nodded and dug in her purse. After a moment, she pulled out a disposable phone, this one labeled with a blue smiley face sticker. She proffered it to Zita. Her elegant nose wrinkled as she eyed the confines of the alley. "I will stand watch. After that, shall we Metro home?"

"That's the plan. We'll hit my place for clothing. After that, I'll go scout the victim drop-off point to see if we can call in a tip on that too." Pressing the number Wyn had looked up earlier, Zita waited for a dispatcher.

Mild-mannered Wyn swore.

Chapter Fourteen

"**Why do I let you talk me into these things?** I could be home in bed with a book and hot cocoa," Wyn huffed. Panting, she tried to keep pace with Zita as they walked on the uneven sidewalk. When they reached the commons and left the circles of light to cross the darkened grass, she drew closer.

Thunder rumbled.

Without her illusion, Wyn's pretty face looked fretful as they entered another spot where the streetlights did not reach. A flowy shirt and matching capris in a deep rich blue hugged her slim form. At least the floral shoes had personality, even if regular running shoes would have been more practical than the odd heeled sneakers she wore.

Zita blinked. *Because I need to act.* "Because Quentin needs help, and you don't want me to destroy more of your clothes when I scout out that building? Plus, nobody will expect me to go home at midnight. I took off from Miguel's office before lunch. If I were on the run, I'd hit my place before they noticed I was missing, and then not come back." A fat drop of rain hit her nose. Her friend slowed even more as she picked her way across the grass, and reluctantly, Zita changed pace to match. *You'd think a person with legs up to her chin could walk faster.*

Tendrils of Wyn's hair sprung free from a bun with the movement. "Please, in the books, they go back like imbeciles, and that's when the psychotic killers spring their trap. I would have preferred to at least park closer so we could do a fast getaway."

"What? We only parked on the other end of the complex from my place. I still think we should have parked at the Metro. It's only a couple miles away, and your car would have blended in there. You'll see. We'll be in, and out, and nobody will notice a..." Zita let the words die, seeing the multitude of coruscating red and blue lights through the breezeway at the base of her stairs. She stopped, her fingers crinkling the bag with the gun. "Caramba." Her shoulders drew tight.

Wyn focused on the lights, then back on Zita. "You were saying? This is like a novel. If you insist on going there, we should teleport in. You can transfer us out afterward, and save us the walk in the rain." She stopped, putting her hands on her hips. Rain dotted her shirt like teardrops as a steady sprinkle began.

Police swarmed around the covered parking area. At the edge of the building, a crowd buzzed and shifted, unusual for her complex this late at night. Strobes flashed, the colors interrupting the steady illumination of the permanent security lights around the building. Uniformed officers stood in a sloppy semicircle, keeping the curious away. One or two officers even guarded the first floor breezeway, perhaps to stop people approaching from the commons, as Zita and Wyn were. All the apartments, except for Zita's, had lit windows. Seemingly all of the second floor residents had hauled out lawn chairs to their breezeway and sat, conversing and watching the drama. With envy, she noticed the spectators had snacks. Her stomach grumbled, echoed by another growl of thunder.

"If someone is in my apartment, they'd catch us, and I don't care to be killed or spend the rest of my life in a research facility... and if anyone knew about the teleporting, they'd probably just kill me," Zita answered, stepping forward for more details. Within the cordon, two nondescript SUVs shifted position, allowing in a coroner's van. A painful lump formed in her throat, and she swallowed, once, twice, convulsively. Her hand stroked over the dampness of the uneven hair on her head, back and forth, then dropped to vibrate at her side. "I need to know what's going on."

A firm grip seized her arm. Without thinking, Zita struck a pressure point on the other person's arm and was following through on an attack when she recognized the fabric.

Wyn let out a yelp and yanked her hand away. She rubbed at her arm. "Goddess. We need to go, can't stay here. Answers can wait until tomorrow." She looked up when another peal of thunder crashed.

Crossing her arms, Zita planted her feet. "Not if it's Quentin in the body bag," she forced out. "Sorry, I didn't realize it was you at first."

Even the poor light of the commons could not hide Wyn's change in expression from annoyed to understanding. "You're right. I'll be fine. Let's go talk to the officer on the breezeway, and I'll see what I can find out. Try not to seem so... well, like you want to punch someone." She smoothed her hair and sailed toward the officer.

In her wake, Zita forced one foot in front of another, and struggled to make her face more neutral and the bag more innocuous. She made it up to the breezeway in time to hear Wyn, who had angled herself to have protection from the water, questioning the stocky cop. Zita stopped several feet away, doing her best to ignore the rain soaking her clothing.

"I'm afraid I'm not at liberty to say, miss," the uniformed officer replied. He had been smart enough to stand under the overhang, out of the rain as well. "The parking lot is a crime scene, so you need to go around." Middle-aged, the cop had the set face of a pit bull, capable of either menace or loopy grins. Right now, he favored them with an expression between the two. Running did not look like of the cop's strengths, but Zita would have bet that he could walk all night in those polished shoes with the worn soles and scuff marks.

"Oh, we were taking a shortcut. My friend's had a bit much to drink so we're going to crash at a buddy's place." Long eyelashes lowered over hazel eyes, then stopped, and widened. "Do we need to be afraid to walk the rest of the way?" Wyn bit her lip.

Zita tried to appear drunk.

Even experienced pit bulls fell for puppy eyes. The cop shuffled his feet, glanced toward the lights, and lowered his voice. "You should be fine, miss. Nobody will try anything with all these people around, but you should hurry to your destination and stay inside. Your friend does look shaky. Do you need help? I can call someone."

Wyn simpered. "Oh, no, he's a building or two further up. We can manage." She stopped, and her hand flew up to her mouth. "Is that a coroner's van? Oh, what if it's John? Please, can you tell me? Please, don't let it be him! He's about our age, brown hair and blue eyes?" She touched the officer's sleeve, the picture of alarm.

Zita stared as tears welled in Wyn's eyes, uncertain if she was frightened or impressed by her friend's acting. "That would be bad," she agreed. She ran a hand over her head again and let her concern for Quentin show on her face. Her foot began vibrating on the pavement. "Can you tell us anything?"

The cop shook his head. "I'm sorry; I can't say anything about the victims. You ladies need to move on." He stared at Wyn's face as though hypnotized. His eyes followed one glistening tear, and he glanced toward the parking lot and back. His voice low, he said, "I don't think it's him."

Biting her lip again, Wyn nodded. "Thanks, officer." *It's not Quentin or Jennifer. Both corpses are too old.*

Tension eased in her shoulders, and her foot stopped the insistent tapping. Sensing the conversation was over, Zita nodded at the cop too. She took Wyn's arm and turned as if to go toward one of the other buildings when Andy came running around the corner. His eyes were dark and wild, and his clothing rumpled. The way he cocked his head to the side made him appear more avian than human. Something sparked in his eyes. Zita's stomach churned.

"John!" Wyn shrieked. Freeing herself, she ran forward and threw herself in his arms. "Let's go to your place."

Zita snuck a glance at the cop. He looked relieved. She hurried up to the others and hugged Andy. He gave them both a hug that started out painful, then became tentative. She whispered, "Yes, John, we should go to your place before he realizes you don't match the description she gave." The eyes that looked back at her changed from one blink to the next from black to the familiar chocolate of her friend. He gave a slight nod.

His arms encircling their waists, Andy whipped around to present his back to the cop. They proceeded down a couple buildings and ducked into a breezeway. He leaned against a wall and exhaled. "I thought you were dead," he whispered. "Oh, God, I'm probably going to get so many tickets. They announced on the radio that two people were found dead in your complex, and given all the messages you left today..." He swallowed.

Wyn shook her head. "We've been in plenty of trouble today, but we're both alive for now. Zita has a plan to change that later."

"I'm glad—wait, what?" Andy said. He regarded them. "Does this have to do with why you were on TV earlier?"

Zita sniffed. "Let's not talk about this here." She scanned the area.

Wyn wheeled and stared at her. "You were on television and didn't tell me? I think we should go to your place. Maybe you can sniff any intruders out as an animal before they see us."

"What was that part about dying later? Some guy was offering a reward, and she was in the background. You couldn't even see her cranky little face most of the time. Miguel looked pissed when he finished speaking and saw she was gone, though." Andy asked. A second later, he mumbled. "Do you know your pants have an enormous rip?"

Wyn giggled. "Sorry, my bad. I forgot I should have been covering that."

"Yes. Thanks." Zita raised her hands in the air in surrender. "Fine. Break me out of that research facility if they catch us." She scrabbled at her clothing to get it off.

Andy's mouth tilted up as he turned to face the faded brick wall. "I figure you'd get upset at the gym facilities and break us out." Wyn nodded in agreement.

Zita grinned. "Verdad. You can count on me. Stay put until I let you know it's safe to move." She shifted, choosing a German Shepherd dog. The explosion of scents that greeted her nose, and the sounds that teased her ears, made up for what her vision lost in color. When she finished, she nosed Andy's hand.

He scratched behind her ears after he turned around. Wyn had already picked up the clothing and bag. When both had their hands in the black ruff of her chosen form, Zita pictured her equipment closet. Other than her gear, the closet was empty, though a lingering scent revealed an intruder had been by the door earlier. Her instincts guessed today, but she could not have said why. The apartment smelled empty and silent. *Open the door for me, quiet and slow.*

Someone—Andy, she noted, as moonlight crept inside to verify what her nose was telling her—eased the door open, and she slipped through. Since her snout was giving her more information than anything else, she let it guide her around the apartment. After two circuits, she growled. *Safe now, but someone checked the place out earlier, including all the closets. I was right to be cautious. Leave the lights off just in case.* Shifting to herself, Zita dressed in the darkest clothing she could find, using the heavy Maglite she normally stashed under the head of her bed next to a knife. With the aid of the flashlight, she dug through a box. She raised her fist in the air in triumph when she located the only mask she owned. When she returned, the clothing and bag were in a heap on the floor of the empty closet. Since she could hear her friends talking in another room, she shrugged and hid the gun inside one of the fake plants in the exercise room. A thought sent her scurrying to grab a camping lantern, after which she joined the others. The soft murmur of Wyn's voice led her to them.

Familiar with her habits, Andy and Wyn waited at the table in the kitchen. Lighting the lantern, she set it on the table with the flashlight and went to the fridge for food. Zita let Wyn take the brunt of the storytelling, though she interrupted to add details.

Musing aloud, Andy commented, "He sounds like Snake Eyes. Did he talk?"

"Very little," Zita answered. She turned and set the sandwich fixings on the table, padding to a drawer to get plates and knives.

"Oh, can't be him then," Andy answered. After foraging through her supplies, he picked up the peanut butter and bread. His mouth kept twitching up.

Curiosity piqued, Zita asked, "You knew a ninja who went by Snake Eyes?" Wyn coughed, so Zita whacked her friend on the back before hurling herself into a chair. With a hummus base, she began building a real sandwich.

Mirth danced in his eyes, visible even by lantern light. "Uh, when I was young" he said. He and Wyn exchanged a look over Zita's head and burst into laughter.

"You have more interesting friends than I thought," Zita said. *Is Snake Eyes single, you think?* She narrowed her eyes. *What is the hilarity for?*

He snickered again. "So, then what happened?"

Choosing to focus on her sandwich, Zita let Wyn continue the narration. When she finished construction, she sliced it in half and picked it up, only then realizing how silent the room had become. She looked up and met two pairs of eyes. "What?"

"Will that even fit in your mouth, my hobbit friend?" Andy asked.

Zita eyed it. Saliva warmed in her mouth. "Hobbit? Never mind. I've had bigger, but this will do the job for now." She began eating.

Both of the others snickered.

She blinked and swallowed. *Poor word choice in front of the perverts.* "Why are you my friends again? So did you get to whose bodies are in my parking spot?"

As she wiped a tear of laughter from her eyes, Wyn answered, "I was reaching that when we noticed the gastronomic monstrosity you built." She swiped a carrot stick in a dab of hummus and nibbled.

Zita rolled her eyes. Her tone held no animosity. "Listen up, I ran, fought, and shifted tonight, one of those forms being a bird. Do you know how many calories flying burns? Me neither, but based on how hungry I am and general zoological principles, it was a heap. So the corpse wasn't my brother?" Her fingers tightened on the sandwich. Hummus seeped out the other end.

Andy looked from one woman to the other. In a typical move, he elected to eat his sandwich rather than get involved.

Wyn declined to answer Zita's less important questions. "The first corpse was a deceased male with graying hair, a heavy build, and multiple tattoos. My policeman friend out there identified a couple prison tattoos mixed with regular ones on both him and the second corpse, a heavyset middle-aged female. Does that sound like your brother or his date? It doesn't match the pictures you have."

Reassured, Zita nodded and took a bite of her sandwich. After she chewed, she answered. "The pictures are recent. Quentin's two tattoos are both from his service. He said any future ones would have to beat the Marines, and nobody does that. Jennifer is in her thirties and thin."

Wyn nodded, her face sobering. "The policeman focused more on the state of the corpses than a description of what they used to be. Someone murdered and mutilated those poor people, but he was uncertain of the order in which those events occurred. He did not want two inebriated girls contaminating the crime scene or being scarred by it." She sent another carrot stick through the puddle of hummus on her plate, and finished it, pushing the plate away. "Here's what the dead man's head looked like." She held out her hand, and a small illusion appeared of a man's head and shoulders.

Squelching her squeamishness, Zita forced herself to examine the image. Recognition took a moment given the condition of the face. "It's Brains! He was at the zoo and came after me here." Her food turned sour in her mouth, and she set it down.

"Someone did a number on his face," Wyn murmured, "but the rest of his body was worse." The image disappeared. She repeated with a woman's face, banishing it when Zita shook her head.

Zita flexed her fingers, guilt flooding through her. "The damage to his jaw was me. The missing ears and other injuries were someone else." She rubbed her hair.

"So what's the next step?" Andy asked.

"I'll verify illegal activity at the address Wyn got from Boris' mind. Then, we call the cops and report the address and our suspicions about kidnap victims. Pues, I should call Miguel too about seeing my complex on the news and a dead body. It's possible he can tell us more." The odds were against him telling a civilian, even his sister, but she had to hear his voice. She didn't know if Wyn was listening or not, but both of the others stared at their mismatched plates. Zita retrieved her cell phone from Wyn's bag, sliding the battery back into the phone... and ran a finger over her sandwich, her stomach protesting the cessation of food. *I will be back for you, my delicious.* After a tap on the keys, she held the phone to her ear. *Say the words.*

Despite the late hour, her brother answered on the second ring. "Garcia. Talk to me."

Zita exhaled, tension loosening in her chest that she had not even realized she held. "Miguel, what's going on? The news story of the hour is about dead bodies at my apartment complex."

"I can't tell you much, but it's not Quentin or Miss Stone. Are you safe?" Concern laced Miguel's voice.

Zita nodded, forgetting he could not see her. "Yes, I'm secure enough. What's going on?"

"They found bodies in your parking spot but have yet to release a cause of death or anything. What I've heard sounds like murder." He exhaled.

She sniffed. "At least my bike doesn't have dead guy all over it since it's in impound. I don't suppose Quentin's turned up? Maybe he and Jen wandered into a hospital suffering from sexcapade-induced amnesia?"

Wyn perked up, no doubt eager to go home. Andy shook his head and left the room with the flashlight.

Miguel sighed into the phone. Papers crackled. "No. Don't ask what's going on with the case. I can't tell you anything, other than Ms. Stone's father hired a private company to search as well once he finished his ill-advised reward offer."

"What can you tell me?" She shook her head at Wyn, who deflated and poked at a carrot.

"Zita, I couldn't tell you any more even if I knew it. As of an hour ago, I'm off the case. Between Quentin's disappearance, the attempt on you, and the unknown victims in your complex, my superiors have decided it's a conflict of interest for me to remain on the case." Miguel's voice reflected her frustration.

She paced. "That idiot Parzarri's not in charge, is he? He was acting like Quentin was a criminal." Upon returning, Andy set her laptop on the table with exaggerated care, opened it, and began tapping keys. He whispered to Wyn, whose answer was indistinct.

"He was exercising due diligence." Miguel's voice sounded as unconvinced as she felt. "Parzarri isn't in charge of the case, but he's a full detective and investigating."

"So do you need to go back to Bumble?"

Her brother gave a disgruntled snort. "No, I'm assigned to consult on cold cases. My boss knows how important it is for me to be in the area for you and Quentin. I have to go home once it's resolved, or if it goes cold, but he bought me time to be here. Are you safe at your friend's place?"

Truthfully, she replied, "It's safe. I'm going back after this." *Once I check Boris' drop-off address for Quentin.* The amendment could only be mental for her brother's continued heart health.

Miguel paused, then issued orders, proving the universe still spun, even with Quentin missing. "Be aware of your surroundings, and lock the doors. Check in with me tomorrow. Go rest."

A raspberry into the phone expressed her feelings far better than words could. "I love you too. Any other morsels of wisdom, macho?" She ran her finger through the hummus on her plate.

He paused. As if he could not resist, he threw in his favorite bit of advice with his farewells. "Take one of those stun guns I gave you everywhere. I love you too. Goodnight."

She laughed and hung up, sucking hummus off her finger. Her mirth ran out as she took the battery out of the phone and hid both in the ornate box by the front door. "Right, so the plan is on." When she returned to the table, she started on her food again. Wyn shook her head, watching the sandwich disappear.

Andy proved his attention was not completely on the laptop or the dishes he set by the sink. "You hid your phone in the box with all the novelty condoms?" He snickered.

Zita shrugged, hating the defensive tone in her voice. "I wanted it near the door, and that was handy. It's not as if I'll move it any time soon with the losers Miguel and... and Quentin have been sending me." Her throat tightened at her brother's name, and she choked. "Bit of food, sorry."

Andy set down his glass, compassion radiating from his eyes. "I can't believe Quentin's been kidnapped. Did you know he still came to the hospital to see us after you left for Brazil?"

Her eyes teared up, and Zita sniffed. "Horseradish is strong, just warning you," she claimed. "That's so like him." She took another bite, despite her complaint.

Wyn nodded, her eyes misty. "He knew how to kiss even then."

"You kissed my brother?" Zita made a face.

Her friend nodded. "Yes, both of them."

She choked again, this time on a bite of food. "Wait, what?"

A teasing grin flirted across Wyn's lips. "I'll tell you about it another time." She pulled out the pencils securing her hair and finger-combed it.

Andy looked between them. "I didn't kiss anyone in your family, if that helps," he proffered.

Zita shook a finger at Wyn, opened her mouth, then closed it again. "I'm not certain I want to know how you ended up kissing my brothers." She chomped on her sandwich while the other woman smirked.

"Fine by me," Wyn said.

After clearing her throat, Zita nodded. "Right, I've got to get going." She stared at her plate. The red dish sat empty, except for a few crumbs and parsley. Munching on the garnish, she deposited the plate in the boring white sink.

Andy nodded, sympathy still on his face. "For the record, I'd like to state this is a bad idea."

"I've only one mask for the three of us, so I need to go alone unless you know a place selling masks at one in the morning," Zita said, assuming that would forestall any debate. When she pulled the mask from her pocket, she spun it on a finger by the elastic. The black plastic mask only covered her eyes and part of her cheekbones, but it would work well enough when combined with the altered face and hair she had used earlier.

Pinning her hair back up with a pencil, Wyn speared her with her gaze. "You're not going alone. If we have to, I'll wear the mask, and you can go in animal form. We can talk mentally, or Andy can go. He's bulletproof and only needs a way to escape. If you hide nearby, you can teleport you and him here."

Andy's head swung left and right between them and the computer. The sounds of his tapping on the keys gained speed and strength. He shook his head again.

"I hate not doing anything," Zita objected. She gathered up leftover food and put it away, the wash of cold from the fridge a welcome respite from the sticky air of her apartment. Filling a water bottle from the sink, she sipped the lukewarm liquid and planned, checking hydration off the lists of needs to fill.

Andy interrupted before they could argue. "Go get dark T-shirts. The miracle of the Internet will teach us Padawan how to create ninja masks from them. We can all go. Zita can teleport us to this traffic cam, and back here when we're done. We'll take my car from here to wherever we want to call the police. I'm not getting left behind, or going in alone." His lips twitched into a smile, a lock of hair falling over one eye.

"Pada-what? The Internet isn't just for porn and shopping? Seriously?" Zita answered. "Huh. Ninja masks are cool. You don't have to go at all. I'll meet you back at your place tonight later, Wyn, so I can rest unless I'm followed. If I'm being chased, I'll shift and sleep hidden as an animal and call you in the morning." Staying away would keep her friends safer.

Even as he enlarged the pictures on-screen, Andy ignored her. "We're in. You're not doing this alone." He muttered about contagious stupidity, but Zita elected to pretend she had not heard.

Wyn shook her head. "We will all go. Andy and I will hide close by, and you will slink around—"

"Scout," Zita corrected.

With a raised eyebrow, Wyn continued. "Fine, sneak around to verify they are performing illegal activities. As soon as you have information we can use to entice the cops, you return, and we leave. I'll wear the mask. Fighting's not my forte, and I'll have my illusion anyway. It'll be my alternate cover if I get too distracted."

Spinning the laptop around, Andy tapped a grainy image. "This is a few blocks from where we want to go. Think it'll work, Zita? What am I doing in your plan, Wyn?"

"You're backup. If anything goes wrong, you go in for Zita, and I'll use an illusion to distract them." Wyn paused and tilted the lamp to shine more light on the petite Latina. "Are those pants purple?"

Zita glanced down and smoothed the cotton on her legs. They seemed fine to her. "Oh, I guess so. They're dark, and I can move in them. The only issue is they don't have pockets, which is why I dug out this old fanny pack. It should be small enough so you can carry it for me." She pulled the laptop closer and peered at the screen. Buildings in the sort of neighborhood specializing in desperation, she assessed. The smeared, uncertain gang sign visible on one wall served as a usable landmark, though.

Wyn protested. "They're purple."

"Camera looks workable." With a grimace, Zita checked her pants. "They're dark purple. Why, do I need to change them? I found black ones, but they have sequins."

Andy patted her hand. "There, there. Wear the purple sweatpants. It's a scientific fact that the purple ones have the most stretch." He made an odd face, between a sneeze and a smile.

Zita pursed her lips. "You realize that makes no sense, right?" Remembering his aversion to people pointing at him, she turned the finger she had been about to point at him into a hand wave.

He shrugged. Andy bit his lip, and his eyes crinkled at the corners. "It's science. One of those things, I guess."

Wyn gave a dramatic exhale. She rubbed her eyes and covered a yawn. "Are there many sequins?"

"It's a phoenix pattern from ankle to thigh on both legs. I like them, but I thought they'd be too distinctive. Oh, and the pants are leather, so not good for this weather." Zita shrugged.

Wyn winced and buried her face in her hands. "Right. Purple sweatpants it is. I'm not even going to talk about the fanny pack. Sartorial decisions aside, let's finalize a plan, and you two can construct masks. Go get those shirts."

"How many do you think I have? Is orange dark enough?"

The answer was a unanimous "No!"

Chapter Fifteen

Bargain basement ninja masks in place, the trio hid in the shadows of a narrow lane between a building and a fence that was probably meant to be a driveway. Lingering scrapes marred the walls with previous drivers' carelessness.

The building they watched was a duplex in a neighborhood that had suffered a bad economic downturn. Most gangs might consider even perfunctory territory battles excessive, and prostitutes and dealers had more convenient and profitable places to be. Many of the stoops sat empty, save for trash, and tattered foreclosure notices hung on multiple doors or boarded-up entry holes. A grimy tricycle, missing a wheel, hung from one rusty railing as if it had tried to jump. The occasional scuttle from inside a building suggested the presence of life, but most of the inhabitants hid. Another driveway went down the side of the target building, and disappeared behind the duplex itself, a house converted into two residences. The basement windows were boarded over, and no light escaped the windows on the ground and second floors.

"I have to say it or explode. I have a bad feeling about this," Wyn whispered. She bit her lip and huddled closer to the dubious shelter of the fence. The silvery hair of her illusion practically glowed even in the poor light.

Andy sighed. "Now we're doomed. Never say that," he hissed back.

For people sneaking around, they talk too much. Wyn keeps trying to stand under the feeble streetlights, too. Zita made a mental note to make a top ten list of ways to improve sneakiness, with limited talking at the top of the chart. Second on the list would be choosing disguises that did not include glitter or light colors. Wyn's dress actually sparkled even in the dim light. She pulled her sweaty mask away from her face, but the muggy air offered little respite. Letting it fall back into place, she inched toward the street. In an undertone, she said, "If you're out, wait in that fast food place while I search for Quentin. Hide behind the roaches—they'll scare off any robbers. I can do this. With any luck, they're all asleep, and I'll be back in ten minutes."

"Stop trying to weasel out of having us here," Andy answered, his voice almost inaudible. "We're fine, just hurry. At what point have we had the sort of luck that would make this go smoothly?"

Regardless of her unhappy expression, Wyn agreed. "Keep us updated." She folded her arms across her chest and rubbed her arms, despite the oppressive humidity.

Zita sighed. *Fine. Focus on not being seen and not talking aloud.* Stored heat seeped through the thin soles of her shoes from the rough concrete sidewalk. Eyes adjusted to the partial darkness, she verified the street was empty, then darted across and into the alley masquerading as a driveway beside the target house. Her nose wrinkled, and she shut her mouth, grateful for the thin barrier of the shirt. Warmed pavement was acceptable, but the stench of urine, putrefying food, and rotten eggs was overwhelming. *This place stinks.*

You should have used your cat form. It would have been easier, and I like your cat shape. It's so... fluffy and huggable. Wyn's laughter resonated over the link.

Andy's soft chuckle resounded mentally. *Yes, it's like having a tame cat.*

Wyn seemed to be having fun at Zita's expense. *Tame cats are mythological. Cats only humor you until they get what they want. Zita in feline shape comes close, though.*

Andy's tone was amused. *I bow before the cat expert. It is true, we don't suffer through the cat butt hello as much when Zita turns feline. Remember when we got her chasing the laser pointer?*

Zita had the mental impression of both of the others laughing. *Focus, haters.* As she padded up the overgrown drive and toward the back of the house, a car rumbled nearby. Lights flared on the street. Relocating to the front, she did a low vault onto the narrow porch, lying down to prevent detection. She suppressed a shiver. A few seconds later, a car careened down the stingy driveway, lights cutting out as it pulled up behind the house.

Car. Wyn's mental voice warned.

Sarcasm dripped as Zita levered herself up with her arms. *Thanks, I noticed.* With a cautious audit to ensure no other oncoming vehicles, she scurried after the car. A dark SUV rattled as it settled down, throwing off heat, while an old Mustang sat quiescent beside it. Despite the fabric tacked up over the duplex windows, two on the first floor leaked light that puddled in the parking lot comprising the entire back yard. An ancient shed squatted in the last bit of space in the yard. The other windows were closed tight, with no light or sound escaping. Stealing near, Zita hid behind a dented trashcan on that side of the house as a car door opened, and footsteps crunched across the gravel to the door. Rotten eggs, chemicals, and sickness overpowered all other scents here, overriding even the odiferous remnants of spoiled Chinese food in the trash. She peeked around the corner of the house. Blond hair haloed a tall man's head. He exchanged a few words with another man inside the building before stepping in. The door shut. The blond man's body and movement looked familiar. *I'm going to get closer and see if I can eavesdrop.*

Leaving the dubious safety of the garbage bin behind, Zita sped across the yard to leap from the roof of the Mustang to the top of the SUV. Once there, she unzipped her fanny pack and pulled her spray chalk. *This is a public service announcement, so when they inevitably hit someone or something, investigators know who's what.* She smirked.

What? Wyn asked.

I am marking the vehicle, per your suggestion, so we can identify it from a distance. Zita snickered. Standing near the edge of the vehicle, she checked her work. The word ASS stood out in white letters on the roof. "My work here is done," she whispered, somersaulting off the car on the side opposite the house. She shadowed up the cement stairs and crouched under the windowsill closest to where the blond had entered the house.

Andy's mental voice held concern. Wyn echoed him a second later. *Be careful.*

Someone inched the windows open for air, and the murmur of conversation and a methodical scratching sound teased Zita's ears. Her vision was limited to a narrow strip where the sheet over the window did not completely meet the frame. Inside, a short man in a surgical mask scraped at matches. He sat at a table covered in pots, pans, and assorted paraphernalia more suited to a science lab than a room with a border of roosters and a dancing pig potholder. Two of his fingers were shorter than the others. Canisters were lined up on the table beside with one of those miniature brown refrigerators she had not seen since college. A door (*basement stairs, perhaps?*) hung open behind him, a bare bulb burning. *Wrong window. This one's either making drugs or into hardcore cooking.*

Both of her friends made disgusted noises in her mind.

Zita moved to the window on the side of the house, noting with disgust that she was just a few inches too short. After a moment, she stretched to the windowsill, and pulled her body up to bring herself enough to peek inside through a gap in the makeshift curtain. She prayed the neglected window frame would hold her weight. Now she was closer, she picked up the thread of the conversation inside. This window faced into a cluttered dining room/living room combination where worn easy chairs, apparently retrieved from the trash, fought for floor space in front of a massive flat screen television. Discarded beer cans and an empty pizza box gave the whole scene a festive slob party air.

Their voices low, people moved inside, and she caught glimpses of a man she did not recognize before the dangerous blond man paced into view. She froze. *It's one of Jones' bodyguards.* He held an envelope in his hand, striking it on his khaki-clad leg as he listened. A shoulder handgun rig rode openly over a plain black shirt, one tight enough to confirm her earlier impression of muscular shoulders and a trim chest. She would have enjoyed the view had the circumstances been different.

Andy asked, *Jones?*

Miguel suspects he is a serial killer. He had a pair of bodyguards, and this looks like the more competent one. The subject of their speculation turned and paced away, exposing a glimpse of a hefty knife belted at his waist, and a firm derriere. *It's a shame. The man is built.*

Wyn snorted. *We're the ones who need to focus?*

The bodyguard frowned. "Where are your guards?" His voice held an accent—South African, she guessed.

Stepping into view, the other man set down a dingy blue refrigerated lunch bag on a small laminate table near the window. He was average in height, weight, and fitness, she judged, with a sullen mouth and hard eyes, framed by stringy brown hair. His thumb gave a sulky jerk toward the kitchen.

Taking a deep breath, setting a hand on his belt, and scowling, the blond bodyguard said, "He seems otherwise occupied."

His companion cracked open a beer. "I sent the rest upstairs after you got here so we could have privacy. Don't worry, Pretorius, he's multitasking. When he starts cooking, I'll get someone else. The new pink ice sells mad good and for three times the amount of the regular kind. For that scratch, we don't need a distracted or tweaked cook. The others are resting up before their shifts." He held out the beer to the bodyguard.

The blond—Pretorius—grunted in negation as he turned back, staring at the alcohol. "The operation should have dedicated guards at all times, especially when you've got guests downstairs. No drinking on duty, either. Make the change. Are the samples in the bag?" He nodded at the lunch bag.

Nodding, other man said, "Yes, the blood is in there. I threw in a small bag of the best of the pink ice too. That shit turned out almost red." He licked his lips and set the beer down.

Pretorius acknowledged the comment and flicked another glance at the man patiently shaving matches in the next room. "Why is he in a surgical mask? Was there a spill?"

"Oh, him? He's paranoid. The guest you came to pick up? She's been running a high fever, and he's worried he'll catch it. Don't worry, we dosed her with extra sleep juice, and that brings it down. Figure it'll break soon." The drug dealer waved Pretorius' concern away with his hand.

Carajo. Some woman they're holding is sick. That might be why Jen's dad was frantic.

Flaxen eyebrows climbed. Pretorius swore in a patois Zita did not recognize, but she understood the tone. Her ears buzzed, and she shook her head to clear it.

When Pretorius ran out of invectives, he let the other man know his opinion in plainer language. "You lot may kill her or make her brain damaged if you've given her that much. The point of taking and keeping them healthy is to maximize profit. Take an extra blood sample and dispose of her. Don't waste any more drugs."

"Shit. That's how they brought her to us. We were trying to keep the merchandise ready to go. She'll be fine when it goes down." The drug dealer ran a hand over his greasy scalp and propped his other hand on his hip. He seemed ready to continue when the bodyguard speared him with a flat, cold gaze.

"Dead or brain-damaged has no value. If she infects the others, we'll go from being short on what was promised to no shipment." Pretorius' voice dropped, and Zita had to press her ear against the window for the next few words. "Do you want to explain that to our buyers or to Sobek?"

His face pallid, his scruffy companion shook his head. Sweat beaded on his brow. "No... No, sir."

Pretorius nodded.

Zita eased down from the window and flattened against the side of the house, shaking out her stiff arms. *We need to get her out before they kill her.* The other two sent their assent, with Wyn's wavering. Her stomach churned. *Is Quentin one of the others she could infect?* After catching hold of the window, she pulled herself back up to continue watching.

The drug dealer stared at the empty television screen and took a deep breath. "Look. I don't have a problem getting rid of her, but we've been using blood samples from the prisoners to make the pink ice. The cost of the drugs is nothing compared to what we're raking in. Regular blood won't work like theirs. Can we keep her until her condition requires too much care or we get another group to use for the pink shit?"

She recoiled. *Eww. They're making a drug using blood from people. They're storing people in the basement.*

Wyn's tone was bitter. *This keeps getting better and better, kidnapped people, drugs, and Soylent Green. I refuse to discuss the unhygienic nature of that or the blood-borne disease vectors that creates.*

We have to help the captives. Andy's tone was somber.

Pretorius tapped his fingers on the oversized knife affixed to his leg. After a moment, he withdrew a phone from his pant pocket. "That's the secret ingredient? Interesting. Perhaps you can keep her for a few days then. I'll check with Sobek, but my advice is to kill her." He sent a quick text, then pocketed the phone. He glared at the other man. "The passage between buildings is upstairs? I'll go

Karen Diem

explain the change in procedures to your men, then evaluate the amount of trouble keeping the woman will cause."

The drug dealer nodded, tension easing out of his shoulders. "Aiight," he answered, the slang term marking him as a local. "She's due for another hit soon anyway. This way." He ambled out of sight.

As soon as Pretorius followed him, Zita dropped to the ground. *Andy, I'm going to need your help. If Jen's unconscious with this fever or the tranquilizers they've been giving her, you may need to carry her. I'll check the basement of the place on the right first, and switch to the left if she's not there. The back door will be unlocked so you can slip inside and join me.* When she stepped near to the darkened door, she pulled out her spare picks, blessing the urge that had prompted her to bring them. Within a few seconds, the door clicked open.

Andy's tone was brisk. *On my way.*

I'll follow in case I need to heal the poor girl. Wyn's empathetic nature had kicked in.

Opening the door as little as possible, Zita slid into the blackness of the kitchen next door. The glow of several cell phones charging provided the only illumination. After appropriating a phone, she clutched it to her chest and continued a few more steps. With the assumption that this kitchen was a mirror image of the lit one on the other side, Zita snuck to where she thought the door would be. When she found a handle, she pulled. Light and cold air engulfed her as she stared into an old fridge filled with test tubes of blood, junk food, and colorful banded bundles of cash. With an internal sigh, she held the fridge open so she could use the light to find the basement door. *Not completely symmetrical row houses.* She closed the appliance.

When she tried easing the basement door open, it stuck. Creaking sounded from upstairs or next door. Zita ran her fingertips over the lock until she felt the bump of the thumb turn. After unlocking it, utter darkness challenged her. Fumbling with the unfamiliar phone, she turned it on and used the light from the screen to see into the basement. Paint flaked under her hand as she touched the metal rail leading down one side of the bare wooden stairs. The basement held an ancient furnace, a fuse box, a table with scattered medical paraphernalia, and two cots. Exposed pipes and wiring ran the ceiling and unfinished walls while the floor had the cool solidity of cement underfoot. A human form shifted on one cot, moving beneath a thin cover.

"Jen Stone? Is that you?" She hurried over to the motionless form. The warmth emanating from the unconscious person, even through the blanket, was alarming. *Hurry, I think she needs a hospital.* Steeling herself, she turned the person onto their back and pushed the phone close to the face. Greeted by familiarity, Zita gasped. Not who she had expected. *It's Aideen! The sick woman is Aideen.*

Surprise came through the link with her friends. *I'm heading in now.* Andy wasted no time.

Zita's brain offered an alternative to a fever, and she felt herself go pale. *We need to get her somewhere safe and nonflammable before she wakes.*

Sounding puzzled, Wyn followed Andy's lead. *Of course.*

A loud thud sounded upstairs. Wood creaked.

When she went to drag Aideen away, something prevented her from moving far. The light of the phone revealed handcuffs holding the cop to the bed. "Ironic, and I don't have the right tools for this," she muttered. She tucked the phone into her cleavage, struggling to work with the weak light glowing through her shirt. Pulling her smallest pick, she set to work on the restraints.

Aideen's eyes fought their way open, pupils dilated and unfocused. She made a querulous noise.

"You were kidnapped. I'm trying to rescue you. Be quiet so I can free you," Zita murmured, slipping into her Mexican accent. The last thing she needed was Aideen to recognize her. The ceiling creaked again. Her eyes focused upward. "You'd think he'd know how to walk quietly since he knows serious martial arts." As the captive's eyes slid shut again, Zita pulled off the blanket to better reach the other cuff.

As the second one released, the door at the top of the stairs opened, and the light clicked on. Tears sprang to her eyes at the sudden light, and she turned partially toward the stairs to give Andy a piece of her mind. Instead, startled, Pretorius and his drug-dealing companion stared at her as they reached the bottom of the stairs. The bodyguard dropped into a combat-ready crouch closer to the furnace; his drug dealer companion opened and closed his mouth. Zita touched her face—the fabric of her mask met her fingers. "Oh, hey, how you doing?" she delayed, inserting a genial tone to her voice. Zita fiddled with Aideen's blanket to cover her movements as she surreptitiously slid the lock pick back into her fanny pack, keeping turned away. The fake Mexican accent had thickened as well. Other people had comfort food or lucky clothing; she had a cheesy accent. *Go figure.* She would have to remember that any last words would be unintelligible due to it. Straightening, she faced her opponents, with Aideen at her increasingly sweaty back.

Pretorius started to go for his gun but paused. He straightened. The dealer stared at her and stumbled over to stand next to the tense bodyguard. Zita liked the way he was in Pretorius' path if the big man chose to charge her.

"So," she stalled, injecting a cheerful note into her voice. Zita smoothed her pants, wiping sweat off her hands. "I'm collecting for the Ninja Widows and Orphans Fund and was trying to see if the lady wanted to contribute. She seems to be a deep sleeper, so would you be interested in donating in her place? Cash only, please." *Hurry, Andy, I have company. Two men, the tall blond one moves like a soldier. The other is a street brawler, and they both have guns.*

The big blond man sighed. "I'm not paid enough for this."

The drug dealer scoffed. "A Mexican ninja? There's no such thing."

Zita sniffed. "Of course, there is. No one has seen us, because, duh, we're ninja. That's our thing. Makes it hard to collect for charity, though." Despite the precariousness of the situation, she grinned under her mask. *Two guys cornered me in an enclosed space, and they both have reach on me. Andy? Where are you, mano?* The fierce heat at her back reminded her she might have other backup if the other woman woke. That or another problem.

"This is why I called your security pathetic," Pretorius said in a calm tone. "If this nut job—"

"Ninja," Zita interrupted, enjoyment easing awake. It was wrong. It was dangerous. But it was fun.

"Can get in, your security needs serious work," he finished.

Busy. Andy's thought echoed on the mental connection.

Brows lowered, the drug dealer continued to gawk at Zita, and drew his gun.

Pretorius slapped the gun down without taking his eyes from her. "Unless you have rubber bullets in there, no, not with what you've got on the other side of that wall, you idiot."

Most of the time I wish people would take me seriously. Now someone is, and I wish he wouldn't. Also, chalk up another idiot who doesn't know how to hold his gun. Does no one know how to handle a firearm these days? She held her hands in the air, a corner of the blanket hanging from one hand. "Don't mind me. Let each other know how you really feel. That shit's good for the soul. I got time."

The drug dealer holstered his gun and pulled out a switchblade. It was a sad and dingy little thing compared to the massive combat knife the other man had belted at his waist.

Never one to let an opportunity pass by, Zita held a hand to her mouth, as if shielding it from Pretorius. "Hombre, you might want to put that away. It doesn't look right next to the knife porn he's got going on," Zita stage whispered, pointing a finger at Pretorius' compensation toy. *Andy? You coming?*

"How many of you are there?" Pretorius demanded.

The drug dealer followed her finger to Pretorius' knife, then back at his own. He seemed... sheepish.

Fighting... Trying not to kill anyone. Andy sent, distraction in his tone. *Stay... alive.*

Aideen stirred behind her. *You too.* Zita shifted position to hide the motion, mind whirling. The dealer would lose it soon; she would keep up the absurdity until then. If he blocked Pretorius from getting to her, her chances improved. "Ninjas? No one knows. It is one of the many mysteries of my people. The problem with counting ninja is someone always sneaks off and hides, and then jumps out to get the census taker. Then they have to start again later because you have to have a massive kung fu fight at that point. Anyone within a mile has to join in. It's required. In the bylaws even." *It has to be wrong to enjoy this so much.*

Pretorius pinched his forehead again as if the pain would aid him. "Right, a comedian. Why is she not already down and giving us answers... or dead?" He shrugged at his sidekick.

"She sounds like she's on the pink crystal," the drug dealer commented. "I don't believe in Mexican ninjas." He was sweating more than Zita was, she noticed, although she had the excuse of standing in front of the human furnace.

"How many of you are in the building?" Pretorius asked.

Zita tried prodding. "Oye, pendejo, the proof is standing in front of you. How dumb you got to be to ignore what's right in front of your face?" She angled her body to present less of a target and scanned the room. Another thud sounded upstairs.

"I can see the tag on the shirt you used for your mask. Real ninjas don't have wash instructions on their head," the drug dealer argued.

Zita resisted the urge to check for a tag, but it was close. She blinked. "Why do you think we need a fundraiser?" Her fingers itched to check.

"Enough humor. How many of you are in the building right now?" Pretorius ground out his question, followed by a glance up at another noise from above.

The drug dealer's face was a mix of emotions, and she wished he would choose an action. "It's just me unless others are horning in on my territory. If they are, they're hiding because, you know, sneaky bastards. So are you going to donate or what?" Another thud sounded, this one accompanied by a shriek.

When their eyes flicked upward, she tossed the blanket at the drug dealer, using him as cover to get to the stairs. Zita leapt, grabbing the rail and pulling herself up. She slid under the banister and came to her feet on the stairs. *Need to keep them from killing Aideen.* "I'll collect that donation for you," she suggested as she took the stairs two at a time. When she reached the top, she glanced around the barren kitchen, deciding at last to slip behind the door. The light from below was enough to keep her from having to work blind.

Heavy footfalls raced up behind her.

When a shadowy shape appeared in the crack between the door and the frame, she slammed it into his face, once, twice, then a third time.

Whoever she hit fell with a series of exclamations and thuds as they tumbled down the steep stairs.

She grinned at the swearing. *Distraction outside, coming up.* After confiscating two cash bundles from the fridge, she ran across the kitchen and flung open the back door. *If you're out back, get out or hide well, Wyn, and not near the cars.*

Feet pounded up the stairs, and the door exploded open. If she had still been behind it, she might have been seeing little birds, or pies, or whatever one saw when concussed. Birds were interesting, but pie had more appeal. Pretorius, blood smeared on his shoulder, panted at the top of the stairs.

"Oh, hey. How's it going? I got your donation, thanks," Zita said lightly, fanning herself with the money. To further annoy him, she tucked one block into her fanny pack in slow motion. The wall connecting to the other half of the duplex shuddered, and wailing began, a panicked, high-pitched sound.

I'm in the living room. Where is the basement? Nervousness trembled in Wyn's words.

"Take off your clothes! Wash it off!" a man—it sounded like Andy—shouted through the wall.

Zita's smile dropped off. She had to get her friends out of the house. *So much for the fun. Get out the front door, Wyn. Forget the basement. I'll teleport with Aideen once we lose these jerks. We can figure out how to lie to her later.*

Pretorius ripped the microwave off the wall. Hefting it in one hand, he threw it at Zita. Her eyes went wide as she ducked, rolling onto the porch. The object flew past her, taking a chunk off the doorframe and landing on the stairs.

Remember Boris was mad about Sobek's new friend with powers? I think I found him—super strong. Get out, Wyn! In preparation to leap, Zita perched on the porch rail, using a hand to hold a post for better balance.

Right next to her, the door to the other kitchen swung open, letting the light inside and the man who had been scraping matches pour out. He sprinted like a frightened rabbit, unwilling or unable to waste breath on screaming, instead displaying his lack of running prowess.

The open door allowed her peripheral vision to see Andy holding a mostly naked man's head under the sink faucet. Her friend batted at a few other men with his free arm, his pants missing, and his boxers displaying in all their Batman glory. The loser in the sink coughed and sputtered. *Are you out yet, Wyn?*

She lost interest in Andy's sudden fetish for dunking drug dealers when Pretorius thundered out the doorway after her. Waiting for him to get closer, Zita vaulted off the porch railing before he could lunge, spinning to her feet.

He jumped after her, landing heavily.

Zita leapt on top of the Mustang to avoid him, shoving the remaining block of cash into her shirt to free up her hands.

Pretorius grabbed for her and missed.

From there, she flipped to the top of the SUV, and balanced, taking a moment to check behind her. The stream of light from the open back door let her see the frustration on his face—or was he glowing? "Are you glowing or are you just that white? The sun's not your enemy, hombre," she goaded him, exaggerating her snicker. *I'll try to distract him so you can get out, Wyn.*

He paced around the SUV, with her turning to face him. Her nemesis moved fast for a man his size, but not as swiftly as she could. Pretorius snatched at one of her ankles.

Evading his grasp, Zita tumbled down the hood and back onto the Mustang. From her shirt, she pulled out the cash (or as she thought of it, the guaranteed distraction) and waggled it at him. "Aww, no mad face. God loves a cheerful giver, you know."

Wyn finally deigned to answer. *No, not yet. Some criminal is running around in here, so I'm hiding behind the curtains.*

Silent, cautious, Pretorius strode to the Mustang. He glared at her. She readied herself to bound to the other car but was astonished when he leaned down and hoisted the Mustang on its side.

Prepared to jump anyway, she tumbled to safety, but the bundle flew from her hand. The landing was harder than she would have liked. *Judges are not impressed by sloppy landings.* Zita recovered in time to catch Pretorius charging her.

She sidestepped, dropping into a negativa, and tried to sweep his feet out as he went past. While her blow was solid, he only stumbled. His recovery was almost instant. In comparison, her foot ached at the contact. *Carajo, is he a man or a wall?*

He kicked, clipping her and sending her staggering toward the old shed.

Oye, I will have bruises tomorrow. If you're safe, Wyn, I'll ditch this guy and teleport to Aideen through a window. Zita ran again, planning her next series of jumps. Intuition warned her the enemy was close.

A deep groan came from inside the house, and flames lit up the dark kitchen. Fire streaked by them. Pretorius snarled behind her.

When Zita reached the shed, she did a quick wall climb up the weathered gray boards and onto the roof. Wood creaked a warning underfoot; this was not a safe place to linger. As she turned to assess her pursuer, she discovered Pretorius had changed priorities.

Brake lights warned her, and she did a pop vault off the roof, rolling to a two-footed stop. The rear of the SUV slammed into the shed. With a groan, the decrepit structure dissipated into slivers.

A fiery female form drifted out of the house, an agitated ball of fire dancing in the figure's right hand. Flames licked at the doorway behind her.

Pretorius shot a ray of light at the fiery woman. When it hurled her backward, the SUV's engine roared as he raced away.

Of course, he has laser beams shooting out his hands too. Why not, when he's already extra strong and tough, and can function as his own flashlight? He probably poops grenades. He's gone. You need to be out of the house. It's on fire. Zita sprinted toward the house.

Not one to waste time, Andy tossed a man out the back door.

The human baseball landed on the ground by Zita. When the dealer got to his feet, he pulled a knife and charged her with a crazed look that made Zita think he had been sampling the merchandise. *Scrawny street brawler, not even an effective one.*

"You know the thing about capoeira?" Zita asked, dodging the blade. "It's more about legs than the arms." She kicked him in the stomach, then danced behind, slamming her foot on the back of his knee.

He fell, clutching his leg.

Zita continued toward the house, when Pretorius' sidekick from the basement staggered out the door, his gun drawn. Blood splattered his face. Seeing her, he raised his gun to shoot. Even with him holding it sideways, she was an easy hit at this range. She skidded to a stop. "Oye, let's not be hasty," she tried.

Something thunked. His eyes rolled up in his head, and he fell to the ground.

Wyn stepped over his prone body, holding a cast iron skillet in both hands. "That's for making me a lame cliché!" she barked, tossing the pan down on top of him.

Water dripped from Andy when he emerged from the other door with three men in an awkward carry. One kicked as he was dragged. Another lay motionless over Andy's shoulder, nearly naked, soaked, and sobbing. The third was unconscious and missing his pants. "We need to get farther away before the flames reach the drugs. The neighborhood is in deep trouble if this place explodes," he said.

"Someone's on fire in the kitchen. Now it's alight as well," Wyn said, gesturing toward the room. Her hand flew to her mouth, and the sorrow in lavender eyes turned to alarm. "Oh, my Goddess, he's getting up! We need to help!"

Zita shook her head. "Remember the hospital?" She inclined her head toward the kitchen.

Spooked, Wyn nodded and got out of the doorway. She hurried to the shed, halting as the dots connected. *Is that Aideen?*

I refuse to answer on the grounds that it might incriminate one of us. Zita wasn't trying to be humorous.

Andy's tone was thoughtful. "Does she just shoot fire or can she control it?"

Zita shrugged. "No clue, why?" She dragged basement man down the stairs.

Andy waved his unconscious man toward the door of the burning kitchen. "If she controls it, she might be able to put that out." *Should we pretend not to know her?*

That was my plan. We always bickered like hellcats and dogs, so I'm not comfortable giving her our secrets. "Hey, fireball! We need your help!" Zita shouted into the kitchen as she dragged the unconscious man into the yard, dropping him near the shed remains. *Move, in case she can't do anything.*

Wyn's thought was musing. *Are you the dog or the hellcat in that simile?*

The creature who came to the door did not resemble Aideen in anything other than build. Her body seemed formed of fire, with dark holes where her eyes and mouth should be. Flames shot out like snakes—burning ones—and coiled around her shoulders, resembling hair, the length the only possible suggestion of gender. A crackle and roar surrounded the woman. She drifted above the ground, not touching, until she stood outside the burning kitchen. "That's not my name," she replied, in a voice made unrecognizable through the distortion of the blaze. One hand rested on her stomach, and she stumbled sideways. Tiny flames licked the porch railing.

Pues, take her earlier form and add drama. Struggling to hide her annoyance, Zita replied, "We don't know your name. Can you control the flames or just shoot it?"

Dark eyes swirled with fire for a moment. "What?"

Andy sighed. *If this is going to be a repeat of the time you pissed off the shrink, maybe Wyn should talk? Aideen never minded us.*

Eyes on the growing conflagration in the kitchen, Zita clarified. "Can you only throw fire and, uh, wear it, or can you put it out too?" Remembering Aideen's competitive streak, she added on a prod. "If you're not powerful enough to make the fire go out, we understand." She shrugged, watching the kitchen burn, even though every instinct was to run and try to extinguish the spreading inferno. If not pushed, Aideen would posture until the house exploded.

For a moment, the slow slide of the snaky locks was the only movement on the blazing woman, who also glanced over her shoulder to consider the kitchen. While Zita watched, flames that were gobbling up the curtains—well, sheets—went out. The fiery woman turned back to Zita. Before that moment, Zita would have sworn fire could not smirk; Aideen proved her wrong. "Fire obeys me. Tell me who you are and what you are doing here."

Surprise came through the party line, so quickly smothered that Zita was unsure of the source. Part of her suspected both of them. *I am totally a people person. Why you got to be hating?* She rocked on her feet, anxious to start moving.

Wyn's mental voice held suppressed laughter. *As friends, we're aware of your strengths and, uh...*

Areas needing improvement, Andy proffered. *Keep talking since it's working for unknown and miraculous reasons.*

Smoothing her shirt, Zita gave the quick version. "We heard rumors about kidnap victims kept here. Before we wasted the cops' time on it, we came to see if the guy who mentioned it was blowing smoke. Umm, not like you. The big blond—you know, the living laser pointer—ordered them to kill a woman in the basement, so we were going to pull her out and call the cops. Everything ballooned up from there. This place is a meth lab too, and if the blaze reaches those chemicals, it'll take out the whole neighborhood. Could you put out the rest of the fire now, please?"

The flaming woman gazed at the kitchen. "Civilian vigilantes," she sighed. "Very well. Remain near and you can explain more when I am done." If she gestured or did anything, Zita missed it. The small fires dancing in kitchen all smoldered and died in a single second.

"Praise the Lord and all the saints," Andy breathed. He set the unconscious man down on the ground next to the dealer from the basement, and improved his hold on the struggling man and weeping one.

Tension unknotted in Zita's chest, and she bobbed her head at him. "You said it, mano. Now we're skipping the explosions, let's see if these creeps know where the other captives are." She nodded at the man trying to resist. "Maybe your buddy, Wiggles, wants to tell us where the rest of the captives are?" She made a face and turned away from the crying dealer. "Anyone got a tissue for the soggy guy?"

Andy dumped the weeping man on the ground, where he curled up in a fetal ball and continued his caterwauling. Wyn knelt beside the guy, murmuring. After giving Wiggles a shake like a recalcitrant puppy, Andy set him down and pointed a finger at him. "Sit. Stay."

A mad gleam in his eyes, Wiggles started to lunge, but froze, his eyes tracking a shape behind Andy.

Zita looked.

Aideen had returned, shedding little sparks, her gaze on Wiggles. "Lie down on the ground and assume the position," she told him. "I'll be asking the questions now." She tossed a fireball the size of a baseball in one hand. Her other hand rubbed her stomach. With a nasty look on her inhuman face, she snarled, "Do you want to test me?"

Andy stomped over and stopped one captive from limping away by scooping him up and dumping him on top of the others by the former shed.

With whirl of pale hair, Wyn knelt by the crying man. At her touch, he turned the remains of his face on her, his skin half-covered in blackened blisters and red oozing wounds. "Let me make it better," she said, her voice soothing. Her hands wove patterns in the air. Green light appeared, and the volume of the moans decreased. *I'm concentrating, so if I miss anything important, let me know.*

Wiggles gulped, and rolled over on his stomach, putting his arms behind his back.

"Good. Now, you mentioned captives? Did you not find them all?" Aideen asked.

Zita twitched her shoulders. "We didn't have a chance to search the entire house. We only found one. If they've got others, we haven't located them yet. There are at least two more victims unaccounted for." She took a second to straighten her mask, pushing aside the dread coiling inside her. *Quentin, where are you? Is that a tag on my head? It is. Carajo.*

Everyone was silent while Aideen thought. "Very well. I freed one female captive. You, on the ground. How many hostages are in the house?"

"J-just one woman in the basement. I swear nobody messed with her other than blood samples. All the others are elsewhere until it's time for the shipment." The reply was muffled by the face in the ground.

Aideen nodded. Pointing to Andy, she snapped her fingers when he looked at her. "You. Where are your pants? And theirs?"

At first seeming irritated that she had pointed at him, Andy looked down. The poor light made it difficult to tell, but Zita thought he blushed. "One threw a flask at me." He waved a hand at the wet man Wyn was healing and the unconscious guy. "Standard procedure," Andy said, "when splashed with an unknown chemical, is to remove contaminated clothing and flush affected skin for at least fifteen minutes. The fire limited the flushing, but I did what I could. They didn't seem to be taking care of themselves, so I helped them too." His voice was barely more than a whisper, probably to disguise it.

Small sparks cascaded, and fiery locks swayed. "What is the blond doing?" she asked.

Wyn did not look up. "I'm healing him. He was hurting. I'll heal you too if you can turn off the fire so I can touch you."

"He's a criminal. He can see a doctor after he's processed."

She did not say that. Gentle Wyn narrowed her eyes, and her expression carved the exquisite lines of her face into the mask of an avenging goddess. Her lips firmed, and she tossed a silvery lock of hair over her shoulder with her free hand. "I don't care who he is, he doesn't deserve to be in agony. I am far too exhausted to deal with your rubbish." The subject of her tirade stared up at her with worship in his eyes. Her other hand continued with the glittery green glow. "If you want me to heal your stomach, you'll hush and let me do this, or your tacky flaming self can continue to suffer."

Aideen opened and closed her mouth. She whirled to face Andy. "You! Search the house for kidnap victims. Let me know whether he's telling the truth. And put on pants." She moved her hand from her stomach and another ball of fire appeared in it. She fixed Wiggles with a glare. "If he is lying, he can deal with the consequences."

A whimper came from the man on the ground. "I'm not lying," he howled, "I swear, mister."

Aideen growled. "I'm a woman." Her aura flared. The temperature in the immediate area soared enough that Zita began sweating.

The scent of urine grew stronger. "Oh, God. I'm so sorry, lady," the man on the ground pleaded. The other dealers stared everywhere but at Aideen.

Andy seemed torn, glancing between Aideen, the man on the ground, and the house.

"I'll do it, mano," Zita said. "You've got the best chance of keeping them under control, and we don't want to hurt anyone." She eyed Aideen. *Keep an eye on Flaming McBitchypants. I'll go before she gets madder that we're not obeying her every command.*

You have the best chance of keeping Aideen from hurting anyone, Andy. Wyn called out, "Be careful." She returned attention to her patient.

He acquiesced with a nod. "All right."

Apparently deciding to ignore their disobedience, Aideen circled Wiggles, who followed her every motion without moving. One ball of fire winked out, and she stepped back, cradling her stomach with her free hand. The temperature decreased. "You! The mouthy one! Get going!" she demanded.

Wyn sent a mental laugh. *That's you, Zita. I'm the beautiful one, Andy's the sensible one...*

Yes, that sounds about right. Andy agreed, his tone amused.

Zita rolled her eyes. *You two are haters.* The temperature dropped further as she entered the house. She left the door cracked open because breathing was a necessary part of more entertaining activities.

We'll be here. She wouldn't dare hurt me, not if she wants healing, and Andy resists the fire enough to rectify any bad behavior. Wyn kept up a running commentary of the interrogation.

Zita concentrated on scouting the house as she would have in an area with known dangerous animals. She had no interest in leaving traces for the cops to find or in being attacked by anyone hiding within. Her caution was wasted; it was empty. The house had only the essentials, most of which were filthy, save for several boxes of brand new men's sneakers, the giant television, chemicals, and baggies.

Their five prisoners sat in a subdued huddle, with Andy between them and Wyn. His mask was more unkempt than before.

Wyn waved. Andy greeted her with a single word, spoken in a hopeful tone. "Pants?" Aideen... floated.

Zita summarized for them. "The house is empty, if nasty. They have a big-ass TV and DVR, mattresses that are the source of all VD in the city, and huge stinky jugs with chemical labels in one basement. I called from their cell phone, so the cops are coming."

Wyn sighed. "We will march these boys into the living room and let them doze while they wait for the police to arrive," she informed Zita. "They were supposed to be extra security for a dawn shipment of captives at the Baltimore docks." *I'll use my sleep spell on them, so they remain present until the police arrive.*

"Pants?" Andy repeated, looking up and down at her. He moped, seeing her bare hands. *You think you can get them all to sleep?*

I hope so. Failing that, we can use their own restraints to tie them up. Wyn pulled zip ties from her pocket. Zita decided not to think about why her friend had picked those up.

Zita shook her head at Andy. "No spare clothing. We need to go soon, so let's herd some snakes." *You know we have to go to the docks, right? We can't take the chance they'll ship Quentin out of the country and turn him into a sex slave.*

"No pants?" His face fell. Andy's mental tone held both disbelief and laughter. *Quentin? A sex slave?* He gestured to the men by the shed. "Come on, let's get you in the house."

Zita shrugged and followed. *The man has skills, based on the unrequested testimonials his dates have given.*

Yet another thing I did not need to know, Andy moaned.

One prisoner called Zita a name when she poked him to hurry.

Zita snorted. "Buddy, I'm no dog. I'm the whole fucking arca. Do you want her to get impatient?" She tilted her head at the flaming woman.

Defiance died with one glance at Aideen, and the men trooped into the house without further protest or insults. Aideen took to the sky as they entered.

From her position bringing up the rear, Zita shook her head. *She gets to fly, too? Dude.*

Once they settled their captives in the living room chairs, Wyn did her gesture and hand-waving trick, and the pink sparkly fog swirled. The drug dealers yawned.

When the rough surface of the wall next to her met the back of her head, Zita shook herself out of her own stupor. She grabbed Andy and staggered out of the room.

He yawned and blinked sleep from his eyes. "Strong magic," he grunted and made a face. They headed outside and sat on the back stoop, taking deep, cleansing breaths.

Zita nodded. "Even at the edges, that pink sparkly cloud has a mean kick." She rubbed the back of her head where it had collided with the wall.

"So what's a whole fucking arca, anyway?" Andy asked.

"Noah's ark. Since I can be pretty much anything," she said.

He grunted, and the pair sat in companionable silence for a few moments before Wyn came out.

"They're asleep." The witch was satisfied. "They should sleep until shaken or hit."

Andy mumbled under his breath for a moment, then hung his head. "We didn't find Quentin, but we stopped these idiots from blowing up the rest of the neighborhood. If Zita's description of the cellar contents is accurate, those chemicals would do a number on the surrounding area too. That's not too shabby for so-called civilian vigilantes." He sounded cheerful.

Zita hopped to her feet. *Things to do.* "I noticed Aideen took off without searching for any other captives. Did she have to turn the flames off before you could heal her?"

Wyn leaned against a post, her body drooping and weary. "Yes, she had our friend here give her his mask." She inclined her head toward Andy. "I made him an illusory one. After I healed her, she practically threw it at him, claiming it was disgustingly wet. He did a decent job putting it back on considering it was dark."

"What did she expect?" Andy complained. "People sweat when they're next to an inferno in the middle of the summer. You know Aideen'll call the cops about the dawn shipment, right? We could go home and rest now."

Zita shrugged. "Fine with me if she tells them." She rubbed her forehead and considered. "If I thought they had all the information, I would leave this to the police. Since they don't, I will find a spot to crash nearby so I can watch how they do. If the cops miss finding them or can't handle Pretorius—the one who shoots lasers—I want to be close by to help Quentin and any other prisoners."

Wyn sighed and rubbed her eyes. "Just when I was hoping to get my beauty sleep."

Her throat felt tight. "If you two don't want to come, I understand," Zita offered.

"What's more sleep deprivation amongst friends? The frat boys might listen for five seconds if I explain that I spent the night with two women," Andy grumbled.

Nodding agreement, Wyn heaved herself away from the post. "No better time than the present."

Relief bloomed. Smiling beneath her mask, Zita added. "Okay, vámonos! Mano, you might want to pick up the remains of your clothing before we go. Oh, and witchy wonder, don't forget your weapon unless you're wearing gloves under your disguise?"

Wyn's shoulders slumped. After a moment, she retrieved the frying pan.

Chapter Sixteen

Zita rose out of a dead sleep and crowed from beneath the lounge chair where Wyn slept. Coarse, woven strips of polyester complained as Andy staggered out of his chair to his feet. Above Zita's head, Wyn mumbled vague threats and flopped over on her patio chaise, falling off.

Awake now, Zita stopped before repeating the call and fluffed her feathers. She peeked out from under the lounger.

Andy blinked at her.

Wyn glared. "What were you thinking? It's not even dawn yet," she hissed.

She clucked. *If I'd known crowing was such a strong impulse, I would have chosen a different shape. I thought dawn would wake a rooster best.* Before she could do more, lights came on inside the narrow home whose patio furniture they had borrowed for the night.

With a gasp, Wyn staggered to her feet. *Run!* She sprinted across the postage stamp lawn, and down the sidewalk.

Andy tucked Zita and her clothing bag under one arm like a football and followed.

A cluck escaped her, and Zita resisted the urge to peck as they bounced across cracked pavement. *Loosen your grip. You're crushing my feathers.* The predawn dimness prevented her from seeing whether anyone witnessed their flight.

When Wyn dropped to a walk, panting hard, Andy slowed to match her pace.

At the slower speed, Zita could make out more of the same old, thin houses, separated by lawns the length of a sedan. Most had backyard chain link fences; the lack of a one and available loungers had been the deciding factor in their accommodations. Zita prayed they had run toward the docks, rather than away. *Wyn, you should reconsider that training regimen I made for you. It would stop you from getting winded so easily. Let me know when I can shift. This shape is terrible for seeing any distance.*

When Andy squeezed her, she pecked at him reflexively. Zita had the satisfaction of seeing him flinch, even though her beak had not pierced his skin. *No penetration, story of my life.*

"Hey!" Andy said. He dropped her in some brush by a wavy wall separating the docks from the residential area. "Lalalala, don't want to know."

With the shrubs hiding her, she grabbed a mouthful of dandelion before shifting to a seagull and taking flight. Once she was aloft, she changed again to a snowy albatross. As she adjusted her wings to soar, Zita cawed in delight at her improved eyesight and the incredible sense of smell. The odor of rank fish was far more pleasant in this form than in human form.

Below her, Wyn put her hand up to her eyes and peered up. "How will we tell you from the other—oh, that is one giant seagull." With a shrug, Wyn handed the plastic bag to Andy.

Zita rolled her eyes or as close as she could manage as a bird. *Albatross. Technically, albatross don't usually travel this far north, but I doubt anyone will know that. People should assume I'm the seagull emperor.*

The smiley face on her clothing bag grinned up at her as Andy fastened it around his wrist. *Why not be a seagull?*

Although flying was mindless if she obeyed her intuition, Zita experimented with subtle variations of her wings. When instinct and intellect combined, the list of possibilities widened; she loved

SUPER 279

nothing better than finding those boundaries and exploring them. *Albatross have an excellent sense of smell, which might help me find Quentin. They're designed to move around rather than sitting still, which suits me.* She circled, noting the change in colors and scents between the port and the aging residential neighborhood snuggled up to it. While she grew accustomed to the movement, she kept herself lower and closer to her friends.

"If it looks like a seagull, smells like a seagull..." Wyn commented, then whispered to Andy. They both snickered and strolled around the wall to get to the port. "Why did we have to sleep there overnight again?"

Andy sighed. "So I could park my car farther away and have less of a chance of it being noticed."

The witch snorted. "The whole rooster thing ruined that plan." She and Andy had reached the outer parking lot and cut across the empty rows toward the main port.

Zita's muscles felt warm and stretched. After calculating the angles, she swooped toward Wyn, pulling up at the last moment to avoid a collision.

Andy ducked and covered his head.

Wyn gave a wimpy shriek and threw her arms up to protect her face. "Hey!"

The homeowners noticed a pair of trespassers. They didn't notice Andy's car, parked a few blocks away. I would have teleported us, but we couldn't find any webcams. Zita ascended on an air current and soared over the port.

An odd, asymmetrical shape, the port had a long side divided from most of the residential area by Broening Highway and railroad tracks. The predawn darkness was interrupted by circles of artificial light, farther apart in the parking areas most distant from the ships, and closer together until the piers shone almost as bright as day. None of the buildings were tall, and the closest areas were another port and a neighborhood of petite houses; she imagined the sobs of police snipers searching for advantageous spots to set up. Zita had to credit the marine terminal for organization; the largest permanent structures—storage sheds, perhaps—clustered on the west side, while outlying areas were primarily commercial parking lots, with personal vehicle areas in the outer ring. Orderly streets broke the area up into sections, with only two or three exits. Stackers and trucks clustered near the ships, with sections devoted to irregular container groupings in between. White lines divided every inch of pavement, designating the size of object that could be placed or parked in any given spot. Nine gigantic blue cranes dangled over the water on two sides of the port, and rail tracks meandered through the facility. With organization that regimented, anything that broke pattern was suspicious. Her stomach twisted at the number of cops she noticed adjusting what she assumed were hidden weapons, and far too alert for third shift dockworkers near dawn.

At this hour, the dock served only three crafts. The giant container ship she dismissed with a single glance; while anonymity provided concealment, it required too many crew. Of the remaining two container vessels, one was half the size of the other. The smaller of the two had its own crane onboard. *Either might work.* Dockworkers with more numbers than skill unloaded both of the smaller ships. More of the suspiciously perky dockworkers grouped by the lesser ships, so she assumed the police agreed they made better candidates as well. Tension and excitement simmered.

These are not the droids you're looking for. You can do it, Obi-Wan. Her wings faltered when she heard Andy's words over the mental connection.

Uh, what? Zita wheeled and headed back toward where her friends should be.

Wyn sent laughter. *Would you believe that worked?* Her mental voice held overtones of relief and surprise.

Andy's held the same. *I knew you could do it. A security guard wanted to know what we were doing. Wyn convinced him to let us continue. So where are we going? We're in a massive parking lot.*

You know you don't have to be here, right? If you want to go home, I won't think less of you. Zita scanned the ground, trying to determine who was present. The resulting number of cops or crooks—people who appeared alert and might be hiding weapons—made her wings twitch. *This may turn into a gun battle. Bystanders fare poorly in those.* After a moment, she identified the pair walking arm in arm as her friends, a familiar bag smiling and swinging from the man's wrist. They had made it through most of the outer parking lot, and a slow-moving figure strolled away from them.

Andy's reply was a mental snort. *We'll go if you do. You're not bulletproof either.* He appeared to be an elderly African American man, with a mustache and beard that held more gray than black on a vaguely familiar freckled face. Broad-shouldered yet slim, he had to be a couple inches over six feet tall. He walked with Andy's martial artist roll and economy of motion. Even if they had split apart, she would have guessed his identity by that gait.

Clasping his arm was an African American woman of a certain age and the bearing of a queen. A hand smoothed hair that glinted with silver as they strolled under the lights. Wyn made a face unsuited to her apparent dignity at Andy. *As if we would abandon the endeavor now? With luck, our presence will prove superfluous if the surfeit of older American sedans in the parking lot indicates the amount of law enforcement presence. That said, I'm delighted to confine myself to the back.*

After a momentary pause, Andy agreed. *Way back. Possibly so far back you couldn't find us with the Way Back Machine.*

A what machine? Why do you look familiar, Andy? Zita ignored the urge to ask about the machine.

He frowned at his companion. *I'm not the one who looks like Nichelle Nichols. Who did you make me?*

A smile teased at Wyn's lips. *Don't worry, you're worthy of being seen with me. We needed disguises that people would not question. I figured I'd pick two people you'd appreciate, fanboy. Keep chatting with me, Morgan Freeman.*

Andy's tone held resignation. *That explains why the guard acted so strange. If you had to pick famous people, why can't I be Wesley Snipes or Samuel L. Jackson?*

Zita ignored their byplay as her attention paused on a white pickup. Tucked between larger trucks near F Street and a service road, the vehicle waited with the engine running. Stomach clenching, she swooped that direction to get a closer look. Nothing stood out about it, other than the fact that someone huddled inside, their face hidden by shadows from the containers on either side. As fleets of white pickups and vans were scattered liberally through the marine terminal, she counted herself as paranoid and continued her flight. She exhaled and adjusted her wing position. *Walk as if you know where you're going. Everything's pretty well-lit close to the docks. Don't slink or do anything odd—I've spotted cop snipers on the few buildings, and an awful lot of people who are criminally slow, cops, or union workers. Once you hit 14th Street, settle nearby and be ready.*

Assent hummed in her mind from the others. After peering at street signs, they headed the right direction.

Wyn acknowledged and added her own opinion. *Got it. People seem to be trickling in, so we don't look suspicious walking here. We'll have plenty of time; dawn won't be for another forty minutes.*

Zita returned to her circuit of the port, gliding low over the containers closest to the smaller ships. The feathers on the back of her neck prickled. Cargo containers, in uniform twenty- and forty-foot lengths, were piled and stacked in spots marked on pavement. Although the containers followed no obvious placement model, creating an odd maze of multicolored metal boxes, each one was precise within the confines of the rectangles painted on the ground. She assumed their location assignments followed a strategy known only to dock planners because it made no discernible pattern to her. Forcing herself to focus, she continued skimming the tops of the containers, pulling up higher as an SUV thundered by, followed by a truck. When she glanced at them, ASS gleamed under the lights as the SUV parked in the lot near the smallest ship. The truck pulled up by the vessel. After reading the street signs, she sent a terse message to her friends. *They're here early. The ship is the small one at G and 11th Street.* Men piled out. She eyed them and groaned internally as the sixth and final form to exit was a tall, familiar blond man. *Oh, joy. They brought Pretentious P, that Pretorius, with them. I hope he's not bulletproof in addition to all his other powers.*

After a pause, Andy sighed on the party line. *We can't see from here. Should we head that way or stay back?*

Zita didn't have to think about her answer, even as she flew closer to the ship. *Stay back. There's a police swarm here; the last thing we need is the bad guys getting away because the police think we're the issue.*

Wyn's mental voice held humor and relief. *If Quentin's kidnappers are the bad guys, why are you so nervous about the cops?*

Perching on an unused crane next to the ship, Zita twitched her shoulders, settling her feathers. *Quentin's kidnappers are meth-cooking drug dealers with a sideline in kidnapping, torture, and murder. Perhaps they are kidnapping torturers with a sideline in drugs, but they're definitely evil. The cops are just authority figures. Even if they're on our side, they might not be competent. That said, use the phone we lifted from the meth place to call in a tip to the cops on the ship. I doubt Pretorius is shipping cookies to his abuela.* She swore. *Now I want cookies.* Antsy, she shifted from foot to foot before sinking into her roost.

The driver remained in the truck while Pretorius and two cronies marched up to a stevedore with a handheld device. Engine idling, the truck next to the ship held a single shipping container, the standard smaller container, at twenty long by eight feet wide. Fans whirred on the refrigerated container. Her head twitched. *Are those rusty rivets or air holes?*

After nodding at the driver, Pretorius spoke to the stevedore.

The dockworker poked at his little machine again and replied. After gesturing to a couple of loitering workers to join him, the stevedore walked to the container truck. They conferred next to the truck.

Pretorius put his hands on his hips.

One dockworker jogged onto the ship. On the deck, one of the cranes began to hum. The arm lurched from one side to the other.

Pretorius advanced on the dockworkers. His steps gained speed as the stevedore with the device waved it at the truck and knocked on the walls of the container.

Another dockworker fumbled around trying to attach the crate to the hooks. Only one dockworker, the one unlocking the container from the truck, seemed to know what he was doing. In a more controlled descent, the crane dropped to the box. The dockworker who had unlocked the container climbed up top and attached a large hook to the crate. After jumping back down, he gave a thumbs-up to the crane operator. The cargo began to rise. Noticing the movement, the stevedore on the ground shouted, and made a slashing, negative motion.

Pretorius yelled back, closing the distance between himself and the lead stevedore. Conversation grew heated; the words were inaudible, but the tones and body language communicated. A gun flashed, and then everything was a confusion of shouting.

Cops melted in and out of view behind cover as they identified themselves and barked orders.

Pretorius bellowed instructions at his men, who swore and fought with the dockhands.

Everyone seemed to have guns, waving them in every direction. The crane creaked to a stop, box swinging in midair.

Wyn must not have been able to see much from her vantage point. *What's going on? That sounds... awful.*

Zita gulped and lifted herself up into the air, rising higher. *Everyone but us has guns. I don't think Sobek's men want to follow the playbook. Stay back. They're taking hostages. Hopefully, they won't shoot near the container.* Her friends were as safe as possible near a gunfight, she reassured herself.

The shouting ceased when Pretorius pressed against the truck, shielded by the tires of the vehicle. Each of his men, save the truck driver crouched at his side, had a dock worker hostage. He turned his head to either side as if issuing instructions. With one hand at his side, he counted out numbers with angry flicks of his fingers. On five, his men ran to the ship, towing their hostages as human shields. Pretorius stepped out from behind the truck, and a brilliant white wall of light sprang up between the it and the rest of the port. He dashed toward the gangplank.

He can make walls of... something glowy. She reminded herself this was for the cops to handle, and she would only watch for her brother. Dark-clad SWAT team members moved toward the wall. The first one to reach it tapped, and yanked his hand back. *Glowy and hot,* she amended.

A cop ordered Pretorius to drop to the ground.

Pretorius shook his head as he ran. With a flick of his hand, he returned a white bolt back in the direction the voice had come from as the wall simultaneously disappeared. He had not aimed so his intention may have been only to delay further police action. After reaching the deck of the ship, he ducked down by the side. One of his cronies pulled the gangplank up behind him.

The police scattered, taking cover behind anything possible. While they dispersed, Pretorius found better cover between two standard crates, ones lacking refrigeration or air holes. Given the way men scurried to truss the hostages, he must have been giving orders. One of his thugs smacked the head of an argumentative hostage with his handgun. Zita's stomach twisted.

The cops behind the machinery and containers settled into an uneasy détente with the boat.

Zita continued to circle overhead.

The airborne crate was suspended partway between the ship and the dock. A crewman emerged from a windowed room toward the front of the ship—probably the bridge—and crept over to Pretorius. His outstretched hand offered a phone to the bodyguard. Without leaving his position, the blond took the phone and held it to his ear. He made a gesture with his other hand. Heavy chain screeched, and water cascaded.

A summer spent working on a cruise ship had taught her the sound of a lifting anchor. *Carajo. They can't leave, especially if my brother is here. Maybe I can steal their keys so they can't drive it.* Gliding into a different air current, she let it carry her down obliquely toward the front of the vessel, keeping the ship's bulk between herself and the cops. When she got there, Zita landed on a railing and surveyed the windowed room. It was a bridge. Unfortunately, one skinny man was inside, but at least one window stood open. The crack had to be about six inches wide, the most allowed by that style of window.

Zita grinned internally. Engrossed with checking instruments and doing mysterious things with switches and dials, the man inside did not notice when she shifted into a cat and joined him.

Once she was behind the man in his white vinyl chair, Zita shifted again, this time to gorilla. Moving so her fur barely whispered, she reached out and seized him, putting him into a chokehold. His hands scrabbled at her muscular arms in a futile attempt while she counted seconds in her head. About the time she started to worry, he stopped resisting and went still. She released her hold, easing his limp form to the ground. When she checked his pulse, it was steady. Relief flooded her. *Practicing safe sleeper holds is difficult when everyone over the age of ten is taller than you.*

Now he was down, Zita examined the bridge. Three of four sides had windows, including her entry point. The whole room reeked like fish, sweat, saltwater, and men who needed to bathe. A row of lockers lined the wall without windows. When she opened a few, she found a handful of snacks, cleaning supplies, and a toolbox. Her eyes lit up at the latter, and she flipped it open. A wrench landed across the room. She lost a second gawking and made a mental note to practice more as a gorilla. Two metal consoles, pale green, were the only furniture other than the two ripped chairs that badly needed cleaning. Rushing to a boxy console, she searched for a key to pull. In the disorder of old-fashioned buttons, dials, assorted odd knobs, and built-in monitors that covered the consoles, nothing seemed like a key. A few buttons glared with dull red eyes at her. Instruments beeped, buzzed, and hummed like a chorus of tone-deaf kindergarteners. As she realized she could not even find a keyhole, let alone a key, she swore; her limited experience with marine vessels had not prepared her for this. When she finally noticed a button with the image of an anchor over it, she pushed it. The button lit to a red glow, and the loud release of a chain winch began. She clenched a fist in victory.

A minute later, she had duct taped the now-moaning sailor and packed him into a locker. After ensuring the locker had ventilation holes, she closed the door, picked up tools and began working. When enlightenment failed to dawn after another look at the confusing electronics, she settled for turning off everything and pulling out any visible plugs or cords. Since only four screws and a wire attached it, she removed the joystick too. While she searched for more ways to slow them down, her hands knotted the various cords into a ball. The heavy metal door caught her eye. *If they can't get in, they can't sail this puppy away.* Spinning a screwdriver in one hand, she eyed it. *Just what I need, a watertight security door.* A chortle escaped as she went to work. She switched to a chimpanzee for improved dexterity. Zita finished with an artful layer of duct tape, one of the most awesome inventions ever, in her opinion. *Nothing says fun like duct tape, a knife, and paracord; throw in the wilderness, a sexy man, and a box of condoms, and you have pure bliss.*

Yay, more treasure to bury in the too much information box. Andy grumbled.

Wyn sounded more uncertain. *Are we still looking for your brother?*

Someone shouted and a single gunshot echoed.

The locker behind Zita thumped and leaked obscenities as its occupant reacted.

Another torrent of shouting—like baboons gone insane, loud, and angry—made her peek out a window as she finished up. A dockworker lay on the deck of the cargo ship. The back of his head was... everywhere but where it should have been.

Zita gulped and pushed down nausea, contentment fleeing. *Still working on rescuing my brother. Their negotiator isn't worth shit. I'm pulling cheap delaying tactics to stop them from leaving.* She rubbed her hands on her hairy arms, thinking about the dangling container.

Whatever happened to observing and reporting, like super-powered mall cops? Andy asked.

Wyn added, *Really attractive mall cops.*

Zita did not bother to answer. Transforming to her human disguise form, she picked up the only other item she recognized in the console. Her hair hung around her like a cape; she hoped it hid her face from any cameras. "Hello," she purred into the intercom. The Mexican accent was definitely a comfort at this point. "This is not your captain speaking. This is just a reminder that the cargo container hanging over the ship has innocent people inside, so if everyone would please avoid shooting it, that would be awesome. Thank you."

The shouting ceased or at least paused. The handle of the door clicked, and an angry man glared through a window at Zita.

She wiggled her fingers at him.

He gaped and pounded on the window. His face flushed red, and he called out to the others. The man began kicking the door, alternating with rattling the handle.

Obeying her instincts, she dove for the floor right before a ray of light went through where she had been standing. *Lasers are an excellent hint to leave.* Zita crept to the window farthest from where the beam had originated. With a hard shove to slide it as far open as it could go, she dropped the ball of wires out. After shifting into a cat, she hopped on the sill and slipped through. With the ball of wires in one claw, she changed again into her albatross form and launched herself into the air. Wheeling above the docks, she dropped the ball of wires near a cluster of police.

Once she had attained enough height, she circled over and around the cargo container, finally perching on it. Chemicals mingled with more human sweat and urine odors coming from the holes in the metal crate. When she took the time to sort through the scents, she could distinguish multiple people inside, none of whom were her brother. *People are inside the hanging crate, but not Quentin.*

A screech of hydraulic brakes distracted Zita, announcing another truck rumbling toward the ship. It stopped, reversed, beeping loudly, and ran over part of the container storage area. Thanks to his slow three-point turn and attempt at nonchalance, the driver took long enough for her to recognize him as the beefier of Sobek's bodyguards. More important to her, the truck held a container identical to her perch. She may have yelled in her excitement as she launched herself off the hanging container and arrowed after the truck. *A second semi with another container is by 11th Street and, uh, 10th Street! Bring my bag of tools. I'll try to stop it before it takes off.*

As she prepared to dive close enough to do—what, she didn't know—Zita saw a flare of light on the drafty top of a blue crane. The sound of the gunshot hit her ears a second later, followed by an echoing, ear-shattering boom from the truck.

It skidded sideways and came to a halt by a giant shed, momentum exhausted.

She glimpsed movement from the crane even as she swooped toward the truck. Having thought the blue crane empty when she scoped out the place, she puzzled at the shot even as she approached the disabled vehicle.

The driver threw open the door and ran.

As Zita neared, she shifted to a chimpanzee when she was close and hit him with both feet. The blow knocked him off balance, and he fell forward with a choked cry.

She landed, rolled to absorb the impact, and whipped around to see if she needed to do more, but he was unconscious on the ground. One of his wrists appeared bent wrong, and she scented blood. His breathing was regular. Reassured, she paced back to the truck, though her stomach curdled at the sound of his moans upon his awakening. The container reeked of more fear, chemicals, and people, overlaid by the burnt stench of hot metal and fuel. This close, the air holes were visible.

Faster than she expected, Andy came running up in his usual form, no longer Morgan what's his name; he and Wyn must have been creeping closer instead of staying back. His mask was firmly in place.

Near the lock for the container, Zita gestured, curling her fingers for her tools. *People are inside that thing. Give me my bag and a minute, and I'll get them out.* Andy tossed it at her. Pulling out the fanny pack, she dug through it.

He faced the container, breathing hard. "They locked people in there?" Horror suffused his tone, and he shivered. His eyes flared, and he shook his head. Seizing the side of the door, he dug his fingers into the seam with no more effort than Zita would have used with sand. Metal shrieked.

Zita found her picks and waved them at him. *Oye, I have the tools right here.*

The door surrendered with a bang, and the entire end of the shipping container yawned open. Andy tossed the twisted scrap of the door aside.

Right here! Zita shook the lock picks at Andy. She tucked the items back into her bag, used a grab bar on the corner of the container, and pulled herself inside. Her eyes widened.

"People don't belong in boxes," Andy grunted and climbed into the truck.

Wyn, wearing her blond guise, staggered up to join them, gasping for air. She put her hands on her knees for a second to catch her breath, then straightened. When she was able to glance inside, a hand flew up to her mouth. "Those poor people!"

The scent of chemicals and urine hung heavy in the stuffy air of the container. Old cots, bolted to the floor, rubbed up against each other, each one holding an unmoving form. The makeshift beds were arranged three across and three long, with coolers set in the narrow space remaining between the last cot and the wall. Each unconscious person had a slow-drip IV secured in one arm. Sympathy propelled a soft hooting sound from Zita. After handing her fanny pack to Wyn, she inhaled and began carefully climbing over the cots to check the occupants. Since a chimpanzee could move more easily in the cramped confines of the container, she remained in that shape. Her knowledge of medicine was limited to sports medicine and her CPR certification, so she could not do much more than basic monitoring. *They're all alive, but breathing and pulse rates are shallow and slow. A tranquilizer? Quentin and Jennifer aren't here.*

Andy, pull one out. If I can revive them, perhaps they know where Quentin and Jennifer are. Wyn visibly took a deep breath, her fearfulness disappearing now that she had a goal.

While Zita finished checking the last person, Andy inhaled sharply and pulled the first cot. Bolts groaned and gave way when he tugged. He hopped to the ground carrying it with no obvious effort. "I recognize this person." He set the bed on the pavement. "How are the others? Can you check, W—uh, blond lady?"

Zita really needed to pay more attention to faces. *Who is it?*

"Oh, my Goddess!" Wyn exclaimed, looking closely at the unconscious woman on the cot. She leaned over. From her own hospitalization, she also knew how to disconnect an IV and did so. Green sparkles grew around her hands. "It's Trixie! She doesn't even live in DC full time. I... I don't know if I can help her, but I can try."

"So they must be in the other crate?" Andy said.

Zita shook her head, rubbing a hairy arm over the top of it. *No, they were not in the hanging crate or any on-deck crate. The threat of imminent gunfire stopped me from checking the hold, but I could try that next. The driver is over there. Maybe he knows.*

Perhaps more loudly than she had intended, Wyn muttered, "I'm glad something scares you."

What? Zita watched her friend working on Trixie.

Wyn's pretty mouth thinned. "I'm petrified. This is crazy, but you're diving into deeper and more terrifying places every minute. You're even enjoying it." Despite her words, her hands and the sparkly light were steady over Trixie.

Pursing her lips, Zita stared at her friend. For once, she was glad her inhuman form lacked speech, as it gave her a chance to formulate an answer. Her tongue was thick in her mouth, and she pushed aside the hurt that Wyn could think she would enjoy her brother's danger. *What happens if the cops fail—if we fail—is worse than any other possible future. If anyone else dies, especially my brother, and I could have stopped it and chose not to, that's worse than my death. I won't play that, not again. Sí, some parts of this, when nobody's being victimized, have been fun for me, to be honest, but the whole saving people thing? Totally worth it. Plus, I found out I got two badass friends, including one who's scared as shit and going ahead anyway. I don't know anybody else that brave.* Zita walked to the edge of the truck on all fours and sat down next to the fanny pack. She hooted.

Wyn looked up and gave her a tremulous smile.

"Freeze!" shouted a cop, stepping out from behind a container. "Step away from the gurney. Put your hands in the air. This is the police." The eager young man and his older partner both had guns drawn. One focused on Wyn, and the other on Andy. Zita gave them credit; both had textbook-perfect hand positions on the weapons. While they wore patrol cop uniforms, bulky ballistic vests sat atop, sealed shut.

With a shudder, Wyn pulled her hands away and the glow disappeared. She blinked at the officers. Her illusory perfect mouth dropped open. If possibly, her milky skin turned paler.

Andy sighed and put his hands up behind his masked head. His shoulders slumped. *Yup. That's what I expected to happen. Do you think they'll let me defend my dissertation from prison?*

Walking to the edge of the box, Zita shook her head at the cops and pointed to the boat. She hooted at them, adding a raspberry in case they mistook her meaning. A male voice behind a box swore, revealing the presence of at least one more cop.

Classy, Zita. Wyn was the first to acknowledge the gesture. Her voice only shook a little as she tried to soothe the police. "They have—had—nine people in this container. The driver's over there, he, umm, a monkey fell on him. We were attempting to render aid to the victims of the crash." *Please don't shoot us.* The words and emotions accompanying them fretted over the party line for a moment before the litany cut off.

One older cop muttered into his shoulder radio. While he was speaking, his gun moved from threatening Wyn to point at Andy, with a waver toward Zita. "On the ground, now," he bellowed. His stomach jiggled, and his movements held none of the threat she'd associate with a real fighter. Still, he had reach on her (who didn't?) and hard eyes that told her he had been a cop long enough to fight dirty. Fair enough, survival was a respectable goal.

On the other hand, his younger partner appeared fair game. The rookie shifted, separating to cover them from another angle and drawing Zita's attention. Color was high in his cheeks, despite his dark skin. While physically fit, he lacked the cynical opportunism of a street fighter. His eyes were so wide that white ringed them, and he bounced with excitement. His sweat stank of adrenaline and nerves. Gesturing at her with his gun, he shouted, "Get your monkey down too!" The older cop shook his head.

Karen Diem

Andy snorted. "You try telling her anything." He knelt. Unhappiness thrummed through their party line. *I can't let them take off my hood, but if they shoot me, it might ricochet.*

A breeze thick with moisture lifted pale hair in soft tendrils around a perfect face. Wyn raised her hands in the air and kneeled. "No need to get upset, officers. We just wanted the people in the truck to be safe. This is all a misunderstanding. We're just bystanders."

The experienced cop guffawed. "Lady, people wearing masks are either going to a Halloween party, kinky, or committing a crime. This ain't no party, and nobody's naked. All of you, on the ground with your hands on your head." He gestured with his gun, dark hands wrapped firmly around it.

"Technically, the monkey's naked," the young one blurted out, his eyes on Wyn. The tip of his gun dipped.

If we get technical, I'm an ape, not a monkey. He's right about naked, though. You know he's going to get an obnoxious nickname from this, like Monkeypants. When her wide smile made the younger policeman flinch, Zita scratched her head and considered. Grabbing her bag of clothing, she clambered onto the top of the truck. The rookie's gun swung toward her but returned to Andy. From the top of the truck, she took in the surrounding area while her thoughts raced. *Can you convince them to let us go, Wyn?*

Her friend's mental voice held notes of exasperation. *What did you think I was doing? I'm trying my best to persuade, not force.*

The voice of the third cop came from the direction of the downed truck driver. "Hell of a shot to stop the truck. SWAT's going to be insufferable. The driver needs a bus, but he'll live." As she peeked over the edge of the truck, she marked him for another experienced policeman, between the other two in age. His movements were efficient and no more than they had to be. While his gun held steady on the bodyguard, the awkward angle of his arms and the amount of sweat coming off him suggested a ballistic vest hid under his dockworker garb. He had his foot in the back of the downed man and spoke in quiet bursts of command. The bodyguard lay on the ground, eyes wide, blood dripping from his nose.

The oldest cop shook his head, his gun steady on Andy. "SWAT says it wasn't them. It could have been the Halloween gang here or their pet chimp."

Andy looked up. "Oh, no, we're all unarmed. We thought you stopped them."

A block or two east, a flicker of light caught Zita's eye. A glowing Pretorius sent first one, then another streak of light toward where the cops huddled outside the ship. She could not tell from the angle if he hit anyone or anything, but shouting began and ended again.

The radios affixed to all three cops began to buzz with distant voices.

"What was that?" asked Wyn. *Was it Aideen?*

No, Pretorius. Zita bounced on her toes, craning her head to see. The bright streetlamps deepened the shadows thrown by all the crates and vehicles, making the area a patchwork of light and dark. Tracking people in it was a challenge; had it been a game of paintball, it would have been an engaging pleasure.

The dockworker cop gestured to the rookie. "I'm on the light bulb. You search and cuff this one," he stated. Once the rookie had his gun trained on the downed man, the third cop broke into a fast walk toward where Zita had last spotted Pretorius. He disappeared into the maze.

The older cop grunted into his radio while the rookie did a cursory search of the driver.

Curling up around his hands, the man on the ground cried out when the rookie attached a handcuff to one wrist. He writhed on the ground, shouting that his wrists were broken.

For a crime lord's bodyguard, he's a pansy. Zita curled her lip in disgust.

The rookie seized the bodyguard's arm, and hauled him to his feet, not touching the wrists or attaching the other cuff. "Come on, sit on the truck," he urged the distraught man, leading him to the truck bed.

"You're going to get to learn extra paperwork tonight. Cuff him anyway," the older cop told his quivering partner. Shaking his grizzled head, he turned to face Wyn and Andy. "I'm going to ask you both to lie down on the ground with your hands on your head. Slow and easy, please. If you can get your pet to do it, have it lie down too."

A couple of metallic clunks sounded as the young cop attached the other end of the cuffs to the grab bar on the container. "That'll hold him until we can get him medical," he said, nodding his head. As Zita watched from atop the cab, she noticed the bodyguard continued to bend over his arms, but his eyes were alert.

Eyes wide, Wyn shook her head. "She's not a pet. She's like a person on a permanent sugar high," she began. "Listen…"

Like a person? Had she not been on top of the truck, she might have missed the next shot. Having crept closer to the police, Pretorius threw another bolt of light at a liquid container. The distance prevented her from seeing what the first shot accomplished, but the second one was obvious when the ground around the tanker turned into a growing puddle of flame. Oily black smoke coiled up in an evil but brilliant conflagration. The building wind poured smoke on the ship and the now-shouting cops outside. When the severe coughing began, the shouting died down. Drawing her lips back from her teeth, she pant-hooted, pointing at the fire. *Pretorius shot a tanker crate and lit whatever goop's pouring out on fire!*

Andy and Wyn both twisted, as did the rookie cop, to look at where she pointed. The more experienced policeman kept his gun on Andy but glanced over when his partner exclaimed. Even a block away, the acrid scent made Zita's nose wrinkle when a gust of wind brought them a wave of it. The bodyguard muttered to himself.

"Fire!" shouted the rookie, pointing a finger and taking a few rapid steps toward the blaze. His gun hung, forgotten, in his other hand. "Fire! It's gonna catch up all the containers!"

His partner murmured into his radio again. Unlike the younger cop, his gun remained on Andy. "Weapon up," he barked at the rookie.

Andy focused on the ground and released a noisy exhale. His shoulders hunched. *Observe and report, she said, and I listened. If I'm lucky, I can turn that on an angle to stop the liquid from spilling out before any of the other containers catch fire.* "Don't bother. I think I need to get that." He rose to his feet, his hands nervously smoothing the sides of his pants.

The patrolmen began shouting at him to get down. Their shouts drowned out the other noise, even the mumbling of the driver handcuffed to the truck.

"I'm real sorry about this, but I have to go," Andy said. Bending at the knees, he leapt inhumanly high over the two cops, before sprinting into the network of containers and vehicles with enviable, but human, speed.

Impressed, Zita murmured her approval. *Way to stand up, mano.* As she gripped the edge of the truck roof, she hung off upside down, on the wall opposite the handcuffed man. A tinny voice buzzed.

The handcuffed bodyguard grunted and whispered again. His thuggishness only increased in proximity, aided by the scents of jerky and chaw. With a wary eye on the remaining police, Zita stared until she located the noise. A deep, echoing boom sounded from the direction Andy was headed.

With the police distracted, Zita squealed and swung over to the surprised man. She snatched the headset from his ear. While skipping out of reach, she stuck it in her own ear and ignored the shouting from both the prisoner and the police. The older cop was aiming at her. The younger one waved his weapon everywhere.

A man, sounding terrified, prattled away on the phone. "Pretorius is having fits. He left the tub to distract them, but the bridge controls are fucked, so we can't leave. We're having a hell of a time finding replacements since half the real crew is now locked in the hold. We didn't sign up for this shit. If you or that freak, Pretorius, don't get here and resolve this, me and the boys are out."

The men on the boat are panicking. The handcuffed thug is one of Jones' bodyguards. Can you find out if he knows where Quentin is? She pulled herself up onto the roof of the truck again, and grunted into the headset, pushing her tone as close to a man's voice as possible. The police seemed to relax with her up there and out of easy reach; she held the opinion that keeping people with guns content was good for her continued well-being. Another bang sounded, and everyone winced.

Her attempt must have been unconvincing as the speaker paused. "Who is this?" he ordered.

Stupid thing, I don't want it anyway. Zita tossed it on the ground at the older cop's feet. When she surveyed him again, Pretorius, glowing, tossed someone else thirty-seven feet away. The skid and bounce looked particularly painful, and she winced in empathy. She gave whoever it was points for the roll at the end of the throw. After a moment, Zita identified Andy by his habitual slump as he trudged back, shaking his head. Something inside her relaxed until an unfamiliar man tried to sap Pretorius from behind.

The blond did not even look, just swatted the person away with one hand. Since a container interrupted the flight, his victim did not travel far. The hapless officer slumped into a jumble of limbs near the flaming puddle. She winced again. *A cop got bounced off a container. Andy was thrown too, but he's fine. If the cop is alive, I'm going move him away from nasty burning death.*

Wyn flinched and grimaced. *That poor man. Go see what you can do. I'll see if I can get anything from the bodyguard. The cops, well, I'm not particularly threatening.* The witch turned her head and studied the bodyguard.

His gun on Zita, the older cop knelt and picked up the Bluetooth. The rookie had his gun aimed at the truck. She took advantage of his distraction to shift to an owl and fly toward the downed cop. Light flashed as Pretorius fired again.

Someone shouted from behind her, but her attention was on the network of boxes below. Cops crept through the crates, some with the measured steps of Special Forces veterans, and a few with just aspirations to stealth. None were close enough to do anything for the injured cop. Zita landed beside him, noting the dangerous liquid continuing to spread. Heat blasted her feathers. *Andy, can you get that container upright so it doesn't leak more? If you could distract Pretentious P, that would help too.* The cop's chest movements were shallow. *This guy's alive. I'm moving him.*

Exasperation dripped from Andy's mental voice. *I'm trying. He keeps pushing it over and hitting me with his lasers, well, not technically lasers, maybe more of a plasma bolt...* Her friend shoved the container up to balance on the short end.

Staying away from the flaming liquid, Pretorius inched toward the water, even as he shook another ball of light into his hand. He tossed this one at the fuel container, punching another hole in it.

Swearing with language that might shock kindergarteners and no one else, Andy raised the container, spinning it overhead to stop the flow from the two holes.

Zita shifted to gorilla, and lifted the cop, trying to support his neck. This close to the fire, burning diesel and scorched rubber overwhelmed all other scents. Vaguely, she recalled the advice not to move back injuries, but letting him burn to death was not an option.

Pretorius turned toward her, a ball of light growing to life in his hand.

Obeying her instincts, Zita evaded the blast with a wild leap to the side. She landed on her shoulder and rolled, cradling the cop like a child in her arms. She grunted.

The injured man groaned at even the limited impact and opened his eyes. Shock and pain swirled on his face. She put a finger on her lips and carried him, zigzagging through the boxes, toward one of the less stealthy cops. "Right. Hallucinations," her passenger said.

Andy growled, the sound loud, rolling, and deeper than his usual voice. "You could have hurt someone." Thunder echoed overhead. Clouds gathered.

"That would be the point," Pretorius replied. Another bolt went off.

Her ape feet moved faster, and she set the injured man down in front of one of his coworkers. The other cop drew on her. His eyes flicked between her and the hurt man she had set down. *Claro, the gorilla handing a wounded man over to a cop's care is more hazardous than any laser-shooting, hostage-taking problems. Have to remember that.* She raised her hands in the air and took a single step back.

"Gorilla's saving my ass," the wounded cop slurred. "Drinks on King Kong!" He let out a cheer.

When cheer drew the other's attention, she shifted back to owl and flew, circling around to see if Andy needed help.

Her friend had the container in an upright position, cutting off the flow of liquid. His eyes glowed white when he strode over to a scorched forklift and snapped off a fork from it. Hefting it in one hand, he stalked Pretorius.

Perhaps sensing the danger, Pretorius ascended into the air, a measured, gradual rise. He smirked down at Andy. "If you're auditioning, you should know that being stronger and tougher is the new average for the servant class. While the eyes are a dramatic touch, you'd have to do better than that." Almost imperceptibly, the overpowered bully's head crooked toward his ship, and his lips turned downward.

With a screech, Andy crouched before leaping up into the air, an impossible jump that brought the two men level for a moment. That was sufficient for Andy to strike Pretorius with the improvised bat, sending him crashing to the ground.

When Pretorius staggered to his feet, blood dripped from his arm and nose. He wiped it off his mouth, his face ugly as he flicked it onto the ground. His body was too stiff, hinting at injury and anger. Pretorius launched himself up into the air, higher this time, but still at a slow incline. His gaze returned to the boat; then, he faced Andy again.

Zita's friend had landed on his feet, his back toward the blond man. Andy pivoted to face Pretorius with a harsh, jagged sound that was both a shriek and a roar. His voice was a deeper rumble as if multiple men spoke in unison. "I am more. You may not deserve mercy." Light rippled over his arms and body, like small lightning bolts. He tossed his makeshift weapon to the ground.

Her eyes widened as Zita realized what was happening. *Andy, keep control! Don't shift! Think of baseball or your grandma or something.* She circled back toward the ship of hostages and the box swaying in the breeze. The storm clouds had built and rain fell, rolling off her feathers in increasing amounts.

Andy? Hang in there. Wyn's voice was soft. *Zita, the driver knows where your brother is, but he hasn't thought of the address yet. They're not here. I'm trying to dig without him noticing or hurting him.*

Fire streaked out of nowhere and exploded against Pretorius, throwing the bloodied man down to the pavement below. He fell at Andy's feet, rolling and gasping and slapping at the flames on his clothing. Glowing with fire, an androgynous figure floated in the air above the boxes, snaky locks writhing around an incandescent face.

Aideen's here.

When Pretorius lurched to his feet again, his hand glowed and blood mixed with soot on his face. One arm held his ribs. He snarled up at the flaming woman, who smiled.

A soft cough came from behind him. He twisted to look, and Andy, sans lightning, smacked him upside the head with one hand.

Pretorius collapsed. The shot Pretorius was holding flew wild, landing nowhere near Aideen.

The shot was, however, near Zita; it nicked the rope holding the container over the ship. A screech escaped her as she launched herself in the air. *He hit the crane rope. The container's going to fall!* She searched her brain, frantic to think of an animal strong enough to stop the people inside it from falling into the water.

Andy gawked at the container and took a deep breath. He ran and leapt, one of those supernatural jumps. His arms and legs flailed as he ascended toward the rope. When he caught it with one hand, the added tension severed it, and he seized the other end of the rope with his free hand and hung suspended. The container swung from one arm while his other hand gripped the rope to the crane. His legs dangled in midair. Rain dripped off his hair and nose. "I got it! I got it. This shouldn't work, but it did. Farnswaggle's Thirteenth Theorem in action!" he shouted to the sky, jubilant.

Oblivious to the contents of the container, Aideen grumbled as she flew over to Andy and inspected his work. Her voice held affront. "This started early! Wait, why are you holding up a box?"

Zita could only hope Aideen had the sense to stay away from the ropes.

Wyn's voice was worried. *Do you need anything? Can we help?*

"They have hostages in the box." Andy's posture relaxed as if hanging from the rope and holding the box relieved a terrible tension. He nodded down to the cops swarming below. *Convince them to let me go so I don't have to hurt them or take off my mask...*

Aideen hovered near Andy. "You people again. Are you the reason for all this mess?"

Zita's friend, holding the rope halves, shook his head. "No, we're helping. Can you put out the fire or is it too much for you?" Andy's tone was chirpy.

The flaming woman sniffed. "Please." She wafted over to the bonfire and posed above it. Lowering her arms dramatically, the flames began to extinguish, even as the rain lessened to a mist.

Andy! Zita! The bodyguard is gone. He ran off during the fight. I'm sorry, I was distracted for a few. Contrition warred with frustration in Wyn's mental tones.

Zita flew without conscious thought. *You hurt?* Reaching the sky above the truck, she was relieved to see her friend, hands on her hips, one foot tapping. The rookie guarded Trixie, who was sitting up and rubbing her head. The older cop paced.

Wyn sounded upset. *Yes, fine. Can you locate him? I almost had the address. He's planning to tell Sobek to kill the hostages and go into hiding.*

Alarm shot through her, and Zita gulped. She scanned the area. A white pickup truck inched down the street. Acting on a hunch, she concentrated on that section, and caught sight of the escaping bodyguard, still on foot. He slipped into a nondescript gray sedan and closed the door, tinkering with the steering wheel.

No time for cleverness. Zita landed beside the car, shifting to a gorilla again. Silent, she curled her fingers around the door handle, hoping to ease it open, then pull him from the vehicle so Wyn could ransack his brain. Incongruously, the ape part of her brain noted the car smelled like fast food and candy. Her stomach released a loud gurgle right before the engine started.

The escaping bodyguard looked up from whatever he was doing in the car and glared at her.

Zita's gorilla form jerked the door open even as he grabbed it and tried to hold it closed. When she resisted, her weight and strength warped the doorframe, stopping it from shutting completely.

Swearing, he floored the gas pedal, and the gorilla had to release it or be dragged. Red lights flared as he braked to avoid hitting a barrier and changed direction.

Quentin! He needs to tell us where my brother is. Shifting to a grizzly bear, Zita raced behind the car and leapt. Her massive black claws scrabbled for purchase on the smooth skin of the vehicle as she attained the trunk, then clambered to the roof of the vehicle. Her weight caused the roof to give a little, enough to impart an odd, springy sensation underfoot. One claw hooked into the sunroof, and she inserted the other claw as well, jiggling and pulling. The roof groaned, then cracked. While glass shattered, the frame of the sunroof tilted up and back at ninety-degree angle. Surprised by the lack of resistance, she lost her grip and fell off the back of the moving car, rolling behind the vehicle.

Light flared from the driver's side as a gun fired.

Zita dodged between the flash and the thunder. *He's going to get away!* She jumped up, changing form again to an albatross. Her wings pushed against the air with effort and emotion. While she wanted to follow him, she could not abandon the others. Quentin needed her, though. In rare indecision, Zita hovered awkwardly in midair, an exercise for which her avian form was not equipped. Fatigue settled over her even as a flaming shape arrived, holding a burning stick with a familiar happy face bag. Despite all this, she kept her eyes on the departing vehicle.

"Which one is he? You're the only giant seagull I see," Aideen asked, dropping the bag and the stick casually on a nearby car. She waved her hand at the stick and the fire extinguished.

Wyn was the first to speak. *Go. He's going to Sobek, and we're out of time. Sobek celebrated this shipment by starting on Jennifer and your brother. We got this.*

The boat...you guys. Zita could track the car as it stopped a block away at a light. The door sagged open, scraping against the ground. The driver yanked it closed again. *Good, he can't go at top speed if he can't keep that door shut. I might be able to tail him, even on the highway.*

Let the cops do their job here. Go save Quentin or at least call in his position to the cops. Andy spoke on party line again. *We'll hang out here, and when I get down, Wyn will whammy them. Go.* He snickered at his own pun.

As Zita glided to her clothes, she flared her wings and seized the bag. She clicked her beak and gained altitude, the bag clutched in her talons. Once her flying leveled out, she went after the battered car, trusting Aideen to figure out which vehicle to follow.

The cop rose higher in the sky. "Try to keep up."

Chapter Seventeen

Dawn's grimy fingers scratched away at the darkness, and rush hour traffic began pushing and shoving its way onto the roads. When Zita's target limped off the highway and into the warren of another dock area, she swooped closer. Even with the slower speed and reduced distance, she lost sight of the car.

Here, buildings and the occasional grouping of decorative trees dotted the streets while cement piers jutted out into the water. Each pier had warehouse buildings hogging the center of the dock, with narrow strips of road and storage around them, then the actual boat docking areas on the outside. Cranes were far fewer than at the Baltimore docks; most of the ships were small ones, tourist rides, or personal, pleasure boats. Forced to make assumptions about Sobek's thought processes, Zita concentrated her search on more industrial areas where drunken partiers would not mistake the murderer's lair for a portable toilet, and witnesses would be easier to avoid.

Aideen might have just been following her around; she flew overhead, but not beside Zita after a near miss.

Remaining in the shape of a snowy albatross, Zita soared above a pier, searching for the car. They had done one quick circuit of the docks, but Zita had not seen or heard anything suspicious other than discussions that seemed more furtive than third shift. Still, she rode the wind closer to take advantage of the lights.

She located multiple dead fish and rats, a canine corpse, and quite a bit of rotting food before she found what she sought. Zita circled and stared at the setup while Aideen flitted higher. At one of the more deserted, tired docks, a weathered metal crate hung from the end of a yellow construction crane's hook, high above the river. The stench of blood, death, urine, and a strange plastic scent was so strong that Zita would have wrinkled her beak had it been that flexible. Rust lined the seams and dotted the container at each bolt. Orange cones scattered around the base of the tower crane, designating the perimeter of the work zone. Despite the cones, she saw no actual construction.

Zita brought her rotation in tighter for details. When she caught Quentin's scent and that of a woman, her spirit rejoiced. Had she not approached to determine the difficulty of picking the crate padlock (easy), she would have missed the small black box tucked into the shadow of the hook. It had a faint hum only perceptible when almost on top of it, and a minuscule red light threw a dim glow. Her avian senses recognized it as the source of the unidentifiable odor; having no alternatives, she accepted what they told her. *Ay, hermano, this crate smells like Sobek's sick games. It figures the only bomb expert I know is the one in the box. I can't teleport to get him since I can't see inside. If necessary, I can teleport with the bomb, but where could I go? I won't leave it where it could hurt someone else, but I need time to escape once it's in place.*

In case the link was still there, Zita threw her thoughts to her friends. *I found them. They're in a bomb-trapped box.*

Wyn was the first to respond. *Please don't shout. We're doing better. The hostage crisis is over, and the cops are lowering Andy. Once he touches down, we'll be on our way, though I don't know what we can do about booby-trapped containers.*

Andy snorted. *What she neglects to mention is the hostage situation ended because everyone on the deck fell asleep after mysterious clouds of pink sparkles descended.*

Delighted, Zita opened her beak in a silent laugh. *You go, girl.*

Wyn sniffed. A giggle undermined her prim tone. *Give us your location. We'll head over when we're free. You can tell us if you finish first.*

Altering her flight, Zita zoomed the length of the crane arm. As she flew past the operator's cab and down the cage enclosing the ladder, she was careful not to snag her precious bag. No further bombs revealed themselves, but she did spot a tool kit hidden in the shadows of the ladder halfway up. She crossed the empty pavement between the crane and the closest structures. Cracks and potholes decorated the asphalt, with a scattering of trash to add small splashes of color and unfortunate odors. A row of two-story warehouse units began next to the pile of dilapidated crates. Ornamented with various graffiti, the stack of crates loomed over the pavement, straight across from the crane. Most streetlights in this section were out, and only a few of the buildings had lights. Near to the ground, she spotted a space between two crates. With a call to attract Aideen's attention, she landed beside it.

Sorry, I wasn't certain the telepathy stretched from Baltimore to DC or Virginia. I flew like a mad bird to get here. When she spotted a sign, she sent the street name and the closest building number. Zita waddled into the space, her bag bouncing against her chest with each awkward step. She shifted back to her disguise form and hurried donning her clothing. Her mane of hair she tied back with a shoelace. Her fanny pack of tools was not inside. She berated herself for leaving that at the docks. Folding the plastic bag up as she walked, she stepped out and nearly burnt herself on a glowing form standing outside. With a yelp, Zita hopped back. *I hate it when she does that.*

Fire coruscated around Aideen, her eyes like spots of darkness in her luminescent face. "Did you find anything?" she asked, impatience dripping from her voice. Even that crackled as if it had ignited. She floated a foot off the ground. Shimmers of heat distorted the air around her.

Zita nodded. The Mexican accent was becoming her security blanket. "Sí, a man, and a woman are locked in a box, and hanging over the river almost two hundred feet up at the end of a crane. Both are alive." She ran a hand back and forth over the top of her head. The smooth, heavy weight of her hair felt strange, but it served as protective coloration, a suitable disguise. Freed by her action, a few black strands fell in front of one eye as she lowered her head and continued her summation. "I could get into the operator's cab of the crane, and lower them to the dock. Unfortunately, the box stuck to the top is probably a bomb. We don't dare move anything until it gets defused. While it makes no sense that a strong wind could set it off, the whole torturing people to death thing is all about the mental illness." Aware she was babbling, Zita closed her mouth.

Tucking the errant strand behind one ear, she studied the crate that held her brother and a woman captive. The urge to punch someone, preferably Sobek, rose. Zita jogged in place as she thought. Her eyes drifted over the faded patchwork quilt of shipping containers and down the row of dull gray warehouses. In the distance, people began to move around, though this particular area showed no activity yet. Exhaust, fish, and saltwater drowned out all other aromas. Something tickled her senses, but she couldn't place it.

Aideen drifted in a circle. "Can you disarm a bomb?" she asked. Her flaming aura rose and fell slightly with her breath.

Zita shook her head, and hair fell over her face again. *Stupid disguise.* "No. I know it could go off if we move the crate without taking care of it first. I think we're going to have to call the cops and hide. If Sobek is here and sees us, he might set it off early for spite," she said, her stomach twisting. Turning her head, she searched again for the source of her disquiet. Something had set off her internal alarms.

The glow dimmed first, then flared brighter around Aideen. Her brilliant head nodded. "When dealing with bombs, it is best to let the professionals handle it. You call. I'll see if I can alert local law enforcement. Have the others contacted you?" She levitated a foot higher off the ground, spreading her arms wide like a midair ballerina. When the movement did not alter her flight, Zita realized it must have been for effect.

"Yes, they radioed." *My brain.* "The cops arrested everyone and are working on the captives." *It worked by the nightclub. Let's see if I can do it again.* With a deep breath, Zita reached for a feline shape but kept her grip on her current form. Her vision sharpened and scents grew stronger. Fire hissed, and the camera on the nearest warehouse hummed. The light on that warehouse shone feebly. Turning from the other woman, she wrinkled her nose and opened her mouth, curling back her top lip and inhaling. Zita took a moment to sort through the cacophony of odors. Aideen's flame resembled those chemical fires that burned without heat, with only a hint of wood smoke. For that matter, despite the warmth she threw off, no smoke followed her. Zita's cat instincts loathed the fire. Heated pavement combined with exhaust and—

Aideen interrupted her reverie. "What are you doing? Are you sniffling?" she demanded, incredulity dripping from her voice. Her dismissive gesture with one hand was followed by the other one rubbing over her forehead. Aideen's voice softened. "Never mind. Since you're upset, why don't you return home? The police will attend to this shortly. I will see if any patrol officers are nearby. If you do not leave, wait here for me until I have completed a patrol." One arm outstretched, she leapt upward and soared away in a flash.

Neither the woman nor the part of her that was feline appreciated the idea. "We hear and obey, oh fiery master. Cops definitely won't shoot a dumbass made of fire that flies up out of nowhere," Zita muttered, with a one-fingered salute at the other woman's departing back. If she had had a tail, she would have swished it.

She jogged over to the crane, unlocked the combination lock and slipped inside, leaving the door ajar. *Why do people bother with such lame security?* Climbing the ladder ate a couple of minutes and retrieving the tools took a few more. Good equipment was hard to replace; she hoped Wyn had retrieved her fanny pack from the truck. As she scrambled back down, Zita skipped rungs and slid part of the way for expediency and amusement. At the bottom, she stopped a couple rungs from the ground at the sight of a familiar black-clad form. Her position on the ladder put them at eye level, so he had to be six feet tall. The mask, goggles, and clothing were similar, though this time his belt hung lower with small, intriguing pouches. While the sharp tang of cordite from a recently fired gun blurred it, their proximity allowed her to identify the complex male scent from before. She tensed, but his hands held only the blocky shape of a small electronic device. *Not a weapon, at least not one I recognize, but then again, I wasn't expecting to get stunned earlier either.*

His first words were a question, albeit one delivered in a robotic monotone. "This crane has the remaining prisoners?" He stowed the device in a pouch as he spoke, displacing a boxy gun. One hand tapped the side of his goggles as he looked toward the crate.

Zooming in, perhaps? If he were working for Sobek, wouldn't he know where they were? How did he get so close without me noticing? Clutching her plastic bag with its stupid happy face and the stolen tools inside, Zita nodded. She tossed on the thick accent again for safety. Something told her this was not a man to be careless about or with. "Sí, but there is probably a bomb on top. Don't—"

He interrupted. "I will handle the bomb. Sobek is near. A pay phone is that way." One hand gestured toward another dock, where the buildings looked newer, and the majority of the lights worked. From her earlier circuit, she knew it had tourist boats, yachts, and a closed snow cone stand. "Go find a phone, collect the fireball, and go home before you get anyone killed," he continued. He stepped closer, pointed the boxy gun up, and it whooshed. Something clunked above them.

The bag crinkled under her fingers as they clenched. This close, his scent was even richer, and she could almost feel his body heat. "You can disarm a bomb?" she asked. Zita was rather proud her voice gave away none of the tension his proximity raised, though she could feel her pulse accelerate. Indecision gripped her until she parsed his words. "You were eavesdropping on us? What do you do, follow us around and wait for us to do the hard part?" She hoped she had not said anything that would give away her identity.

A derisive exhale escaped him as if he had stopped himself from snorting at her last question. He pressed a button and sailed upward. One arm rose and pointed at the other dock in the distance.

She swore, placing hands on her hips. Zita looked up and up again. His dark form perched on a rung, then shot again and continued up. Not only was his time better than hers, but it seemed like more fun than scaling the ladder as well.

"I so want that grapple gun. Por favor, dale," she muttered. Another glance upward revealed he was out of her range of sight. She growled and began climbing. Shifting and flying would have been faster, but she refused to have this conversation while naked.

Once at the top, she looked for SWAT Ninja Man. *He needs a shorter nickname.* Even though she had not spotted him, she knew where he would have to go. After removing her shoes, she shoved them into the bag. Zita flexed her feet, the warm metal soothing. Her steps were measured as she learned the sway and feel of the crane arm underfoot. With a deliberate inhale and exhale, she called on her focus. *Less give and padding than a balance beam, but wider. I have to run, though, given his lead. I've done worse. This isn't that different.* After one more deep breath, she let instincts and practice handle the balancing, and picked up speed as her toes warmed and her footing improved. *Hopefully, Quentin goes home tonight, and I can return to mildly illegal base jumping and climbing. Masked vigilantism can be fun sometimes, but it isn't really my thing.*

The masked man paused and swiveled to face her, almost immediately after she'd spotted him. Her speed was better than his, some part of her gloated.

Despite the distance between them, Zita fancied she could catch a faint scent she recognized as his beneath the metal and river odors whenever the wind picked up. She fumbled for words while padding closer, her hands held out at her sides. "Oye, Freelance. Look, I don't know who you are, but are you sure you know what you're doing?"

He nodded and started to turn away.

"Hang on, I wasn't done. If they die because you screw up with that bomb, I'll find you." Zita paused. "Assuming you survive and all." She glared at him. For reasons she would never understand, she pointed two fingers at her own eyes, then turned them toward his goggles.

His head tilted at her again.

She blinked and lowered her hand.

Freelance sighed, as if bored, and gestured for her to continue.

Zita turned red, a fact she hoped her dark skin and mask hid. *Oh, right. He wants the rest of the threat. I didn't think that far ahead. What frightens a seasoned mercenary killer?* She pressed her lips together and gave him the unfriendly stare Miguel gave men she dated. Even if the ninja mask hid it, she hoped the attitude conveyed. "I'll hand you over to the cops as a terrorist. They'll believe a well-armed macho like you could be one, given your physique, sweet grapple gun, and whatever else is in your pants. It'll be years before you walk free again, especially if I tip off the IRS too."

Her index finger whipped out and pointed at him, shaking with each word that followed. "Even if none of your gear is illegal, you'll be well past your prime earnings potential years when they let you go, and your professional reputation will suck. The pecuniary damage alone will ruin you. And if you kill me, my friends will do it. On the other hand, if the prisoners live, you can collect a huge reward for returning them home safe." Hands at hip level, she nodded and bounced into a ready position in case he struck at her. Her bag, attached to one wrist, slapped her thigh with the movement.

Despite his goggles and mask, she thought he focused on her for a moment... and nodded, once.

"Well, then," Zita replied, with a brisk nod as if they had come to an agreement. Mentally, she castigated herself for the lame threat; she had a firm policy against compounding her own stupidity whenever possible. Her return down the crane arm was on autopilot.

Tall, dark, and mercenary's eyes burned into her the whole way, but she resisted the urge to turn.

Prime earnings potential? What was I thinking? He's probably laughing his ass off. Squaring her shoulders, she prayed he was as accomplished as he seemed to think. After sliding down the ladder (much faster and more fun than the ascent), she slid her shoes back on before touching the ground.

Given how little she knew of Freelance, she ran toward the nearest warehouse. *I do like that name for him better than SWAT Ninja Man.* If the bomb squad showed before the device exploded, that was preferable to depending on an unknown. Cameras meant electricity and phones, and the warehouse was far closer than his suggested dock.

Aideen's intercept caught her off guard. "They were not helpful," the other woman informed her.

She blinked. Zita was glad the mask hid her expression. "You are aware you're flying around on fire, right? I've heard cops hate weird stuff, especially if it's near the end of their shift and means more paperwork."

The fiery woman opened her mouth as if to protest, but no sound came out as she rethought whatever she had been going to say. Instead, Aideen inclined her head. "You turn into a seagull, and you call me names?"

Zita shrugged. "Yeah, but if the cops don't know about something, they can go home on schedule. Not to mention, fire is dangerous to everyone but you. Seagulls, not so much. I'll head into that warehouse and use their phone to call the bomb squad." She took a step toward the silent building. The excess heat emanating from the other woman made the muggy morning even more uncomfortable.

Hands settled on flaming hips. "Why have you not already done so?"

Refusing to allow the other woman to cow her, Zita waved a hand. Her eyes flicked to the container. "Got held up." She strode toward the warehouse. A thought struck her. "You may want to stay back so you don't scare anyone inside... in case it's not empty."

Aideen nodded.

Turning her back on the living fireball, Zita strode to a gray metal door. Cameras whirred and focused on her. *Might as well try to do this as legal as possible, especially with Aideen and camera oversight.* She knocked and waited. No one answered.

After a few moments, Aideen called from behind her, "Do I need to melt open the door for you?"

One glance over her shoulder, and Zita tried the doorknob. "No, I got it. Thanks." It turned without protest under her hand, opening into a dim, cavernous area. As she stepped inside, she pushed the door as far open as it would go to ensure no one waited behind it. Wrinkling her nose, she scanned the room. "Hello?" Zita called out, Mexico flavoring her greeting. While screens glowed from a desk on a raised platform, the rest of the room held little light. The bulk of the warehouse seemed deserted, though darkness coiled in the corners, too much for even her feline eyesight. Fifteen feet up, dirty film coated large rectangular windows. Despite her misgivings, she entered anyway, because sometimes progress required stupidity, followed by a clever recovery. If that was what it took to get Quentin back, she knew she could do the first, and prayed she could do the second. Blood and fear were undertones in the wave of metal, sweat, and cement washing over her sensitive nose. The hair on the back of her neck rose. "Hello? Can I use your phone?" She stepped farther inside, eyes on the lit screens. If the computers were at that desk, any phones would be there too.

"Do come in," a male voice invited. Someone squat moved by the desk, his head backlit by the screen.

When Zita was a few yards inside, concentrated light came on with a brilliant flash. Tears sprang to the corners of her eyes in the harsh transition, and she raised a hand in an involuntary action. Something whispered near her, and even blinded, she twisted away. A pilfered tool clunked out of the bag on her wrist. A click and buzz suggested what that might have been. Zita dove for the next patch of shadow and blinked, trying to recover her sight. When it returned, she almost wished it hadn't. She faced a large man with a bandage-clad wrist standing where she had been a second earlier, holding a Taser.

Fluorescents buzzed and hummed in the ceiling as light increased throughout the room. A pair of shipping containers gaped open, one half-full of boxes, and the other empty save a throne-like chair and small table. A drop cloth lay discarded near them, and some wooden pallets cluttered a corner. This warehouse was barren of life, save for herself and the man by the door. The bodyguard tossed the Taser to the side, and it skidded along the floor until the weapon met the white cement block wall.

Slam. Click. The door shut and latched. A red light above it reflected on the polished metal of an ancient fire extinguisher moldering next to the exit.

In the improved light, the escaped bodyguard stalked toward her, the ends of the bandage fluttering with his movements. A multitude of cuts covered his face. The creep pulled a knife with his uninjured hand. Duct tape covered his nose at the bridge, a temporary treatment, she guessed.

"I'm having a bad day. At first, I thought perhaps your interference was the next phase of my audition process, but

Pretorius informed me he would be my only conduit to immortality. My friend here has to redeem himself, so you two get to divert me. Winner might get to live." The voice she recognized as Jones, but the bodyguard was the only visible person.

I found Jones and the driver who got away. They're assholes. Zita scanned the room again, searching for Jones. She thought she caught a glimpse of movement by the computers again. *I'm going to play stupid. People tend to assume I'm an idiot, anyway.*

You're playing? Andy chuckled.

Shut up, jackass. I'm busy here. Zita gave a helpless grin and spread her hands to seem harmless. Fabric rubbed against her cheeks, reminding her of the presence of her mask. Having cold feet wasn't cliché in this situation. The thin soles of her slippers provided little protection from the cool, damp concrete. "Sorry, I don't know nothing about no acting jobs, but that menacing thing is right out of a movie. I'll put in a word for you if I run into any movie people. I needed a phone to call my ride. If you would unlock the door, I'll be on my way." Since she could guess what his response would be, she eased her hand inside the bag, wrapping her fingers around the screwdriver.

Wyn sent a brief message on the party line. *We're coming. It may take a few.*

Jones' voice came again, echoing down as if he were high up. "You may begin."

Before she could reply or do anything, the bodyguard rushed at her, each step slapping down on the concrete.

She dodged the first swipe, dancing a ginga to the side, and ducked the jab he threw at her head with his good hand. Perhaps he was unused to fighting people her size since the blow might have missed even had she remained stationary, but the power behind it made her anxious to end the fight. Zita continued to circle and dodge as she assessed him. *I'm faster, and stronger than most my size thanks to the partial cat shift. He has weight and strength on me, but he's injured and as coordinated as a drunken bull on ice. Ay, no time to linger on crazy times in Iowa. Gracias a Dios this place has room for me to stay out of reach!*

"More blood, less dancing," called Jones.

"It's not my fault if he got no rhythm," she retorted. The bodyguard tried rushing her again, but she did an aú batido, cartwheeling over and kicking him in his chest, twice, as hard as she could. He had more bulk than her so the move failed to knock him down, but he staggered back a few steps. His greater mass threw her backward, but she used that momentum to increase her speed and flip into position. While he was recovering from that, she followed up with a low, hard sweep with one leg to knock him off balance.

He almost fell, but avoided it, though he lost his blade to the ground.

Zita whirled around, giving another low kick, this time at the knife handle to spin it off and under a container.

He recovered, even as she retreated again, toward the container with the chair. The bodyguard followed while she debated if she could climb up the side before he could reach her.

Before she could decide, her opponent attacked in another frenzy of one-armed punches that drove her closer still.

Although she dodged as many as possible, the few she blocked propelled pain radiating down her arms; they'd be black and blue later. *His overhand punches are nasty.* Zita swiped at him with her screwdriver, aiming for his arms. She scored a scratch down one arm, but her reluctance to kill stopped her from taking advantages of openings in his defense. With proximity, she realized the chair had creepy shackles set in the arms and feet of the stained black wood. Blood and excrement clung to chair in a fearful miasma of scent.

"You need new furniture. That's unhygienic," she suggested while she continued dancing, hoping Jones would give away his new location. Zita risked a peek to see if she could find him. A soft noise sounded somewhere near the container of boxes, and a series of taps by the door. She glanced that way.

Taking advantage of her distraction, the bodyguard tried a sweeping haymaker, thundering up from behind her.

Zita turned in time, ducking under the powerful punch and scooping his leg out from under him. Grunting with the exertion even with enhanced strength, she shoved his leg up and rolled him over her shoulder. She smashed him into the ground.

He landed on his side with a crack and a cry.

With an internal wince, Zita stomped on his bandaged wrist, and she ran for the drop cloth.

The bodyguard shrieked, curling up.

She flung the oily material over his dazed body and rolled him into the container while the disorientation lasted.

He howled again every time weight came to bear on his injured arm.

Slamming the container shut on him and the noxious chair, she threw the locks and put her back against the door. Her breathing was harsh in her ears, and her heart was racing. Venturing one step forward, she inhaled, trying to bring her breathing back under control. Frantic, she searched for Jones.

A woman sobbed, babbling incoherently.

Zita jerked her head toward the muffled sound.

Quentin murmured something.

With rapid steps, Zita jogged toward the monitors. En route, her nose recoiled at the pungent stink of sour sweat and bitter swamp water. As she searched to locate the source, something barreled into her from above, knocking her to the concrete. Pain arced through her body, both from the hit and the subsequent collision with the floor. When a boot headed toward her face, she spun away, not soon enough to evade the kick completely, but enough to avoid it crushing her face into the cold surface. *Side, shoulder, and cheekbone. At least my ribs don't feel broken.* She swore, knowing the pain would increase when the adrenaline wore off.

A hand seized the back of her head, fingers knotting in her mask and the thick hair of her disguise, yanking her head up higher. *Can't let him cut me.* Fumbling, she stabbed behind her head with the screwdriver clenched in her fist, even as she writhed and squirmed.

Flesh gave way under the tool, and it pulled from her hand as the other person withdrew.

Zita used the reprieve to regain her feet and locate her assailant. Save the weeping, the warehouse was quiet again. *Camera and audio from the captives' container. Moronic of me not to have realized it sooner. I can't make the top of the box with these injuries.* No sound came from the bodyguard's container. Inching sideways to get next to a wall, she spotted her screwdriver, dripping dark blood into a small puddle.

Racing there and scanning left and right for her attacker, she seized it and held it defensively. "So, you ready to surrender yet?" she gasped, enunciating around her swelling lips and cheek. Her nose told her the wet and sticky substance adhering her mask to her face was blood.

Something rustled nearby.

Her breath released in a pained hiss as the volume of the babbling woman suddenly amplified from noticeable into agonizing. In an involuntary action, her hands clasped over her ears. Her side and shoulder throbbed with the arm movement. Disoriented, she ran to the wall and put her back against it. Zita sucked in air, her hands still over her ears. With distress, realization hit. *I don't know if I can avoid lethal at this point.*

The earsplitting volume decreased to painful.

"I have to improve my recruiting standards. You're not nearly as difficult to take down as he made it look. That's probably what's been slowing my ascent. Not to worry, though, it's only temporary. The world will tremble before Sobek soon," Jones commented, stepping out from behind the other container. He held a Colt M1911 handgun in the classic Weaver stance, advancing until he stood seven paces from her.

Chapter Eighteen

Zita froze, except for her mouth. "Sobek?" she questioned, more to stave off death than any real surprise. *Miguel, right again, hermano.*

Jones grinned, all sharp teeth, glee, and lamentable breath. Darkness stained one of his arms, probably where her screwdriver had scored him. "Fitting, don't you think? Though I'll be concentrating more on the power and less on the whole impregnating thing once I take my place."

Put like that, mythology sounded like an ancient form of bad telenovela or other television show. "Sí, sounds like a plan. You'll want to keep all that, uh, you, to yourself," she agreed. "So what's with the horror house soundtrack? And did you file your teeth? That's, ah, dedication to your theme."

He chortled, letting another pile of steaming psychosis escape. "I like to keep tabs on my object lessons. The girl is so emotional and irrational that she is a delightful confection. I had planned to use another, but she can wait. It may be for the best since I may have to do a quick job on them, thanks to you. All it will take is one touch of my phone to end them."

"They have an app for that?" Zita cursed her mouth even as the words escaped.

He continued raving as if she hadn't said anything. "Someone annoyed me. He will pay, first with his brother. I've promised my informant good money for the pictures when he finds out they are dead. I may frame the photos." The gun did not waver, though his eyes looked through her as if viewing a euphoric future. His smirk grew, along with the madness in his eyes. "After I'm a god-king, he will watch the excruciating glory of my expertise on his sister."

As if unable to stop, her mouth opened up again. "So, you're going for the crazy Olympics then? From what I've seen, you've got a good chance of winning, though you never know with those French judges." Zita edged a few steps so his gun no longer lined up with the center mass of her body.

Jones snarled. Gesturing with the blued gun barrel, he signaled her to move away from the wall. "I will have respect. Enough delays. Why have you targeted my operations?"

With a placating gesture she had seen Wyn use, Zita held out her hands. At the same time, she angled sideways to present a smaller target and calculated her chances of getting the gun away. She sidled toward the wall. Probably yelling at Wyn again, she attempted to send an update. *Jones is Sobek. He's trying to talk me to death. In case I don't survive, Jones has some phone app that he can use to explode Quentin.* "Just lucky, I guess?"

He clicked off the safety on his gun. Removing one hand from his pistol, Jones fumbled with his pants. When he pulled a zip tie from his pockets, a small amount of tension dissipated from her shoulders. "Answer me, and you can have a speedy death. I don't have time to give you the full lesson, but I can make your end agonizing if you don't comply."

"Hombre, this conversation is already painful." Zita kept her eyes lowered, watching him through her lashes. *When he comes closer, I'll shift and take him. Bear might work because if I can't disarm him, a handgun is less dangerous to a bear. I won't leave without Quentin and Jennifer. Maybe I can teleport in using the video feed, then teleport out with them. Since it only works going home, places I can see, or to major landmarks, it'll be interesting.*

Jones took one measured step toward her.

She tensed. Behind him and to the side, the center of the door glowed with a dull red light as the edges warped. With a loud bang, the door flew open and off its hinges. Whether it was reflex or adrenaline, Zita did not even wait to see the results before she ran. Her side howled in pain, but only a whiny hiss escaped as she took cover behind a container.

Aideen strode in, fire crackling around her. "You took too long," she addressed Zita.

"Impatient, much? I ran into Some Beak here and his pet thug," she replied.

Perhaps favored by the good fortune evinced most often by the innocent or insane, Jones appeared unscathed by the blast or the flying door. "Sobek! I am Sobek!" With a shocking disrespect for banter, Jones turned the gun on Aideen.

Zita had to give him credit for prioritizing the threats in the room correctly.

He fired a three-shot burst at Aideen, then another and another until the gun clicked empty. His breath hissed as he jammed in another clip.

Tiny sparks lit up the air around Aideen with each bullet, fading away. The woman of fire examined her fingers. "Sobek... why is that name familiar? This is the drug-dealing kidnapper?" she commented.

Searching for something to throw, Zita offered. "It's an Egyptian frog monster."

"Crocodile god, not a frog creature, you idiots," he snapped.

With a flick of Aideen's incandescent fingers, Jones' gun began to glow an angry red in his hands. He threw it away with a yelp.

Turning her uncanny eyes to Jones, Aideen stared at him. She pointed. "Whatever. Get on the ground and put your hands behind your head." Another ball of fire grew in her hand. "Do not make me incinerate you. It complicates things and I hate paperwork."

Looking between the two women, Jones bent his knees and vaulted up to the warehouse windows. Sliding one open, he bared his pointy teeth.

Well, that explains how he was able to knock me down if he dropped from that height, Zita mused.

Aideen shrieked and tossed a fireball at him.

He dove out the window before it hit.

Snarling, Aideen flew out the door. Her hands filled with more light as she exited.

"Wait! Don't kill him," Zita called to the other woman, racing after her.

When she burst outside, Aideen drifted a couple feet off the ground near the warehouse door while Jones hunkered down at the edge of the dock. "His phone explodes people! Don't let him set it off!" Zita shouted. From the corner of her eye, she noted the camera on the door had melted. "Don't kill him! You can't risk the victims!"

Aideen threw her fireball.

Jones shrieked and jumped, or fell, off the edge of the dock.

Blowing smoke from her fingers as if drying a manicure, Aideen strolled toward him. Another knot of fire formed at one hand.

Zita sprinted back to the warehouse and seized the fire extinguisher and the fallen Taser. Coming from behind the glowing woman, she sprayed her with the coolant.

Aideen spun toward her, getting coolant in the face.

When the flames had extinguished and the other woman coughed and bent double under a thick layer of foam, Zita shot her with the Taser.

Aideen collapsed.

Throwing a "sorry" over her shoulder, Zita dashed where she'd last seen Jones. Sparing a glance upward at the swaying container, she prayed. Below her, Jones clung to the ladder with one arm, mostly submerged in the brown water, and resting his head against the rungs.

Zita's fear was palpable. *Quentin.* She dropped both the extinguisher and Taser and increased her speed. The fetid odor of burnt rubber assaulted her nose, superseding the scents of bitter river water and scorched meat as she climbed down the ladder to him. Water concealed most of his body, so she could not tell the extent of his injuries. Her own screamed as she hauled him out of the water. She made a disgusted sound at the reek. "Crocodile, my skinny brown ass! He even smells like burnt frog," Zita complained.

Scalded red and blistered, his face was barely recognizable. Seeing a spot less oozing than the others, she reached out to check his pulse. One arm snapped up and seized her hand. His eyes opened, all sanity gone. She had only a few milliseconds to register teeth before he pulled them both into the water.

They hit with a hard slap and nasty water invaded her unprepared throat. Jones towed her deeper while she fought the disorientation. When he released her, she was shocked but didn't waste time determining the reason. Choking on the foul brown liquid, she shot toward the surface. Sputtering and gasping, Zita sucked down as much air as possible and swam toward the dock.

One hand had just grasped the bottom rung of the ladder when she was yanked under and dragged through the water at high speed.

Zita fought, kicking, punching, and at least trying to slow his progress, but the water softened even the strength of her feline-enhanced blows.

Without warning, the grip on her ankle released, and she jetted back to the surface.

She gulped down air and swam again, noting her attacker had brought her even farther away from the dock this time. Splitting her attention between swimming and watching for him—as if watching for sharks while reef diving—she stroked toward the shore. The reprieve allowed her to track Jones and recall her free diving experience.

Jones followed behind her, mostly underwater.

He had to be planning something. Zita calmed her breathing and focused, conserving her oxygen. When she reached the ladder again, the attack from behind was predictable. She twisted her legs and kicked at his face, hitting once or twice. New rounds of torment began in her side with the movement.

His answer... a pained grunt.

Her tactic delayed his grab enough for her to take a deep hit of air before he pulled her under again. Her mind raced through possible changes, looking for the right one.

Precious time and air fled while he dragged her back toward the middle of the river. His croaking, distorted by the water, warned her before his grip increased and Jones began an underwater roll in the murky river depths.

Zita stopped fighting and threw herself in the direction of his barrel roll, even using her free limbs to move faster. At least the cool water relieved her various sore spots, even if her shoulder protested the movement.

For no apparent reason, he paused, and the sound stopped. His face drew closer to hers.

Asshole thinks he's a crocodile? She took advantage of the cessation to jab at his face, her fingers like claws. His grip slackened, and she slipped free. Even though her lungs burned for air, she swam for the shore again.

This time, he did not let her reach the dock or even the surface. He snatched at her, catching a handful of her sodden pant leg.

Black spots danced before her eyes. Desperate, she undid the waist tie and kicked her sweatpants off into his face, blinding him. She broke the surface and inhaled. The answer came to her.

Predictably, he surfaced next to her and grabbed at her.

She cackled while her form changed. *Didn't you ever read up on crocodiles? They don't mess with everything in the water.* Her remaining clothing tightened and ripped as her form curved and enlarged.

His hands slid off during the transformation. Realization chased the surprise from his face. Jones spun away. Throwing her pants at her face, he raced through the water toward the shore.

Zita felt... buoyant. Ignoring the cloth on her nose, she emptied her lungs with a fountain of water. As she slipped through the current, she gained speed until she was directly behind him. His expression at seeing two thousand pounds of sleek, round flesh so close was priceless when he looked back to locate her. She lunged the last few feet and rose from beneath, capturing him on her wide snout. Keeping her mouth shut so as not to expose the tender flesh within, she flung her head and tossed him onto the concrete near a pile of rusty chain.

He landed hard and lay unmoving at the edge. Her sodden pants landed on pavement farther away with a squelch. Jones turned his head, and their eyes met. His breathing had a hard, jagged edge, and he gave a pained groan.

In case he had missed the object lesson, she exhaled, splattering him with water. Zita permitted her mouth to gap open in jollity as well.

Jones glared, but made no move to reenter the water. Instead, he pushed himself to his feet, one arm wrapped around his ribs as he lurched away.

Guess he's not a fan of hippos. Wonder how he feels about other animals. Hey, no escaping on my watch again. Zita, now at the edge of the dock, switched to gorilla. Her preference would have been to flip up onto the pavement, but she suspected her injuries would disapprove. Although she hurried, Jones had appeared hurt enough to be an easy catch.

By the time she made her way up the ladder, Jones stood frozen, back rigid with tension, with Aideen between him and the warehouses. The cop's form was ablaze again, and twin balls of light glimmered in her hands. "You have rejoined us. Search him for weapons, Arca. Will Mano and the blond be here soon? I assume you let the criminal who struck me escape."

Zita blinked at Aideen. *Mano? She must have heard me call Andy that. Where is she getting Arca from? If she thinks someone else knocked her down, that's fine with me. I don't want to be a kebab. Mmm. Kebabs.* As much as it galled her to obey, she searched the quiescent man, relieving him of his waterlogged phone and a pair of knives. The screen on the phone was dark, and she risked a glance up. *Once Jones is secured, I can tell Freelance to leave the bomb alone, too.* The container still hung from the crane, with no smoke or sign of the mercenary. A relieved hoot escaped, and she realized the other two were staring.

Neither emanated friendship.

Struggling to not shout, but think loud, she sent to her friends. *We caught Sobek. Need the police to come get Quentin and Jen down. Then, I can go. Not to flirt, Wyn, but I need your healing touch again.*

Jones hissed and lurched to the side with a yelp when his foot touched something.

Checking what had startled him, Zita saw slag steaming where she had dropped the Taser.

Jones bent his knees, but she grabbed his arm, giving a warning growl.

The villain appeared rebellious.

Fire swirled in Aideen's fists, and Jones relented. The glare he gave both women promised vengeance, but at this point, Zita preferred that to his happier expressions.

Zita dragged him back inside the warehouse. Aideen made a token protest but offered no alternatives, so Zita shoved him inside the remaining container. It had air holes already, after all. Her back turned to the entrance, she was locking the crate door when words penetrated from the speakers.

"We're moving! He's coming for us again!" Jennifer screamed. "First the water, then the pain!"

Snatching up the bloody screwdriver from the floor, Zita was almost out the warehouse door when she remembered the two captive men. She paused and gestured at Aideen. Pointing to her own eyes with two fingers, she then directed them at the containers. She repeated the sequence again but did not wait for the result, instead running outside toward the crane. *Please don't let them blow up. I wanted them to see a human when they got out, but Wyn's not here yet, and my clothes are destroyed. Aideen would do more harm than good. Perhaps a talking parrot would be reassuring?*

The crane whined as the cable lowered the container. The makeshift prison touched ground with a soft thud, and Zita stopped by the door. With a combination of the screwdriver and brute gorilla strength, she unlocked the cargo container. Throwing open the door and stepping sideways, she wanted to avoid panicking them. Her foot squished in something cold. When she glanced down, she identified her sweatpants. Shifting to a raven, she snatched them up and flew to the top of the crate.

The interior was hushed. Impatient, she sidled over to the opening, and peered in, upside down.

Quentin stood in front of Jen, his arms spread, and his weight balanced. Joy exploded at the sight of him, even unshaven and filthy. He was alive and moving on his own. While strain showed on his beloved face, he seemed to have no more than minor bruises and nasty cuts, red and swollen, at his wrists and ankles.

His companion shivered and panted as she peered around him at the open door. Crusted blood stood out in stark relief against the ashen skin of half her face and part of one breast. Jennifer wobbled from side to side as if she could not bear to set both feet down flat.

Zita swallowed and bobbed right side up again. She shifted to her human disguise form. Atop the crate, her hair cloaked her body as she crouched above the opening. Emotion thickened her throat, and she fought for a moment to speak. "You can come out if you want. Sobek's tied up and the cops are on their way. If you want to wait in there, that's fine. If not, we'll hang out to make sure you're safe. Don't worry, we'll stay back from you." As a precaution, she thickened her accent before shifting to a raven.

Quentin stepped out of the container. When he assessed the street, his eyes blinked and watered in even the dim light of dawn. A choked sound came from within. He peered around. "No one's here!"

Bare feet slapped on metal, a halting and inconstant rhythm, when Jennifer scuttled out of the container, and stood, naked, in the middle of the street. She rubbed her hands on her arms and stared. Her head turned as if listening to someone else. "No, they're here, they're here, they're all going to get us." The injured woman dropped to her hands and knees and fondled the cement. "But I can feel it sing again."

Quentin exhaled. "Listen, Jen, it's going to be okay. Hold it together a little while longer. Sit down, and get some weight off your feet." His tone was soothing. Despite his words, he checked left, right, and behind the crate as if expecting someone to be there. He stopped next to the edge of the dock and rubbed his sunken eyes. His shoulders set, he stood upright. Somewhat belatedly, Zita realized he was nude as well.

A police siren echoed, approaching fast.

Jennifer gave a humorless bark. "No, they're coming with heavy treads, and they're going to lock us up again. I won't do it. I won't let them." She rose to her full height and clenched her fists. Dirt and something darker covered her feet.

An odd grumbling noise surprised Zita, and the ground shuddered. She took flight as the container jittered beneath her.

The street gave way with a crack, and a streetlamp, already nonfunctional, toppled and smashed to the ground, narrowly missing an oncoming white vehicle. Oblivious, Jennifer continued shouting her defiance, and the tremors worsened. Car alarms shrieked. Windows broke all along the warehouses, and small pieces of the roof fell. Part of the dock crumbled into the water, and a parked car slid into a new crevasse that extended from under the warehouse to the water. Other fissures opened in the ground, and the nasty box continued to slip toward the water.

Quentin wove his way back toward the distraught woman, trying to avoid the various cracks and falling debris. "Jen! Stop! The police are coming, and we can go home." He stretched a hand to her.

"How could you?" Jennifer shouted. "This is your fault."

Stone and sections of concrete speared out of the ground, attacking Quentin.

He took one giant step back, then two more, as another spike rose near his legs. Within seconds, Quentin was dancing backward to try to avoid the rocks. "No, Jen, no!" he yelled.

Shivering and muttering, Jen rubbed her own arms. Distress showed on her face, and she licked cracked lips. "I trusted you," she screeched. Another sharp claw of stone swiped at his feet.

Rising higher in the sky, Zita dove at Jennifer, cawing and rolling aside before impact.

Jennifer shrieked and ducked, throwing her hands up to protect her face.

As Zita swooped for another pass, the ground opened beneath her brother's feet.

Quentin shouted something inarticulate as the earth gulped him down, closing over his head. The vertical section of rock near him crumbled into grapefruit-sized rocks. One hand twitched from the pile of dirt and ruined asphalt; the rubble buried the rest of him.

Jen squeaked and slapped at her shoulder. She whimpered, and collapsed. The tremors stopped.

A harsh, avian cry filled the air as Zita dove and landed. *Quentin! Mano!* From the corner of her eye, she noticed something streak by, but her attention was on the mound of dirt where her brother had been standing moments ago.

Shifting to an oversized badger, she assailed the pile, launching rocks and dirt several feet in every direction. His free hand served as a keystone, allowing her to guess where the rest of him was suffocating below. Already disturbed by the tremors and whatever Jennifer had done, the soil was loosely packed. Zita's panicked digging was rewarded when more of Quentin's arm appeared. She nosed him, then went back to her frantic excavation.

At the touch of her fur, his arm jerked and waved.

He's conscious! Hang on, Quentin. Oblivious to all else, Zita slowed only enough to ensure that her long, curved black claws did not tear into his flesh. When a chunk of dark hair came out under her nails, she slowed, switching back to gorilla to scoop it out from around his face.

When she reached that area, his eyes, and his mouth were shut. Fear raced through her. The arm above the ground hung limp.

Quentin's mouth fell open with a pop and a half-vocalized gasp. He snorted, dirt and mucus blowing out and over her fur. Opening his eyes, Quentin stared. "A gorilla?" he coughed.

She rumbled, breathy with joy, and raised her hand to touch his hair. The sight of her simian fingers reminded her he had no idea who she was. Her heart clenched, and she hid her exultation. Zita continued digging, scooping dirt away from his head and neck with her powerful hands.

Sirens howled nearby even as she freed his shoulders, cursing the red clay and cement. She risked a glance up. Jen was gone. Flaming bright, a form exited the warehouse windows and circled. It pointed at her and soared into the clouds. She sent a quick message to her friends. *Meet me at my place? The cops are almost here. Quentin's safe.*

Will do. Mind the volume. Zita was happy to hear Wyn's response, even though it included chastisement.

Zita shifted to a raven. "Oye," she cawed to her squirming brother. Under other circumstances, the combination of the accent with the strident raven voice would have been amusing. "Sobek and one of his minions are locked in two containers in the warehouse right there. The one is normal, but Sobek has extra strength and can jump a few stories high and pretty far too so they should be prepared. And he breathes underwater."

Her brother peered at her. "Huh? Weren't you a gorilla a moment ago? These dying hallucinations are loco. Aren't I supposed to relive my life in a series of memories? Was looking forward to sections of it." With a grunt of effort, he freed his other arm from the confining dirt. Muscles bulged as he began to try to lever himself out of the hole, panting, and grumbling.

"You're not dead. You're welcome and adiós," she answered, hopping into the air, flapping hard, and landing with a pained thud when her shoulder refused to fly another yard. Shifting to jaguar, she scooped up her sopping pants with as much dignity as she could muster, and limped off behind a jumble of crates. She teleported home as her brother's voice called out behind her.

Chapter Nineteen

"Oh, hey! I brought pizza and juice," Zita announced as she invaded Wyn's living room that night. "You want some?" Bottles in a bag bounced against her leg when she set the two pizza boxes and bag down on the glass table with the Celtic design. Andy hovered behind her.

Wyn shook her head and reseated herself on the sofa, a plush, dramatic thing in deep scarlet. As she reclined on fussy white pillows, she exhaled. "Welcome back. So, what did you tell everyone about what you did last night and this morning?" One of the little floral cups sat on a saucer in front of her on the low table. A plate of chocolate balls and miniscule cookies was by the pizza, with a stack of glass plates and napkins waiting nearby.

Zita shrugged and took a blissful, pain-free breath. The air smelled of cats, lilac, and real food. She gave her friends an impish grin. "Miguel was the only one to ask. Since I showered and crashed before calling, it was all true when I told him I slept in a lumpy chair and got up early to spar. Thanks again for the healing, though; injuries would have been harder to explain. Plus, being hurt sucks big hairy... no me importa." She plopped in the white chair with red stripes, balancing on the edge; while otherwise comfortable enough, her short legs dangled like a child's if she perched anywhere else.

A laugh escaped Andy while he claimed a slice of cheese pizza, juice, and the other half of the sofa. "Weren't you under the chair rather than in it?"

"The story has elements of veracity," Wyn observed. "How is poor Quentin?"

Fruit juice burst on her tongue as she took a sip. Zita put the cap back on and set the bottle on a coaster. She wondered if Wyn had cheated to have the coasters and plates ready for their arrival. "They're keeping him overnight for observation because of his concussion, but the doctor said time, fluids, and antibiotics should fix everything else. When I left—"

"Was kicked out," Andy supplied. The remote had found its way to his hand, and he cycled through television channels in masculine contentment. A cat perched behind him, on the arch of the chair, contemplating the glass bottle and plate he had set down on an ornate side table.

Zita continued. "When I left, he and one nurse were flirting. That's pretty much how he handles stress. He'll survive. Why you gotta assume they threw me out? Is that how friends treat each other?" She cocked her head and made a face at Andy.

Andy snorted. "Because I gave you a lift here from the hospital, and you had a giant foam finger, a piñata, and a security escort. The piñata and finger are still in my car."

Wyn giggled.

Pushing her snub nose up in the air, Zita sniffed. "Maybe the guard was checking me out. Some men like their women tiny and tight like me." She grinned. "Thanks for the ride and all, though. I smacked the kidnappers with the helmet, not the bike, so you'd think the cops would at least release my ride. Shouldn't they be done with all that now?" Soft fur brushed one of her calves. That was sufficient warning to move the takeout boxes. With the cap on and the thick carpet underfoot, the juice bottle would be safe enough on the table. A tail slapped her leg as the cat meandered toward easier prey.

Wyn patted her arm. "You have excellent legs, what little exists of them," she teased, her eyes sparkling. "I'm glad Quentin will recover. Did Miguel have any information about the missing woman?" She sipped her tea, more of the flowery kind she favored. Selecting one of the chocolate delicacies with the grave deliberation of a death penalty jury, she nibbled.

Zita wrinkled her nose at her friend, who giggled again. "Her dad flew her to some fancy private hospital somewhere and told Miguel that Jen wasn't doing well mentally, so the cops can't talk to her yet. Hopefully, the expensive doctors know how to deal with her. The poor woman's feet were real messed up." Zita served up a slice of the loaded pizza and put the box back.

Andy frowned. "I thought you said she vanished." A cat inched closer to his pizza and juice bottle.

Still holding her plate in one hand, Zita lifted both hands in the air. "By the time I dug out Quentin even partway, they were gone. Ninja SWAT Man must have carried her off. Miguel said Jen's dad showed up later with information about her." Zita hopped out of her chair and paced.

Rubbing a charm on a silver bracelet, Wyn arched an eyebrow. "So you're saying the ninja you met earlier disarmed the bomb, lowered the prisoners, then absconded with Jennifer? You're the only witness, and the woman he fled with has magically reappeared?" She toyed with her hair, twining a glossy brown lock around her finger.

"How would you even know it's the same man? I mean, ninja," Andy asked.

Zita thought back. Her mouth curled into a smirk. "Has to be. What are the odds that two physically identical men dressed themselves similarly in SWAT ninja getups? Then they both chose to interfere in the same escapade as us, with the same movement style, voice changer, and sweet grapple guns? They even smelled alike." She'd always remember that scent, too, all man, gun oil, and wilderness. Putting a finger to her mouth, she bit the tip. "He might be our mystery shooter from the Baltimore docks, too, even if the cops are giving the SWAT team all the credit." Mystery solved, she raised a juice up into the air in victory, then had another sip.

Wyn's tone was dry. "You mean the person no one believes exists except you?"

Setting down her drink, Zita folded her arms over her chest and sat again. "I might be wrong about the clothes, but I am not mistaken about the rest. It would have been a sin against God not to notice the body, and I'm a very good girl. Plus, I really want that grapple gun. It's awesome." She relaxed and took a bite of the gooey pizza.

Wyn snickered. "Is that what you're calling it? I bet you do, Zita," she said.

Andy shook his head. "Most people outgrow their imaginary friends by your age, though I suppose the ninja/SWAT combination was to be expected from your imagination," he said dolefully. He was unable to maintain the somber look and laughed. Although he made a face at her, fun twinkled in his eyes. "You have more interesting imaginary friends than Wyn."

"Hey!" both women protested at once.

"Why are you my friends again?" Zita complained.

Wyn curled her feet beneath her and spoke to no one, or perhaps to her cats. "I'm glad it's over. Did Sobek say why he attacked the hospital? Did the authorities find the notebook?"

Rubbing the top of her head, Zita paused before answering. "Miguel never says much about cases, but he told me to stay vigilant. His bosses pulled him from the Sobek case for obvious reasons, and the hospital is an active DMS investigation. From what I overheard during my incarceration at his office, the hospital attack was organized and professional. They had this whole flowchart on the probable expense of the hospital operation compared to Sobek's estimated income. It was out of his league. He was a drug dealer and smuggler who added human trafficking to his sick portfolio. I wasn't able to find out anything about the notebook or the destination of the kidnapped people."

A cat leapt onto the side table and licked the mouth of Andy's bottle. Stealthier, the other feline eased his plate toward the edge of the table. He looked at the juice and sighed. Purring, the first cat challenged his stare and licked a drop of condensation. Andy rolled his eyes and screwed the lid back on tight. "Overheard? It sounds as if you went through their files."

Wiping succulent sauce off her mouth and licking a drop from her bottom lip, Zita grinned and held up two fingers, an inch apart. "Perhaps a little. I was bored, and went into the wrong conference room once or twice on practice runs before I actually snuck out."

Wyn threw a chocolate at her. "You were bored and jonesing for action."

"Why would I let bad things happen to anyone if I could stop them? That said, I like to enjoy myself, not cause trouble." Catching the food, Zita eliminated that ammunition from Wyn's arsenal forever. She bounced, remembering something she had overheard. "Oh, and Wyn? Boris survived. He's in protective custody, begging for a plea bargain."

Wyn beamed.

Before Wyn could do more than open her mouth to reply, Andy jerked his chin at the television. "Ears burning, anyone? They're talking about us again." He rescued his plate seconds before one of the sneaky cats could nudge it onto the floor.

The trio turned their attention to the television. Familiar with wild animals, Zita kept some of her attention on the food so the cats could not steal it.

When the newscasters announced the police were seeking leads to persons of interest, Wyn fetched a small glass bottle from the kitchen and poured a dollop into her tea. Zita and Andy both refused when she offered them some.

Wyn was the first to speak after a sip of her adulterated tea. "I'm not surprised security camera footage of Zita and Aideen is blurry, but I had expected better coverage of you given how long you hung from that rope, Andy. The news helicopters were circling by the time we escaped."

"At least we know your illusion holds up well under video cameras, though. You're in most of the shots," Zita offered. She crunched and chewed, letting the flavors swirl over her tongue. When the reporter gave a description and showed a bad image of Pretorius, she nearly spat out her food. "Wait, I thought you took Pretentious P down?" she asked, turning to Andy.

"He ran off after Andy grabbed the rope. Everyone was busy watching that, and you went after the driver. Pretorius might've been faking unconsciousness," Wyn suggested. She paused, teacup halfway to her lips. The perky TV commentator had changed the subject to persons of interest. When the reporter declared the unknown blond woman led the gang opposing Pretorius, her mouth fell open. While they had no name for Wyn, they identified her associates as Fireball, Arca, and Mano. Shaking her head, Wyn added another dollop to her cup.

A line etched itself on Andy's forehead. He swallowed another bite of pizza and frowned as he chewed. "Why is she the leader? And how come they are calling me Mano and you Arca?"

"How pissed do you think Aideen is to be included with us and under Wyn's command?" Zita snickered.

"I can only answer two of those questions." Closing her eyes, Wyn massaged her forehead. Concentration stilled her features. "Zita called you Mano in front of Aideen and some of those drug dealers, and she made a comment about being an arca. They must've given statements." Opening her eyes, she hummed at one of the cats stalking Andy's plate. She took a sip of her tea as the cat at her feet began grooming.

"Oh, right. Aideen referred to you as that at one point too. Wyn's the most photogenic, so of course she's in charge." Zita took another healthy bite. Bird practice earlier must have burnt thousands of calories. She was starving.

Andy snorted. "I see. Still, what kind of name is Mano?"

"It doesn't matter who they say ran things or what they call us, provided they're wrong. At least now my gang has other members." Zita grinned. "Seriously, when will we ever have to do that again?" She popped the last of the slice in her mouth.

Andy groaned and hid his face in his hands. "We're doomed. I better think of a name."

Spanish and Portuguese Glossary

These are definitions of the words as Zita uses them in the book, and may not include all possible variations. The Spanish is primarily Mexican in usage and slang. Needless to say, anything marked with "Vulgar" should not be used in polite company.

abuela: Spanish. Grandma.

adiós: Spanish. Goodbye.

arca: Spanish. A chest or ark. Zita originally used it referring to Noah's ark in *Super*.

aú batido: Portuguese. Capoeira defensive move. The practitioner performs a handstand, twists at the hips, spreads their legs, then kicks with the instep at their opponent as they descend from the handstand.

ay: Spanish. An interjection, similar to "Oh."

bandeira: Portuguese. Capoeira move where a fast cartwheel is immediately followed by a side flip.

basta: Spanish. Enough.

buey: Spanish. Dude.

capoeira: Portuguese. A fast, fluid Brazilian martial art known for its acrobatic and dance-like kicks, spins and other techniques.

carajo: Spanish. Shit. Vulgar.

caramba: Spanish. A mild interjection of surprise or dismay.

chilaquiles: Spanish. A Mexican breakfast or lunch dish with salsa or mole and any other ingredients (such as eggs or pork) on top of strips of fried tortilla.

chingado: Spanish. Fucked or fucking. This has other meanings as well, but this is how Zita generally uses it. Vulgar.

claro que sí: Spanish. Of course.

cojones: Spanish. Testicles. Vulgar.

comprendo: Spanish. I understand.

Dios: Spanish. God.

fique tranquilo: Portuguese. Don't worry, be calm.

fuba cake: Portuguese. The real name of this light, sweet, cornmeal cake is bolo de fubá. Usually eaten for breakfast or as an afternoon snack with coffee.

ginga: Portuguese. The most basic capoeira footwork, a moving fight stance.

gracias a Dios: Spanish. Thank God or Thanks be to God.

gringo: Spanish. Foreigner, especially from the US.

hasta: Spanish. Later.

hermano: Spanish. Brother.

hombre: Spanish. Man.

loco/loca: Spanish. Crazy man or woman.

macho: Spanish. Man or manly.

mano: Spanish. Bro. Abbreviated form of "hermano" as Zita uses it.

mi amor: Spanish. My love.

mija: Spanish. Abbreviated form of "my daughter."

momentito: Spanish. Just a moment.

negativa: Portuguese. Capoeira defensive move where the practitioner drops low to dodge an incoming attack.

neta: Spanish. Really, for real, you know.

ni madres: Spanish. No fucking way. Vulgar.

no hay bronca: Spanish. No problem.

no lo creo: Spanish. I don't believe it.

no te preocupes: Spanish. Don't worry about it.

oye: Spanish. An interjection that can be used as hey, listen, or yo.

papi chulo: Spanish. Hot guy.

pendejo: Spanish. A jerk or asshole. Vulgar.

perfecto: Spanish. Perfect.

por fa, por favor: Spanish. Please.

pues: Spanish. An interjection, equivalent of well, then, or since.

sí: Spanish. Yes.

tía: Spanish. Aunt.

vámonos: Spanish. Let's go.

From the Author

Thank you for reading!

Please consider leaving reviews for any books you've enjoyed. Reviews assist other readers in finding books, and let authors know what they've done right (or wrong).

For the latest on past and future releases, monthly chatter, free short stories, and the occasional other freebie, subscribe to the newsletter on my website, www.karendiem.com. You can also use the website to contact me, browse free content (cut scenes, sample chapters, my abbreviated autobiography, and more), or find me on social media sites (Twitter, Facebook, etc.). Since I'd hate to read the same stuff everywhere, I do try to put different content in each place. New release notices are the exception and go everywhere.

Arca Chronology

Super
Washout (Short Story)
Octopus (Short Story)
Human
Tourists (Short Story)
Power (Upcoming)
Pie (Upcoming Short Story)

Made in the USA
Lexington, KY
15 November 2018